A TIME TO EMBRACE

Lilli Palmer

A TIME TO EMBRACE

Translated by Carey Harrison

Macmillan Publishing Co., Inc.   NEW YORK

Macmillan Publishing Co., Inc.
866 Third Avenue, New York, N.Y. 10022
Collier Macmillan Canada, Ltd.

Library of Congress Cataloging in Publication Data
Palmer, Lilli, 1914–
    A time to embrace.
    Translation of Umarmen hat seine Zeit.
    I. Title.
PZ4.P1738Ti   [PT2631.A36]   833'.914   80–13014
ISBN 0-02-594640-4

10 9 8 7 6 5 4 3 2 1

Designed by Jack Meserole

Printed in the United States of America

All things have their season,
  and in their times all things pass under heaven. . . .
A time to embrace,
  and a time to be far from embraces.

ECCLESIASTES III: 1, 6

BOOK I

Chapter 1

Sophie fell off the chair, the spoon still in her hand. She landed on her side, banging her temple on the carpet, and the chair spun sideways, falling after her. Porridge dribbled from the spoon, unnoticed. With all her strength she tried to say, "Look, Lutz, I'm eating—I'm eating porridge—to put on weight, just as you told me to—can't you see, I'm trying hard—you can't say I'm not trying—I'm eating my porridge—it's not my fault there's so much left—"

She had to stop then; a fuse had blown. Her hand, the hand that held the spoon, was lying on the floor, but the route to her mouth was blocked.

She gave up, let herself drift. Felt one last sensation of relief enter her mind, that he would at least see the spoon, full of porridge, full of evidence, not pushed down the toilet—sign of goodwill—there, look—not my fault. . . .

Lutz, who was opening a tin of stewed fruit in the kitchen, had heard the thud, and found her lying on the floor. He saw at once that she was unconscious, left her as she had fallen and ran to the phone. He called Werner Hensch, his doctor. Sophie didn't have one; for years she had refused to let a doctor so much as peer down her throat.

After he had phoned, he knelt beside her, took the spoon from her hand and lifted her onto the sofa. No effort; she weighed no more than eighty pounds. He sat beside her, studying her. Othello, the cat, came purring and jumped into her lap. Lutz made to chase him off, but at once Othello flattened himself, as he always did, across her belly, like an apron. Perhaps he'll keep her warm, he thought; she's always freezing, even in this heat.

He felt neither alarm nor grief; he had long expected this. In fact, it was overdue. During the last few weeks she'd hardly eaten anything, was always lying to him, claiming she had just now, or would later. Once he'd brought Werner Hensch to the house, but she simply refused to answer any questions. "All my life I've been too fat," she yelled at the doctor, "and now at last I feel at ease in my skin. Why don't you examine my husband now that you're here? He's anemic and a queer. Can you do anything about that?"

The ambulance could now be heard from afar, the siren coming

3

slowly closer. Lutz got up and began to straighten up the room, lifting the chair onto its legs again, scraping the last porridge from the carpet, taking the dishes out into the kitchen. As he returned, the siren was screaming, close now; it gave a final blast, and stopped abruptly. Silence. He looked around the room: everything was in place, including the motionless figure on the sofa, the cat pancaked across its lap.

Had he called Hensch and the ambulance for nothing? Was Sophie taking no more than her afternoon nap? He ran to the sofa, knelt at her side and listened to her breathing. Definitely changed. The breathing came in strong, uneven surges, clearly inconveniencing Othello, who let himself be lifted off without a protest, to be shut away in the kitchen.

Thank God, thought Lutz, thank God I haven't troubled Hensch for nothing. That would have been rather embarrassing.

The doorbell rang.

It would take a good half hour to reach the hospital, Hensch had said. At such short notice there was no room available nearer at hand. Lutz sat on one of the bench seats with his back against the pebble-glazed window. Sophie had been strapped to the bed so that she wouldn't be thrown from side to side on the journey.

Hensch had made no more than a cursory examination—heartbeat, pulse, blood pressure—and then nodded to the two attendants, who stood gazing down indifferently. Hensch himself would come later to the hospital, in his own car, but would instruct those responsible so that all would be ready and waiting. He offered no further information. "I can't tell yet," he had said to Lutz. "It's not a seizure, or a heart attack. We'll find out in due course."

To the automatic question—"Doctor, is it something . . . something . . ."—he had answered, "I don't know. At any rate, it doesn't look too bad."

Sophie herself didn't "look too bad," though she was still unconscious. On the contrary. Lying there, so peaceful, unusually relaxed, she seemed less emaciated to Lutz, less wasted. But perhaps it was only a trick worked by the unfamiliar setting and the street lights, flickering past. For weeks he had seen her only next to the murky ocher sitting-room wallpaper, holding herself erect, yet shriveled, hollow-cheeked, a boneless bag of bones. Now she seemed to have shape once again, lying very straight, her face distended, released.

4

He gave a start when she suddenly opened her eyes. For a little while she looked at him reflectively, without speaking. Then her gaze strayed to one side of him, and she spoke clearly, with some impatience: "Oh, go away, Egg. We've got no use for you right now. As if you didn't know!" And closed her eyes at once, to cut off any chance of conversation.

Later, when she opened them again, she glanced at the empty place beside Lutz, to make sure that the Egg was no longer sitting there.

"Lutz," she said quietly, "can I trust you?"

"You know you can."

"This is something special."

"All the same."

She was silent for a moment, as though trying to gauge his trustworthiness.

"If it should turn out to be serious, don't let them operate on me, to prolong my life. Suppose I was unconscious or something, then they'd ask you. Promise me that you'll refuse permission. Promise me."

Her voice was level, her eyes calm and dry, though full of urgency. "Swear," she said. "Swear by Jonathan's memory."

He said nothing.

"You're right," she said, and all at once her voice was gentler than he had heard it for a long while. "Take your time, think it over. I know you'll keep your word, if that's what you decide. For Jonathan's sake."

A mean trick, Lutz thought. Why Jonathan? It's been months since I thought of him. Now it'll start all over again.

Jonathan, his younger brother, had been seventeen years old when, one night, he'd let himself be locked inside the grounds of the zoo. It was easily done, with the clumps of dense shrubbery to hide in, as the keepers made their evening rounds to clear the grounds of visitors. At six o'clock, next morning, he had shot himself outside the cage of the great apes. The huge gray gorilla had stood motionless at the bars, watching as people ran from all sides to busy themselves with the bundle of clothes that lay on the ground, a few yards away from him. Then he had turned abruptly and ducked inside, under the flap that led to his indoor quarters, though in summer he rarely entered them.

Neither Lutz nor anyone else had ever managed to discover why

Jonathan had done it, least of all why he had done it that way, in front of the gray gorilla's cage. How had he spent those last twelve hours? What had he been thinking? What had been tormenting him? Lutz had discussed it with several psychiatrists. One had proved helpful and had tried to convince him that very possibly Jonathan hadn't felt tormented; had been looking forward to the shot, instead, like a reward. In the end Lutz came to accept this version of it, as one comes to accept the dubbing of a foreign film, rendered comprehensible by the translation. Now he could deal with it without recourse to sleeping pills. Yet he never forgot that what he carried inside him was a dubbed version. The original text remained undeciphered.

All this had happened thirty years ago. No one remembered Jonathan now, and it was years since he and Sophie had spoken of him. But she clearly knew that he was still preoccupied with the original text, if she was asking him to swear by his brother. For Jonathan was the one inviolable and untainted thing in Lutz's life. Except for the Egg, of course, but she was sacrosanct. Sophie would never have let him swear by *her* memory.

"Well?" she said after a while. "Do you need any longer?"

He nodded.

She closed her eyes. "Do you suppose he's still around, the big gray gorilla? How long do gorillas live, anyway? Perhaps he's still alive, and remembers it. I'm quite sure he remembers it—if he's still alive."

After a while Lutz said: "I swear. By Jonathan."

.

He was sitting downstairs in the hospital canteen, over his third cup of coffee. Outside, the light was fading. A change of shifts seemed to be taking place; nurses and orderlies flocked in, and one or two young doctors, residents perhaps. Hard to tell from their starched white uniforms, so poorly ironed. Here and there a button missing. Disgraceful, thought Lutz. Were things missing in the operating theater too? This pulled him back into his thoughts, into the round he had been trying to escape, in vain, during the last few hours. Operating theater. As yet there was no question of an operation, although Sophie had been taken directly to the X-ray unit. No one had yet stated what was wrong with her. And there was no sign of Hensch.

Around him, crowded metal trays, plates jostling with cups and saucers, filled up the tables. There weren't enough tables; six people were squeezing into a table for four, but nobody tried to join Lutz. They wanted to stick together and enjoy their break. They recognized only too clearly the troubled face of a relative waiting for news, and possibly eager to ask questions. Would the doctor (or the nurse) happen to know, by any chance, what was going on in room number so-and-so? What answer could they give, even if they knew, other than "You'll have to ask the doctor in charge."

The eager, noisy, laughing conversation at the next table began to have an effect on him. That's what hospital life was like! People didn't come here only to die, they were cured, discharged, left the place healthy and happy—it was perfectly possible, as it was possible, too, in Room 384, where Sophie lay. He saw her rise swiftly to her feet, get dressed and come out into the corridor, taking him by the arm and saying, "Don't walk like an old man, Lutz. Come on, let's get out of here quickly—I must go to the hairdresser's—have you fed Othello? We'll get a taxi—come along, for goodness sake—"

Was that what he wanted? Would that be a good idea? Back to the flat, Sophie in the bedroom, himself on the sofa, Othello in his basket —and when five o'clock came she'd be at the front door in her hat and coat, saying: "Back at seven-thirty, same as always." Then the light tread of her high-heeled shoes, down the front steps. Later, at seven-thirty, would come the heavy, dragging footsteps, the key fumbling endlessly in the lock to find the proper notches, and then the door slowly opening to reveal her gray, drooping features. Was that what he wanted? Would that be a good idea?

.

Upstairs, in Room 384, Sophie opened her eyes and took stock. She was in a private room, then; not the general ward. Would the Health Service pay for that? Her head was fairly clear; she found she could reconstruct, to some extent, the missing hours: lunch at home, then suddenly inside an ambulance with Lutz—something dramatic must have taken place, just as she'd always expected it would. In fact, she'd been waiting for it now, from day to day, with indifferent curiosity, if there was such a thing; indifferent toward the illness, but curious to know what was going to happen. The all-important thing was that Lutz had given his word.

The door opened and a nurse with a cap over her gray hair stepped inside. She planted herself next to the bed and took Sophie's wrist, gazing at the ceiling as she checked the pulse. Then she carefully replaced Sophie's hand and bent down to study her face, for outside it was growing dark and nobody had yet turned on the lights. She seemed to be waiting for something, but Sophie merely watched her.

"Your husband is downstairs," said the nurse with added precision, to make sure Sophie understood. "Would you like to see him?"

Sophie shook her head and shut her eyes, heard the door open and close.

When she opened them again, a young man in a white coat was sitting beside the bed. She could only partially make out his face, since he had directed the small bedside lamp onto the book he was reading. Sophie watched him as he carefully turned the pages, making no sound. After a time he sensed that she was looking at him and put the book aside.

"There now. How are you feeling?" A gentle, singsong voice. With a trace of accent on the "th." Yes, that awkward "r," she thought, not even the Egg—after so many years—could say it without rolling it.

"Do you feel pain anywhere?"

Yes. She felt pain, or rather, she felt an uncomfortable pressure on her chest, constricting her breath. She hesitated before answering. They weren't exactly pains—

"Do you need the bedpan?"

Sophie concentrated.

"Yes. But—why isn't the night sister here with me?" she added impatiently.

"I'm your night sister, Mrs. Reinhold," came the answer. "I'm on night duty on this floor. Won't I do?" He said "night sisturr," and Sophie couldn't help smiling at it, as much as at the simple, trustful question that followed.

"Of course," she said.

"Then let's give it a try," he said, and pulled the pan, discreetly covered with a cloth, out of the lowest drawer of the bedside table. "Anyway, I'm stronger than a sister. Makes things easier—I'll show you!"

He raised the section of the bed beneath her head, stuck one arm under her shoulder and propped her up, pushing the bedpan underneath her with the other hand. To her surprise she toppled forward like a rag doll. After several attempts he managed to keep her sitting upright.

"Oh, God," she said, hanging there helplessly, supported only by his arm. "I'm so sorry to be so—so—"

"There's no reason to apologize" he said, and she found herself smiling again.

"Finished?"

She nodded, and he carefully let her sink back onto the pillows before pulling the pan out from underneath her and carrying it to the adjoining bathroom.

When he returned and slowly wound the bed back into place, she had time to have a closer look at him. The white smock hung loosely on him. Short, thick black hair, a dark skin, eyes soft and dark behind the steel-rimmed spectacles. He smiled down at her as she sank down by slow degrees, away from him, and she felt a need to stroke his face. Instead, she said, "Thank you—you do it so nicely, but . . . I still find it rather embarrassing."

Patiently, he shook his head. "A few more times, and you won't find it embarrassing any more. That would be plain silly. It's my job, after all. No such thing as 'embarrassing' for us. All the same, you know—it's a good sign. If you were in really bad shape, you wouldn't find anything embarrassing, believe me."

Without waiting for her answer, he went into the bathroom again and came back with a basin of warm water, a piece of soap and a small towel. Unhurriedly he removed the bedcovers, turned up the coarse-woven hospital nightdress, washed her with firm, even strokes, dried her solicitously, and replaced the covers. He gazed probingly into her eyes for a moment before taking the basin and the hand towel to the bathroom.

Returning, he sat down once more beside her bed. She kept her eyes closed; the brief burst of activity had been surprisingly exhausting.

"Are you in pain?" he asked softly. "I can give you an injection, and you'll sleep through peacefully until tomorrow."

"What sort of injection?"

"Morphine-based. You're not allergic to morphine, are you?"

It was just as well, she thought, that the bedside lamp wasn't shining on her face. Just as well her eyes were shut—though she had a feeling he would be able to read the excitement right through her closed eyelids.

Thinking she hadn't understood him, he slowly and clearly repeated, "You're not allergic to morphine?"

She didn't trust her voice, and merely shook her head. Not too emphatically, she hoped; she was sure that any reaction would provoke suspicion. Best to lie quite still and make no sound.

"Are you in pain?"

She nodded.

"Where?"

She gestured weakly, vaguely, at her chest.

He left the room, and she crossed her arms, hugging her shoulders as though to restrain herself, afraid of bursting apart for sheer elation. So Lutz hadn't said anything about it! Had he forgotten to? Possibly. After all, it was so long ago. Or had he refrained deliberately? To let her have one last fling, now that it didn't matter anymore?

The young man came back in. She turned on her side, away from him, as though to make it easier for him to find her haunches with the needle. That way he wouldn't see her face.

"Did it hurt?" he asked.

Hurt? What did he mean by that? She lay perfectly still, face pressed into the pillow, tracing the familiar steps, so dearly loved, so long denied, following the old road slowly, slowly but irrevocably. She lay so still that he cautiously turned her over to inspect her face. What he saw reassured him. She smiled, her eyes wide open.

"Is it already taking effect?"

She nodded.

"Well, that was quick. So much the better. Now you'll soon be asleep."

He sat down in his chair, turned the light toward his book, and began to read.

Sophie watched him through half-closed lids, her face in shadow. How handsome he was! So dark and quiet, and peaceful. I love him, she thought. And what could be better than to have found, just now, someone I can love? She felt just like him, dark and quiet and peaceful. His twin. . . .

A low buzzing sound. He reached quickly into the pocket of his coat, and the buzzing stopped. Instinctively she shut her eyes, sensed that he was studying her face, from close to, and for a blissful moment she even thought she could feel his breath. Then she heard the muffled opening and shutting of the door. Of course. He was on duty, she wasn't his only patient. What a pity, she thought, and felt her eyes fill with tears. If only he could sit here all night by my bed, how lovely that would be! In any case, I won't get to sleep now, thanks to the painkiller, the killer of all pain. And I *am* free of pain, she thought, so free from head to toe that I feel I could get out of bed and go dancing . . . but why bother when *he* will be right here beside my bed, looking after me? That's what he's here for, no one can take him away from me. Even waiting for him to come back makes me happy. It's a long night, take your time. . . .

The door opened, and the young man came in on tiptoe.

"You're not asleep?"

"No, but I feel fine."

"No more pain?"

"No."

"Well, try to sleep," he said, and picked up his book again.

Shortly afterward her voice startled him, no longer hoarse and labored, but clear, almost gay: "What's your name?"

"Kostas Karanogliu."

"I couldn't possibly pronounce that."

He laughed.

"Are you a doctor?"

"I've still got three months to go, as an intern."

"What am I to call you, then?"

"Must you call me anything?"

"I'd like some way of addressing you. I can't very well call you Sister."

He pondered. "All right then, call me Brother."

"Brother what?"

"Nothing. Just Brother."

She lay in silence. What an extraordinary thing! Brother. All at once Turhan was back again. Brother was what he had always been to her, not half brother, as Papa had insisted, with such malicious emphasis: "Your half brother is . . . your half brother has . . ." Brother. Such a long time since the word had entered her thoughts.

"Brother," she said out loud.

"Don't you like it?"

"Yes. Yes, I do. A glass of water, please, Brother."

He poured her half a glass, slid his arm under the pillow, and lifted her so that she could drink. If only he wouldn't take his arm away! She longed to stay there, propped up with his face so close to hers. Carefully, he let her down again.

Before he could reach for his book, she asked quickly, "Where do you come from?"

"I was born on Crete."

How lovely, she thought. The word "Crete" filled her with an overpowering sense of bliss, for here was further proof that he was her twin, her brother.

"My mother was Turkish," she said solemnly, as though this raised her to a plane where they could meet as equals.

He looked, indeed, surprised, and pleased.

"Really? I'd never have guessed."

"I know," she said, apologetically. "I look like my father. He was a German. Blue eyes—" She stopped, then added grimly, "And red hair. Like mine. That is, like it used to be. It's white now, but I dye it red."

He nodded, and felt obliged to pursue it. "A German . . . and a Turkish girl! How did they meet? On a journey somewhere?"

She slowly shook her head.

"I'll tell you about it—if you'll listen very carefully."

"Wouldn't it be better if you tried to sleep?"

She smiled, and for a second the glitter in her eyes took him aback.

"Have you ever had morphine before?"

"Yes."

"As a painkiller?"

"I had appendicitis. And peritonitis, later on." No lies so far, she thought.

"And—do you always react this way? It doesn't put you to sleep?"

"No."

He was going to say: Be careful, you could find yourself addicted one day. But he thought of her X-rays and wondered if there was any point in warning her.

She gave a contented sigh.

"It's really a simple story," she said slowly, and gazed attentively up at the ceiling as though her text were written on it. "Don't worry, Brother, it's quite straightforward—you'll soon understand—"

The buzzing started again, and the young man stood up automatically, in spirit already outside in the corridor, without even noticing that he had cut her off in midsentence.

Her gaze slid from the ceiling to the empty chair, but her sense of well-being remained unclouded, filling her from head to toe. Her thoughts flew out, surging up in all directions until they lay spread out before her like a landscape seen from an airplane, neatly arranged, ready to be reviewed, unrolling slowly, slowly, almost imperceptibly under her eyes.

Strange. The book she had always wanted to write about her life had presented a totally different landscape: jungle, jagged peaks, ravines, deserts, here and there an oasis. And whenever she addressed it, in her thoughts, she found it altered. Like the title. For some time she had wanted to call it *A Tangled Life*; later she preferred *The Turkish Mother*—but then she might just as well have called it *The German Father*, or even *The Stepmother*—but that would have set the book off on the wrong foot. But now the right title suddenly came to her: *A Time to Embrace*, she thought, and laughed aloud. It fitted everything, from Anita onward, to—to the young doctor here, whom she would have liked to embrace. . . .

Only the opening sentence had always remained the same, in all versions, and it would still serve now in this sunny, peaceable landscape: "In the spring of 1903 the German merchant Johannes Berglund made his fourth journey to Constantinople." That said it all. And she decided to go on calling him Johannes Berglund as long as possible, rather than "my father"; at least until the stage when she actively entered the story. Perhaps longer; perhaps until her first clear memory of him, on the Wannsee, in the sailing boat, shortly before the First World War. Until then he would be Johannes Berglund, a man in his middle thirties, a man whom none glanced at casually or with indifference—unless they had something against red hair. His was a darkish red, but his beard and matted chest were blond—just like a yellow blanket, she used to think, as she rested her head against it on the beach. He was very tall, and sturdy, and broad-shouldered—later on he had a potbelly, thanks to the Cognac that accompanied him everywhere. Even into bed.

His eyes had always made her feel ill at ease, and as a child she'd wanted to hide from them behind the Dahde—but she'd better not bring in the Dahde now, or the story would get all mixed up.

Brother came in softly, and sat on his chair. She was still awake;

apparently not in pain. Her wide-open eyes gazed at him, but he wasn't sure whether she knew that he was sitting next to her again. He pulled the book out of his pocket and rearranged the lamp so that the beam fell directly onto the page.

"His eyes were large and round and blue and they protruded slightly," came her voice suddenly from the shadows. "When he was angry he looked like a basilisk. But he had a beautiful nose. So have I, I've got a beautiful nose—but his was even better, because it was bigger. His mouth . . . that's debatable. It was basically a good mouth, broad and flat, but with the years it grew narrower and stingier, until in the end it was no more than a long slit. Earlier, at the time of his fourth journey to Constantinople—I've still got a photograph of him, it's on my bedside table at home—he was in his middle thirties then, and that was surely his best age. Everyone has their 'best age,' don't you think, Brother? Do you know which yours is?"

"I think I may not have reached it yet," he said cautiously. "It's still to come."

Sophie lay in silence. She'd almost said: Mine too! Mine too is still to come—but something laughed inside her and stopped her in time.

"Brother?" she asked breathlessly.

He took her hand and held it firmly. She gazed at his face but said no more. After a time he freed his fingers and turned back to his book. When he looked at her again, her lips were moving faintly, like someone playing the piano without fully depressing the keys.

Chapter 2

In the spring of 1903 the German merchant Johannes Berglund made his fourth journey to Constantinople. He took a train from Berlin to Vienna and that evening climbed onto the Orient Express. When the luggage had been stowed away, he stretched out on the sofa in his compartment and reflected that he really only dealt in antique carpets in order to bask in the pleasure of the Orient Express. Three unbroken days in this rolling, comfortable room, with its mahogany, mirrors and velvet plush. Twice a day he strolled to the dining car; the rest of the time was spent looking out of the window or browsing through books and portfolios, photographs and drawings of old Persian carpets. Little by little, he liked to believe, he had become an expert in the field, yet where Mustafa Karabey was concerned, he'd more than met his match. Mustafa would always be able to pull a fast one on him. Nevertheless, Berglund bought from him alone, and Mustafa, knowing that Berglund had no illusions about him, had no reason to pretend, and loved him for it.

Berglund, in turn, delighted in the old man. Why did he always think of him as the old man? Mustafa probably wasn't that much older than he was—forty-five, fifty, perhaps. It was hard to tell. His face was mostly hidden by a matted undergrowth of hair, beginning at the shaggy brows, which, like a sheepdog's, all but hid his eyes from view, unless they glittered with a sudden anger. Under the bulbous nose, mustache and beard seemed to grow into one another, leaving no room for lips, only a dark opening when he spoke. The pepper-and-salt beard was certainly a glory. It hung low over his chest, culminating in two white strands, pointing in opposite directions, despite all the old man's efforts to weave them together. Perhaps it was his small, compact figure, scarcely reaching Berglund's shoulder, and his way of walking, a cumbersome, oddly dignified waddle, that made him seem older. He would be at his summer residence now, on the Bosporus. Berglund would send him a message as soon as he arrived; and there would surely be an invitation to visit Mustafa there again, and to inspect the treasures laid out for him in the great hallway. Only once—the first time—had Mustafa received him at his business premises, in the city. The old boy had taken to him right away. Love at first sight—without illusions.

On the third day the train drew in, only a few hours late, at the Sirkeci station in Constantinople. Porters, fez on head, crowded the platform in their multicolored jackets and dirty white breeches. Dozens of them, jostling, shouting, cursing, hands stretched out for his luggage. From the window Berglund calmly watched the seething throng; he no longer hurried to get off the train, to keep up with the victorious porter, as he had the first time, for fear of losing both man and bags. Since then he'd learned the porter's code: kicks for their fellows, loyalty for the effendi. If he had lost track of his man in the crowd, he would be sure to find him again next morning, on the station steps, faithfully asleep beside his luggage.

Outside the station buggies were available, horse- or donkey-drawn, according to your purse. Berglund stood still for a moment in the tumult, breathing in the smell of the city—the mixture of fog, smoke, dust, onions and salt seawater—that he loved. Then he stepped into an open carriage, sat and stretched his legs, weary after the long journey. The horses battled through the crowd, hundreds of men in fez and baggy clothes, and a very few heavily veiled women, for the most part leading children by the hand, and scuttling past. As the horses led his carriage over the Galata Bridge, Berglund once again felt it sway beneath him, as though about to collapse. He turned back to look, in the last light: Constantinople, ailing, magnificent, straddling two continents, Europe here beneath his feet, and Asia over there beyond the Bosporus.

From the first he had installed himself at the august and venerable Pera Palace Hotel, just after the Galata Bridge in the lofty Beyoğlu district of the city. They always gave him the same room, on the fourth floor, furnished in the "French style"—with a plush sofa, gas lamps, and two small potted palms—though the only thing that mattered to him was the balcony, and he dealt curtly with the eager hotel manager, anxious to be rid of him and step outside before it was quite dark.

The view excited him as much as ever. He knew every minaret, every cupola, though he didn't know their names, except for the Blue Mosque far on the horizon, and the church across from it, the Hagia Sophia, reddish in the dying light. Apart from these two, he could identify only the Topkapi Palace, the sultan's residence—but who could fail to recognize that, over by the Golden Horn, not far from the railway station.

The gas lamps were being lit below, on the streets. Someone knocked on his door to do the same to his room. Hurriedly he wrote a few lines in French and sent them with the lamplighter to the night porter, so that they would reach his friend Mustafa Karabey that very evening.

·

The answer arrived promptly, on his breakfast tray. Mustafa would be honored to entertain to lunch his friend Monsieur Johannes Berglund, whom Allah preserve, and begged leave to collect him by carriage, at noon, with a view to dining together at a restaurant—his own cook being presently indisposed with malaria. Thereafter he hoped to receive Monsieur Berglund in his humble abode, where some worthless carpets, scarcely deserving of his attention, awaited him.

The morning mist still hung over the Golden Horn and the sun still lurked behind an ocher haze. The golden crescents crowning the minarets were the first to catch the light, which spread little by little across the roofs toward Berglund's balcony, to blaze at last on his forehead. They would have to ride in the closed carriage, he and Mustafa; his red-haired pate could not tolerate such intense sunshine.

After the third call to prayer from the minarets, Mustafa's coach arrived outside the Pera Palace, and Berglund climbed in. His friend sat, grave and dignified, and very erect amid the upholstery, greeting him formally with "*Salaam aleikum*" and a slow movement of the hand from lips to brow.

"*Salaam aleikum*," Berglund rejoined, with his only bit of Turkish.

Mustafa disclosed, in French, that he was taking his guest to a restaurant dedicated to fish, a nourishment pleasing to Allah and also, he hoped, to Monsieur Berglund.

Through the open window, he celebrated his happy return to the stream of barrows, laden with vegetables, or unleavened bread or slippers, pulled through the alleyways by bawling street vendors; to the donkeys and sneering camels blocking the horses' way; to the woolly-headed urchins hanging from the carriage window, each with a diminutive fez, shouting "*Bak-shi-ish!*" until he swept them off the running board like flies. Mustafa paid no attention to the bustle around them, and meditated instead in dignified silence in his corner, until the carriage stopped in front of an old wooden shack on the Bosporus.

Berglund was gratified to note that many of its laths hung loose, and that half the planking was propped up by worm-eaten posts emerging from the water. It all promised a first-rate, and expensive, meal.

It was dark inside, with only a handful of small tables beneath the tiny slanting windows. A waiter dragged in several pails with fish swimming around inside them; those selected reappeared shortly afterward, cooked in herbs and served on wooden platters brightly lacquered in red.

"Allah bids us enjoy fish in silence," announced the old man, and they set to work on the fish bones, arming themselves for the forth-

17

coming duel, Mustafa with tea, Berglund with white wine. From now on, he knew, he must be on his guard.

Even so, the first skirmish took him by surprise: the old man had called out, but when the waiter arrived with the bill, Mustafa's attention was suddenly distracted by some lingering herbs caught in his beard. There was a pause. The bill hung uncertainly in the air. Berglund hesitantly put out a hand, looked at the figure on the dirty slip of paper and murmured involuntarily: "Good God."

The old man looked up. "You look pale, my son."

Berglund searched for his host's eyes, beneath the bushy brows, but couldn't find them. "Allah's food is richer than I expected!"

Mustafa waggled his head in sympathy. "If you could manage to create within yourself a small column of air, and give it voice, you would at once lighten your burden and praise Allah."

By the time they rose to leave, Berglund's wallet, rather than his stomach, was the burden lightened.

As they drove along the left bank of the Bosporus, Mustafa suddenly became voluble on the subject of the miserable carpets—the best in the country, mind you—and the trouble it had cost him to gather them together, on receipt of the letter announcing his friend's forthcoming visit. Berglund prayed silently that he had brought enough money. He looked out of the window, and his bad mood vanished at seeing, once again, at the waterside, the lovely painted wooden houses intricately adorned with carvings, used by the well-to-do as a summer retreat from the heat of the city.

From the outside, Mustafa's was no different from the others. The main entrance was at the side, and the little garden, filled with flowers, lay behind the house, invisible from the street. As always, Berglund's eyes went straight to the upper story with its many tall, narrow windows behind a curving grille—a mere tracery, paper-thin, by the look of it, but Berglund knew it was in fact wrought iron and guarded the most precious part of the house: the harem.

Two servants helped Mustafa out; a third held open the carriage door for Berglund. The old man turned to him in the open doorway, ceremoniously bade him welcome, and asked for Allah's blessing on the health of his guest, and the outcome of their business.

Berglund stopped for an instant on the threshold. The hallway lay before him, crossing the house from the entry to the garden door, his favorite spot in all Constantinople. It was a particularly fine one of its kind, with a high ceiling domed like a cupola, a floor of polished wood, and in the middle the time-honored fountain. There were small alcoves, to the right and left, like secret drawers in an old desk. A cool, bright place, quiet except for the lazy-busy babbling of the fountain in the slanting sunshine.

Mustafa waddled ahead, pointing at the far end of the hall. There, in the subdued light from the garden, a dozen carpets of differing sizes lay close together. Some had a woolen, others a velvet hue, intricate patterns on a brightly colored ground. There were prayer mats among them, easy to recognize by the unadorned strips for the believer's knees and feet, and equally plain corners, where vessels were to be placed. The Muslim was a practical soul, decorating with the most gorgeous embellishments that which Allah was to see, but wasting neither effort nor space on art which He couldn't see anyway under a lot of garments and copper bowls.

As always, Berglund chose quickly. He knew from experience that it only became harder if he let himself begin to weigh one design against another. His first judgment was usually the final one. For form's sake, however, he examined the weft with furrowed brow, and even smelled it. Mustafa stood a little way off, with the imperturbable expression of the connoisseur who allows his wares to speak for themselves.

This one here—wasn't it a prayer mat from Kazakhstan? Mustafa nodded. Say, a hundred years old? Mustafa nodded. Berglund was proud of himself. And that one—wasn't it an ancient Persian horse blanket? Mustafa nodded once more, and gave him an appreciative glance. Berglund sighed deeply and made his choice. So be it.

The old man clapped his hands. Two white-slippered employees appeared from nowhere, rolled up the remaining carpets and carried them off like so many huge, cracked cigars. Berglund crouched for a moment beside his newly acquired property, gazing at it, running his palms through the firm bristles of wool, so soft to the touch. Then he stood and joined Mustafa, who was already waiting for him in his favorite alcove.

.

They sat opposite one another on the floor, each on a leather cushion, Mustafa crosslegged in the Turkish manner, Berglund, less comfortably, with his long legs tucked to one side. Both had reason to be satisfied, Berglund with his old prayer mat and antique Persian horse blanket, Mustafa because the prayer mat was barely twenty years old and the blanket had been woven by his head groom's wife. A coffeepot and a tiny cup and saucer lay to hand, on a low table; a cigar in a silver capsule was beside Berglund's cup; beside Mustafa's, his hookah. It had been like this each time once business was over; they would sit and smoke in silence, both of them running through the sums once more, in their heads.

And each time it was Berglund who broke the silence, asking Mustafa whether he might not be allowed to look at the harem. Just one look! He knew that *harem* meant "no access" in Turkish, but after all, the old man had told him on each visit that he loved him "like a son," so why couldn't a "son" have a look? One brief look? So far, the old man had always merely shaken his head and stuck the hookah firmly back into his forked beard.

This time, however, he paused, plaiting his beard contemplatively. Berglund was about to repeat his question, more distinctly, when the old man rose laboriously to his feet and waddled off without a word across the polished wooden floor toward a small door, so unobtrusively tucked away in a corner that Berglund had never noticed it before. As noiselessly as possible he followed.

To his surprise, it wasn't even locked. A passageway behind it led to dark, narrow stairs. With Berglund at his heels, Mustafa climbed them slowly, step by step, puffing and groaning. At the top he paused to catch his breath. Here, too, no window. Only the faint glimmer of its golden inlay showed the low door ahead of them. The old man kicked it open with his foot.

The sudden glare blinded Berglund, and he remained standing on the threshold for a moment while Mustafa strode grandly inside. Among the potted plants, the low tables and pillows, sat some ten or twelve large bundles of brightly colored material, stiffening in surprise to see a strange man on the threshold. With a single, simultaneous gesture, they veiled their faces. Here and there a patch of forehead and a pair of eyes peeped out.

Berglund bent low, and took a step into the room. The bundles sat motionless. Then a dark shape freed itself from the knot of figures, drew erect, and marched on naked feet toward Mustafa, completely swathed in brown, a large walking cocoon; probably the first wife, thought Berglund, as he watched her kiss Mustafa's hand. But when he heard her harsh, rasping voice, he changed his mind. A eunuch, perhaps? But Mustafa explained—this was the Dahde, a sort of nursemaid, and the others were some of his wives and daughters. How many did he have, then? The old man counted on his fingers, and raised nine of them. Nine daughters. That one, over there, was the eldest. He called out something, whereupon one of the bundles, a mass of yellow muslin, raised itself slowly out of the cushions and reluctantly, hesitantly, approached them.

In later years, whenever Berglund thought of Amina, it was this first image that rose to mind, this first glimpse of her, undulating slowly toward him, like an underwater creature, or like a figure in a dream, faceless, mysterious, incandescent as a firefly. By Turkish standards she was tall. The low brow and huge, dark eyes were uncovered. She did not speak, but made a bow—a faint one—to her father; of Berglund she took no notice, and as of that moment he was lost.

Mustafa said something to the other women and laughed, and the women too laughed, and squealed, and waved their arms about, well aware that their veils flashed and shimmered in the light.

The Dahde brought a silver tray, with cups on it. Amina raised her arm and a hand like a pale rose petal emerged from the muslin sleeve. She handed Berglund the first cup, gave her father the second and took the last herself. Her hand flew slowly and gracefully through the air, and Berglund followed each movement in a trance. He emptied the sweetish mint tea in one gulp, though he knew it would make him feel sick; one was supposed to drink the stuff in small sips. But so bewitching were the enigmatic eyes and the thin, tranquil, almost transparent fingers, he refused to be distracted by the rise and fall of a cup of mint tea.

The Dahde pushed the empty tray toward him, as if to indicate that his visit was now terminated. He placed the cup on the tray, felt her eyes full of suspicion and hostility, even through the veil, and took an involuntary step backward, while Mustafa and his daughter drank in silence, to a slow, leisurely rhythm. Around them the bright, airy room rang with giggles and twittering cries, like a sunlit aviary.

.

That same evening Berglund asked for Amina's hand.

Mustafa did not seem unduly surprised, just kept on thoughtfully plaiting his beard. They were once again sitting in the alcove, each on his cushion. Was the old man flattered, perhaps, by the proposal? Did he feel insulted? Or was it all the same to him?—he had nine daughters, after all. At last he drew himself up, crossed his arms and began to do business. No beating around the bush: an eldest daughter was far from cheap, and how much did Berglund wish to invest? When it came to business, his otherwise limited vocabulary was suddenly transformed into a stream of guttural but fluent French.

For once, Berglund took no pleasure in it and barely tried to beat the old man down. Gazing at the door that led to the harem, he would gladly have agreed to whatever sum the old rogue asked. But that would have been bad manners. He made, for his part, one unyielding condition: no delay! He would not leave Constantinople without Amina at his side.

In that case he would have to stay on for a while, said Mustafa, waggling his head from side to side until the white tips of his beard shook like tassels. The necessary officials would have to be "recompensed" for the haste, and certain religious dignitaries "appeased," and of course a period of convalescence, after the circumcision, would have to be taken into account.

Somehow Berglund struggled to his feet and drew himself up to his full height. He looked for a moment as though he were about to strike the old man. Circumcision? At his age? Mustafa blinked up at him and nodded slowly. From his silence Berglund knew that on this issue there would be no bargaining.

He took a step back, anxious to be rid of the leather cushion, to be out of the alcove, stretch his legs.

Out in the hall he began to walk rapidly up and down, circling the central fountain. He paused to light a cigar. If only he could take off his jacket! Circumcision! Some stranger snipping away at his most precious possession—what on earth had he let himself in for? This morning he had been a free man—and now, simply because he'd seen a certain figure swathed in yellow veils, a fragile hand, two dark eyes . . .

He realized that he was trembling and stood still, amazed. Nothing like this had ever happened to him. As for the women in his life, he'd barely given them another thought, once they were out of his sight. All at once his neck felt quite stiff, and he turned his head from side to side and way back to gaze up at the cupola crowning the hallway. Even his head wasn't working properly—in fact, he couldn't even remember the price he'd just agreed to pay for the girl!

His mother suddenly appeared in his mind, red-headed, with that cold white skin—would he finish up the same way as his father? He wiped the sweat from his forehead. Best to break off the negotiations, and go home, back to the hotel, pack his things—or at least gain a little time to think it over. . . .

He turned and looked across at the alcove. The old man was still sitting as Berglund had left him, drawing on his hookah. Now he raised his hand and waved to him.

"Monsieur Jean!"—"Johannes" was too much of an effort.

Hesitantly, Berglund set himself in motion. The old man gestured at the cushion, always preferring to bring the giant down.

"You can have an anesthetic," he said. "Here, in town, it is used a great deal now. Of course, with us this usually takes place when a boy is five years old, so that the event is stamped on the memory. It is a moment of honor for the child. His family celebrates the day with sweetmeats and shadow plays. We would of course provide the same for you, with music, and flags—and Punch and Judy shows." He smiled disarmingly, untroubled by the black looks he was receiving from his friend.

"I have been told there is no mention of circumcision in the Koran."

"But there *is*, in the commentaries—and for us they are the deciding factor." The eyes grew serious under the bushy brows, and the voice lost its mocking tone. "I am not a pious man, and Amina is not my favorite daughter, but she shall not be given an uncircumcised husband."

There was nothing left for Berglund to say. He felt as if that afternoon he had jumped into a torrential river and found himself powerless against the current rushing him downstream.

Mustafa allowed his future son-in-law a short breathing space before administering the coup de grace: the Dahde would of course accompany Amina and remain by her side till the end of her days, Allah be praised.

Chapter 3 When he reached his hotel, Berglund ordered a bottle of Bordeaux to be brought to his room. It was late, and he had taken nothing since lunch except the mint tea. But he wasn't hungry.

Up in his room he stepped out onto the balcony and gazed at the dark, hushed city. It must have rained while he was fencing with Mustafa, for the streets glistened like wet silk in the gaslight. A sedan chair was slowly gliding toward the hotel. A figure in a white burnoose walked beside it. Probably a married man with his wife wrapped in her veils and tucked away behind the closed curtains of the litter. No half measures, thought Berglund, and bent forward over the parapet in the hope of glimpsing a hand or perhaps part of a foot as the woman emerged. Ridiculous to make so much of a hand or a foot! Simply because they were hidden in the sly wisdom of Muslim ways. When the sedan chair stopped, all he caught was the glimmer of a bright garment, which then trailed a few steps behind the burnoose, in proper humility.

Berglund drew back, sat on a wicker chair, and poured himself a glass of Bordeaux. Best not to think about it at all, fortify oneself with half a bottle, that should be enough. He already felt a little drunk, definitely lightheaded, and uncertain on his feet.

In the distance the golden crescent of the Blue Mosque showed pale in the moonlight—but his thoughts ran off, back to Mustafa's house on the Bosporus, to the fountain in the hallway, to the little entrance, the narrow staircase, the door that had opened. . . .

He got up, fetched the German-Turkish phrasebook from his bedside table and held the heavy type up to the moonlight. *Allahi akbar! La ilahu illa'llah!*—God is great! I say there is no God but Allah! So they shouted five times a day from the minarets. That wasn't what he wanted. He turned the pages: "Suggestions for Pleasant Conversation in the Brothel"? That would do. Beginning with *Seni seviyorum* —I love you.

Seni seviyorum—would he be able to remember those syllables? *Seni seviyorum*. He must beat that into his brain, so as not to miss it the first time *she* said it to *him*.

The appendix listed a chapter called "Turkish Customs and Practices." He had studied it, eager and unsuspecting, on his first visit to Constantinople, five years ago. "Wedding Ceremonies." That one he had always skipped, having had no intention of getting married— least of all to a Turkish girl.

"Both families must be in agreement." No problem there.

"Bride and groom must be Muslim." Mustafa had generously waived that condition.

"Groom must be circumcised." Will be done, dammit.

"Groom must endow the bride with jewelry." A necklace, perhaps. Pearls. Two rows.

"Groom must pay the bride's family a previously arranged sum." Will be done.

"Bride and groom begin their preparations three days before the wedding. The groom celebrates with his male friends and relatives; eating and drinking." For three days? "On the last day he is led to the bathhouse and thoroughly washed." Berglund laughed out loud, and clapped his hand over his mouth. One didn't laugh alone, in the dark. "The bride spends the three days among her female relatives, who wash her and anoint her with oils and scented herbs." Why not? "They paint her hands and feet, her brow, and her buttocks, with henna." A pity. He would have preferred Amina without the henna. Red hindquarters—like a baboon—most off-putting. "Makeup is artfully applied, and the bride is shaved everywhere—"

He snapped the book shut. He would have a word with Mustafa, first thing in the morning. The old boy had better understand that he, Berglund, was not relinquishing *all* his rights—not to him, or to her. He noticed with dismay that the mere thought of her had made him start to tremble again.

He stood up and leaned once more over the parapet. In the distance a clock struck: two o'clock. No point in going to bed—not in this frame of mind. He had never let anyone or anything come close enough to affect him like this; had guarded against it all his life, instinctively at first, and later, consciously. Not to be beholden! Neither to possessions, nor to people. His friends couldn't live without one particular woman, or without tobacco, or alcohol—and, stranger still, they didn't seem to mind the enslavement, they actually enjoyed it. He filled his glass once more, and wondered why it was that his defenses went up whenever he grew too fond of someone or something. Father and the wing chair! That was it. That's where it had begun, from the moment he had found himself standing, at the age of twelve, before the wing chair in Father's study. He had slipped into the room where Father took his nap after lunch, hoping to beg a one-mark piece from him. But he was too late, Father was already asleep. In his blasted chair. He had watched him sleeping there, ridiculous, slumped, obscene, his open mouth pressed into the upholstery.

Father couldn't live without this chair. So he said. For him it was no mere piece of furniture, it was his best friend, was cosseted, stroked and embraced with a tenderness accorded to no other member of the family. And rightly so. Had Father dared make any such advances to his offspring, neither he nor Vera would have hesitated to take advantage of him with all the ruthlessness of children who know they are in the saddle.

For Father was a natural dependent, a slave by temperament. Only his friend, the wing chair in his study, treated him with respect, molded itself to his small frame, protected him from drafts, warmed him, and, when he went out, waited patiently for his return. No one else waited.

And Mother? Was she like that, because of *him*—or was he like that, because of *her*? Who was "like that" first? What had they been like when they first met? There was a big oval oil painting of her as a young woman, dressed in an off-the-shoulder evening gown, her red hair piled high above her head, pearls around her neck and a rose in her hand. A white rose—but Mother's shoulders were even whiter. Like chalk. Father must have fallen for her; and she must have put up with him, because the little man smelled of money.

Those days were never mentioned, they had left no anecdotes, not even a wedding photograph, and the children never asked. Neither Vera nor he was interested in their parents as a couple. You kept out of Father's way because he made you feel embarrassed, and out of Mother's because there was no peace when she was in the house—exuding a kind of electrical current which penetrated doors and could give you a hefty shock at any moment.

Father appeared only at mealtimes, when he stuffed himself hastily and with as much food as if he were off to the wars. The study was the only room where he was allowed to smoke his pipe, and he would retreat there at once, and sleep for an hour in the arms of his friend. Then slip soundlessly down the stairs to the front door. On tiptoe. He loved old, well-worn shoes, with soft soles, and never bought new ones. He did, however, sometimes have to wear new shoes—not his own, his wife's. She was so large and he so small that they took the same size in shoes, and she loved new shoes, provided they weren't too stiff. And so, five or six times a year, a pair of brand-new shoes with high heels and buttons all the way up were to be found in front of the wing chair, with the buttonholer beside them, awaiting Father's return. He had to put them on and wear them all evening, to break them in, by tripping up and down the stairs with dainty, cautious steps, like a child. Vera and he were used to the sight, and no longer laughed. Sometimes Father toppled over, and they would prop him up again.

Berglund stepped back from the parapet and dropped into the wicker chair. Why was his father pestering him tonight? Was it because he himself was well on the way to being trapped? Nonsense. He wanted to possess this girl, and that was all. The price—circumcision, marriage—was exorbitant, admittedly. As was the ridiculous trembling that came over him when he thought of the fluttering yellow veil. Only once had she looked him full in the face—and he had known immediately: these were no soft, trusting calf's eyes, they were knowing eyes, with shifting lights in them, for all that they were black. A virgin she might be—she wouldn't be worth a farthing otherwise—but she knew what it was all about, he never made a mistake on that score.

He opened the phrasebook once more, vaguely remembering that there was a specific ritual by which the bridegroom expressed his satisfaction, the morning after the wedding, with the irreproachable condition of his purchase. "Groom takes a pistol and shoots into the fireplace." That was it. But that would be difficult. For he had his own, quite specific, plans. . . .

According to custom he must spend the night with Amina under her father's roof, so that all the occupants, upon hearing the pistol shot, could break into vociferous rejoicing.

But Berglund intended to take Amina away as soon as the wedding feast was over. They would drive directly to the station. He would spend his wedding night on the Orient Express.

Chapter 4

Mustafa seemed to be expecting him, for the servant showed him into the long hallway without delay. The old man was sitting on the rim of the fountain, and the Dahde was about to place a footstool beneath his slippered feet. As soon as she saw Berglund she hurried away, hastily pulling the veil across her face.

27

He permitted Berglund to help him to his feet, in order to ex-change the threefold greeting—hand toward heart, lips and brow. And now—to withdraw into the alcove? Oh no, thought Berglund, not the alcove, where he had fallen too often into Mustafa's trap. He lifted the little man into the air and deposited him once more on his cushion on the rim of the fountain. And sat down beside him.

Mustafa spent a while in silence, to regain his dignity, and finally observed that Allah was great, and was the one true God. Berglund had nothing to offer against this; on the contrary, it provided a cue for his opening gambit.

"Allah," he remarked thoughtfully, while lighting his cigar, "must surely have designed the world with a master plan full of divine wisdom, wouldn't you say, Mustafa Karabey, effendi?"

The old man looked at him with astonishment. He was fully pre-pared for his future son-in-law to visit him today and do his best to knock a few thousand off the exorbitant price he had set on Amina. Nothing unusual or dishonorable in that. But why begin with his pious hymn to Allah? Was it possible that the man wanted to be converted to Islam? He could tell that Berglund was smitten, and had raised the price accordingly, but was he so eager to oblige Amina that he would change over to her religion? How incredible! It was of no great importance to him, Mustafa, nor for that matter to Amina, but the idea had a certain sporting appeal. It might be amus-ing. He joined the palms of his hands, and gave three pious nods.

Berglund toyed with the water in the fountain, letting it run slowly through his fingers.

"Men and women, I take it, have also been designed according to divine plan, then?"

Mustafa hastened to concur with this no less devout thought—indeed, every worldly particular had been worked out and marvel-ously realized, down to the smallest trifle. And he ran his fingers through the splendid beard with which Allah, in his wisdom and attention to detail, had equipped him.

"In that case," said Berglund, his blue eyes turning an abruptly stony gaze on the old man, "why does the Turk seek to correct Allah's design?"

Mustafa sensed that Berglund's conversion was up the spout—but it left him even more in the dark. Furiously knitting his shaggy brows, he discovered that the French language suddenly failed him. And his hearing, too, seemed to have developed a fault—but his future son-in-law knew and treasured his every trick, and so wasted no time repeating his words or speaking louder. Instead, he brought out his Turkish phrasebook, and looked up the appropriate page.

"Why do you paint the bride's behind with henna?" he asked fiercely, pointing to the sentence in question. "Why do you shave her?"

Taken wholly by surprise, Mustafa's mouth fell open, leaving a yawning black hole, with here and there a yellow tooth, between the tangled hairs.

"Or did Allah make a mistake, perhaps, when he created woman?" continued Berglund remorselessly. "Are you so ashamed of his work that you get your women to improve it, secretly, in the women's quarters, before allowing it to be inspected? Is Allah then a bungler?"

He had gone too far. Mustafa swayed back and forth in indignant protest, and fell off the fountain altogether. Two servants rushed up and lifted him back to his feet while Berglund watched impassively, without raising a finger.

The old man bellowed in Turkish, appealing to heaven with fists raised, and allowed himself to be half carried and half dragged out, hands waving wildly in the air. No one paid any attention to Berglund, who remained sitting on the edge of the fountain, watching the water eddy out from the spring. It was so beautifully cool, sitting there—probably for the last time. Still looking down, his gaze traveled away from the fountain and came to rest on a pair of naked brown feet on the polished floor. The Dahde! Crept in, no doubt, on old Mustafa's orders, to show him the door. He raised his eyes, finding himself already at a disadvantage—she could look down at him at leisure, while he had to look up at an inscrutable dark-brown pillar.

She raised her hand—to usher him out? No, the brown fingers were pointing not toward the entrance door, but—was it possible?—to the tiny portal that led to the harem. Berglund jumped up—and the hand at once made a peremptory gesture meaning "no" in any language and pointed instead to one of the alcoves at the far end of the hallway, beside the door leading into the garden. As Berglund started toward it, he looked around, but she had vanished.

This alcove, too, was furnished with a pair of cushions on the floor, beside a low table. Berglund sat and waited. Sweat shone on his forehead and upper lip, though he continued to mop at them with his handkerchief. He arranged the cushion so that he could keep an eye on the entrance to the harem. This time there would be no sudden apparitions, barefoot or soft-slippered; he would see the door open, and be able to see her approach, gliding softly toward him—

"Monsieur," came a low voice behind him.

The Dahde and Amina stood behind him in front of the alcove; two statues, one dark, the other white, both motionless, ghosts in daylight.

Berglund sprang to his feet. The garden door! So the women were allowed into the garden. A pity; he had rather liked the idea of Amina caged in that bright, sunny room.

In his confusion, he bowed and at the same time reached automatically for Amina's hand, to kiss it; but the hand—the rose petal—had flown in Turkish greeting to her heart, her shrouded mouth and exposed brow.

He recovered his composure and moved back to invite the women into the alcove, offering them the cushions to sit on. But they remained standing where they were. He cleared his throat, racking his brains as to how he should address Amina.

"Mademoiselle—" he burst out finally. "I am sorry to have upset your father."

Presumably she understood French; she had called him "Monsieur," after all. What else could he say to her?

"Monsieur," answered the white statue, "do not leave."

He stared at her. He had said nothing about leaving.

"Be patient. You will receive message, by hotel."

The voice was a young girl's, but the manner was surprisingly mature and her French not at all bad. Berglund could find nothing to say, and continued to stare at her, without a word. Perhaps misconstruing his silence, she took a step toward him, and her voice sounded almost anxious.

"Monsieur—I am coming with you." But when she saw the ecstatic expression on his face, she stepped back again.

"Yesterday was my father winning. Today is you."

He could offer no reply to these enigmatic words, and merely nodded. After a short pause she added: "I read Victor Hugo," as though this explained everything, both yesterday's events and today's. Her hand was already fluttering through the parting gesture —in reverse order: brow, lips, breast. Then she was gone, slipping through the garden door. The Dahde waddled after her.

.

The promised message arrived the next day, at the hotel: a roll of parchment sealed with wax, which testified in ornate lettering that the girl Amina would be delivered in pristine condition ("*dans l'état naturel*") and without any "embellishment" to the highly respected Monsieur Johannes Berglund, whom Allah preserve, in return for which the highly respected Monsieur pledges himself to be circumcised, in honor of Allah, and to pay the sum of sixteen thousand gold ducats, in favor of Mustafa ben Karabey.

.

The wedding took place a month later, in Mustafa's house, at exactly five o'clock in the afternoon, as decreed by law. The Hotscha, a little black-robed priest, united the bride and groom, Amina heavily swathed in veils, Berglund in black dress suit and starched wing collar. Hundreds of guests gathered in the great hall after the wedding meal; mostly men, with here and there a shrouded female figure of an older vintage. The Dahde, parceled in brown as usual, waddled gravely from guest to guest with the silver tray, offering them mint tea and heaped sweets as brightly colored as their costumes.

Berglund towered head and shoulders above the crowd. At least it allowed him to breathe freely, but among the billowing white skirts and colored and embroidered waistcoats he felt like a huge black beetle. He had to hold out until the last guest had left the house. On that condition alone had he obtained old Mustafa's permission not to spend the night under his roof. No friend or relative must witness the shameless way in which his daughter left her father's house!

In the rising heat, Berglund thought he would shortly strangle in his stiff collar, and withdrew into a far-off alcove to undo the top button. He looked back at the guests, searching for Amina, but she was nowhere in view. He had not been allowed to see her since their conversation at the garden door, an endless-seeming month ago during which he had been duly circumcised, a nasty little operation, performed at his hotel, though, thank God, necessitating three days in bed. The bride remained in purdah for the four weeks before the wedding. A last turn of the screw, a final whetting of the bridegroom's appetite.

Mustafa pushed his way through the crowd, to join him in his alcove. He lowered himself to the cushion with a groan.

"The bride is upstairs in the harem," he said in answer to Berglund's searching eyes. "The bride"—now no longer his daughter; no longer his property. "She is bidding farewell to her sisters." After a pause he added: "Her mother is dead. She cost a great deal of money, but she only lived a short time. She came from Alexandria. Amina is like her. Troublesome. If I may offer one piece of advice, my son: don't spare the whip. Nevertheless—I wouldn't say you'd made a bad buy. You know what the sultan said, when he was asked which of his slave girls he wished to be brought to him that night? He said: 'Pour a basin of cold water over each of them; bring me the one who gives off steam, and sizzles a little.' I think you'll find, my son, that Amina sizzles a little."

I'll never begin to fathom the man, thought Berglund. There he sat, his father-in-law, a dignified old man—talking about his daughter as if she were a cheap slave girl. . . .

"I was unlucky with my wives," the old man went on. Till now he had carefully avoided any reference to his private life. Perhaps the wedding ceremony had made him feel nostalgic.

"The first four either died or proved barren. Those who followed produced nothing but daughters. Let us hope Amina will strive to give you a son. Let me know at once. No need to bother if it's a daughter."

The Dahde approached with her silver tray. Berglund and the old man shook their heads, and she disappeared once more among the milling guests.

"Give the Dahde a sleeping place not too far from Amina, my son."

"She will have her own room," said Berglund.

"I wouldn't advise that," said the old man with a frown. "You don't want her to be lonely, do you? Put her mattress outside Amina's door."

Berglund nodded, though he didn't find it an enticing prospect.

"What is she called? *Dahde* simply means 'nanny,' 'nurse' . . . isn't that right?"

"She has no name. She was a slave when my father bought her. He needed servants, so he bought a village, some twenty people or so, with their furniture, their camels and their goats. In Libya somewhere, quite cheap. The Dahde was an orphan. The village elders threw her in, free of charge. She was four years old. Later I bought her freedom—and when I married, I took her with me."

"Does she speak only Turkish?"

Mustafa stared at his son-in-law.

"Only Turkish? She hardly speaks at all, my son—she is a good Dahde. Be grateful that she neither reads nor writes and should cause little mischief. Do not disturb her on her prayer mat, and feed her daily."

He struggled to his feet.

"The Hotscha awaits." He sighed. "I have yet to pay him. He is very expensive." With that he left Berglund and headed for the priest, who was standing apart, waiting gravely with his hands hidden in the wide sleeves of his robe.

Gradually the numbers began to dwindle; some of the guests took the trouble to seek out Berglund in his alcove and take their leave, with a faint bow and the greeting in reverse order—brow, lips, breast. Berglund responded in kind. He liked the gesture and had practiced it in front of the mirror, at the hotel. In no other way would he greet Amina. The very thought of exchanging a European handshake with her seemed like sacrilege.

.

It was dark by the time the last guests had gone. The Orient Express did not leave until ten o'clock, but the Sirkeci station was some way away, and Berglund was anxious to leave. He had "arrangements" to make at the wagons-lits, and they might take time. In this country one didn't like to be hurried.

Amina's old-fashioned chests and leather bags stood in the hall; Berglund couldn't help being moved by the sight. She had never been anywhere before, never seen a station, or a train. She had only Victor Hugo to go by.

In no time at all the servants had removed all trace of the wedding celebrations, and the tall, spacious hallway was once again cool and serene. Mustafa sat quietly enthroned in his favorite alcove, smoking his hookah. He had not summoned his new son-in-law to join him, and Berglund sat a short distance away, on the edge of the fountain. It

33

was deathly silent now—only the water bubbled on importunately—and he was waiting, alone, a little numbed by the violent contrasts of the day. He dipped his hand into the cool water and dabbed at his face.

The portal that led to the harem opened at last, and the Dahde appeared with a bundle under her arm. The prayer mat, thought Berglund. Amina followed, wearing an embroidered dress, and over it—despite the heat—a sleeveless coat. On her head an embroidered fez, from which the all-obscuring veil hung to her shoulders.

Mustafa squirmed to his feet, put down the hookah and went over to the women. Berglund too had risen, but held back, waiting. Amina lowered her head. The old man raised his hand as if in blessing, and she touched brow, lips and breast, a little less casually, perhaps, than before, kissed his hand, and turned to go. No words had passed between them. Perhaps everything had already been said. The Dahde stepped forward and also kissed the old man's hand.

The servants carried the luggage out into the waiting coach. Both women stopped in the doorway and watched as Berglund approached his father-in-law. He made the Turkish greeting, but Mustafa stretched out his hand and laid it heavily on Berglund's shoulder. A wave of emotion coursed suddenly between them, and Berglund almost gave in to his feelings and embraced the old man. He quickly turned and followed the women out of the door.

But no sooner had he taken his place beside Amina in the coach than a strange thing happened: the Dahde gave a sudden hoarse and piercing cry and clambered out of the coach, running back toward the house as fast as her sandaled feet permitted. Mustafa was standing in the doorway. An oil lamp above him cast a gentle light on his tangle of white hair and the red shoulders of his ceremonial jacket.

Berglund rose to go after her—but to his surprise, Amina laid her hand on his arm, and he sat back, as startled by the firm pressure of the "rose petal" as by the Dahde's sudden flight.

The Dahde had now reached the doorway and was kneeling before Mustafa, throwing her arms around his knees and pressing her head against him. The old man bent down and murmured in her ear. Then he straightened up and placed his hand on her head. For a time they remained, unmoving; finally, he took his hand away, she rose laboriously to her feet and padded slowly back to the coach.

Berglund had watched the scene intently and now turned to

34

Amina, who sat calmly ensconced in the upholstery, gazing out of the window on the other side of the carriage, as though the whole affair was no concern of hers—or she already knew its outcome.

He reached out and helped the Dahde back into her seat, opposite the bride and groom. The dark-brown upholstery swallowed up the dark brown of her wrappings, and it seemed to Berglund as if, all of a sudden, she had disappeared.

Chapter 5 One hour later they arrived at the station. By then Berglund had had his first lesson in the art of silence; for when he tried to start a conversation Amina had merely answered yes or no, or not answered at all. Eventually he gave up and sat, stiffly, somewhat at a loss, listening to the clip-clop of the hooves on the paving stones. Yet little by little he began to feel that the silence in the carriage was not an uncomfortable one. Indeed, it felt almost natural. The veil didn't exactly invite conversation—for, without an answering smile, without eloquent eyes to address, it was like speaking into a void. Only the faint, occasional flutter of the material assured you that there was someone alive and breathing behind it. No doubt that was why Turkish women giggled so much. Amina at least did not giggle. He began to enjoy her silence.

Light broke into the semidarkness of the carriage, and she pushed her face against the window so as to see, through her veil, the lights of the Topkapi Palace. Berglund sat up, straightened his hat. They would soon be there.

In the noisy maelstrom of the station, Amina and the Dahde pressed close against each other. As the porters took their luggage away, the Dahde reached after them imploringly, and although Berglund made reassuring noises, she cried out despairingly in Turkish. Berglund's concern was short-lived—for there, beside the platform, he saw his beloved Orient Express, awaiting him.

What a pity that neither of the women could possibly know the difference between this and any other train. They barely looked up from the platform as they hurried along behind him, in silence, past carriage after carriage, to the two wagons-lits sections. A mustachioed official stood outside the women's compartments, directing the porters, for not even a married woman was allowed to share her husband's quarters.

No. 7b: compartment with double bed. Berglund had realized that Amina and the Dahde were not to be kept separate during the eighty-hour journey to Vienna, at least during the day. He only hoped that the Dahde would not put up a fuss when Amina was secretly collected at night and brought to the men's sleeping car, compartment No. 5a.

They both stood now, irresolutely, on the steps of their sleeping car. Mustache turned to Amina and spoke Turkish to her. All three turned to Berglund.

"Monsieur, should I escort the ladies to their compartment?"

Berglund bowed to Amina, nodded to the Dahde and said casually to the man: "Very good. I shall wait here for you."

Mustache gestured toward his colleague, who was standing on the steps of the neighboring sleeping car, helping the male passengers with their luggage.

"No," said Berglund pointedly. "I have something to discuss with *you.*"

The man gave him a suspicious look, and without a word offered his hand to help Amina up into the carriage.

Berglund remained waiting on the platform.

Twenty minutes later, as the bell announced their imminent departure, he was still waiting. At last, cursing, he climbed into the men's carriage and slammed the door behind him. Rumbling and hissing, the train lurched forward. He ran down the corridor to the connecting door between the two carriages, to find it locked, of course.

For the first time ever, he felt lonely in his "room" amid the mahogany and the velvet. The bed had been made and the curtains pulled, but he could not bring himself to undress.

A knock at the door—and the familiar face of the conductor, an old friend, who also sported a mustache, but a cheerful one. Berglund waved him into the compartment. Perhaps . . .

"Would you sit down for a moment?"

The man twirled uneasily at his mustache.

"Herr Berglund—it is not permitted."

"Could I have a word with you?"

The conductor shut the door and leaned against it, gazing attentively at him.

"Monsieur," he said when Berglund had explained, "you can't do anything about my colleague next door—he is a widower, and stubborn as a mule. But if you could be patient, tomorrow night, in Bucharest, he will be replaced by a friend of mine. Then something could be arranged, if you follow my meaning."

Berglund did, and brought out two gold ducats. The conductor swept them elegantly off the table and into his pocket, and withdrew respectfully.

Now he felt in better heart to take off the dress suit and the stiff collar. He climbed into bed and ran his palm across the smooth mahogany partition. Tomorrow!

.

The train stopped for a full hour in Bucharest. This suited him, it wasn't dark enough yet. The window should be open, and the night air blowing in, when Amina entered. . . .

The bucket with the champagne, the two glasses, the dish full of sweets, the vase of roses—all hastily rounded up by the conductor while the train waited in the station. He forced himself to settle back into an armchair, and stretched his long legs. Come now: calm . . . equanimity . . . composure.

The train moved off with a violent jolt, and he could hold out no longer in the armchair. Too hot. He leaned out of the window and cooled his face in the rushing wind. It was long past sunset, but until the train was out of the city it would not be dark enough in his compartment. Patience . . .

Pulling his head in, he caught a glimpse of his disheveled red hair in the mirror, and combed it with care. Should he undress? He knew he looked impressive in the dressing gown, he had often been told as much—but what about the nightshirt beneath it? Not the most seductive of garments—though he'd have to put it on sometime. Was it perhaps a little too direct, to receive Amina in his dressing gown? What would *she* be wearing? Most of all he would have liked her to come to him in the yellow muslin she had worn the first time, in the harem, as she rose and walked toward him.

It was truly dark at last. Now and then a faint light swept the compartment, as the train passed a signal box or a cluster of houses. And he began to undress, without noticing. All at once it seemed perfectly natural: no nightshirt, just the dressing gown. Then he groped his way back to the window.

37

By the time the knock came, he had very nearly regained his usual nerve. Friendly mustache looked in—the light in the corridor revealed his smirking face—then he widened the opening, for something white to slip through, before once more shutting the door.

The wedding dress. He recognized it at once. But a different veil, leaving the upper part of her head free, and in the split second that the light had fallen on her, he had glimpsed her eyes. She remained standing by the door, made no attempt to advance into the compartment.

"*Venez*, Mademoiselle." He went across, took her arm and led her to the chair beside the window; then drew up another and sat next to her. There would be time, in the morning perhaps, for addressing her in the familiar *tu*. Not now; after all, she was a stranger. He had bought her as he had often bought women before, yet this was no whore but a young girl with whom he had barely exchanged a dozen words. She had said she wanted to come with him. Why? To escape from the harem, to lead the life of an emancipated woman (Victor Hugo!)? Or because she had taken a sudden fancy to him? Hardly. And at that moment, if he was honest with himself, he didn't really care. There she sat, his property, while the Orient Express rushed through the night. The Thousand and One Nights.

He reached for the champagne and filled both glasses in turn, but she shook her head. Of course—the Koran! No alcohol. He drained his glass, then drank hers as well, and suddenly felt a frenzied agitation mounting inside him. But what was *she* feeling? She was leaning back in her armchair, hands in her lap. Those hands! He took them, stroked them, found that they almost slipped through his fingers, paper-thin, all but weightless. He raised them and pressed his face to her palms. "Oil and scented herbs . . ." A signal box flashed past, and he caught another glimpse of her eyes, gazing calmly and composedly at him.

What if he now stroked her arm—up to her shoulder, then her neck, and then up to her chin, still hidden by the veil? She offered no resistance, and neither pulled back nor stopped him.

He stood and raised her to her feet. His fingers felt for the fastening of her dress, they searched beneath her veil at the nape of her neck for the hooks and eyes he had always been adept with, be they ever so small. But this time he searched in vain, running his fingers up and down the seams, exploring the material from side to side, clawing at it despairingly with his nails.

All at once he felt Amina's hand pressing against his chest. He had tipped her forward, and she lay there, leaning on top of him like a rag doll, as he worked at the dress. "I am sewn up," she said calmly.

His fingers jerked away from her as if he had been stung. Sewn up? He gazed at her, appalled. There was nothing about this in the Turkish phrasebook. Sewn up? How—and where?

Was she deliberately keeping him in suspense? When she spoke again, he thought he could hear suppressed laughter in her voice.

"Bride always sewn up in wedding dress. Groom opens seam with dagger."

The train lurched violently as it entered a bend, and he had to grab hold of the window with one hand, putting the other around the girl, to keep their balance. How defenseless she felt! As soon as he could straighten himself, he propped her carefully against the wall and groped his way to the washbasin. He had no dagger. Nail scissors would have to do.

But as he came back toward the window, brandishing the little scissors, Amina stretched out her hands imploringly, as if to ward them off.

"No!" she whispered. "Scissors cut happiness in two."

"I haven't got a knife," he said helplessly, dropping the scissors onto the table.

She took a step toward him and reached for his hand.

"Only dagger," she whispered, and placed his hand against her breastbone. "Here!" He thought he could feel something narrow and sharp, under the dress, against his palm.

"Bride must not touch," she said urgently, as if in answer to his unspoken question. "The Dahde brought dagger—hidden here. You must take out."

She dropped her hands and stood patiently waiting, as he struggled to fit his large hand into the gap between her neck and the material, then find the blade and, without hurting her, extract it between thumb and forefinger. It was less than six inches long and no wider than a fruit knife, tapering to a deadly point.

Amina gestured to the nape of her neck. He turned her around so that the faint, infrequent light from the window might help reveal the all-important seam.

They stood, waiting, in silence; at last a signal box—and as it rushed past, just enough light for him to see where her fingers were pointing. There it was, the seam, that was where it started! He covered the spot with his forefinger so as not to lose it; he could feel the place quite distinctly now, but decided to wait for the next hamlet, so as to see it, too, since the dress was tight against her body, and the blade was sharp.

It never occurred to him—nor, apparently, to Amina—to light the gaslamp in the compartment. For the time being, no hamlet came in view, but he no longer felt impatient. In the darkness he held his finger poised against the seam, and, as he waited, he was reminded of an image from the Sistine Chapel, Michelangelo's vision of the creation, which had always intrigued him: Adam, lying drowsily in the grass, just completed, still wet as it were, and God the Father on His cloud, solicitously propped up by angels after His exertions. The last link between the Creator and His work were their forefingers, barely sundered. . . . And Berglund's own finger, touching the seam he was shortly to rip open, seemed to him as lightly yet as fatefully suspended.

The train passed through a small town, and slowed down, as if to make his task easier. Now there was ample light. Carefully he inserted the blade—and the true meaning of the old custom became suddenly clear to him as he slowly, slowly but with a steady hand undid the stitches one by one.

.

When he awoke, it was as if he had been so deeply buried that he could make his way only very slowly to the surface. The rattling and shaking of the train told him at last where he was. A few seconds more and he could identify the weight against his right arm: Amina.

There was something jabbing into his shoulder. He reached up carefully—it was a metal clasp, the one that gathered her veil together behind her head, now twisted and tangled in her hair.

It was still early, five o'clock at the latest, and no longer completely dark. He could make out the blackness of her hair against his arm, and her face, still hidden by the veil. She was fast asleep, breathing quietly and steadily. He pushed himself up slowly onto his left elbow, and watched the fine material across her face waft up and down. Soon it would be light enough—the window was still open— and he would remove the veil. . . .

Last night, once the dress had been split open, she had stepped out of it unaided and placed it neatly on the chair, together with the undergarment and the curiously pleated leggings that lay beneath. Then at last she turned slowly to face him. Narrow breasts, full hips—his heart sank: he preferred it the other way around, yet he found himself affected, and impressed, by the calm way she stood before him, gazing past him out of the window, naked except for the short veil which flapped up and down in the gusts from the window, now sticking against her face, now billowing out like a soap bubble.

Then she raised her arms, unhurriedly, to release the veil from its fastening behind her head—and he could only reach out imploringly to stop her, could not find the right words. For a moment she had looked at him, surprised, almost suspicious, her arms two white triangles above her head—then she suddenly understood, and slowly let them drop. He could have sworn that her eyes were smiling at him. He had not been mistaken, then! She understood instinctively or knew already, knew things he could never have explained to her.

Morning was approaching fast, or else his eyes were growing accustomed to the darkness. Cautiously he released the metal clasp beneath the dark hair on his shoulder. The veil lay still across her face, now free to be peeled away. He lifted it stealthily, leaned forward and gazed in rapt excitement at her pale and sleepily puffy face.

So this was what she looked like!

Perhaps she felt he was looking at her, for her breathing seemed less steady now, but she still lay motionless. He studied her features, taking his time. It suddenly occurred to him that he would not have recognized her in the street. Some of her features he knew already: the long, arched eyebrows, as thick and black as befitted a daughter of old Mustafa, recognizable by his bushy brows alone. Her eyes, which had seduced him from the first moment he saw her, were hidden by faintly flickering lids. The nose was new to him, and he studied it in detail: it was straight and broad, though not too broad. No one could say it was a classical nose, but it wasn't one of the potato-shaped ones he had seen so often in Turkish bordellos. The upper lip, very short; the mouth full, dark, and firmly etched; the kind of face that lost its charm with its youth. But she was young, very young, just sixteen.

Her pupils moved beneath her lids, and Berglund was now sure she was awake. He lay back on the pillow, satisfied, feeling no urge to greet her yet, to talk and smile. He felt content. At peace. Peaceful, tranquil, as never before.

It was light now, but he fell asleep once more. Without his knowing, Amina sat up soundlessly, leaned across, and began to study his face.

BOOK II

Chapter 1 Later, when he thought back to these first few months, he saw them as one sunlit, unbroken parade of days beneath a cloudless sky; beginning that first day, when he woke once more at nine o'clock, to find Amina sleeping at his side. Waking her, he jumped out of bed, opened a small case, took out a pistol and brandished it before her. She understood at once, and laughed, then gazed questioningly at him. No fireplace. Well then, he must fire into something else, but fire he must. Naked, with a pistol in his hand, the oriental custom seemed to him entirely proper. Should he shoot out of the window? But then nobody would hear it. He slowly turned full circle—Amina pulled the blanket over her head—eyeing prospective targets, and decided that the center mirror, above the sofa, should have the honor. He aimed, fired and laughed aloud above the bang and the sound of splintering glass, one shard of which embedded itself in his thigh. Satisfied, he pulled out the chip of glass and was about to wash the small cut it had made when several fists began to knock urgently at the compartment door. He took his time, put on his dressing gown and combed his hair. Outside the door, three pale, alarmed faces—one of them the friendly mustache, the others two young men from the next compartment. The conductor understood at once, saluted by way of congratulation, and pocketed another gold ducat from Berglund as he gathered up the shattered glass. The young men, two brothers from Austria, required something rather more elaborate by way of explanation, while they stared amazed and curious at the bed and at Amina's shape buried beneath the covers.

Spending the night in Vienna would have meant arriving at the Hotel Sacher with Amina and the Dahde and the chests and bags, so he decided instead to take the next train to Berlin. They traveled together in a first-class compartment, Amina in her traveling outfit and yashmak, the Dahde still from head to foot a brown parcel.

Along the route he tried to draw Amina's attention to this or to that, but could obtain no more than a syllable or two, albeit favorable ones, in response. "Look, Amina, a ruined castle from the fourteenth century." "Very pretty." "We're coming to the frontier now,

45

the German frontier—you can see the German sentries, with their rifles, over there." "Very pretty."

He even tried to involve the Dahde, but when in the middle of his description of the confluence of the three great rivers in Passau she gave a loud snore, he abandoned the idea.

After a time there was silence in the compartment. One by one they had fallen asleep.

The arrival in Berlin, the journey home in two cabs—he and Amina in the first, the Dahde and the luggage in the second—the welcome waiting for them at the house on Ruemelangstrasse, in the Tiergarten—it all seemed to him to glow, in retrospect. His telegram had said that he had married a Turkish girl, and his housekeeper, Frau Glaubitz, was prepared for everything. There was a full reception on the front steps, with herself and Peelke, the manservant, on the lowest step, and behind them, one step up but still hidden by them, Gerhard the gardener, a dwarf.

As the first cab drew up, and Berglund helped Amina out, Frau Glaubitz dug her elbow into Peelke's ribs. Just as she imagined it: one with a veil! When the second cab arrived with the Dahde, however, her Berliner nose was severely out of joint. A black! She crossed herself, and wondered whether to apply for an increase in salary.

What sort of food did they eat, these shrouded creatures? Berglund solved the problem by letting the Dahde convert a second-floor room into an oriental kitchen, with an open fire—to the horror of Frau Glaubitz, who wrung her hands. The entire house would go up in flames! But after all, the houses in Constantinople hadn't all burned down, and the Dahde—of this much he was certain—could be trusted with a fire.

His house now contained two separate zones. Frau Glaubitz and Peelke continued to rule undisturbed below, while above them the Dahde reigned, and cooked, filling the air with fatty, aromatic smells. Berglund didn't mind. It reminded him of Mustafa's house. His old way of life remained unchanged, except that he now rarely visited his sailing club, and saw his friends less often. He gave a reception so that they could meet Amina, and they came eagerly, in full strength, only to find that Amina wore a yashmak! Poor thing. Shy, of course. What a bore for Berglund.

No bore at all, and Amina was anything but shy. He loved the yashmak and insisted that she keep it on, at least at night. During the day, when he was out of the house and there was nobody to see her but the Dahde, she took it off.

He resumed his working day soon after their return to Berlin. The premises where he both stored and displayed his antique furniture and carpets was too far away to return home at lunchtime. He had never minded this; nor did he now. He loved the old building in the Rankestrasse. His office was a tall, spacious room on the second floor, with his clerk—a pallid youth called Gerstenkorn, known as Gerste—installed in one corner. When important clients called, Berglund was informed by means of a speaking tube and descended in an ancient elevator to the showrooms on the ground floor. There he made his entrance through a strategically placed Spanish doorway. In the evening he went home by cab—but now, perhaps, he would purchase a motorcar. He had seen no reason to indulge in one before, because he didn't know what to do with a chauffeur during the day. Now he did.

The car and the chauffeur—one Gaston, from Alsace—were duly added to the household, and Amina and the Dahde took daily drives through Berlin, when Amina felt well enough. For she was pregnant. She had informed Berglund, six weeks after their arrival, and without any fuss. When he asked her whether she had let her father know, she vigorously shook her head.

He sometimes wondered how she actually spent the day. She never complained at having no friends, no girls her age to talk to, no one in the city she knew. She wouldn't visit the Turkish embassy—the women there were "different." When he came home, he would find her lying on a divan, in the bedroom, or on the terrace, reading Victor Hugo. Thank goodness the man had written so much! On one occasion he brought her a book by Zola, but she returned it a few days later. "*Non,*" she said, emphatically.

At the beginning his friends' wives had tried to make contact with Amina, out of curiosity or else egged on by their husbands, but her monosyllabic answers and the presence of the Dahde had nipped their goodwill in the bud. People wondered what on earth poor old Berglund found to do with her. They could have spared themselves their concern. It wasn't only the yashmak he loved; he loved her lack of industry, her indolence, her indifference toward everything that happened during the day. It even pleased him that she had made no flattering comments about his house, or his garden. They couldn't

47

compare with Mustafa's, so why should she? To please him? He liked the way she never did anything "to please," never feigned enjoyment. She was polite, never interrupted, listened attentively—or was she, perhaps, not listening at all?—greeted and parted from him with the Turkish salutation. His friends professed their admiration for her graceful bearing, her rose-petal hands; what more could he want? When he arrived home in the evening, she welcomed him with a smile and let him play with her hands. Then he read the newspaper while she leafed through the magazines he had brought her. She merely looked at the photographs, made no attempt to learn German, and that too pleased him. They could make themselves understood in French to one another; that was enough. Now she would have a child and be kept busy. So much the better. It made no difference to him whether he had children or not. Perhaps if he had examined his feelings more carefully, the answer would have been: preferably not.

The months of pregnancy brought nothing new into Amina's life. She did not have to start "resting," like other women; she merely continued resting, as before. Whether an unseen change was taking place, an inner effort of preparation, or a sense of pleasurable anticipation, Berglund could not tell. There was no sign of it, and he sensed that the yashmak would not have been sufficient to hide it, for although the Dahde waddled around as heavily shrouded as before, she seemed to him to waddle much more cheerfully. He would have dearly loved to know what she looked like behind that tantalizing shroudedness, and he pressed Amina for particulars. Well, she was a Negress. That, as far as Amina was concerned, was all there was to say. But Berglund persevered, and the girl was obliged to reflect deeply. She never "saw" the Dahde any more, she declared, and could scarcely remember, for here she wore the Petsche, the all-obscuring veil, and besides she was so used to her that she couldn't really describe her at all. The Dahde's skin was very, very dark, she had very, very many teeth, and they were very, very white.

When she was five months pregnant Amina declared that she no longer wished to go out driving—she did not feel well enough, and the way the car lurched around in the snow and slush was far from pleasant. From then on she left the bedroom settee only to stand, every so often, at the window, watching the driving snow.

48

Around this time the first discord arose, and shortly afterward their first, and only, quarrel. Berglund wanted Dr. Schweikart, his family doctor, who had brought Berglund's sister Vera's children into the world, to keep an eye on Amina during the later stages of her pregnancy. But Amina would not hear of it. The Dahde would look after her, now and later; the Dahde would rear the child. And the delivery itself? The Dahde. No one else.

Berglund said nothing. The best course, he thought, would be to have the doctor visit them, of an evening. He and Amina would get to know one another socially, in a relaxed and friendly spirit. She would see at once that she could safely place herself in his hands.

But when Dr. Schweikart entered the house, they found the bedroom door locked. How did she know? The Dahde, of course. And how did the Dahde know that the kindly-looking old man with the pince-nez and the gold chain across his ample belly was a doctor? The Dahde, after all, couldn't understand a single word in German; couldn't even tell the time. Yet she could tell one coin from another, even German ones, by smell, most probably. And as for the doctor, she had simply smelled him out.

When Schweikart had gone—"Don't worry, my dear Berglund, when the time comes she'll call for me herself, you'll see!"—he found the bedroom door stayed locked, although he pounded on it. He swore under his breath, and knelt to peer through the keyhole. Brown. Dark brown. The Dahde was standing guard, within.

There was a spare key to the bedroom, in a kitchen drawer somewhere, in case of emergencies. He came down into the drawing room, rang for Peelke, and turned to the window and the snowbound garden beyond, in order to hide his anger.

"Peelke—bring me the spare key to my bedroom." Without turning around.

"At once, Herr Berglund."

Noiselessly he went upstairs again, inserted the key and turned it quickly in the lock, kicking the door open. The Dahde fell backward, as he had hoped, and Amina, cowering in the bed, gave a small cry of alarm.

It was not a good idea to beard Berglund when he was angry, but the Dahde tried. She picked herself up and placed herself between him and the great brass bed.

"Tell her to leave the room. At once."

Amina hesitated, but not for long. For the first time the china-blue eyes looked threatening, and hard as pebbles. She whispered a few words in Turkish and the door closed again, behind him.

But before Berglund could open his mouth, a waterfall of words began to tumble from Amina, first in French, then, abruptly in Turkish. The gist, despite the wild, confusing torrent, was clear enough, however. The Dahde had brought more than a dozen children into the world, no, none of her own, those of the wives in the harem— other households sent for her, too, because she knew so much about it —no man other than her husband should ever come near a Turkish woman—doctor or no doctor—disgrace—defilement—ruin—suicide—

Berglund let her scream at will. But when she suddenly burst into violent sobbing, buried her face in the pillows and pounded the bed with the "rose petals," he found himself becoming anxious for her. After all, she was pregnant and could at this rate lament her way, perhaps, into a miscarriage. He sat beside her on the bed, stroked her hair, and promised that the Dahde, and the Dahde alone, would bring the child into the world. The sobbing eased forthwith, and he left the room.

When he came to bed later that night, he found her waiting for him, with the yashmak before her face.

Chapter 2 The last few months of the pregnancy were peaceful. That was the best you could say for them. The magic rings that had encircled him so tightly, as soon as he set foot in the house, had spread to such an extent that he suddenly felt a chilling draft between the gaps. Well, that's the way it was, when a woman was "expecting" she became shapeless and inaccessible. Even the rose petals were swollen, and he was no longer allowed to play with them.

The Dahde's life, on the other hand, took on a new meaning. Up and down the stairs, all day long, carrying flowerpots from the garden greenhouse to the bedroom—she had made friends with Gerhard, the dwarf—and dozens of silver trayfuls to Amina's bedside, back again to her kitchen, and to the bedroom once more. As she trotted past him, preoccupied, in a hurry, and so patently glad, Berglund sometimes felt a real need to talk with her. One day he grabbed her fast by her brown calico, surprised to find her hard to the touch and not at all flabby, and smiled at her as broadly as he could. She stood still, before him, but as for what was going on behind the thick folds of her veil . . . If only he could see her eyes! But she always remained fully veiled beneath the Petsche, indoors and out. He proceeded to make a few friendly noises in French, meant to convey benevolence toward her and concern for Amina. After a short silence, she uttered a couple of muffled sounds, which he believed to be meant in the same spirit of goodwill. He let her go and she waddled hastily away.

Still, he did not feel entirely easy at leaving Amina so completely in her hands, and decided to seek advice at the Turkish embassy. Perhaps there, too, they had similar problems with their women. But apparently not. The sultan's envoy—a bald, well-groomed man in a black suit—listened attentively, shook his head, and said briefly but politely that Berglund had clearly been unlucky in his choice. Many Turkish women were more progressively minded. His own, for example: you could have taken them—all four—for Frenchwomen. Their twelve children had been born in Berlin under the most modern conditions, including the administering of ether. He would send his first attaché to Berglund's house, with instructions to sound out the Dahde.

A few days later—Amina was now in her eighth month—a young man in his middle thirties with a thin pencil-mustache, a monocle, and a hint of a paunch appeared in Berglund's drawing room and presented himself: Dr. Kemal Edib, of the Turkish legation.

But how was he to entice the Dahde down from her upstairs kingdom to be interviewed? What words could he call up the stairs? He had no choice but to ask the elegant young man to come up to the Dahde's kitchen with him.

In the corridor upstairs, all the doors were closed. As always, sweet-smelling vapors wafted out from under the "kitchen" door. Dr. Edib smiled forbearingly, indicated to Berglund that he should stand back and leave it to him, and knocked on the door, calling out something in Turkish. Silence. The young man waited for a moment and then knocked once more, sharply this time, and called out in a less friendly manner and at greater length. Silence. Even the vapors ceased to waft. The Turk stood for a little longer where he was, his nose against the unyielding door, and called out for the third time, briefly and threateningly. Then he turned and walked past Berglund, down the stairs, visibly upset and heading for the front door. Berglund caught him just in time and pressed him once again into the drawing room, where liqueurs and coffee were waiting. The young man refused to sit down, though he condescended to swallow both, in stunned silence; the rebuff to which the Dahde had treated him seemed to have affected his powers of speech and movement. Finally, however, he declared that he would not leave Berglund in the lurch when the time came, Dahde or no Dahde. There were, he confessed, still a few such creatures left, in his country. Here and there. Hadn't Berglund mentioned that she had been a slave? So she should have remained.

In these last few weeks before her confinement Berglund saw his wife only in bed. She no longer wore the yashmak, and even so she had to struggle for breath. Her face had swollen up and Berglund again assured himself that this must be the case in pregnant women. Soon she would be weaving toward him in her yellow veils again, lithe and slender. He pictured her in the garden, when it was warm enough again. There was a surprise waiting for her there: a fountain he had had secretly built. The idea that the garden would also contain a squealing bundle in a perambulator rarely occurred to him. Surely the Dahde would find a proper wet nurse and keep the child largely in her kitchen, surrounded by the sweet-smelling aroma of the herbs. And motherhood, he hoped, was something that Amina would take in her stride. She would lay the infant aside, and resume her old life.

He thought it better to mention that "by chance" he had met a certain Dr. Edib, from the Turkish legation. Was he married? asked Amina with a sudden spark of interest. Yes. To a Turkish wife? No, to a German wife. The spark died.

Chapter 3 At the beginning of April, as Amina entered her ninth month and barely turned her head toward him when he came home at night, Berglund brought off a carefully prepared coup. He owed it largely to his new friend, the Turkish ambassador—though he himself paid for the considerable expense involved. It so happened that the sultan, after much deliberation and many diplomatic exchanges on the subject, had at last granted permission for his famous Karagöz puppet troupe to tour abroad. Karagöz and Hazivat were the protagonists of an ancient sequence of puppet plays, comic, grotesque, and obscene, that had delighted the Turks for centuries.

Their first performance abroad, in the ballroom of the Turkish embassy, was almost a disaster. The entire diplomatic corps and their ladies sat before a linen screen on which marionettes, fifteen or sixteen inches tall, hopped to and fro—that is, their silhouettes did, or else Islam would have banned them long ago. Silhouettes, however, were not human images, and hence beyond the law.

The invited audience understood none of it. At least, they behaved as if they didn't, sitting in solemn silence throughout even when the proceedings on the screen were quite unmistakable. Apart from the embassy personnel, no one present had any idea what these strange figures represented, whether they were whores or kitchen maids, knights errant or bath attendants, and why they were constantly yelling and beating each other up. During the entire performance, the ambassador held a handkerchief over his mouth and coughed into it a good deal, shoulders heaving convulsively.

The icy atmosphere began to filter through the screen to the performers, who broke off after the second piece and were only persuaded with some difficulty, and by the ambassador himself, to give one more performance on the following night—in a different place.

The next morning Berglund delayed his departure for the office and sat down beside Amina, on the bed. She looked at him out of sluggish, dark-ringed eyes and hid her hands under the covers, so that he could not take hold of them.

"Amina—there's someone coming to see you and the Dahde, to-night."

She stared at him. Didn't he know she hadn't been receiving visitors for weeks now?

"Someone from the embassy?"

He shook his head.

"Baba?" she said softly. Baba was her father. From the way she asked, he could not tell whether or not she would have been pleased by the sudden appearance of old Mustafa.

"Karagöz and Hazivat are coming to see you."

Her lips opened, and she gaped at him for a moment, then flung her head back into the pillows, with a loud cry. The Dahde rushed in and fell to her knees beside the bed. They clasped one another as Amina whispered and sobbed and laughed, and the brown colossus grunted the strangest cadences, in which one could, nevertheless, detect a definite excitement.

When? When?

At six o'clock that evening.

Which pieces were they going to perform? Having no idea, Berglund assured them that they would be "new" ones. By their response he realized that he had made the wrong choice, and quickly added that they would play the old ones as well.

She never once asked how it was that Karagoz from Constantinople was suddenly going to appear in her house in Berlin. He would be there, nothing else mattered; and she promised to remain quietly in her bedroom until the stage had been built and everything prepared, downstairs.

Punctually at five o'clock that afternoon, two carriages arrived outside the house, and six heavily muffled figures carried chests and boxes into the drawing room, from which everyone was then barred for an hour. At five minutes to six Berglund was allowed in, and Gaston and Peelke set out an armchair for Amina and a chair beside it for the Dahde. Berglund intended to sit some distance behind them, in order to give them the feeling that the performance was for them alone. Peelke decided to watch from the doorway, so as to be able to slip out unnoticed. The furniture had been pushed back against the walls and the room was divided into two by a curtain of unbleached calico, the "curtain of instruction" as Dr. Edib had explained. It was already lit from behind. The players could be heard making a few exploratory noises, one of them worked a marionette quickly across the screen—then they were ready to begin.

A gong sounded. Upstairs the bedroom door opened, and Amina emerged, half supported and half carried by the Dahde. Berglund hastened halfway up the stairs to meet her and took her by the elbow. She seemed feverish, with glowing eyes and hot, dry skin. For the first time she was wearing the yashmak again; everything was to be as it had been in Constantinople, when Karagöz was invited by Mustafa to give a performance in the harem. Berglund let her carefully down into the armchair, where she bulged like a taut, overripe fruit, and he saw her dig her fingers into the Dahde's thick brown calico arm at her side.

The gong sounded once more, the lamps in the room were extinguished. Frau Glaubitz squeezed herself into her place beside Berglund and giggled nervously, while Gaston sat on the other side. Peelke stood stiffly at the door.

And then Karagöz catapulted into the center of the screen with a loud, joyful cry, shaking his round beard and billowing cap, and Amina struggled to her swollen feet, crying out: "*Salaam! Salaam!*" And when Hazivat, with his pointed cap and pointed beard, joined his partner on the screen, she waved and shouted and blew him a kiss, and the Dahde too rose to her feet and bowed and clapped her hands. Berglund could not take his eyes off his wife. He had never seen her behave like this, would never have believed that she could reach out her arms so longingly, and laugh, and cry, even before the performance had properly begun.

He had a rough idea of what the plays were about, thanks to a bashful summary by Dr. Edib. Apparently the fables were all much the same; the main thing was that there were plenty of sound thrashings. In this instance, it concerned some whores who trick a rich man, tear off his clothes, and leave him stark naked on the doorstep; Karagöz happens along, tries to help and is, in his turn, robbed and stripped; a drunkard comes across the two naked men, mistakes them for wild animals and is about to kill them when a handsome brigand arrives in the nick of time and saves them.

Berglund had been told that the dialogue was littered with obscenities which could be suppressed, on demand; but he had deliberately raised no objections, so as not to spoil the two women's pleasure. The result far surpassed his expectations. The Dahde gave one loud squawk after another and occasionally hid her already shrouded head under her mistress's shawl. Amina pounded the arms of her chair, swaying to and fro with shrieks of delight.

Frau Glaubitz and Gaston sat stiffly upright and made no sound. Berglund could not make out whether they were stunned because they didn't understand or because they did.

It lasted two full hours. In between there was a short interval to let Amina recover. When the lights were doused once more, Berglund noticed to his surprise that Frau Glaubitz, Gaston, and even Peelke had returned for another bout.

At long last it had to end, and Amina, exhausted and happy, waved goodbye to the screen as if to a departing friend. Then she let herself be carried, unresisting, to the bedroom. She had no desire to bid the puppeteers farewell; they had brought her Karagöz, and apart from that they held no interest for her.

She fell asleep at once, one hand clutching the Dahde's skirt.

Chapter 4

He had agreed with Dr. Edib that he would let him know when the labor began; if nothing else, he could spend a few hours in Berglund's drawing room over his host's liqueurs, cigarettes, and pornographic Persian books. Until one could feel sure that the Dahde had everything under control.

Dr. Schweikart had also promised to be on the qui vive, in case of any sounds of distress—via Dr. Edib—from the Dahde, at the front line.

One evening, at the end of April, Berglund returned from work, and realized that the moment had come only when he saw the Dahde carrying successive caldrons of hot water into the bedroom, pushing him unceremoniously aside when he got in her way. Should he hurry to the bedroom and say something to Amina? What, for instance? A quick kiss on the forehead and "Good luck, *chérie*"? A smile and a last wave from the doorway? "See you soon" or "I'll be downstairs thinking of you"? Nothing of the sort. The Dahde stood guard in the doorway and growled in unmistakable menace. Over her shoulder, though, he caught a glimpse of the rose petals clutching at the brass rods of the bedhead, heard a suppressed moan, realized that words would be ridiculous—and withdrew relieved and with a clear conscience to the drawing room below. He left the double doors open and moved his armchair so that he could see the stairs and part of the landing above.

Dr. Edib arrived, as arranged, and devoted himself to the liqueurs. Berglund passed him the Persian books, but these he did not deign to look at; it wasn't, in his eyes, a suitable moment. His host either stood at the window, gazing out into the darkness of the garden, or else sat at his desk and turned unseeing the pages of a newspaper. They were both listening for any noise that might come from above, but all they could hear was the opening and shutting of doors and the heavy, shuffling tread of the Dahde.

At eleven o'clock Berglund sent the chauffeur to fetch Dr. Schweikart. They sat for a while, all three, smoking in silence. Then Schweikart and Edib played a game of chess.

Once, around midnight, Berglund thought he heard a muffled cry. He ran out of the room to the stairs, stood listening at the banister. Silence. The gaslamps flickered on the floor above, but the Dahde was not to be seen, and all the doors were shut.

The Turk was the first to fall asleep, and then the doctor, each in his armchair, each holding an extinct cigar between drooping fingers. Berglund paced noiselessly back and forth between them. Once, he stopped and studied the carpet beneath his feet. It was the first one he had bought from Mustafa—five years ago—little realizing—

He lifted his head. That was surely a cry! Now he was certain. He shook the doctor awake, and both climbed the stairs up to the landing, to listen. Silence.

"My dear Berglund," said Schweikart, fighting back a yawn, "it's all very well, I mean, all this consideration for the feelings of your wife and this—this person, but it seems to me the time has come to do something."

"Such as?"

"Well, I would suggest waking the Turkish gentleman. He could perhaps try to catch her when she comes out of the room, and ask how things are going."

Berglund woke Edib, who surfaced slowly out of a deep sleep, rubbing his stiff limbs. Reeling slightly, but resolved to see it

57

through, he took the stairs one step at a time, while Berglund and Dr. Schweikart remained at the foot of the staircase, following him with their eyes.

Having reached the landing, the Turk stood for a moment, uncertain what to do next. There were four doors, and he wondered which to try. At that moment a long-drawn-out, moaning cry rang out from a door to his left, and Dr. Schweikart sprang with sudden agility up the stairs and past the Turk, pushing him aside and raising his fist to knock on the door, when it was opened from the inside. He almost collided with the Dahde, who was emerging with a basin.

"Take hold of her!" cried the doctor, and vanished into the bedroom.

The Dahde dropped the basin, and a pool of bloody water spread across the floor. Edib seized her by one wildly flailing arm and held her, until Berglund reached him and secured the other, behind her back, over her sobbing, furious, protests.

"Speak to her, man!" he shouted at the Turk. "Ask her what's happening—how my wife is—has the child arrived—*ask* her, for God's sake!"

A deluge of words descended on the brown colossus, who started to wail incoherently.

The bedroom door burst open once more, and Dr. Schweikart rushed past them down the stairs, to return, two steps at a time, with his large medical bag.

"Let her come in!" he cried as he ran past them, pointing at the Dahde. "I need her. But tell her, Herr—Herr—tell her to behave, or there'll be a disaster. . . . The ether—she's got to help me hold the tubes—"

He disappeared into the bedroom, leaving the door open.

Dr. Edib did his best; but she seemed not to hear him and went on moaning, at which Berglund abruptly let go of her and struck her in the face with all his might—that is, he struck blindly at the veils, which gave a muffled thud. But the blow must have somehow found its mark, for she fell silent at once, and as the Turk shouted something further in a voice that in the sudden silence rang like a trumpet blast up and down the stairwell. She set off behind Berglund, who shoved her in at the bedroom door. He remained for a few seconds in the doorway, saw Dr. Schweikart kneeling on the floor rummaging in his bag, saw two white knees, red-spotted bedsheets and a fraction of a cheek, partly covered by tangled strands of dark hair.

He walked slowly back down to the drawing room, Edib behind him, and went silently to the corner cabinet to pour himself a double brandy. The Turk, too, poured himself one, as Berglund had forgotten him.

An hour later Dr. Schweikart came down the stairs, and Berglund knew by his heavy tread that it was all over. The doctor lifted his leather bag and brought it down so harshly on the table that the instruments inside rang with a faint clatter.

"Still, the baby's strong enough," he said, and let out a long, heavy sigh. "It's a boy."

What now? What should he do? Go upstairs, kneel by Amina's bedside and cry? Or do what he would so much rather: stay here, where he could cling to the presence of the two men.

Dr. Edib stood up and planted himself before Berglund's armchair, gave a deep bow and expressed the embassy's condolences, to which, if he might be permitted, he would wish to add his own. After which he remained standing there, hovering uncertainly as though awaiting instructions.

Berglund made a vague gesture, past him and toward Schweikart, who was leaning against the table, staring ahead.

"Go upstairs and speak to the—that person." An order from the doctor to the Turk, who hesitated, dreading the task. All three raised their faces, listening, but there wasn't a sound from above.

"What are your—what is the custom in these matters?"

"Women are not usually supposed to see a dead person," began the Turk, but added hastily, "although of course in *this* case—" He broke off, and turned to Berglund. "Do you have a Koran in the house?"

"Yes," said Berglund, and stood up at last. "In German."

"That's no use," said the Turk with a touch of censure in his voice. "We also need a *kefen*—"

"A what?"

"A cloth, to—what is the word—"

"A shroud," said the doctor.

"Yes. Well—I'd better talk to the Dahde."

"You do that," said Berglund, and watched him valiantly climb the stairs, only to pause uncertainly on the landing. He had once again forgotten which was the bedroom door, and now no cry rang out to guide him. Helpless, he put his ear against the nearest door, and then at the next along—

"The third, on the left!" came Berglund's gruff voice from below. The Turk knocked cautiously, opened the door, and disappeared inside.

"Thank God," said Berglund and sank back again into his chair.

The doctor stared at him. "I beg your pardon?"

"What? Ah yes—I mean, because—the Dahde needs someone now who can talk to her—comfort her and so on. Won't you sit down, Doctor? It's already three o'clock."

But the doctor shook his head and continued staring down at the table.

"How old was she? Seventeen? Only sixteen? My God."

"How did it happen? Didn't she have the strength—"

"Cesarean. There was no other way. The contractions had ceased. She was already very weak. Didn't come around after the anesthetic."

Berglund sat up sharply.

"Did the Dahde—was it *her* fault, that Amina—"

"No. She did all she could. Perhaps—if I had gone up earlier—but that would only have upset the girl and she would have fought the anesthetic. No, no, it would be unfair to reproach the nurse."

Berglund dropped back into the chair. He would rather have liked to have had somebody to blame. Amina—gone. No more yellow veils. My God—Mustafa! He would have to send him a telegram. What did one say, in such circumstances? "Deeply regret to inform you— inconsolable to have to inform you—"

"Wouldn't you like to have a look at your son? Splendid specimen —eight pounds!"

"I'd rather wait a little till the Dahde—" he broke off.

"She's perfectly calm," said the doctor. "I don't believe she even cried—hard to be sure, of course, with all that stuff in front of her face. On the whole, she helped me out extremely well. Almost hospital standard. Now, I must see to a wet nurse, right away, or your son will start making his presence felt."

He closed his bag and fetched his hat and coat from the wardrobe in the hall.

"I'll be in touch, my dear Berglund—and I need hardly make you any speeches—you must know how deeply I grieve with you. Good-night."

Chapter 5

Berglund remained standing by the stairs even after the door had shut behind Dr. Schweikart. He thought that never before in his life had he felt so utterly incapable of forming a resolve—even a resolve to move; to do something, anything. The next, simplest, most immediate thing. Why was that? Was he completely empty? Or full to bursting? It came to the same thing. Here he stood, holding on to the handrail. Suddenly he heard a timid voice from the far side of the stairwell.

"Forgive me, Herr Berglund, but we should so much like to know —after all, we feel very much involved, even if we—might one ask—"

He slowly turned his head toward the kitchen quarters. A shaft of light—and Frau Glaubitz in the doorway. He cleared his throat, searching for the words, for the tone. She took courage and came toward him in her slippers, noiselessly. And peered into his face.

"Oh God—oh God—" And when he still said nothing, "But that's dreadful!"

She seemed a stranger. He had only ever seen her in her blue-and-white uniform, with her hair pulled back severely in a knot underneath the white cap. Now it hung loose and streaked with gray over her woolen nightdress, giving her a helpless, almost childlike air.

"The baby's all right," he said. "A boy. Eight pounds."

The corners of her mouth turned up automatically—and fell back again.

"Oh God, oh God!" she repeated, and since he said nothing further, she backed away and disappeared.

Still bracing himself against the banister, he tried, as objectively as possible, to examine what his feelings were. Dog-tired, he thought, I'm dog-tired, and that's all.

The bedroom door opened, above, and Dr. Edib came down the stairs. He looked bleary-eyed, but once more under control and resolute. After all, he was a Turk. Losing a wife was always something you had to allow for. For this very reason the Prophet, in his wisdom, had advised taking four of them, to improve the odds.

"We need the Koran—although I have already recited the main prayer—and the *kefen*, the shroud, I mean. It has to be forty feet long, and seamless. I shall see to it myself."

He collected his coat, and Berglund automatically handed him his hat and his walking stick, realizing that he could not detain him any longer.

"I'm very grateful, Dr. Edib, and I must find some way of—showing my appreciation. I shall certainly tell the ambassador how very much—how greatly your presence has helped."

Edib bowed, turned to go, and then turned back once more.

"She is quiet now—the Dahde. You don't have to worry. You can go upstairs."

The bedroom lay in semidarkness, though the curtains had been pulled back; it was not yet full day outside. He came to the foot of the great brass bed and took hold of the cool metal rods. Amina lay covered up to her chin, the yashmak half across her face and half across the coverlet. Only her forehead and closed eyes were visible.

He turned his head. The Dahde was sitting in one corner of the room with a small white bundle on her lap. He didn't mind her sitting there in the dark corner. On the contrary, he felt less alone. Besides, he knew that it was to please him that she had placed the yashmak over Amina's face. For the first time, he felt a sob welling up in his throat.

He moved slowly around the bed and sat on the edge. Carefully, as though the action might wake her, he drew back the veil and studied her face—as he had done less than a year before, in the Orient Express, and at the same time of day, in the gray light of dawn. She looked peaceful, he saw to his relief; no grimace of pain. Her mouth was slightly open, giving her a somewhat surprised look, as though she couldn't quite grasp what had happened to her.

He bent over and laid his cheek against hers, only to pull back with a start, for it was already cold. He sat up again. Should he try to draw back the covers, to look at her hands and touch them once more? No, they too were probably quite cold by now, and even stiff. Should he kneel by the bed and cry? His knees showed no inclination to do so, and what if the tears wouldn't come? Most of all, he would have liked to have continued sitting there, beside her, and pretended to gaze at her—though he realized that he was seeing nothing now. Simply staring.

After a while he managed to get to his feet. He walked slowly toward the Dahde. Reaching her, he noticed that she was gently rocking the white bundle, and as though the child knew that its father was gazing at it, it now made a couple of whimpering noises. The brown hand drew back the covering cloth, and he saw the baby's round head, its black hair, tightly closed eyes, and sharply defined mouth. Amina's mouth.

He bent down and stroked once the hard brown hand that held the child. Her head remained bowed and she made no sound.

Chapter 6

Mustafa's answer arrived a month later. A long letter whose first part was devoted, in great detail, to the newborn child and Berglund's luck in having so promptly brought a son into the world. It was undoubted proof of Allah's exceptional favor, in whose honor the child should be called Turhan, and raised as a Muslim.

Before he got to the end of the letter, Berglund had resigned himself to Turhan, but there was no question of his having a Muslim for a son.

The second, and brief, part of the letter offered condolences over Amina's demise, and wondered at Allah's eternally unfathomable decisions.

The third part startled Berglund to such a degree that he sent the chauffeur away and walked to the office. He needed time to think, and some immediate activity to work off his agitation—and it was, after all, a beautiful May morning.

He walked down the wide avenue of Unter den Linden, reaching into his pocket every once in a while, to be sure Mustafa's letter was still there. The old man had written—why hadn't Berglund thought of it himself? It was the next, the natural, step. The obvious one. The logical one. Wait a minute: was it logical? Yes, it was perfectly logical, but above all it was *wise*! As if Mustafa knew exactly—and all Berglund had sent him was a telegram—to what extent he had been impaired.

The old man had written that after all, he had eight daughters, but even ruling out the ones under ten years of age, there was, for instance, his daughter Yasmin, whose mother he had purchased in Haifa. She was only two months younger than Amina, had turned out very well, and would be cheap into the bargain, since he would regard Amina's price as sufficient (in view of her sudden demise) to cover a second daughter. Of course, in the event of *her* entering Paradise before her time according to Allah's inscrutable plans, a new price would have to be agreed upon in respect of a third daughter, and, needless to say, he could be trusted to set a fair price.

It made perfect sense.

Or was it utter madness? To marry a girl he hadn't even seen—not even once! But then, what about his married friends, with their carefully chosen partners? They had sniffed around and around each other long enough—and what had they learned? Why hadn't Georg Wertheimer, his best friend from childhood onward, scented the fact that his intended would shortly became a heavy drinker? And his cousin Wolfgang Berglund—why had he never suspected that his future wife was frigid? Now and again, though only very rarely, someone got lucky, and his marriage partner turned out the way she was expected to. Had his adventure with Amina been that much more of a risk? Rather the opposite. Since she spoke no German, there was no wifely chatter to get on his nerves; and being so utterly alien, she had discouraged any competition, two marked advantages already, without even mentioning veiled nocturnal benefits. It would be the same with Yasmin.

As he passed the Brandenburger Tor into the shadows of the tall trees, he saw himself step once again through the low door into the harem, into the tide of brightly colored veils, out of which one had detached itself, the one beloved yellow shape, weaving toward him. . . .

Yasmin must have been sitting there among them too. Would she remember it? Of course she would—it was less than a year ago. Did she, too, read Victor Hugo? Would Mustafa have asked her, before writing to him? Surely not. The old fox—who loved him "like a son"—only pretended that the bridal price was of importance. He knew damn well that it was a matter of complete indifference to Berglund whether the cost of Amina could be amortized or not. It was the girl, the girl Yasmin, that mattered.

He stopped and took the envelope out of his pocket; read it through again slowly, sentence by sentence. There was nothing else about Yasmin, only that she existed, that she had turned out well, and that her mother came from Haifa. Jewish, then; half Jewish. He put the letter back and looked around for a cab. Now all at once he couldn't get to the office quickly enough, couldn't wait to be dictating to Gerste his letter to Constantinople. Everything fell into place and he could visualize it all: Yasmin would be there, silently and smilingly waiting for him at home every evening, yashmak over her face. Amina, Yasmin, the difference would be infinitesimal. She would be a mother to—what was he to be called? Turhan. She would be a mother to Turhan. For the time being, the Dahde was still at home in the nursery, but ever since Amina's funeral she had been waiting for some departing embassy official who would accompany her home to Turkey. Dr. Edib was due to go on holiday next week and had promised to take her with him.

He had not seen much of the Dahde; only, in fact, when he visited the baby's room, where a newly acquired fat Polish wet nurse called Anuschka was also to be found in peaceful coexistence with the Dahde. He didn't go there to see the child; he had little left for screaming bundles at the end of the day. Yet he looked forward, every evening, to the moment when the door of the baby's room opened and Anuschka descended to the kitchen. Then he quickly climbed the stairs.

The nursery was lit by a single nightlight in one corner. The Dahde squatted, somber and motionless, in another. Berglund sat down opposite her on Anuschka's tiny nursing chair, and smiled at her. Sometimes he forgot to bend first over the cradle and gaze at the sleeping child. Then a silent reproof bored through the brown veils and forced him to his feet. Only when he returned, his duty done, and sat down once more, did she begin to emanate the dark, velvet tranquillity that since Amina's death he longed for, all day.

Yet when at last he was sitting opposite her on that squat, ridiculous chair, breathing in the mingled smells of soap, milk, sleeping child and burning candle—the Dahde had no particular smell of her own—he rarely held out for more than a minute or two before standing up again, to bid her *salaam*. And the Dahde would nod. The audience was over.

That evening, after Mustafa's letter, he could hardly wait to climb the stairs to the baby's room. He ignored the child, waved her silent reproof aside and drew the nursing chair toward her. He then tried to communicate the contents of the letter to her, speaking in German, and extra loud, as if the volume could make up for her lack of comprehension. She raised a warning hand, pointing at the cradle— too late. The baby had woken with a yell, and began to howl at once. She stood up and picked the small parcel out of the cradle, returned to her seat and rocked it to and fro on her knees. It gurgled, grumbled a bit and fell asleep again. Berglund pointed to the letter he had brought out of his pocket, said "Mustafa" several times, as distinctly as he could, and then, in a querying tone: "Yasmin?" And again: "Yasmin?"

Her knees, absorbed in their placid task of gentle rocking, abruptly froze. One hand remained holding the child; the other, with one rapid gesture, pulled her veil aside, as if it were suddenly blocking her vision. It happened so suddenly that he stared at her, open-mouthed; she too seemed taken by surprise, for she let out a faint, woeful moan and let the veil fall back across her face. But there had been time enough to see what, for so long, he had wanted to see: the face of the Dahde, a wide, coarse, darkly tinted Negro face framed by short gray curls. Only the eyes surpassed all expectation, deep-set, unnaturally large and exceptionally beautiful, and for that instant they had been focused on him with a biblical intensity, leaving him with an immediate sense of guilt, though he didn't know why. But what was perfectly clear was that she had understood him.

"Yasmin?" he whispered once more, but she did not react; neither nodded nor shook her head; but bent instead over the envelope containing Mustafa's letter. He guessed what it was she wanted, took out the letter and unfolded it for her. She touched it carefully with one finger, as though it might be likely to crumble, and then placed the flat of her hand against the written page for a moment. Finally she stood up and placed the child back in the cradle.

He sat downstairs over a glass of brandy and brooded. What had she meant by putting her hand against Mustafa's letter like that?

"What my lord and master commands, is well done"—perhaps. And perhaps not. Should he ask Dr. Edib to come and ask the Dahde about Yasmin? Awkward. Very awkward. In any case, he had already posted his answer to Mustafa that morning, gratefully accepting his proposal. A whole year, the period of mourning, would have to go by before Yasmin could take her sister's place. Her half sister; Amina's mother had been Egyptian. Would Yasmin look like her, in any way? Perhaps he could ask Mustafa for a photograph—but then again, what would he be able to make of the portrait of a girl in veils? Yasmin would perhaps—probably—wear a different color. Should he spend the wedding night on the Orient Express again? No, it should be something else, on the high seas perhaps . . . shimmering sails . . . shimmering veils . . .

A few weeks later, the Dahde left for Turkey. In the early morning, long before Dr. Edib arrived, she was already in place in the hall, sitting waiting by her leather bag. Berglund had not been present at her farewell to the child. Perhaps she had cried. There were times when it was good to have a veil in front of one's face.

Edib arrived punctually in a cab, but this was paid for and sent away by Berglund. Gaston dragged the Dahde's leather bag out of the hall and dumped it on the seat beside him in the car. Then Edib got in. The Dahde hesitated, bowed to Berglund, growled something resembling "*Salaam*" and bundled herself onto the seat beside Edib, in the rear of the car. Berglund shut the car door; Gaston climbed into the driver's seat. But before he could press the starter, Berglund abruptly opened the front passenger door and sat down on top of the Dahde's leather bag. "Ready!" he said.

At the station he accompanied them to the train. Edib shook hands once again and climbed in. Gaston, behind him, carried her bag into another compartment.

The moment had arrived. Berglund took the Dahde's hand and said twice: "*Salaam!*" in a husky voice. The tears that wouldn't come, at Amina's death, now sat thickly in his throat. The Dahde said nothing more, but she seized his hand and kissed it. Then she scrambled up the steps, without any help, and vanished into the compartment.

The train pulled slowly out of the concourse. Berglund stood and watched it. No one waved.

Chapter 7 A year later, early in June 1905, he drove to the station with Gaston. Everything had gone smoothly this time: no bride price to be paid, and he was already circumcised. For a while he had toyed with the idea of returning to Constantinople and marrying Yasmin there, but the thought of crossing that threshold into the harem once more and facing another wedding reception in the crowded hall had held him back. The girl was to take Amina's place, not to eclipse her memory.

It was far too early, the platform was empty, but he had not been able to wait any longer. At home everything was prepared, although he had put off telling Frau Glaubitz till the last moment. It was for her to inform Peelke and Gaston, and he in turn would tell the garden dwarf. Rather that than march all four of them into the room to tell them to their faces that Amina's sister would now occupy the great brass bed with him. Frau Glaubitz's expression when he told her had been quite enough.

He felt completely isolated as it was. All his friends, without exception, thought he was mad, and some had even said so to him. Not one could understand how one could contract a marriage without even seeing the bride. This was Germany, after all, not darkest India.

Only his sister Vera, who had recently returned from New York with her family and had never known Amina, had taken it differently. "What a lark!" she said, and nudged him in the ribs. "I never thought you'd find *one*—and now you've managed to procure yourself two in one year! If only I had a veil through which to see my Friedrich!"

By now he had walked at least ten times up and down the long platform. Here and there, other people were coming up now. Gaston had been left outside the station; he wanted nobody standing beside him.

Mustafa had written that he was not to worry: Yasmin would be escorted by a Turkish consul and his wife, who were traveling to Vienna. There the girl would spend two days' rest in the consulate, after the long journey, and then they would put her on the train to Berlin.

68

No doubt they had shown her Vienna. Her first excursion around a European city! The thought annoyed him. Her first excursion should have been at *his* side. He pictured her black eyes—what other color could they be?—gazing over the yashmak at the Ring, at Kaerntnerstrasse. Perhaps she was shy—perhaps she wore the all-enveloping Petsche. That too seemed thoroughly acceptable. At home, at the appropriate hour, he would unpack her.

He looked up at the clock. Three minutes to go. Would she have Mustafa's thick eyebrows, like Amina? Enough! He stopped for a moment and made a solemn vow not to compare the girl to her predecessor. He would not do her the injustice of measuring her by certain standards. . . .

He walked on. How must it be, then, for a Muslim, once he'd gathered his four wives under one roof, one after the other—how could one prevent them from either surpassing and dominating one another, in turn, or submitting and resigning themselves. . . .

He stopped halfway down the platform. The train uncoiled slowly out of a distant curve, and chose its track. The huge locomotive ground steadily past him, shrouding him briefly in steam, jogging on hesitantly until one final creaking jolt brought it to a halt. The first-class carriages were usually in the middle of the train, opposite where he was standing. She would probably be sitting timidly in her compartment, all alone, waiting for him to come and find her. Patience! Wait until most of the passengers have emerged. . . . He forced himself to stay where he was, watching the welcoming embraces, the cries, the waving, the calling for porters, and the people all around him, walking slowly away together. Little by little the train emptied.

Taking his time, he walked over to the doorway of the nearest first-class carriage. As he grasped the rail to pull himself up the steps, his gaze was caught by a familiar silhouette in the middle window of the carriage, halfway down the corridor. The Dahde! Standing there next to a woman in a huge feathered hat, and wearing, as ever, the swathes of dark-brown calico, with the Petsche covering her head.

He hauled himself up the steps. The Dahde! So Mustafa wasn't going to let this second daughter leave without her, either. He had no time to ask himself whether he was pleased or not, but only thought how stupid it had been of him not to foresee this. And where the Dahde was, there also would be—he almost said "Amina"—there

69

would be Yasmin. No doubt the Dahde was standing guard outside her compartment. He entered the corridor and called exuberantly, "*Salaam aleikum!*" as he hurried toward the brown figure.

She turned toward him, bowed, and answered silently with the Turkish greeting, breast, lips and brow. The woman in the feather hat also turned to him, and said, "Good afternoon," in slightly accented German.

"Good afternoon," replied Berglund with cursory politeness and took the Dahde by the shoulder. "Yasmin . . ." he inquired urgently.

"Good afternoon," repeated the woman in the feather hat. When Berglund turned to her, uncomprehending, she added with a smile, "I am Yasmin."

Later, at home, when the worst was over and he sat alone in the drawing room before a glass of brandy, he wished he could remember what he had said to her after she spoke those words. He had probably gone on staring at her, as he was staring at his brandy now. Uncomprehending.

She had understood at once—that is, he hoped that she had only understood a fraction of what was going on in his mind, for she struggled to pronounce the word "surprise," and couldn't manage it. She gave up and said instead: "I have learned German." In a guttural accent, but perfectly comprehensible. And all he did was stand there —he had no idea how long—like a man numbed by a blow to the head. In the end it was the Dahde who had been the first to move, stepping to the window and waving for a porter—with some difficulty, in view of her veil. But at least she had done something to help get them out of the corridor.

Out of the carriage, in search of a porter. He had to walk the whole length of the station, for they had all disappeared, and it was just as well to have to walk, even run, to get the blood pumping, to force some of it into the brain and get it working properly, to go and fetch Gaston and return to the platform, where the Dahde and the woman in the feather hat who had said she was Yasmin stood all alone beside the empty train. Just as well the woman had so much luggage, all of it brand-new, that he had to help Gaston to carry it and load the car. It gained him time.

Once inside the car, with the Dahde in front beside Gaston, he had recovered sufficiently to ask her something—and now he remembered what that first question had been.

"Why"—he addressed her in German—"are you dressed like that?"

She had not fully understood, for her German was still uncertain, and he had repeated it in French, in which she had answered fluently.

"Madame Karabekir, the consul's wife, took me shopping in Vienna, and dressed me from head to foot. She enjoyed it so much. These clothes are all the rage there—don't you like them?"

"Yes, of course," he said mechanically, and she laughed and tossed her feathered head.

It was as though the plumes, whipping past his face, had swept him back to consciousness. Until then the lines had been down between eyes and brain, as though blinded—but in the mind, not in the eyes—for now, at last, he registered what it was that he saw. She was smaller than Amina, that is, she was of medium height, black hair, black eyes, narrow waist—good God, a corset! He wanted to kill somebody.

All the way home she prattled like a child, not seeming to notice that he hardly ever answered. She had taken daily German lessons all year, Father had given her permission, didn't he think she spoke well, he'd soon find out how well, only she was still too excited . . . Madame Karabekir had smuggled her out of the consulate because the Dahde wouldn't allow her to wear "that" sort of clothing, and had threatened to go back to Constantinople, but she couldn't, could she—after all, she had no money! And the beautiful luggage—Madame Karabekir had seen to that too, she'd been certain the future husband would approve, she would send him the bill, he would be so pleased . . . one couldn't go around in veils and a yashmak in Berlin . . .

Oh yes one could, thought Berglund; and he now knew whom he wanted to kill: Madame Karabekir. One could; and one should. But how was he to set about putting Yasmin into reverse? He wanted to be fair, it probably wasn't her fault that she had already, in one short hour, got on his nerves. He took another gulp of brandy. Would he be able to put *himself* into reverse and start afresh, once she had taken off the corset? And how were they to conjure up some Turkish garments, and a yashmak?

The answer came to mind before he'd even finished the question, and he stood up and left the room. In the stairwell, he listened for a moment. Silence. She was asleep. Thank God. Though it was only nine o'clock. Worn out by the journey, the excitement, the wretched corset. The Dahde, too, was asleep. With his own hands he had put her mattress outside the bedroom door, but she had dragged it away at once, into her "kitchen." It seemed she would not sleep outside Yasmin's door. In the old days she had always known when he was shutting the door for the night, and promptly dragged her mattress down the corridor. For the first few weeks the rustling and scraping sounds, as well as the thought of her lying so close, against the door, had irritated him. And then he had grown accustomed to it. A kind of overture, before the opera.

She clearly held something against Yasmin. Not so Frau Glaubitz. At her first glimpse of the feathered hat she would gladly have fallen on Yasmin's neck in surprise and delight. Even Peelke looked less severe. As far as the garden dwarf was concerned, there was no way of telling; his face was as deformed as his body, and only when he laughed, revealing perfect teeth, could one be sure where one stood with him. However, Yasmin's arrival had not made him laugh.

He decided to be ruthless and wake the Dahde; she would forgive him when she understood the plan.

He knocked softly on her door. She opened it as promptly as if she'd been waiting for him. He led her down the corridor, to an attic door at the far end. Behind it were stored trunks, unwanted furniture and a huge wardrobe. She anticipated him and opened the wardrobe doors. There they were: Amina's clothes, her shoes, her silver slippers, and beside them, on tissue paper, her yashmak. With one sweep of her arm the Dahde plucked the clothes from their hangers and carried them to the stairs. Berglund followed with the shoes and the veil, with its little clasp at the back.

Downstairs in her "kitchen," the Dahde carefully draped the clothes over the back of a chair, for there was no wardrobe in the room. He placed the shoes beside them, and pressed the yashmak into her hand, looking meaningfully into her veiled face. To his relief she nodded. He could leave it to her. It would not be easy.

Nor was it. He had slept downstairs on the sofa, and waked to muffled sounds of crying, and occasional shouts of rage. The door flew open and Yasmin could be heard struggling to emerge, her shrill cries mingling with the Dahde's threatening growls. He went into the hall and looked up to see the girl, held fast in the Dahde's iron grip, flailing out with her legs beneath the nightdress. And then she saw him.

"Monsieur!" she cried, pulling one arm free and extending it imploringly toward him. "Monsieur! Won't you tell her to give me back my lovely clothes—she'll have to, if *you* tell her to! Please . . ."

He wavered. It was even worse than he had feared, and then she delivered the coup de grace: "Monsieur—I can't put on *her* clothes! I am not Amina, Monsieur, I am Yasmin!" This last she cried in German, so that Frau Glaubitz and Peelke, brought running by the noise, gazed up at her, appalled. Then they noticed Berglund in the drawing-room doorway, and hurriedly withdrew.

No point in hiding behind the Dahde any longer. He slowly climbed the stairs.

The Dahde let go of Yasmin when she saw him coming. The girl rushed toward him and threw her arms around his neck, sobbing incoherent sentences in several languages at once. But he knew what she was trying to tell him. He freed himself gently from her embrace, and with a nod to the Dahde, led the girl back to the bedroom, one arm around her shoulders.

The room looked like a battlefield. Amina's clothes strewn on the floor, torn and trampled, the shoes scattered about the room, while the new clothes from Vienna lay in a heap in one corner. He pressed the trembling creature down onto the edge of the bed, and sat next to her.

It hadn't entered his mind, it was the very last thing he'd intended as he had climbed the stairs. He had been meaning to talk to the girl about the clothes, about the feather hat, about the corset—but now she lay there in his arm, the corset gone, crying, yielding, soft. He pressed her back into the pillows, raising her nightdress. It was daylight already; he felt no particular desire for her, but he'd been starved for so long and suddenly felt bare flesh under the thin material, and took her quickly, far too quickly, almost in haste. Even a little brutally. He felt ashamed when it was over and she lay beside him, sobbing. She hadn't stopped crying for one instant, he thought angrily. But then he hadn't given her much time to do so, had hardly even looked at her. Except once. And in that particular and decisive instant the expression in her eyes had quite bewildered him, they

73

had been begging him, despairingly, and yet with a certain longing. But at that moment he simply couldn't take it in.

.

Shortly afterward he left the bedroom, alone, and called for Gaston and the car. He drove to the Turkish embassy, reflecting how glad he was that he had maintained his relations there during the year of mourning. The ambassador was not available, but Dr. Edib appeared. A year ago he had made Edib a party to his plan, and shown him the new marriage contract. The Turk had shown no surprise, but merely murmured that "such things" were perfectly common in his country, though not always successful. This Berglund had pretended not to hear.

"Dr. Edib," he said now, avoiding the man's eyes, "would it be possible to procure some Turkish clothes, and everything that goes with them—here in Berlin?"

Edib was a credit to his profession. In the last five years convulsive struggles had been taking place in thousands of Turkish households, struggles not merely concerned with the question of women's clothing but with the ever-growing influence of European customs on the traditional Turkish way of life. Fathers were becoming increasingly violent, daughters fled their homes. Edib guessed what had happened in this instance, but he behaved as if it were no more than a matter of tailoring. Yes, of course it would be possible. One of the ambassador's wives—the eldest—sometimes wore these kinds of clothes, in private, and had them made up by a local dressmaker.

That same afternoon the dressmaker arrived at Berglund's house. Yasmin had stayed in bed. The Dahde had hidden all her Viennese clothes, including corset, shoes and hat, up in the attic; but Yasmin "would rather die" than put on Amina's things.

Berglund was not present when the measurements were taken, but at the foot of the stairs he waylaid the dressmaker and offered to double her wages if she would go to work at once and manage to bring something ready to wear in the morning. From the bedroom above came muffled sobs.

.

The worst of it was that there was no one he could talk to, no one he could turn to for advice except his sister Vera, and that wasn't worth the trouble. She could be very entertaining, with her absurd, contrary chatter, but a serious conversation with her was out of the question. Nor would any of his friends have offered much other than "Serves you right" or "Send her back again—and the marriage contract with her."

Too late for that. Besides, he couldn't do such a thing to Mustafa. And in truth he had little to complain of anymore, in Yasmin: she had stopped crying, and wordlessly put on the new Turkish clothes. Under no circumstances, however, would she wear the yashmak, and she asked him whether he found her so ugly that she should hide her face. No, of course not. Nor was she ugly, far from it. She had a round, snub-nosed child's face and an extraordinarily beautiful skin, of a pale-golden color.

It would work out somehow, he told himself, once the documents were signed, and the ceremony over and done with. At the embassy. No need for a reception, just the bare essentials of the Muslim rites. Then a week's honeymoon on a Mediterranean liner. Somehow it would work out.

And to some extent it did. The ship was crammed, Berglund discovered several acquaintances among the passengers, and Yasmin became very quiet. Perhaps it was the clothes that brought her down —she felt ugly and old-fashioned and barely showed her face on deck. But as long as she was silent, Berglund put up with her company, even occasionally in their cabin, alone.

.

She was neither stupid nor thick-skinned. When they left the ship at Genoa to take the train back to Berlin, she knew he didn't love her, and never would. The day the red-haired giant had walked into the harem, she had sat in a corner drinking him in with her eyes. *There* was a man! The kind she had read about in the books she loved, not only Victor Hugo, but Balzac and, secretly, Maupassant. But although she knew that *she* was Mustafa's favorite daughter, she had held out no false hopes for herself, once she saw the way he looked at her sister. A year later, when Mustafa had brought the news of Amina's death, she had burst into tears and embraced him with a force of emotion that, as he perhaps guessed, was not entirely for her sister's sake. Mustafa was wise; he had not deluded her that it would be easy in Berlin. Whatever there had been between Berglund and Amina would only burn the brighter for her premature death. This was why she had seized on her new Viennese wardrobe with such excitement, hoping thereby to replace her sister's image with a bolder, more modern one.

And it had all gone wrong, irredeemably wrong. When she finally understood, she tried hard to undo the damage, even wore the hated yashmak at night. But not even that could help now.

In Berlin she discovered to her horror that she was pregnant. That something concrete should emerge from the sterile gymnastics she had practiced with Berglund seemed to her downright sinister. Right from the start he had said to her: "Once it's over, it's over, don't you think? All that cloying nonsense afterward—I always call it 'affection time.' Do you need that sort of thing?"

"No, no." While every fiber inside her yearned, "Oh yes, please!"

No affection time. Only the bleak, miserable few seconds of the physical side-by-side. Every time he approached her bed she had closed her eyes tight and tried to flee in her mind to the man whom she had once watched crossing the threshold of the harem. Every time she had tried to escape from his dreadful mechanical haste into absolute rigidity, or else she would have screamed and jumped out of bed. All these memories—they were really only one, for they were all similar, all similarly appalling—she had wanted to burn out of her thoughts. And now she would have her nose rubbed in it until the end of her life! She would have to face it that all these terrible things had indeed happened to her, for there would now be a living creature to remind her of it every day, who would perhaps look at her out of Berglund's eyes, demand from *her* "affection time."

She cried much during the first few weeks, but this was thought to be normal. Anything that pregnant women did or did not do was "normal." The Dahde was obviously delighted and looked after her like a mother. Yasmin sometimes called little Turhan, now taking his first steps, and played with him. There seemed to be nothing of Berglund in his face, nor even of Amina, except for her dark eyes staring out of his thin, secretive little face.

Berglund now mostly slept in the spare bedroom, and she came to terms with that as she seemed to come to terms with everything. Her one joy was her daily German lesson. A German student, found by the embassy, came every morning at eleven, and she liked his company and made good progress. He had fallen in love with her, despite the pregnancy, and she found that his meek, hungry eyes comforted her.

Berglund spent little time at home. He went more often to his sailing club, and passed whole evenings with his friends, as he had done as a bachelor. Yasmin, the Dahde and Turhan went on excursions in the car. Yasmin visited the embassy wives—time passed. Sometimes she would sit in the garden without reading, simply listening. It seemed to her as if she were waiting for something that was about to happen, something that had nothing to do with being pregnant.

She soon began to swell up, and now the Turkish clothes were positively welcome. Berglund wanted her to be treated by Dr. Schweikart, and she had nothing against this. When the doctor congratulated him on his clever and charming wife, he never noticed the look of amazement he received in return.

Nine months after the honeymoon, and without fuss, Yasmin gave birth to a daughter, while Berglund was at a regatta.

The child was named after Berglund's mother, Sophie.

BOOK III

Chapter 1

At seven in the morning there was a knock at the door, but Sophie didn't say, "Come in." She was staring with rapt attention at the wall opposite her bed, where the shadow of a branch with five leaves hanging from it was slowly creeping across the plaster, moving with the morning sun. She consulted the oracle: if the first leaf reached the mirror before someone came in, that someone would be Brother. . . .

A second knock. The nearest leaf was still an inch away from the edge of the mirror. The oracle had spoken. Brother never knocked.

The door opened a crack, and Lutz came in cautiously and sat on Brother's chair. Sophie turned her face to the wall.

"Are you in pain?"

Without moving, she said slowly: "Lutz—I've got something very important to ask you."

Dear God, he thought, let her stay lying the way she is, she'll only read it in my face. . . .

"You've got a—slight inflammation of the lung. On one side. The left lobe of the lung." Last night Dr. Hensch had told him that the left lobe no longer existed, eaten away.

Sophie dismissed this bit of information with a wave of the hand before turning her face to him.

"Lutz—see if you can remember: did the Egg ever tell you what it was like when she was sent back to Constantinople?"

"Why?" He was on his guard at once. "Why do you want to know that now?"

"I need it," she said impatiently, "I need it for my book. That's right, yes! I'm writing it at last. I've got at least a hundred pages done—I spent the entire night on it. I've just got to where I come into the world—but there's a gap now. I know she went home when I was very young, but I don't really know why. Did she ever tell you?"

"I can't remember now, exactly."

"Think, Lutz," she insisted, coughed, shutting her eyes in pain, but continued, struggling for breath: "I know . . . you've got a good memory . . ."

"She mentioned it once—we were talking about the concentration camp, and she said it wasn't the worst experience she'd ever been through . . . at any rate, she'd never thought of killing herself there, whereas on the train to Constantinople, those three days, she'd stood by the carriage door a couple of times, at night, and even taken hold of the handle."

"What stopped her?"

"For goodness sake, she was only seventeen, with her whole life still ahead of her. She wasn't short of courage, as you know!"

Seeing her eyes, he hated himself. Why couldn't he have kept his damn mouth shut? She was right, he had a nasty tongue, it was the queer in him, "with all a woman's worst attributes"—and it didn't help that he always felt sorry afterward. Well, he'd better make her laugh now, somehow.

"Your father, of course, insisted on a Turkish divorce"—stentorian tone; he had a real gift for mimicry—" 'Yasmin Karabey Berglund—return to your father's house!' Three times over, to avoid any misunderstanding."

She laughed a little, and it hurt so much that she stopped at once and closed her eyes.

"Sophie, isn't the . . . the writing too much of a strain? You've got to sleep. I mean, you aren't *that* well—"

"Oh yes I am," she whispered, barely audible. "I'm wonderfully well—d'you understand?" He nodded; of course he understood. There was a faint remaining glitter in her eyes, which he had never seen before, but he could guess. "I don't ever want to leave this room, d'you hear me, Lutz? I feel well in here, at last."

"What about Othello? He wouldn't even drink his milk this morning." Wasn't it perhaps important to feel a "will to live" and to try and get out of a hospital? Nonsense. Sophie was right, he was a hopeless case, always seeing both sides of the coin.

Once more she waved her hand, as if she wanted to efface everything that lay outside these four walls.

"Lutz—I've fallen in love. I know you'll be happy for me—"

"With the young doctor?"

"He's called Brother, I've been waiting for him for hours—the pain's come back. I need another one . . . tell them outside—you know what I mean."

He stood up, left the room and returned with a nurse. Sophie closed her eyes at once and managed to make a rattling sound come from her throat. The nurse drew back the sheet, turned her carefully onto her side and bared her hipbone. There's nothing left of her! thought Lutz.

"I'll stay here till she falls asleep."

The nurse nodded and went out.

Sophie was still lying on her side. He went around the bed, so he could see her face. She smiled at him with huge, shining eyes. Okay, he thought, let her have the stuff. I'll take the responsibility.

"Find Brother for me." And when he was slow to react, "The young doctor, the one from Crete—"

"He's only on night duty, Sophie. He'll be asleep now."

Oh. Of course. She closed her eyes.

"Go home, Lutz—I've got to get on with my book."

He tiptoed out of the room.

Chapter 2

She had only one photograph of her mother, taken in 1906, before her return to Constantinople. Wasp-waisted, hair piled high, one gloved hand on a lace-bordered parasol, and a defiant smile on her face, as if to say: "Don't try to give me orders."

Orders were shortly to be given: "Yasmin Karabey—out!"

It must have been dreadful. So dreadful she could never talk about it. Except, much later, to Lutz. He wasn't a son-in-law for her, he was her adopted son.

What a pity Lutz had already gone. She had meant to ask him how Yasmin had picked up the threads of her life in Constantinople. Damaged goods, returned unwanted. She could imagine her arrival: Mustafa in the hallway—arms wide open, Yasmin in tears throwing herself into them. In Turkish clothes and yashmak or, as in that last Berlin photo, corset and piled-up hair? Have to leave that question open, thought Sophie, sorry, dear reader, but I can't help you, I simply don't know. I can see the hallway, I can hear the fountain— but Mustafa and Yasmin clasp each other in a double image, like two photographs printed on top of each other, an oriental version and an occidental one. And I also don't know how she spent the following fifteen years, in Turkey—she never spoke of them either. But perhaps Lutz knows. It's all the same to me now, that she loved *him* and not me. On the contrary, I'm happy for him. *Somebody* truly loved him. Why was I ever jealous? I can't understand it. It's all so clear and right and well arranged, love has no given quota, it's inexhaustible, there is plenty to go around, enough for everyone, even for me.

When Brother comes back, I must tell him about my first memories of Papa: I'm standing in the bow of a big sailing boat, holding onto his white trousers, which rock back and forth, and gazing up at him, and seeing, way, way up above me, a curious sight: a triangular piece of chin, and above it yellow strands of beard blowing strongly in the wind, and above *that* the two dark caves of his nostrils—and blue sky all around.

No. It doesn't work, I can't always describe him from beneath, from the worm's-eye view that was mine for so long, forever perhaps. But then, he was so much bigger than other men. Remember, Brother, that it's Papa I'm speaking of, but I simply must go back to calling him Berglund, and from now on I am Sophie, which gives me more elbow room and I can leave my worm's-eye view and watch the pair of us from all angles, even from above.

After Sophie was christened, Berglund went on a journey around the world, by ship, with a few friends. He would be gone for six or seven months, he had announced. He would write. Postcards. One or two actually came, at least to start with. And Yasmin now knew that whatever she had been waiting for was about to burst in on her. One day, when a whole month had passed without a postcard, she ordered the Dahde to bring her the Viennese clothes. And the Dahde obeyed without remonstrating, ironed the clothes, repaired where necessary, and combed out the ostrich feathers. She guessed what was coming.

Next day Yasmin went for her first drive along Unter den Linden in the corset and the feather hat. Instead of the Dahde she took the young student with her. German lessons.

Through the curtains of the children's room, the Dahde watched her go. Then she placed Sophie in the pram, gave Turhan his hoop to hold in one hand, took the other firmly in her brown paw and strolled up and down the Siegesallee. It was her favorite route. She was certain that the huge white marble figures of early German kings that lined the avenue must be the country's native gods, so she shuffled slowly from god to god, stopping to bow before each of them. Here she felt safe. One of the statues, Albrecht the Bear, even received the Turkish greeting. What it was about him in particular that appealed to her, no one knew.

·

When Berglund arrived back in Berlin, he was in excellent spirits. Two cabins on board ship were crammed with works of art from all corners of the earth. Gerste worked late into the night making an inventory; the Herr Direktor had made magnificent acquisitions. Persian carpets, though, were not among them.

To welcome him home, Yasmin put on a French outfit by Worth, dark-brown velvet with pleated chiffon frills. Berglund took it in without a word.

Soon afterward he invited Dr. Edib to dinner at the Hotel Esplanade. But this time Edib was mulish, addressed the liqueurs and remained obstinately silent. Berglund finally had to spell out exactly what he wanted from him. Edib raised his eyebrows and avoided his host's gaze. Berglund hinted at an endowment in favor of Turkish orphans—Edib finished his last cup of coffee and, for the first time, opened his mouth. What emerged was brief, blunt and unambiguous: he could not help him in any way, nor did he want to. The girl was very young. To send her home as a divorced woman would be downright cruel; no Turk would marry her. And to remove her from the child—

"She can take the child with her," Berglund interrupted quickly, and earned himself another hostile look. He gave up and sat back in his chair. There was nothing more to say, he was a scoundrel. Amen. As long as somebody would talk to Yasmin . . .

Next he tried his sister Vera, who had been to tea with Yasmin a few times, and seen the Turkish clothes give way to French fashions. The children had been brought in, Turhan pale and fearful, clutching the Dahde's knees, the red-haired baby placed on its mother's lap. Though somehow Yasmin had managed not to touch the little girl. Clearly she couldn't stand her.

And now her brother was proposing that she, Vera, should tell the young woman to go home to her father and take the child with her? "Why don't you let her stay here? You can get up to whatever you like, she won't get in your way."

85

Wrong. She did get in his way. He only had to see her, and it spoiled the house for him. The quieter she was, the more she avoided him, the worse-tempered he became. The whole thing was bungled, botched, irreparable.

.

It was at this time that the boy Turhan had a serious bout of bronchitis. It was the first of many, and in the years that followed, the children's bedroom was always to contain a kettle full of healing herbs in boiling water, whose balmy odors belonged to Sophie's first sensuous memories. Dr. Schweikart was called, and arrived to find both the Dahde and Yasmin sitting by the boy's bed. After his examination, he took a walk with Yasmin, in the garden. Gerhard the dwarf was raking up the leaves that fell from the tall elms, and the young woman lifted up her long dress above her buttoned boots to wade through the small pyramids of rustling yellow and brown leaves. Like a child, thought Schweikart, and watched the leaves scattering from the neat piles that the dwarf had so carefully accumulated.

"Autumn," he said. "A beautiful season—dahlias, pears, grapes—" Yasmin kicked her way through the next heap and the leaves flew even higher in the air. "Don't worry about the boy. They're quick to run a temperature at his age, and your little girl should only have to spend a day or two in your bedroom—or will your husband mind?"

"My husband doesn't share my bedroom."

Schweikart stopped. Yasmin walked on, and assaulted the next pile of leaves.

"Frau Berglund . . . is this a temporary measure? Have you had an argument with your husband? Forgive me if I'm intruding—"

"You couldn't intrude if you tried, Doctor. We're not at one, my husband and I. There's plenty of space between us."

"May I ask, since when—"

"From the beginning."

"Would you like—shall I have a word with your husband?"

"If you wish. He'll tell you he'd like to be rid of me."

"You're sure of this?"

"Yes."

"What are you going to do about it?"

"I'm waiting for the morning when I wake up and say, all right, today I'm up to it. Then I'll pack my things very fast and take the train."

The doctor studied her in silence, her pale, still slightly puffy child's face with its lips pressed firmly together and trembling eyelids.

"But what will happen to the boy, if you take the Dahde and the baby with you? How will he manage without the Dahde?"

"The Dahde and Sophie are staying. They're all staying. I'll go on my own."

"You're going to leave your daughter here?"

"I'm going home. Back to my father."

.

The doctor felt it was his duty to tell Berglund. Perhaps there was still a chance—but to his astonishment he found himself clapped on the shoulder and embraced. "Schweikart! My dear fellow—did she really say that? I'll write to Mustafa right away."

"To whom?"

"To her father. My old friend. He loves me, you know—he's had seven wives—Yasmin is his favorite daughter, he might be glad to see her back."

"And the child?"

Berglund hesitated for a moment, and sighed. Yet another wailing child.

"She can stay here, I suppose. There's room. The Dahde will look after her. You can't imagine what a help you've been, Doctor." He hugged him once again, radiant with loving kindness and relief.

The doctor disentangled himself and reached for his bag.

"Tell me, Berglund—nothing to do with me, of course, but what exactly have you got against that charming young woman?"

"Nothing, nothing at all, my dear doctor. She *is* charming. But not my type, you understand. What's more she's frigid, poor thing—nothing one can do about that. It's all my fault, if you like, but that's neither here nor there. The whole thing was a mistake, right from the start."

.

Shortly after, Berglund had a long talk with the Dahde, or rather they sat in silence together for longer than usual when he made his nightly visit to the children's room. There was another letter from

87

Mustafa in his pocket. The old man had taken the news of Yasmin's impending return philosophically, though he misunderstood the reason. Mustafa thought Berglund was divorcing Yasmin because she had produced a daughter instead of a second son, perfectly legitimate grounds for complaint. He himself had allowed all the superfluous women of his household to stay, out of sheer kind-heartedness, and because there was plenty of room.

The offer of a third daughter was given no more than a casual mention; Mustafa guessed that his son-in-law was fed up with his Turkish adventures.

Berglund sat down once more on Anuschka's little nursing chair, opposite the Dahde. Everything was the same, except that now there were two children's cots against the wall. The Dahde waited, silent and somber as ever, but with her head raised as though scenting something out of the ordinary. In Berlin she could talk to no one now, and had developed the sixth sense of the deaf and dumb.

He unfolded the letter, said slowly, "Mustafa," and—as before —she placed her palm against the handwriting, as though greeting her master.

"Yasmin," said Berglund curtly, sharply, and pointed at the door. The Dahde sat up stiffly and turned her head in the direction of his outstretched finger, as if Yasmin was about to walk out of the room this very minute, on her way back to Constantinople.

.

Mustafa wrote at once to his daughter when he received Berglund's letter. And she, in turn, lost no time, and appeared the very next morning in her husband's bedroom. She would take the evening train to Vienna; her bags were already packed. There she would spend the night at the consulate and then—back to Constantinople. There was a particularly good train she could catch, called the Orient Express. Had he heard of it? Would he kindly book a compartment for her? All this in a quiet voice, with eyes downcast.

He stood up automatically, and took a step toward her. She moved back toward the door and said firmly: "Monsieur—recite the words of divorce. Then you'll be free." She added, more softly: "And so shall I."

The words? She pointed to the German-Turkish phrasebook on his desk. He hunted through the index quickly, bypassed the "Marriage" chapter, and found the next item: "Divorce."

In a low, embarrassed voice, he spoke her name three times and ordered her to return to her father's house. When he looked up from the phrasebook she was already gone.

Chapter 3

Sophie's earliest memories were all dark brown. Dark brown the Dahde's hard fat hands, washing, combing, holding her, dark brown the stiff cloth of her djellaba, to hang on to, dark brown the waving folds of the Petsche, to be tugged at, dark brown the Dahde's firm, chubby cheeks, which she could bite at leisure.

And later, the sailboat—the one place without a speck of brown. No brown hand to take hold of her, no growling noises which Sophie understood perfectly, though without any idea what sort of language it belonged to, Turkish, Arabic, or simply "Dahde." Nor was Turhan's mouse face to be seen there, since even the Wannsee made him seasick. Berglund wanted no one on board whom he'd have to worry about. No one had to worry about Sophie. At the age of four she would paddle fiercely through the water like a puppy, her red hair darkened by the water and slicked down against her small head, the pale eyes wide with strain and effort, obsessed with the determination to please her father. "Papa, look!"—she didn't dare call out to him, and instead struggled back and forth in the cold water, trying to catch his gaze, until a woman's voice called: "Sophie! Come out at once. Your lips are turning blue."

The woman's voice changed so often that it seemed, in memory, to belong to no single person. Voice after voice, like those of successive governesses in other children's lives. They rang out on deck every Sunday, friendly, eager to make an impression on "the child," then one day they were gone, to be replaced by a new voice, usually the following Sunday, a long chain of assorted womanhood, some of whom brought bribes, fed her secretly with chocolates, or gave her dolls. No sooner had the friendly ladies gone than Sophie threw the dolls overboard; her only interest was in how long they took to sink.

At home the Dahde ruled unmolested, as before, on the top floor. Her grunts were the children's ten commandments. She punished rarely, and then only for lying, or—a memorable day—when Turhan pissed into the copper pot usually filled with spices which stood on the edge of the prayer mat beside her knees as she performed her devotions. Sophie's idea, but she left the execution to Turhan; he was a better shot. When the Dahde, rocking backward and forward in solemn prayer, put her finger in the copper pot and drew it out wet—watched by the children with bated breath—she never stopped rocking and praying for a second. In time she stood up, without hurrying, carefully washed both hands and pot, and rolled up the prayer mat. Then she turned to the children. First Turhan received one around the ears, but her heart wasn't really in it; next she grabbed Sophie firmly by the hair, laid her across her knee, pulled down her drawers and gave her a good sound beating. Then she buttoned her up again and took both children for a walk in the Siegesallee, as usual, taking not the slightest notice of their howls. As she made her way, swathed in her veils, from statue to statue, other children called out behind her back, "Witch! Ugly old witch!" but she never seemed to hear their cries and jeers.

.

Berglund employed private tutors for the children; he didn't want them to go to school. How would they explain about their mothers, or the Dahde? As a result they had no friends and were left to their own devices. Sophie, though two years younger, was a faster learner than Turhan, and when she discovered this she inverted their age difference and elected herself his protector. That was fine with him; he wanted to be protected by everybody, by the Dahde, by "downstairs" (Frau Glaubitz and Peelke), by the garden dwarf. Even by Father, though there he was not indulged. You had to impress him if he was to so much as notice you, and Turhan soon gave up trying. Sophie never did, never ever. She made it her daily task to win him anew, never gave up hoping that he would have time for her, perhaps even praise her.

When Sophie became a "person," as her father put it—and for him Turhan never became one—she began to feel that his eyes did actually come to rest on her sometimes, and not without a certain amount of pleasure. It amused him to see how much she grew to look like him. She was eight years old now, and tall for her age. His red hair sprouted from her head like a symptom of some strange disease, orange-yellow at the temples, where the sun had caught it, then

gradually darkening above to a brick red. The color of her eyes, however, didn't come from him. Like a dark amber, it struck him one
day, and really rather beautiful, he thought, watching her sitting on
deck, staring up at the sun. She could do this without blinking and
without tears coming to her eyes. It had been remarked on before
and much admired—and now Papa had discovered it! She sat there
staring up into the sky long after he had disappeared into his cabin.

.

Early one Sunday morning Sophie noticed a new young sailor on
deck, leaning against a mast, whistling, making no effort to help the
others scrub the deck. Curious, Sophie crept nearer and hid behind
the lifeboat without the sailor noticing. Now he was lighting a cigarette. Sophie sprang like an Indian from her hiding place and planted
herself firmly before him.

"You! The crew aren't allowed to smoke on deck."

The young man looked down at the child, its cheeks flecked with
red spots of excitement, hand and forefinger imperiously extended in
a gesture he thought he recognized.

"Even on a lovely Sunday morning like this?" The fellow smiled
and took another deep pull on the cigarette.

"I'll tell my father!"

"Sneak."

Oh God, the man was right. Sneak! Scum of the earth. Not even
Turhan sneaked. Tears welled up inside her, and the outstretched
hand sank down to hide behind her back.

The distress in the amber eyes, which had blazed so imperiously at
first, was not lost on the young man. But he went on smoking in
silence.

A cabin door opened behind him, and Berglund emerged onto
the deck. Sophie saw him first and hissed, "Quick—put it out!" But
the young man only laughed, bent down and kissed her on the
mouth. Then he turned and walked toward her father.

The warm, tobacco-scented kiss still on her lips, Sophie stared
after him, wanting to save him, to cry: "Papa, he's new, he doesn't
know the rules, please don't be angry with him, don't send him away
—I love him!"—the thought came like a bolt out of the blue. Too late.
The new sailor had reached her father, had given a military salute,
right hand raised to the peaked cap. Papa returned it with a smile,
the sailor took the cap off, long brown hair fell down over his broad

collar, Papa put his arm around his shoulder—her shoulder. Then they both laughed and came toward her, arm in arm.

"This is Anita," said her father. "Get to know each other." And strolled away.

The woman sailor sat down on the bulwarks to try to light another cigarette, but the wind kept blowing out the flame despite all her attempts to shield the match with her hands. Sophie waited impatiently. "Get to know each other," Papa had said. Two childish fingers, strong and white, suddenly clasped the sailor's thin brown hands, as if to make a more effective shield. The match flared, the cigarette caught.

The sailor looked up, smiling. "Thanks." Quickly, Sophie pulled back her hands, didn't know what to do with them, hid them behind her back again. "Watch this," she said, and stared at the sun with wide-open eyes.

"*I* can do that," said the sailor, looking up at the sky.

Sophie frowned. "Easy for you," she said. "You've got a fringe over your eyes."

The sailor woman had such dark, thick lashes that her eyes seemed to be in shadow even when they were wide open.

"What do you see, when you stare at the sun?"

"Red circles," said Sophie. "And you?"

"I see fiery torches, yellow and red, and sometimes a dark purple color."

"I'd like to see fiery torches, too."

"Give me your hand. We'll try together."

Returning from the quarterdeck, Berglund saw Anita and Sophie standing hand in hand at the rail, heads stretched way back, eyes wide open, tendered to the sun.

•

From then on Anita was to be found not only on deck but at home too. In the evenings, though, she would leave; no one knew where she went. She refused to be accompanied, saying she was glad of the walk, on her own. But first she always came into the children's room to say goodnight. Sophie would fling her arms around her like a pair of tongs, Turhan shyly offered a hand. Only the Dahde stood there as before, dark-brown and doom-laden.

Anita brought neither dolls nor sweets, but often sat with Sophie and talked to her. Sometimes the things she said left Sophie worried.

"You mustn't tell Gerhard that you're already several inches taller than he is."

"Why mustn't I? It's true."

"That's why. It upsets him because it *is* true. Take care how you handle the truth, Sophie." And with that she went out of the room. Sophie sat, perplexed. As far as truth went, she had never had easy relations with it, had no gift for it at all. Deceit was second nature to her, lies flowed out of her before she even had to think of them—to the Dahde's sorrow, for she laid great store by the truth. Turhan never lied. He spoke the truth as involuntarily as Sophie lied, and consequently the Dahde's rumbling "Pants down!" rang out only for Sophie, whose rearquarters had gradually grown hardened as time went by. But recently there had been a certain improvement. Now and again, with a supreme effort, she had squeezed out "the truth," to the delight of the Dahde, who grunted with pleasure and let her off her punishment. When she saw the effect, Sophie had increasingly choked back her ready inventions, and "lied" the truth.

And now here was Anita saying she should "take care" with the truth! The following morning, Sophie waited for her at the garden gate. Anita usually came at midday and ate with them, in the children's room, untroubled by the Dahde's dark-brown silences.

As she came around the corner, Sophie rushed up and blocked her way.

"Anita—what does it mean, being careful with the truth?"

"Can't that wait till we get home?"

Strong shaking of the head, the red plaits flying. "Tell me, Anita, tell me now."

"All that really matters is that *you* know what the truth is—even if you tell lies till you're blue in the face, as you've been known to do, haven't you? But when someone else is involved, then think twice. The truth can hurt just as much as a spanking from the Dahde when she's caught you lying to her. D'you understand?"

The strong, resistant little hands sank back. She felt the flush creeping up her cheeks, across her whole face and up into her hair.

Anita studied her silently, as the girl stood before her, gulping, the forehead freckled like a field of tiny buttercups, the amber eyes full of tears, the short nose, not yet fully formed, the firmly etched, resolute mouth, starting to twitch, uncertainly.

She thought: I'm beginning to love her.

·

That was no news, everyone in the house knew it. Even the Dahde, who did not put up a fight, perhaps judging that the time had now come when she needed a helping hand.

As, for instance, the day the huge china doll in the children's room fell and shattered. Sophie and Turhan had screamed with fright and seized hold of each other, trembling. The doll's face had burst in pieces, one good eye still goggling cheerfully up at them out of a pink sliver of cheek. Silence. The Dahde was in her kitchen. No one came, the doll's eye went on goggling. Now that she was dead, the least she could have done was shut her eyes—she did that when you laid her down, and there she was, lying down. Sophie tried a little laugh, Turhan bleated faintly behind her. Still nothing, no one, silence. There was no need for words; they both knew what remained to be done. Sophie broke off the arms and legs, Turhan tore out the blond curls, the torso was jammed into the waste-paper basket.

But what about the clothes? The doll was life-size, and Papa had brought it, exquisitely dressed, from Paris. Sophie thought it over, undressed Turhan and crammed him into the clothes. They fitted. Then she lifted him into the doll's carriage, stuck the lace bonnet on his head and tied the pink ribbon beneath his chin. Gasping, sobbing with laughter and excitement, they felt as if they had done something truly monstrous, at once murder and masquerade. Sophie ran the doll's carriage around and around in circles, while Turhan, his mouse face framed in lace, squeaked with delight and dizziness.

The door opened, and the Dahde appeared. The carriage stopped with a jolt, almost spilling Turhan. Sophie pressed her hands to her eyes, swaying blearily, stoically waiting for the brown Nemesis to strike.

Instead the door shut again. The children stared, gazed anxiously at one another—the Dahde was gone. What did it mean? Cautiously Sophie began to push the doll carriage once more, but Turhan, scared, began to whimper.

The door opened a second time, and the Dahde was there once more—with Anita beside her! The Dahde, bringing her enemy, her rival, as a reinforcement? Why? Surely not just because of the broken doll; she didn't bother much about such things. And why wasn't Anita laughing as she watched the Dahde pull Turhan out of the carriage? Didn't he look a scream in his long silk dress and little bonnet? No, Anita wasn't laughing, she was watching the Dahde, who had thrown back the Petsche in her agitation, tears running down her face. Sophie giggled, studying Anita attentively—what was she thinking? After all, Anita had never seen the Dahde's face. But she was behaving as if she'd known it all her life, and helped to pull the silk dress off the flailing child. Naked, and crying, Turhan crept under his bed, while the Dahde wiped her cheeks with the doll's dress. But before she could draw the veil across her face again, Anita took her by the arm. The Dahde slowly raised her eyes, huge and still full of tears. Anita bent forward and kissed her quickly on the cheek, then she took Sophie firmly by the hand and led her from the room.

Down the stairs, and through the empty drawing room, out onto the terrace. Only then did she let go of her hand, and sat on the stone wall. Sophie placed herself expectantly between her knees. Something important had clearly taken place: the Dahde had never cried before, and Anita had kissed her. Why? Anita lit a cigarette and gazed obstinately past her.

Sophie decided to break the ice.

"Why can't Turhan ride in the doll's carriage?"

"Because he's a boy. You shouldn't put doll's clothes on him, Sophie, it makes a fool of him."

"Turhan likes playing doll."

"Do you like having a doll for a brother?"

Sophie chewed at her lower lip.

"Why not?"

"Wouldn't you rather he was like Papa?"

The yellow eyes stared malevolently.

"*I'm* like Papa."

"You're a girl, Sophie, and you look like him, but that's a different matter."

The little head with its red plaits sank forward in silent anger, then shot up again, defiantly.

"It isn't fair, Anita—"

"What isn't?"

"Turhan likes to play dolls. I don't. Perhaps I'm a eunuch."

95

"Where on earth did you get that idea? Do you know what a eunuch is?"

"Frau Glaubitz says a eunuch is something halfway between a man and a woman. She says the Dahde is a black eunuch. Perhaps I'm a white one."

"The Dahde is black, but she's not a eunuch. Nor are you, Sophie, you can take my word for it."

Chapter 4

A pity, thought Sophie. She'd rather like to have been one—it sounded so nice. But if the Dahde wasn't a eunuch, what was she, then? Once when she was bathing her and had pulled the Petsche back, Sophie had stared up into her dark face and asked: "Dahde, where do you come from?" And at once, the veil had fallen down again, like a curtain.

Questions got you nowhere. Some time ago, she had plucked up the courage to ask her father: "Where does the Dahde come from?" He had looked at her in surprise, and thought about it for a while. Then he had said: "I don't know, Sophie. I did know, once, but I've forgotten it. But she comes from somewhere—very far away."

From very far away. If only she too had come from "very far away," instead of from Ruemelangstrasse in the Tiergarten. One evening she read in a book about someone who had traveled "very far away" to find the Stone of Knowledge.

"Anita, could the Dahde be the Stone of Knowledge? Papa says she knows a great deal, and she is very hard to the touch. What do you think?"

"Yes," said Anita, without hesitating, "you've guessed it. But don't tell anyone, do you hear? It's a secret. No one must know we've got the Stone of Knowledge in the house, or she might disappear."

The Dahde—disappear? Now that Anita was there, the thought was no longer so unbearable. For the first time she grasped the idea that things came to an end in life; one person arrived, another left. A sad thought? Yes. But not without a certain appeal.

August 1914. She was nine years old when the war broke out and wrought a fundamental change in everybody's life. Sophie could see no good reason for this. Anita was there. That was all she needed. The only worry was that Papa might be called up—the phrase itself was disturbing enough, as if a hook were to descend on a long rope and suddenly haul him aloft.

Papa was old now, forty-six, and "in the Reserves." Reserves, according to Frau Glaubitz, were the money you kept aside in case of an emergency. Which meant that Papa would not be hauled away until the Kaiser was in trouble and needed his spare assets. In the first two years of the war it seemed he was in funds, and Papa remained at home.

But other familiar fixtures in Sophie's life were hauled away. First Peelke, and then the private tutors. And so for the first time both she and Turhan were sent off to school. On that memorable day, Sophie came home for lunch, glowing, having already made a friend who had carried her satchel for her. Turhan had long since been returned by the school custodian. He had never stopped howling and "disturbed the lessons."

.

In the evening, when the children were asleep, Berglund sat morosely in the drawing room with Anita. Here it comes, she thought, here we go. She was prepared, knitting away at a scarf, for the first time since her schooldays. Military gray, a sullen color.

Berglund sat in his favorite chair, the only one that wasn't too small for him, and chewed at his cigar.

"I don't know much about children, but there's something wrong with that one, I can tell you."

All right, thought Anita, let's start with the children. Aloud, she said: "With Turhan, you mean?"

Berglund said nothing. He had been about to say that he couldn't imagine where on earth the boy had got it from, this minginess—when he was suddenly reminded of his father. Didn't heredity sometimes jump a generation?

"I ought to send him to Constantinople, to his grandfather. But I don't even know if he's still alive. Haven't been in touch with him for years." He fell silent. For a moment Yasmin's memory intruded.

"And Sophie? Would you send her too?"

Berglund glanced briefly at her, long enough to see the fear in her eyes. He shook his head. After a while, he said casually: "Perhaps we ought to get married. What do you think?"

At last, thought Anita, and went on knitting.

"We don't have to decide right away. I mean—we could talk about it, in principle, without committing ourselves."

More or less as I imagined it, she thought. The knitting needles clicked on in the silence.

"Any reason why we shouldn't?" said Berglund and sighed. The sigh was a mistake, it had slipped out.

The clicking stopped, but only because a stitch had dropped.

"No? I suppose I could have put it differently."

"For instance?"

"I could have said: 'Anita, I love you.' "

She laughed. "No, that you couldn't have said, Johannes."

"Why not?"

"Because you don't know what it means."

"Do you?"

"Yes."

"I thought you didn't love your first husband."

"I didn't."

"Who, then?"

"None of your business, Johannes."

He sighed once more, this time without regrets.

She got a cigarette out of her bag, and he bent forward to offer her a lighted match.

"Thanks," she said. "Well—I feel honored by your proposal, since I know why you're making it: you're going to be called up soon, and you want someone to look after the house."

"Not 'someone.' *You*. But I must admit, I'd hoped you couldn't knit."

She stared at the gray rag in her lap, had to laugh, and threw the knitting into the waste-paper basket. Then she looked at him reflectively for a while, her hands folded in her lap.

"I really wouldn't advise it, Johannes. That is, I'm willing to look after your house, but apart from that . . . I'm a jealous person, and not particularly—well, let's call it levelheaded."

"Neither am I."

"I know. But you don't know enough about *me*. If I were to marry again . . . " She left the sentence unfinished. "It's twelve years ago, but I can still feel the dread, inside me. I had no idea I could hate, I'd always thought I was a nice girl. Then all at once, blind hatred . . .

I didn't hate *him* for very long, you can't hate anyone who suddenly finds himself flat on his back, with helpless eyes and gaping mouth, unable ever to stand up again. It was in *me* the hatred lived, unconnected, independent and went on living, for years, until I gradually made peace with it, and with myself. But it's still sitting there, somewhere, deep down. It makes me—somewhat unreliable. That's what I'm afraid of. So be warned, Johannes."

They sat for a time without looking at each other. Then she stood up slowly, stretched as if after strenuous exercise, and left the room. He sat for a moment longer, stubbed out his cigar and followed her into the hall. Leaning against the wall, he watched her adjust her hat before the mirror and insert the hatpin. Perhaps I'll be strong and never come back, she thought.

"Adieu, Johannes."

She offered him her hand, but he shook his head.

"Do take that dreadful hat off, Anita. And come here."

.

The telegram, calling him to join his regiment within a fortnight, arrived a few days before Sophie's eleventh birthday.

"Sophie," said Anita, as she helped her put on her apron after school, "what would you say if I told you that your father and I were going to get married?"

The girl's head fell forward until Anita could only see the crown and the white curve of her forehead with just a few buttercup-freckles.

"Wouldn't you be pleased?"

The small head jerked upward. No.

"Why not?"

"Because—" Lips tightly compressed; but the tears had already started to come. "Because now you belong to me, and Papa too." She saw the doubt in Anita's eyes. "Yes, he does! A little bit of him, anyway. But if you get married, I'll lose even that little bit. And I'll lose you. Completely."

"Look at me, Sophie. In reality, your papa and I have been married for a long time. It's simply a matter of signing a piece of paper now. It won't change anything, believe me."

"Everything changes, once you get married."

"Who told you that?"

"The Dahde."

The Stone of Knowledge, thought Anita.

"Then you don't want to come with us to the registry office, next Monday?"

Sophie reflected, carefully catching the last tears with her tongue. "Perhaps—I could *cycle* there."

It was a moment before Anita understood.

"You mean: if Papa gives me a bicycle for my birthday, you can get married."

Eye to eye. Troubled brown, confronting stubborn dark yellow. Gradually the yellow brightened, till it shone innocent and sunny.

"Wouldn't it be fun, if I came on my bicycle? Gerhard's taught me how to ride, as a surprise for Papa." And since the brown eyes remained impenetrable, she added generously: "It'll be my wedding present for you both."

Chapter 5

A man in uniform arrived to collect Berglund. (Sophie, hiding behind a curtain, waited in vain for a lasso to come and haul Papa away.) And gradually a change came over her familiar and well-regulated life. It seemed to grow a little more confined and meager each day, but you only noticed it when you suddenly stopped and remembered how it had been before. For instance, no more parcels came from Turkey, for the Dahde. The house smelled different now. When she got back from school, Sophie sniffed in vain for the aroma that once had streamed out of the kitchen. The Dahde herself seemed to be crumpling slowly inward, she was shrinking—or was it that Sophie was growing? No, the Dahde looked positively deflated and thinner, and she often went around now without the Petsche, so as to breathe more easily. She knew they were "at war," and often held the weekly magazines, with their photographs of soldiers in trenches, close up before her eyes, though sometimes upside down. Turhan had become her child. She growled with pleasure as he did his homework in her room and reported to her in her language, which only he and Sophie spoke, about his day. He did badly at school and had no friends. The singing teacher was the only one who liked him, for his clear, beautiful voice, and gave him solos to sing. Every evening the Dahde sat at his bedside and listened with rapt attention while he sang Schubert songs to her. He still had a peaky mouse face, grew too fast, ate too little, and hurried, hollow-chested, down the shady side of the street, since he couldn't stand the sun.

Sorrow struck now and then in Sophie's class, reminding her there was a war on, and that one should grieve. Sometimes a girl was absent, and then reappeared, dressed in black, and Sophie joined in the crying. But on her way home she skipped and whistled through the streets, full of the blissful, ever-present prospect of Anita sitting in the bow window, watching, waiting for her.

Every few months she didn't skip, but walked home slowly and reflectively. Sometimes she stopped, thinking hard; you should be pleased, she told herself, Papa's home on leave, you should be happy. But of course it meant that Anita would not be waiting for her in the bow window.

Papa always brought something back, sardines, perhaps, or chocolate. He wasn't fighting at the front, lying in trenches; he had something to do with supplies in the Belgian sector, that was all she knew. Sardines and chocolate. Hurrah! She began to skip again—then stopped. Anita wouldn't be there in the bow window. . . .

The evenings were the worst. He wanted to spend the evenings alone with Anita in the drawing room. Sometimes she took refuge with Turhan, who now had his own room, but he was always busy sticking stamps into his album or singing to the Dahde. So she walked up and down the corridor, up and down, not knowing what to do with herself.

And Anita never even noticed, she had better things to attend to. But were they better? Anita always asked herself that, when Berglund was home on leave. It wasn't wise to be so happy, it wasn't safe. But God knows it was hard to keep oneself in check, during those few days. And it almost seemed as if Berglund felt the same way. Was it possible? Did miracles happen? Was it the war? It couldn't be—and yet he insisted that she should sit beside him, close against him, he wouldn't let go of her hand, even while smoking the cigars he had filched from the camp. He told her little about his army life, and only shook his head when she asked: "What's it like, Johannes, *tell* me what it's like?" It was that bad, then.

At night she lay in his arms, frightened, unable to sleep, not even wanting to; she preferred to stay awake and enjoy every last hour. Fear. Fear that something would happen to him—telegram—a hero's death—died bravely for the Fatherland—it could happen any day, even behind the front line, in the Belgian sector. Fear of becoming too dependent on him, of asking too much of him, love, faithfulness; much too much.

The mornings of his departure, Anita and Sophie would stand silently beside him in the hall, and together—since neither would give up the privilege—bring him his uniform jacket, his coat, his cap, his bag. Sophie couldn't understand herself. What made her wail all of a sudden? What made her hug Papa so tight and stick her nose deep in between his neck and his military collar, where he always smelled so good, when she knew all the time that she was glad he was leaving?

Anita didn't cry. Only when the front door finally closed behind him, she sometimes burst into tears, blindly crying, "Johannes! Johannes!" and leaning her head against the door. Then Sophie would flee into the garden, in her nightdress—with Anita in pursuit. Sophie would let herself be caught, and they would clasp each other tight, and cry together. But for different reasons.

.

During the last year of the war, Papa managed to come back only once on leave. Strange—other fathers seemed to have the usual amount of leave, as Sophie gathered from her classmates. She was twelve years old now, and looked older because of her height and a growing bosom, small as yet, but the envy of the class.

And then, when he did come home on leave, it was somehow no longer the same, right from the start, even though he not only brought chocolate and sardines, but a bottle of wine and two pairs of stockings for Anita. He looked particularly well, she thought, really handsome, despite the first white hairs in his short red mane, and in an excellent mood, asking all sorts of questions, even addressing himself to Turhan for a few minutes, which left the boy bathed in sweat.

In the evening something very odd happened. Papa suddenly wanted Sophie to stay in the drawing room (Turhan had locked himself in the bathroom), saying that she was grown up now and he saw far too little of her. Her first reaction was delight—until she saw Anita's face. She glanced uncertainly from one to the other, and stood in the doorway for a second or two, in order to be quite sure, for she was about to make her first adult decision.

"I'm tired, Papa. Sorry. Goodnight," she said firmly.

As she climbed the stairs, the ecstatic feeling grew with every step, the confidence that she had "handled it" right. Without help. No one had prompted her.

She entered her bedroom, head high, and stood, feeling neither lonely nor excluded but so thoroughly proud of herself that she went at once to the mirror. She was a person now, a decision-maker. Perhaps it showed. She bent forward and inspected herself. No, it was still this morning's face, too round, too many freckles—but the nose was beautiful. Papa's nose. She unbuttoned her blouse, slipped off the bodice and turned to see herself in profile. Perhaps her bosom had grown. She checked it every Sunday morning. Today was Tuesday. No change.

Voices from below. She dropped to the floor and pressed her ear to the boards. Anita's voice, worked up. Now Papa's, calm, but not friendly. Now Anita's again. She had never heard her make such violent noises. Silence. A door was opened and immediately shut again. Footsteps coming up the stairs. Sophie jumped up and grabbed for her nightdress, but the footsteps headed off in the opposite direction, Anita's footsteps. They went into the bedroom, alone.

Chapter 6

She didn't know how long he'd been sitting there, engrossed in his book. Why did everyone in hospitals creep in and out so silently? Why not just open the door normally, with a good sharp click—so that people knew someone had come in and could react accordingly, talk, or complain, or smile, or pretend to doze, whatever they felt like?

Aloud she said: "Take that thing off, that thing on the door."

He looked up from his book.

"I can't do that—it's part of ward equipment, so you can take a quick glance at the patients without disturbing them."

"But I want to be disturbed—by you, that is, Brother. I've been waiting for you so long! Where were you? At home? Have you got a home? A wife?"

"I've got a room here, in the staff quarters."

"No wife?"

"No."

"Would you like one?"

He wanted to cut her short, but couldn't find the words, and shook his head in silence.

"Oh, don't be such a wet blanket," she said as he went back to his book. "You see—I made you laugh. Come on, tell me. There's so much I've saved up to tell *you*, and we've got the whole night together, haven't we? How wonderful." She closed her eyes and shook her head gently from side to side, sighing with pleasure; and suddenly frowned.

"Are you in pain?"

"Only at a distance. It doesn't worry me, I'm happy the way it is. Where were we? Have you got everything I've been telling you about Anita?"

He hesitated. She opened her eyes and gave him a sharp look.

"Listen, I'm not just writing this for fun! You're the first person to know about it. Nobody else has read it yet. What was the last thing I wrote—it was about Anita and Papa, isn't that right?"

He nodded, hoping she wouldn't pursue it.

"Have I already mentioned why she was so upset that night? I haven't? You see, we got stuck there, I can't remember why."

She was silent for a moment, then the corners of her mouth turned upward, half amused, half embarrassed, and she giggled.

"You won't believe it, here I am, a—let's say an *experienced* woman, and there you are, a doctor, who knows it all—you *do*, don't you, Brother?"

"You mean medically? I've got a bit to learn yet."

"Good Lord," she said crossly, "sometimes you can be downright stupid, Brother. I'm talking about *people*, about what can happen between two people—" She stopped and listened as if somebody had just said something, nodded, smiling. "And the way things turn out quite differently, not what one had in mind at all—you know all about that, don't you, otherwise I couldn't tell you any of this, you'd only misunderstand it. I can't explain it for you—that is, perhaps I could, but I don't want to." She gave him a serious look. "I'd only embarrass myself, and I'm too old for that. You understand, I'm not trying to *teach* you anything, I just want to talk to somebody who *knows* about these things. As an equal. You do understand, don't you—because when I first saw you sitting here, I thought at once, he *knows. . . ."*

He thought of her X-rays, and shut his book. He would give her the night; not try to stop her talking. He knew the strength of the morphine injection she had been given an hour ago, when the nurse on daytime duty, making her final rounds, had found her moaning and apparently unconscious. The fact that the morphine had this effect on her, instead of calming her and putting her to sleep—well, that wasn't his business. Her husband had said nothing on the subject, and he wasn't obliged, as a doctor, to delve into her past.

"I hope I know what can take place between two people—I can certainly understand it, whatever it is."

"That'll do," she said, satisfied. "If you can understand it, then you know about it. Now and forever. And if it ever happened to *you*, you'd remember, even though it couldn't be exactly the same—after all, you're a man, but you've known, Brother, you'd recognize the *feeling*, you'd recognize it right away, like an old friend. That's why I've got to describe it to you as carefully as possible. Now, where were we? You tell me."

"Anita and Papa . . . " It was like being at school again.

.

Right. Yes, that was a bad night, Brother, a terrible night. In the middle of the war, remember, the streets all dark, Papa home on leave, and all we could gather from him about what was happening "out there" was bad news, things were going wrong, we might not even win the war—though none of that really interested me. All I was concerned about was what was happening in our house that night, once Anita had gone into the bedroom on her own. I was old enough to understand perfectly well what that meant: Papa in the guestroom downstairs, and Anita alone upstairs in the huge bed, where she was so lonely while Papa was in Belgium. She used to wrap herself in the nightshirt he'd worn on leave, or else she couldn't get to sleep, she said. So just imagine, she'd been waiting seven months for him, with nothing but his nightshirt to smell and to kiss, and now Papa was *there*, and didn't come to her. I knew, because I'd turned out the light in my room and opened the door a little. I heard everything. I heard Papa go into the downstairs bathroom, I heard him *whistle*. Just a few notes and then he quickly stopped, he must have felt ashamed, but it showed me exactly how

105

he was feeling. He was feeling good. He only whistled when he felt good. And at the same time I heard Anita crying; it sounded as if she had something stuffed against her mouth, so that no one would hear. Then silence, and Papa shut the door downstairs. I went into the corridor, tiptoed to her room, and knocked. No answer. The door was locked. I knocked again, and whispered through the keyhole: "It's me, Sophie." First she called: "Go away Sophie, go to sleep!" But I said: "I won't. I'll go to sleep here outside your door and catch pneumonia." It made her laugh a bit as I'd hoped, and then she came and opened the door. By then I really was shivering with cold, I only had my nightdress on and no slippers, so she led me to the bed, in the dark, and it was warm there. I felt something long and woolly next to me and knew at once: Papa's nightshirt. I sat up and tugged and pulled at it—one half lay under her and the other under me. "What are you doing?" she said, but I wouldn't let go till I had the whole thing in my hands, and before she could get it away from me, I hurled it with all my might into the darkness.

"How dare you!" she cried, but as she made to turn the light on, I threw myself on top of her—I was already quite strong—and forced her back against the pillow.

And suddenly—that's why I'm writing it in such detail—suddenly I was someone quite else. Perhaps that evening I simply burst out, like a ripe chestnut—remember how I spoke to Papa, earlier—I only know that I felt I was in the saddle, like a man; I was in command. I pressed her back against the pillow and said: "Anita—stop crying this minute. You don't have to sleep alone, and you don't need that old nightshirt—you've got *me*."

And to my surprise she stopped struggling, stretched out beneath the bedclothes, sobbed a few more times—and stopped. I stretched myself alongside her, and she put her arm around me. First she pressed me against her shoulder, then I put my arm around her too, and we lay like that for a while, close and warm.

I said: "You see, you don't need Papa anymore. I'll stay with you."

She didn't answer, and I soon fell asleep, with her arm around me, and mine around her. I don't think I moved once, all night—I always sleep like that, like a sack of potatoes—because I woke up in the same position. When I turned to look at her I saw that she was staring at the ceiling, eyes wide open. I could see her quite clearly in the early light.

I raised my arm and stroked her face, and I knew the time had come to ask: "What's the matter with Papa? Doesn't he love you anymore?"

She wasn't angry, she gave me an answer, but she didn't look at me, just at the ceiling.

"He's found himself another woman. In Antwerp. A Belgian girl. The wine's from her, and the stockings. Nice of her."

All very calmly.

"And does he love her now? Did he say so?"

"Yes."

I hadn't stopped stroking her face, but I must admit, it was as if someone had given me a box around the ears. Papa had found himself another woman, a stranger, someone nothing to do with *us*, with Anita and me, and Turhan and the Dahde and our house and Frau Glaubitz and Gerhard—after all, we were all one thing, Papa too, he belonged to it, to *us*, and how could anybody come between us? Then I remembered how it was *before* Anita; with everything already there, the house, the rest of us, and yet we none of us belonged to each other the way we did now. But that seemed an eternity ago, I was still a child then, with no idea what it was like to have someone waiting for you in the bow window.

"Anita, this woman, the Belgian girl, will she be coming here to live with us?"

She turned her head to me, so that I was now stroking her hair, and looked at me as if I had said something crazy.

"What do you mean?"

"You said he loves her, that means she'll come and live with us, doesn't it? As you did, remember? First you were on the boat—and then you were suddenly in the house and I knew you belonged to us."

She sat up, detaching herself from me, and played absently with a long strand of hair. Then she looked at me and tried to smile. And that was so sad, Brother—I nearly burst into tears, but I knew that would be bad for her, so I dug my fingernails into my palms as hard as I could, so that the pain would distract me. That was an old trick of mine, it stopped one laughing or crying when one wasn't supposed to.

"I think it'll be some time, Sophie, before she comes and lives with us. Who knows, it might never come to that."

That was all I wanted to hear. I threw my arms around her neck, and kissed her. "Perhaps he'll come upstairs again tonight and sleep here," I whispered, but she freed herself and shook her head.

"No, he won't. He's not that kind of man, your father." As if bestowing praise on him.

Then she slowly got out of bed and said: "Perhaps it would be best if he left right away."

I agreed. Off with him. Back to his Belgian girl. We'd all stay the same as before, and Anita would be waiting in the bow window.

I too got up, and went to my room. But then I thought of something and ran back to the bedroom. She was standing by the window, in her nightdress, looking down at Gerhard, who was gathering up the fallen branches in the garden. I picked up her warm bedjacket and put it around her shoulders; like a husband, it struck me.

"Anita—don't forget, you're not alone. I'll sleep in here again tonight."

And that was when it happened.

•

The young doctor sat up in his chair. "When what happened?"

She turned to him, and he could see by the glitter in her eyes that the morphine had reached its peak.

"It was quite wonderful, Brother," she said slowly. "It seemed perfectly natural, and perhaps it *is*, perhaps many people have had a similar experience."

"What experience?" he said, impatient for the first time. But she was not to be hurried.

•

I was late for school, as you can imagine. I could think of nothing but Anita, and got some very low marks that day. Finally, the teacher asked what was the matter with me. I lied, said I had a headache; my forehead was hot under her touch, and I got away with it. White lie, I thought—justified, in an emergency. All I wanted was to get home as fast as possible, see Anita, make sure she wasn't crying.

But when I reached home at last, out of breath, running the whole way, Frau Glaubitz told me Anita had gone out. Papa too. But not together. We ate lunch alone, Turhan, the Dahde, and I, and not a word was spoken. As we got up afterward, however, Turhan said emphatically: "Papa really is a bad person." But the Dahde shook her head and said in her language: "A man is neither good nor bad.

He's what he is." And she went out at once into the Siegesallee, on her own.

But it didn't do any good. Later that afternoon, while I was struggling with my homework, the doorbell rang: a telegram for Papa. It lay waiting for him on the silver salver in the hall, and when the Dahde returned from the Siegesallee, she saw it lying there. For a while she stood over it, and then, without touching it, shuffled slowly off up to her room.

Shortly afterward Papa came home. I heard his key in the lock, and watched from above through the banister as he went to open the telegram. Then he looked up and saw me, before I could hide.

"Sophie," he called softly, "is the Dahde alone in her room, or is Turhan with her?"

"She's alone, Papa."

He came up the stairs, telegram in hand. "Mustafa is dead," he said, and seeing my uncomprehending face, added: "Your grandfather." I made no attempt to pull a sad face, I didn't know anything about him, no one had ever mentioned him.

Papa stood there holding the telegram, as if waiting for me to tell him what to do next. "Stay here," he said. "I may need you." Then he went to the Dahde's room, and shortly after called me in to join them. The Dahde was sitting on a chair, with the telegram in her lap. She had pushed back the Petsche, and was swaying back and forth, the way she did in her prayers, only much less vigorously. Papa stood before her, and I must say, he looked unhappy.

"Sophie—there's something the Dahde wants to tell me. You must translate."

I went over to her and put my head next to hers. She sat still and whispered in her language: "Ask your father to write to Constantinople for me—I want to be buried at his feet. Ask them to keep a place for me."

I told Papa, and he nodded. Then he bent down and stroked her head. She was right, he was neither good nor bad, he was what he was.

.

Anita didn't come back until after dinner, and then went straight up to the bedroom. I don't think she even saw Papa. He was in the drawing room with his friend Georg Wertheimer, and I heard them talking, laughing too, but perhaps that was Georg.

I undressed and waited. Georg left, at last. I heard Papa lock the front door and come back to the bathroom, back into the guestroom —and then the door was finally closed. But I waited a little longer, he might still decide to come up to Anita—perhaps he had something more to say to her.

The house was very quiet. Extra quiet, as though everybody was holding his breath, each in his separate room. No door opened downstairs. I thought I could hear Papa snoring.

I slipped out of my room and went softly toward Anita's door. It was locked again. But I'd told her I'd come! "Anita!" I called angrily through the keyhole. "Open up."

"Go back to bed, Sophie."

"Certainly not, I am staying here till you open up. You need me."

"No," came her voice, "I don't need anyone. Go to bed."

I rattled the door, by now I didn't care if someone heard me—but everything stayed quiet. Then I did something really sly, Brother, the devil only knows how I thought of it. I floated a sob through the keyhole and said with a trembling voice: "I want to see you, Anita— my grandfather's dead." Crafty, wasn't it? Not yet thirteen years old, and already bound straight for hell.

Anita opened the door, and I threw my arms around her, managing to squeeze a few more sobs out of myself. She led me to the bed, and I huddled under the warm covers, forgot Papa, forgot the Dahde, forgot Grandfather—whoever he had been—forgot everything, wanting only Anita, her warmth, her arm around me. But the arm didn't come. She turned out the bedside light and stretched out beside me, stiff and straight, without touching me. I waited, listening hard—was she crying? No, her breathing sounded calm. I propped myself up on one elbow, reached out for her face, and felt wet cheeks. She *was*, then! I leaned over and began to kiss her eyes, her cheeks, her forehead, her nose—that tickled her and made her laugh a little, and she turned her head to one side, but I turned it firmly back and kissed her mouth—she resisted, tried to say something, opened her mouth —and I began to kiss her open mouth with a quite new, quite different and savage delight.

She was, I think, just as surprised as I was, transported all at once into a different climate, a completely different landscape.

I suddenly noticed that she was returning my kiss—and I took

fright. I remember very clearly that it frightened me because someone was doing something to *me*, and at that instant it didn't matter
that the someone was Anita. I froze, and pulled away, but now it was
she that wouldn't let me go, that held me powerfully, jamming her
mouth so hard against mine that I could hardly breathe, it was as if
she wanted to punish me—and perhaps not only me! I can see that
now, but at the time I simply felt scared, because she was actually
hurting me. I fell back onto my pillow—she let go of me—but all of
a sudden I could feel an emptiness inside me, a void that insisted on
being filled, or rather, I had a feeling that I had been lit, like a match,
and yet I somehow couldn't burn. I reached for her again, trying to
find her mouth, I wanted to fill the emptiness, I wanted to burn—
didn't quite know what ought to happen next, or what was already
happening—and at the same time knowing exactly what was happening: she was slipping off my nightdress, and I could feel her hands on
my skin. I recognized that quite clearly but I was also—probably because it was the first time—forging blindly ahead, along the pre-
ordained path—or was it a stream I was rushing down? I only know
that I was impelled, irresistibly, toward a goal.

Which was quite quickly and quite easily reached, without the
least effort. It was astounding how thoroughly it filled the void. I lay
absolutely still, next to Anita, but severed from her, alone with myself.
It didn't occur to me that *she* had had anything to do with it, or with
me. But this only lasted a matter of seconds, and then my brain came
back to life and I understood what had happened to me.

What now? Sit up, put on my nightdress and say thank you? Was
that what one did?

Anita's arm arrived and pressed me to her, before I could get
around to doing anything. She began to cry again, and that disappointed me. I'd assumed that, just like me, she was feeling good,
filled to the brim, utterly content.

I stroked her arm, but a little distractedly, my mind was so full of
thoughts I couldn't really concentrate on her unhappiness. Or
wouldn't. There was so much I had to sort out, and most urgently, of
course, the question: had I taken Papa's place just now, in some
sense—or not? Was I—what was the right word—was I merely an
object of affection for her? Or more than that? Far more?

I came to no conclusions that night. A woolliness came over me, and my thoughts seemed to flow into one another. I think I fell asleep at once.

.

When I woke up, it was light and the place beside me was empty. I ran to the window and saw her at the very back of the garden, walking back and forth under the plane trees. There was no time to do anything but hurry to my room, get washed and dressed, pack my satchel, and dash off to school.

When I got home at lunchtime, Frau Glaubitz, opening the front door, told me once again that Anita wasn't at home—but that Papa wanted to speak to me. Before lunch, too. Right away. In the drawing room.

I was no coward, but my heart was now beating so loudly that I stayed by the door so that he wouldn't hear it. He was sitting in his favorite chair, smoking, looking as if he'd been waiting for me for some time.

"Come here, Sophie." He pointed to the other armchair, opposite him. "Sit down there."

I sank into its hugeness, my legs hanging down without reaching the ground. I knew how ridiculous I must have looked, with my old school shoes dangling on the end of my legs.

"Where were you last night?" Quiet, but dangerous. That was what always paralyzed one, the cool voice and the baleful eyes. "Your door was open. I came to tell you something."

I couldn't breathe. Last night! Had it perhaps not been a master stroke, after all? No giant step forward? No infinitely blissful experience? Had I simply got myself into trouble? I could hear the Dahde's voice: "Pants down."

"I know where you were." Still quiet. I thought I was going to burst with fear. "I want you to tell me the truth."

Yes, Papa, yes—if only I could! I opened my mouth and gasped for air like a fish on dry land. He saw I couldn't speak under his gaze, and looked away, carefully tapping his cigar over the big ashtray on the desk, beside him. "I won't punish you, as long as you tell me the truth."

Air in my lungs again, at last. And thank God no tears on the way, he hated tears. But no solid ground, as yet, beneath my feet. I slid deeper into the chair, fishing in vain for the floor. If only I could have found it, it would have made it so much easier to return his gaze, firmly and candidly. But I couldn't, I had to draw myself up in midair, as it were. In any case, I knew there was only one thing to do: tell the truth. The whole truth, if it came to it—which hopefully it wouldn't.

"I was with Anita. All night." Clever to have volunteered the last bit, it smacked of nothing to hide.

"I know. Why?"

"Someone had to be."

"Do you also spend the night with her while I'm in Belgium?"

"She doesn't need me then, she's got your nightshirt."

"My nightshirt?"

"She sleeps with your nightshirt, Papa."

He turned the china-blue eyes full on me and looked at me in silence, for a long time. Dear God in heaven, don't let him ask for details—

"And tonight? You'll spend the night with her again?"

"Yes, Papa."

"Come over here, Sophie."

I eeled my way out of the chair and placed myself before him. My face was at the same height as his. From close to, his eyes weren't really quite so frightening.

He reached for me with both hands, sat me on his knee and hugged me to him. I found myself slipping down once more, and lying with my face next to his shoulder. Until now I had always been the one who hugged him, and he had put up with it, but now *he* was holding *me*—and it gave me the strangest feeling, *his* arm around me—and last night *mine* around Anita. . . .

Did he realize?

"Sophie," he said softly, so softly that later I couldn't be sure he'd really said it, "you're very dear to me, you know. I hadn't fully realized—I think perhaps you're dearer to me than anyone else in the world."

Instead of dissolving with bliss, I felt my stomach turn cold. Oh God, I was dear to him, and I'd betrayed him—with his own wife!

•

"What?" the young doctor interrupted hoarsely. "You really thought you'd—"

"I didn't think, I *knew*—or are you going to tell me it wasn't a betrayal? Someone had slept with his wife. I was that someone. It could have been somebody else, of course, the milkman, the lodger—what are you staring at me for? A betrayal's a betrayal."

"Well—yes. I suppose one has to call it that. And—did you tell him? In so many words?"

"He didn't ask me any more about it, thank God. I don't know if he suspected and just didn't want to know, or whether he assumed a twelve-year-old would chastely share her stepmother's bed like a good little girl. On the other hand, he knew perfectly well I wasn't a good little girl, I was *his* daughter, and I'd had an oriental mother, so I was probably early developed—in Turkey girls get married at my age! But if such thoughts entered his mind, he pushed them aside—like so many cuckolded husbands." She giggled. "He said: 'I'm glad you're looking after Anita'—that's how cozy it all became between Papa and me; and then he really took me into his confidence, as though I was already his ally: 'I hate to make her so unhappy,' he said. 'I suppose you know what's happened.' I nodded again, traitor and ally. 'It was sheer chance—they assigned the girl to me as some sort of bookkeeper—her husband was killed early on, she's still young—perhaps it'll all blow over, I don't know, I hope so—no, dammit, I don't, I hope we stay together, I like her—you understand, don't you?' "

I thought, Oh yes, *now* I understand.

He let go of me, and stood me on my feet again. His tone changed, became dry, matter-of-fact.

" 'In the end perhaps *she'll* break it off and the whole thing will have been a wartime affair like thousands of others. Who knows. We'll see. Everything's about to be turned upside down—best to grab what one can. Meanwhile, it's a good thing you're looking after Anita.'

"Which brings me to our third night together."

She was silent for so long that he stood up and leaned over her to see her eyes, but they were wide open, glimmering in the darkness like two cigarette ends.

"Brother—" she breathed, and raised her arms. They stuck out of the wide sleeves of the hospital smock like two bleached bones. But her strength failed her, and they fell back. Her mouth began to tremble, and the dark, glowing, amber eyes filled with tears. He took both arms, holding them gently by the elbow—they weighed hardly anything—and lifted them around his neck, knotting the fingers together so that they wouldn't fall back again.

A few tears rolled across her cheeks, smooth cheeks, the skin spread taut across the bone, like ivory. She really was no more than skin and bones. Why had she waited so long before admitting herself to the hospital? He wished he knew. Bent over her, with her arms around him in a lover's embrace, she was no longer his patient, it was as if she were his mother or his sister or a former love, or, above all, his child—the child he had only once held in his arms, since it wasn't officially his. Though it *was* his, he would have known it at once, even if the girl hadn't winked at him so significantly with her dark, slanting eyes. They had spent no more than a few nights together, while her husband was away—an old friend of his, and yet he had betrayed him without hesitating. In his own bed, too. A year later he had returned to Crete, on leave. And there the child had been, and his old friend, who had welcomed him with enthusiasm, knowing nothing, and never to know. Even his father confessor had agreed that it was better that way. That had happened five years ago now, and he rarely thought about "his" child. But now it was suddenly in his arms again, in the shape of this old woman, who felt as light as the child had, and who was smiling at him, now, just as innocent and newly born.

He kissed her very gently on her smooth, wasted cheeks, freed her fingers from behind his neck, and sat beside her on the bed. Then he took one of her hands and laid his on top of it, so that she wouldn't suddenly feel lonely.

"You see," she said, looking down at his protective hands, "you see—I've got you now. I knew I would. I've always been able to get anyone I wanted, I've had them all, because I'm a beast. Don't stare at me like that—you've known that all along, and it doesn't worry you—although you're one of the kind ones. I knew it as soon as I saw you. Someone like me can smell the kind ones. My husband's one—or he was once, when we were first married. In any case, I don't think it's a virtue, it's a gift, that's all, I'm sure of it, you're born with it, like good teeth or good digestion. I'm not kind—maybe I'm noble but I'm not kind. And I never wanted to be. Which was wrong of me, perhaps, because in the end it's always possible to work at being kind, even if it never comes out like the original, never quite spontaneous and natural. But now, for instance, now that you're holding my hand and we're sitting here so nice and quietly, in the darkness—I would so much like to tell you something truly splendid about me, to have you sit up and marvel. I'm pretty sure I've already got under your skin—a little, anyway, though you're still resisting it—and it would make all the difference if you could now discover some rare and admirable trait in me." She paused for a second and grinned. "Instead I'm going to tell you the story of my third night with Anita—and then perhaps you'll take your hand away."

"Tell me anyway," he said.

"Do you have a sister?"

"Two of them."

"Older than you?"

"Younger. Much younger."

"Can you remember them when they were twelve or thirteen?"

"Of course."

"Can you imagine either of them, at that age, as a fully fledged lover?"

He shook his head, smiling.

"The older one is a lay sister, the younger one's fourteen now, and just as pious. She's a sweet child, not very bright, I'm afraid. Helps my mother with the housework."

.

Then you'll find it hard to understand what I'm going to tell you. I wasn't pious, and I didn't help anyone with anything. I was quite bright, I think—but above all eaten up with passion. I use the word "passion" deliberately, because there's something innocent about it, and I was absolutely innocent. I only felt guilty toward Papa, for having usurped his place without his knowing. But my night of love with Anita had been just that, a night of love, spoiled only by her tears—and my only worry was that she had gone on crying for Papa. I decided to love her even more, and could hardly wait for evening to come.

Papa left the house early, to dine at the sailing club. Anita still hadn't returned. Where on earth could she be? Where did she always disappear to? I undressed and went to her bedroom. It was freezing cold. By now, in the fourth year of the war, there was no more coal, and every day Gerhard cut a branch or two, no more, from the trees in our garden, to burn in Turhan's stove and mine. Anita gave her ration to the Dahde. She was old, Anita said, and used to a warm climate.

I crept into the huge bed and lay shivering. The wild excitement I had felt all day began to falter and wither away. The bed was like a large, yawning black pit.

Gradually I became afraid. What if Anita never came back tonight? What if she never came back at all? My teeth were chattering and I began to sob. I could have gone back to my own warm little bed—but I'd made up my mind to freeze here in her bed, as in an icy grave. Perhaps she'd find me in the morning, stiff and cold—but she'd understand, she'd know I froze to death for *her*.

I heard the front door open, and sat up, shaking with cold and excitement—someone with a key! It could of course be Papa. Or was it—

Soft footsteps on the stairs, footsteps I knew well. I dropped back, dug my face into the pillow.

A second or two later, the light came on. She walked to the bed and turned my face around toward her, saw my tear-stained eyes, felt my cold hands.

"Child," she said, and sighed, then sat on the edge of the bed.

I put one arm around her neck. She didn't stop me. I pressed my cold face against hers, and warmed it. Slowly her warmth began to spread through my whole body, until my brain too began to thaw out and the turmoil and the need to have her in my arms surged up again. I was very glad I hadn't died.

I got onto my knees and tried to take her coat off.

"Let go, Sophie," she said, and stood up. "Go back to your room, it's much too cold for you here."

"Come and warm me up," I said and stretched out underneath the covers. "Come. I've been waiting for ages now."

.

"That night *I* was the seducer, Brother. Don't forget, I was an exceptionally quick learner, and also completely—you could call it shameless, but I tell you I was innocently shameless. I had only the one thought in my head: tonight she isn't going to think of Papa, she's going to feel how much I love her, so much so that I wanted to die for her. Smile if you like, Brother, it was a serious matter, to me. Perhaps you've forgotten how intensely *you* could feel, aged twelve —under certain circumstances. I don't think I was exceptional; children feel torn apart by jealousy or hate or malice just as strongly as adults—and by love too, of course. In time, one tends to forget, or even finds it embarrassing, and refuses to admit it ever happened. Few people care to examine what they felt, as children—and I'll tell you something, Brother, very often that was the only time they really loved or hated. Later on both have shriveled up. Is that the case with you?"

"I don't know."

"You've never loved, then?"

He realized he was still holding her hand. He let go of her and stood up, went to the window, and looked out. No stars. Raining a bit. Why resist? Why not face the fact that here was someone who— instead of letting herself be nursed—was about to crack him open like a nut, and that he was more than ready to let it happen? God knows there was enough "drama" on his ward, people dying, either on schedule or quite unexpectedly; tears, pain, both physical and spiritual, and, like his colleagues, he had gradually developed the protective shell their work demanded, or else they would be broken by it, instead of bearing it with stoicism and a carefully rationed quantity of sympathy. A limited quantity, the supreme law of survival. But this woman had pushed through those limits and forced him to suffer with her, to bleed as much for her fate as for his. She poked un-caring into all the distant, rediscovered corners of his soul, making him vibrate whether he wanted to or not, each time she pulled the strings. Was he endangering his Hippocratic oath? But then, it was probably just her obsessive need to get things off her chest, making *him* want to "confess" as well, and not only sit there listening.

He turned and went back to the bed. All this time she hadn't said a word. She was cunning, all right, she knew when to say nothing.

He sat on the edge of the bed and took her hand again, filled by a sudden sense of impending loss. One day, one day soon, he would come into this room to find some other person lying in this bed. . . .

"You're right," he said, and stroked her hand. "I haven't loved anyone yet. Naturally, I've had—attachments. I'm involved in one now, with one of the student nurses working here, in the laboratory. She comes to my room at night when I'm off duty, and it's very nice, I like it—that is, I like *her*. Perhaps I can't love in the sense *you* mean."

"Of course you can," she said, and fixed him with her drugged, brilliant eyes. "You love *me*. You can sense something and you don't quite know what to do with it and you think: ridiculous! Some old woman who'll soon be gone—what's she to me? But you'll see, you'll never forget me, because you've discovered that you *can* love—I may even have spoiled your chance of being happy with some other girl, because you'll secretly compare them all to me. Oh, how I'd love to think so!"

A buzzing from his coat pocket. He stood up automatically, carefully freed his hand.

She said nothing, turned her face to the wall.

Chapter 7

Berglund left early next morning, without having spoken to Anita again. Downstairs in the hall the entire household gathered around him as he put on his coat, Sophie nearest to him, the Dahde and Anita a good two yards away, and behind them Frau Glaubitz. Right at the back, Turhan.

Papa kissed Sophie, embraced Anita and the Dahde in hearty and identical fashion, and shook hands with Frau Glaubitz. Forgot Turhan, who had ducked.

In the front doorway he turned and said to no one in particular: "I'll be back soon. I trust they won't need me there to the bitter end. Two, three months at the most—and I'll be home."

The door shut behind him, and Sophie stood looking at it, trying to straighten out the warring factions of hopes and fears that were simultaneously assaulting her. Uppermost, let Papa come home safe and everything be the way it was before—but lurking underneath, a sudden flush of panic: then what will become of Anita and me?

Her eyes fell on Anita, this time neither crying nor steadying her head against the door, but standing calmly by and looking back at Sophie. Their eyes met and each knew that the other had been thinking the same thing. Anita gave a short laugh, turned slowly around and strolled into the drawing room. Through the bow window she could see an orderly stowing Berglund's suitcase on the back seat of the army car. He was already installed in front, never once looked back toward the house.

Sophie approached and stood beside her, and they both watched in silence as the car started up and drove off into the early-morning darkness. Sophie put it into words. "What will happen to us when he comes back, Anita?"

"Perhaps he won't come back *here.*"

What? Papa coming back—but not coming home? Did that mean she had to choose between Papa and Anita? Anita turned abruptly, went out and up the stairs, Sophie behind her. But as she made to follow her into the bedroom, Anita stopped, blocking the doorway.

"No. Go and pack your satchel, right away. You're leaving for school much too late these days. That's got to stop, d'you understand?"

"Anita—please!" Quavering voice, wet pleading eyes. "Just one question, otherwise I can't possibly go to school—"

"Well?"

"Anita—couldn't you love Papa *and* me?"

"Off you go now, Sophie. We'll talk at lunchtime."

Sophie heard the door being bolted from the inside, and now the lurking panic deep inside surged up into a single, burning wish: that the war would last, so that Papa wouldn't come home! She shut her eyes in shame at such a sinful longing, her head throbbed, any minute she was going to be sick . . . she turned her head from side to side, tried to take deep breaths, repeated tonelessly: "But I can't go to school like *this* . . ."

A sound came from the dark corridor behind her—light too had to be rationed these days—and a pair of heavy, shuffling footsteps.

The Dahde came slowly toward her, the veil pulled back, the huge, inky black eyes probing and ominous.

"I'm going, Dahde," she stammered, and ran into her room.

When she emerged again into the corridor, satchel in hand, she found the Dahde standing in the same place, staring at Anita's door. Slowly she turned her head and looked at Sophie—who took one deep breath and shot sideways past her, down the stairs, and out the front door.

·

The agony of school lessons! The minutes crept endlessly past in a vacuum, without sound. She could see the teacher's lips move, she even thought she could understand what she was saying. Yet she did not truly hear anything. And answering was quite impossible. Only

when she saw the other girls' faces turn toward her did she realize
that it was her turn, that it was her they were all waiting for. She
stood up and said: "I'm sorry, Miss?"

"I asked if you were feeling ill, Sophie."

"I don't know."

"Does it hurt, anywhere?"

"Yes, Miss."

"Where?"

"Everywhere."

The class laughed, but the teacher remained serious. The girl
looked very pale, with dark rings around her eyes.

"Put on your coat and go home, child. Gertrud will accompany
you."

Gertrud was at the top of the class, and no friend of Sophie's. It
was now a matter of pulling oneself together, of walking down the
pavement with her, slowly, the way one would if one hurt everywhere.

"What's the matter with you, then?" asked the top of the class.
"You've been acting up for days. Are you really ill or just pretending?"

A low thrust that had to be parried.

"My father's been home on leave. He left this morning." The plain
truth and, all the same, a lie.

"Really?" said Gertrud, and her cool gaze melted a little. "Does he
mean that much to you?" And when Sophie didn't answer, she went
on: "Mine's almost become a stranger, I hardly know him anymore."

I've got to know mine for the first time, thought Sophie. I've de-
ceived him, and I shall go on deceiving him. . . .

"You don't look at all well to me," said Gertrud. "But I doubt if it's
got much to do with your father. You've probably caught something."

If only she'd stop looking at me. I'm sure it's written all over my
face. The Dahde saw it!

"Perhaps it's infectious," said Gertrud and edged away from
Sophie.

"No," said Sophie, "I'm sure it's not infectious." And burst out
laughing. The idea was too funny. The top of the class gazed coldly
at her.

"I'd say you were a bit cracked."

"That's right," said Sophie, and laughed even louder.

Gertrud stopped.

"Where do you live? Have we got far to go?"

"It's over there. The white house on the corner."

"Well, you can get there on your own now. I'll stay here and watch till you reach the front door." Top of the class. Conscientious.

"Bye," giggled Sophie and shot off as if unleashed. In the doorway she turned and waved to the small figure waiting at the other end of the street, who didn't wave back.

·

Anita was at home, said Frau Glaubitz. In Turhan's room. Why? She hardly ever went there. *Because she doesn't want to be alone with me.*

Sophie managed to walk past Turhan's door on the way to her room. She took off her coat, removed her school smock, washed her hands, dried them, washed them again, with no idea what she was doing. She stood by the window looking down into the garden. Sallow grass, a few early buds on the bushes, no one in sight. If only Gerhard were working somewhere down there, something human to attach her thoughts to and distract them, block them out, *not* press her head against the windowpane and moan!

The gong sounded, downstairs. Lunch. She heard Anita emerge from next door, talking to Turhan as they went down the stairs. No one called: "Sophie!" The Dahde was not to be seen.

On the table bowls full of yellow turnips and mashed potatoes, also some stewed apples, the rest of last year's crop. Anita nodded to her, friendly, neutral; she had a lot of questions to ask Turhan about his role in Handel's *Messiah*, which the school choir was going to perform at Easter. He wasn't used to so much attention, and poked nervously at his food. Sophie wrestled down her stewed apples, stared at the wallpaper: yellow roses, lovingly entwined on a blue ground. Anita would keep her word. "We'll talk at lunchtime." Consult the oracle once more: count the roses—an even number, and everything would be all right. One, two, three, four, five, six—twenty-three roses. Oh God. Oh God. If only she could find something to hold on to, someone to turn to. . . .

Right in the middle of Anita's musical observations she suddenly said: "Is my mother still alive?"

Anita was just forming the word "harmony," and her mouth froze on the "o." The question was so unexpected, and the eyes in the small white face so desperately serious, that it was a few seconds before she managed to answer.

"There's no reason to suppose otherwise, Sophie. She's still young, younger than I am, I think. You must ask the Dahde."

After that she didn't, or couldn't, return to the *Messiah*, and Turhan saw his chance, and fled.

"Come, put your coat on," said Anita. "Let's go into the garden."

.

Her mother had, in fact, nothing at all to do with what she wanted to discuss with Anita, but once she'd started down that line her thoughts got stuck there. She'd never talked to anyone about her mother, except to the Dahde, long ago, and that had been a total failure. Asking Papa about her was out of the question. But instead of her mother becoming a tantalizing secret, she had gradually lost all interest in her. She didn't suffer, watching other children hugging their mothers, didn't envy them; she had other things, Papa, the Dahde, the boat—more than enough. And then Anita had fallen into her lap, out of a blue sky, the ultimate blessing.

But now, over lunch, it had all collapsed. She had *nothing*. No one cared about her—least of all Anita. And suddenly the grief had come into her mind and remained there.

"Anita—has Papa ever talked to you about my mother?"

They were walking side by side along the garden path, under the tall, bare trees. The sky had brightened, and a pale, early-spring sun was struggling to trace the shadows of the branches on the lawn. But it was still cold. Anita had turned up her fur collar; only her eyes were visible.

"Right at the beginning. Apparently they didn't stay together long. She was much too young, sixteen, I think—"

"Three years older than I."

"Yes. But she'd grown up in a harem. Your father had nothing to talk about with her."

"Could he talk to Turhan's mother? She too came from a harem."

"She died, before he—before she—"

"Before he could get bored with her?"

Anita didn't answer. Aha. *That's* how it had been; now she knew. Her mother had bored Papa. Poor Papa. A good thing she'd never met her; she wanted nothing to do with her.

"What was she called?"

"Don't you know?"

Sophie blushed. But why? Must one feel ashamed, if one's boring mother didn't interest one?

"She was called Yasmin."

Yasmin. Beautiful name. Didn't really fit the picture.

"Listen to me, Sophie." The tone was brisk—but at the same moment she felt Anita's arm around her shoulders. "What's happened between us—it's got to stop. You know what I'm talking about. That doesn't mean I don't love you anymore—do you understand me?"

She had prepared herself for it, she'd had all morning to face it, to arm herself against it—with bravado, if possible, something like: but of course, Anita, I was just going to suggest the same thing myself! Far from it. She fell into the black hole that had been lying in wait for her all day.

The arm around her shoulders held her tighter, almost lifting her off the ground, and that helped. It helped so much that she managed to leave unsaid the last hope, the last childish plea: "Please—just once more!"

Silent and hugging close together, they walked down the path, turned back at the greenhouse, and when Anita's arm left her shoulder for an instant, Sophie at once pressed herself in again, eyes all but closed. And so the arm held her tight, all the way back to the house.

Chapter 8 At the end of August, when Sophie returned home from school, Frau Glaubitz whispered in high excitement even before she let her enter: "Herr Berglund is in the drawing room—in civilian clothes!"

"Sophie!"

He found her taller, but too thin and too pale. Just as well he'd brought a whole bag of provisions with him. Anita was sorting them out in the larder.

For her part, Sophie thought he looked better than ever, even without the handsome uniform. She sat in the armchair opposite him—and now at last her feet *did* touch the ground—watching him calmly and cheerfully describing his adventures on the journey home. You could see how happy he was to be home; no question of his going home "somewhere else." How had they greeted each other, he and Anita? she wondered. Would they be as in the old days again? She shut her eyes for a moment. Four months had gone by, four long, barren months. Anita's bedroom had stayed locked, had never once opened in spite of her desperate pleas through the key-hole. She had fallen on her knees outside the door, during the first, hardest night, unable to sleep for loneliness and longing, and had pleaded and whined till the early hours of the morning, and halfway through the second night—till all at once the Dahde suddenly stood beside her, candle in hand. She had been sobbing too hard to hear her coming, and now there she stood like the Last Judgment, eyes glowing in the candlelight like coals. She couldn't move, lay cowering on the floor like a sick dog and hid her face in her arms. The Dahde lifted her up and carried her back to her room, sat down beside her on the bed, and began to pray, holding her hand and rocking back and forth, eyes shut. Her lips murmured the Suras of the Koran. Back, back to her earliest childhood, when it had been the last thing she saw before falling asleep: the Dahde kneeling on her prayer mat, swaying and humming. It had always soothed her, had healed many a childhood sorrow. Even now, after all this time, it eased the pain. It had finally rocked her to sleep, and she had never gone and groveled outside Anita's door again.

Papa lit a cigar, one of his final pieces of booty, drew deeply on it, and studied her.

"You don't seem at all well to me," he said. "I'd like to have old Schweikart take a look at you. You're not just undernourished, you look as if there's something wrong with you, quite different from last time. Has something happened? At school?"

"I—got a bad report."

"Why? You've always found it so easy."

"I don't know, I've had difficulty paying attention—I'm glad you're here, Papa."

"Come here," he said, and when she stood before him, he stroked her face. "You used to look like me, now you look like a thin sliver of wartime soap."

She had to laugh, and thought how really glad she was that he was home again, now that everything was lost anyway.

.

After lunch Papa and Anita went out onto the terrace to drink the coffee he had brought back. Sophie and Turhan strolled around the garden, each with a bar of chocolate from Papa's bag.

"He's going to tell her now," remarked Turhan, and sat on the grass in the shade.

"Tell her what?" She stretched out beside him, folding her arms behind her head.

"That it's all over."

"How do you know?"

"I know a lot of things you don't know. Now don't get all worked up," he said with a smile, as she sat up, glaring. "*I* didn't know, the Dahde sniffed it out, as usual. Ever since he got back she's been sitting on her mat talking to Allah. But I don't think he'll be able to do anything either."

Sophie said nothing. Once again, the tangled, conflicting turmoil inside: pity for Anita—yet vindictive delight. Serves her right, she ought to love *me*! *I* wouldn't leave her in the lurch. Anger with Papa—vacillating, fickle—yet he loves *me*. In a different way, of course, but in the only way he can. He hasn't much of it to give—I've known that for a long time. *I* have, though—

"What'll happen now?" said Turhan, chewing reflectively on a blade of grass. He's beginning to look different, thought Sophie. His hair no longer fell across his forehead like frayed black thread, it had a parting in the middle and a blue-black gloss to it. The face was beginning to lose its mouse look, and beneath the narrow, curved nostrils could be seen the first trace of a mustache.

"He's got one in Belgium," said Sophie.

"*One?* That would surprise me."

"He's getting old." It had never occurred to her till now, that you could *talk* to Turhan.

"I think it's the war. He's not so—dashing, anymore. With any luck Anita'll go along with it, and won't go rushing off—"

"Oh God!" She fell back into the grass and covered her face with her hands. Turhan watched her for a while, chewing on his blade of grass.

.

"It's hot," said Berglund, although he was sitting in the shade with his cup and his cigar. "This suit's become too tight for me. D'you mind if I take my jacket off?"

"Not at all."

How formal they were with each other. She moved her deck chair into the sun and looked up at the cloudless sky, suddenly remembering the day on the boat she and Sophie had first stared at the sun together.

"Not much of a cigar," he said, and eyed the gray-brown sausage between his fingers. "But I'm lucky to have got any at all before the whole camp was abandoned. Everyone grabbed whatever they could carry."

Anita nodded absently, still staring at the sun. The bursts of flame flashed out in all directions, yellow, red and deep violet. Berglund watched her as she lay there in the deck chair, in a white dress, her slim brown face raised upward, the dark eyes wide open—she was still very beautiful. Pity he was no longer interested.

He cleared his throat. Here it comes, thought Anita and kept her eyes on the streaks of flame, shooting off sideways or making circles that grew larger and larger—

"I haven't been able to part with Keitje," he said, as though it was the end, not the beginning of a conversation. He paused to see if she was going to say anything, but she remained still, staring up at the sun. "That is, I've parted *from* her, for the time being, since she doesn't want to leave Belgium. Hates Germany, of course. On the other hand *I'm* not prepared to leave everything here and move to Antwerp, if only because of the business. I want to open up again as soon as possible. She really expects too much of me. We seemed to have reached an impasse." Anita still said nothing, and he went on with a touch of impatience: "I'd rather hoped *you* might have a suggestion to make."

Anita stood up, went past him into the drawing room and out toward the stairs. He overtook her at the door.

"What's the matter? I told you about her a good couple of months ago—"

Instead of an answer she lifted her hand, as if to strike him.

"You actually want *me* to solve your problem for you?"

He caught her hand and pulled it down, forcing it behind her back and pressing the length of her body against him, as though he were tenderly embracing her. She fought, and tried in vain to get free, turned her head aside, tears streaming from closed eyes. He bent down and leaned his head against hers.

"Anita," he said softly, "you're my friend. I didn't mean to hurt you. I didn't know you were still—come, be my friend! Help me."

She opened her eyes, leaned her head back as far as she could and looked at him as though he belonged to a species she'd never seen before. Her lips trembled, tried unsuccessfully to form a smile.

"You poor man," she said tonelessly.

He let her go, and she wiped the tears from her cheeks.

"Can't you be my friend? Don't you want to?"

She looked at him for a long time, and there was something in her gaze, beneath the thick, wet lashes, that he found unsettling. Hatred he could have understood, would scarcely have begrudged her, but there was something new in her stare, something insidious, almost calculating, in the dark eyes that wouldn't let go of his.

"Come," he said again. She had never heard him speak so pleadingly, and didn't resist as he put his arm around her and led her to the sofa. He sat down beside her, took her hand.

"Let's not talk about it anymore. I—it'll sort itself out somehow, I'll find a way out of it." She stayed stubbornly silent. He looked out past the terrace to where Sophie and Turhan sat, at the bottom of the garden, on the grass beneath the tall trees, too far away to have heard anything.

"Sophie looks dreadful, don't you think?" She nodded. "If Schweikart agrees, I'd like to send her off somewhere, to recuperate a little. To the sea, perhaps. Salt water." She nodded again, and gazed indifferently out into the garden.

An idea suddenly presented itself to him—and was rejected at once. Why, though? It was an ideal solution, really, it would help Anita through a difficult time . . . and Sophie was too thin, no question of it. Well, then? But he hesitated for a few more seconds, amused and aghast at himself. Moral scruples? Good Lord.

And then he said it aloud: "How would you like to go to Venice, the pair of you, for a month or two? Would you enjoy that?"

She slowly turned her face to him—once more with that strange look he found so disturbing.

"Yes," she said slowly. "Yes, I would."

128

BOOK IV

Chapter 1

The best room at the Hotel Fenice for "Signora Berglund and daughter." There were only three available anyway, the rest were still shut, their windows barricaded. Below, the dining room had been hurriedly cleared, card tables and a few chairs put in place. Anita took a quick glance and decided to eat upstairs; if needs be, whatever was left of their traveling provisions.

It had taken forty hours. In Milan they had found a one-armed porter, who carried both their suitcases to the Venice train, and then Sophie, on his back. She knew nothing about it, fast asleep, head pressed into the back of the man's neck.

"*Che carina*," he said, and carefully let her slide down onto the seat in the first-class compartment. Then he folded her neatly into place, like a rag doll, arms in her lap, knees pushed decently together, dress pulled down and smoothed out. Finally he eased her head into the corner by the window, studied her for a moment as she lay there sleeping, defenseless. "*Che bella fanciulla!*" He leaned forward, couldn't resist it and touched her hair, no longer sternly plaited but hanging long and free. "*Capelli d'oro rosso*," he whispered, and tiptoed out of the compartment.

Another eight hours till Venice. Anita was waked by the conductor jogging her shoulder, Sophie was still lying as the one-armed man had left her. Dead? A moment of blind terror! Absurd. She was breathing peacefully, sagged forward into Anita's arms, opened her eyes, and stammered a few disconnected words.

"We're there, Sophie, it's Venice."

Was it morning or evening? Early evening. A porter, both arms present and correct, appeared, and they tottered sleepily beside him to a lonely cab, waiting outside the station. The compartment had been empty, too; few people were traveling much, as yet, in Italy in October 1919.

The room in the Fenice: two beds, two chairs, a sort of kitchen table, a chest with a jug and basin in it, and finally a huge, ancient cupboard without doors, yawning wide like an angry old mouth.

Anita emptied the paper bags from the traveling case onto the table, while Sophie sat waiting on the edge of the bed. When Anita looked up, she had sunk back onto the pillow, asleep. She took her shoes off, covered her, and turned the light out.

A street lamp outside the window shone dimly into the room, and she ate the last of the sandwiches, already stiff and stale, and an apple; undressed silently, stretched out on the mattress beside Sophie, stared at the ceiling, and felt no desire to sleep. She propped herself up on her elbows and looked at the sleeping girl. The hazy light from the street lamp fell on the *capelli d'oro rosso*, the red-gold of her hair. She stroked it back from her forehead, enjoying the silence, the near-darkness, the isolation.

"*Che bella fanciulla!*" Ominous words. Here, in this very city. How many years ago? She closed her eyes and sank back on the hard pillow, which smelled of moldy flour. On honeymoon with Rudolf—a suite at the Hotel Bauer-Gruenewald, on the first floor, overlooking the canal—red velvet armchairs—tables inlaid with gold—four-poster and canopy—red velvet too, with gold tassels—arriving at lunchtime and at once into a gondola—Canale Grande—and Rudolf's forefinger, which never stopped pointing for a moment, this palazzo here, that church over there—the gondolier, small, thin and wiry from a lifetime of standing and rowing, with a bulbous nose, sly little eyes, and ears that stuck out sideways like sugarbowl handles from under his straw hat, a face forever imprinted on her memory.

As they turned off the broad waterway into a narrow, dark, silent one, and Rudolf's forefinger settled down at last, the gondolier had smiled at her, sitting there on her cushion, so shy and proper.

"*Che bella fanciulla!*"

"What did he say?"

"He said I was a—beautiful child." Stammered out, burning with embarrassment. And worse to come: now he was smiling at *Rudolf*. How could he know, poor man, poor gondolier! Signor Papa must be so proud of her, he said, and spoke extra slowly so that the gentleman would understand as well. This time she didn't have to translate, the word "Papa" easily got through to her new husband, without help from his Latin or Greek. He had drawn away from her and hadn't uttered another word while the gondola carried them back to the hotel. As he helped her out, the gondolier gave her a worried look. He may not have understood, but he suspected something.

And yet it had been Rudolf who had insisted on marrying her, straight out of school. "You'll make me young again." Fatal mistake.

Back to Berlin from this honeymoon—his third—and shortly after, the first heart attack. No doubt *che bella fanciulla* had that on her conscience.

And now "Signora Berglund and daughter," and this time *she* was la Signora Mamma and Sophie *la bella fanciulla*.

So soon. So soon . . .

A rushing sound, as she woke up. Water! she thought. Of course. Venice. Flowing past, flowing . . .

But it was Sophie, who was emptying a jug into the basin and washing her face.

"Wake up, Anita, I must eat something or I'll die."

Quickly, on with the clothes and down to the dining room. The place was still dark, not a soul in sight. Sophie's lower lip trembled like a child's.

"I must have something to eat. Quickly! Please, Anita."

"Sit here by the window. Don't run after me, d'you hear? I'll see what I can find."

The porter was snoring in his booth, head on the table, next to his cap. She gently passed her hand across his bald pate. He started, and looked up at her, confused.

"Don't worry," she said. "We just wanted something to eat. Break-fast."

He shook his head. The signora could have anything she wanted, antique Murano glass, a seventeenth-century prayer stool, a necklace —real pearls—that had belonged to the late Countess Benzoni—

"Bread!"

He sighed. "*Mamma mia.*"

"Coffee."

"Not even His Holiness the Pope"—he crossed himself—"gets coffee."

"Milk? An egg? You still have chickens, don't you?"

He looked at her, without speaking. She understood and opened her handbag; Johannes had tracked down some dollars. The man saw the first green note and put his cap on.

"Come with me, Signora."

Anita ran back to the dining room. Sophie was sitting sobbing by the window.

"Count, Sophie, count to a hundred—I'll be back by then. I'll bring something to eat, I promise. But count slowly!"

133

The porter was already waiting at the entrance, looking around anxiously in all directions.

"Quick, Signora."

She ran behind him across the small square outside the hotel. The lamps were going out, in the first morning light. He ducked hurriedly through a low ancient archway, up a couple of steps, across a narrow bridge, down the steps and along beside the water, squeezed tight against the walls of the houses. She slipped and fell, got to her feet and ran after him, only to lose him in a sudden patch of mist over the water—and nearly knock him over, he bobbed up so unexpectedly. He was standing before a low wooden door, next to a huge stone portal which was boarded up. He knocked; the small door opened.

"Quick, Signora."

He pushed her over the threshold and shut the door behind him. A fat, black-haired woman in a nightdress stood waiting for them in a dark passageway, motionless as a statue, a candle in one hand.

"My sister, Signora."

The nightdress gaped wide over a huge bosom; candlewax dripped onto it, but she didn't move. The brother stormed and swore till at last she vanished, rumbling darkly, and taking the light with her. In pitch darkness, Anita leaned against a damp wall, remembered that they had come here for their health, and laughed softly. The porter mistook it for a whimper.

"If you hear noises, Signora, don't be alarmed, it's only the rats. We have rats everywhere. The water! You understand. Even here in the palazzo. My sister's the cook here, the family are down in the country, there's more to eat there—"

The light reappeared, and the fat woman in its wake. She was carrying a round, flat country loaf, a jug of milk and a dish full of eggs. As she had no hand free, she had stuck a small jar of honey high up between her breasts.

A rustling noise at Anita's feet, and two rats materialized, on their way to the water, pressing against the wall, in the candlelight. Their caviar eyes glanced quickly and uncertainly from one to the other. The porter stepped politely aside, and they shot past him and out of the door through an invisible hole.

The fat woman glanced at Anita. "Those are small ones, Signora. We ate the big ones in the war."

"I like rats," said Anita, and looked around as if she hoped one or two more might show up. "I had a white one once, it was quite tame."

The woman gave her a long look and handed over the bread, jar, jug, and dish. Then she turned to her brother and pointed at Anita, arm outstretched. "She can come back when she's hungry."

.

As she opened the dining-room door, Sophie sobbed indignantly at her, "Two hundred and thirty-four—two hundred and thirty-five—" and made a grab for the bread.

"Wait a moment! The porter's cooking some eggs. At least wait until he's brought a knife."

Wait? The heavy country loaf wasn't to be broken; Sophie dug her teeth into it and tore a piece out, chewed, swallowed, and stroked Anita's arm.

"What about you? Aren't you hungry?"

"I can wait."

"I can never wait," said Sophie and tore out a second piece.

.

Anita helped the porter put away what was left. "Do you still have gondolas here in Venice?"

"We have everything, Signora, except food."

"How do people survive?"

"Like you this morning, Signora. Somehow."

When the sun came out, they left the hotel; it was suddenly as hot as a midsummer day. Anita crossed the little square and made her way unhesitatingly through the alleys, branching right or left every so often. Sophie stopped.

"You know your way here?"

"Yes."

"Why are you running?"

"Am I? Stop me, if I'm running."

"Where are we going?"

"To the biggest and most beautiful living room in the world."

"A room?"

"It's got no ceiling, it's open-air."

"That's good," said Sophie. "The lanes are so narrow—I could do with some air."

"You must imagine we're going down a long, dark corridor, a sort of antechamber, and where it ends, right down there, we enter the room."

The corridor grew narrower, twisted, opened out—and before them, as if a giant gateway had opened, lay St. Mark's Square.

Anita stopped and nodded, smiling, as if someone had said good morning to her.

There it was. Hugely spacious, and still contained. It gave no sense of dispersing in all directions, it was neatly raveled up at all four corners, yet it never lost its grandeur. Looking at it, she always had the same feeling of existing on an exalted scale.

"Is this your living room?" Sophie had walked on a few paces, under the colonnade, and turned.

Anita came slowly nearer, took a deep breath. The immense square was full of people, hundreds of colored dots—where did they all come from? Had there ever been a day, during the darkest times, when it had been empty? What was it like, when it was empty? The pigeons, at any rate, were always there.

"Is this your room?" Sophie pressed.

"Not mine. Napoleon's. He called it 'the European living room.'"

Reverently, dutifully, Sophie looked and looked up and down the square. What am I doing, thought Anita, she's much too young! They stepped out of the shady colonnade into the harsh sunlight.

"Look at all the pigeons!" cried Sophie excitedly, and squatted on the stones. Several dozen came rushing over to her.

"Twice as many as there are people living here," said Anita, gazing coldly at the blue-gray swarm around her feet.

"Don't you like pigeons?"

"Cruel beasts."

"Are they different from doves?"

"The same family."

"But doesn't one say 'tender as a dove'?"

Anita kicked out at one of them, which had come too close. "Here in the Piazza," she said, "I've seen them peck a sick pigeon to death. It was hopping around on one leg, over in that corner there, it had hurt itself somewhere. First one came running, to make sure it was good and lame, then it called the others and they all fell on it, one even landing on it from the air, so as not to miss the fun. Wolves are a lot less cruel, I can tell you."

Sophie, still squatting, listened to her open-mouthed. A small, dark pigeon jumped onto her arm and walked daintily up and down. She brought her arm up to examine the smooth satiny bird's face from close up. The pigeon blinked fiercely at her and gave an expectant bob. Sophie jumped so abruptly to her feet that the bird beat the air indignantly with its wings before flying off. She followed it with her eyes.

"Everything's quite different from what you think when you grow up."

A sudden sadness came over her, as if a black cloth had descended on her, here, in the sunshine, amid the brightly colored crowd, right beside Anita. "Why are you laughing? Are you making fun of me?"

"No. You're right, everything *is* different from what you think, and it doesn't matter how old you are."

Sophie came up to her, studied her face. She's exactly as tall as I am, thought Anita, she's caught up with me.

"You're trying to warn me, aren't you? You're telling me to be on my guard, aren't you?"

"Haven't you learned anything in the last few months?"

Sophie shrank back as if she had been struck. The yellow eyes flickered.

"Does that mean I mustn't make love to you here?"

"No, it doesn't. I just want you to watch your step."

"With you?"

"Don't make any exceptions." She leaned forward and stroked the pale, sun-blinded face. "You're standing in the most beautiful spot in the world, and you haven't looked at it yet. Take a look around. Just spin slowly round, you won't see a single flaw. Nothing but perfection."

What did she mean by perfection? thought Sophie, turning obediently. All those houses with the columns in front of them? The tall, thin tower? The church with the curious onions on it?

"That'll do, Sophie, no need to spin like a top. Come, we're going to the jetty, perhaps we'll find a gondola."

Hand in hand they crossed the Piazzetta, past the Doges' Palace. Anita stopped. It had been right here, standing on this very spot. Rudolf talking, talking, Doges' Palace, architecture, inspired inversion, filigree below instead of on top, finally asking her: "Well, what do you think of it, Anita?" "Marble sugar icing," she had said, and he

137

had called her a silly child, and a few other things. When he was finished, she had said: "But—I'm your wife!" He had walked on, without a word. It had been here, right here, that she had thought to herself, for the first time: I'm a woman, I've got a life, and I don't like it.

"What's that over there, Anita?"

"The Doges' Palace."

"Am I supposed to say something?"

She's cleverer than I was then!

"No, you don't have to say anything. There are the gondolas, over there, d'you see them? By the poles?"

"You're running again, Anita."

"Sorry."

Half a dozen gondoliers rushed up and besieged them, assailing Anita, threatening one another with wildly raised fists, and then fell back just as suddenly. An old gondolier of powerful build emerged as victor and took up his oar. They stepped into the gondola and sat down next to each other on the worn, patched cushions.

"Stick to the little waterways," said Anita, and he turned off into a narrow canal. Shortly they were gliding under the first bridge, and Sophie gave a loud whoop. The black cloth of sadness had lifted as abruptly as it had landed—and they were back out in daylight again. She sighed happily.

"Anita—it stinks here."

"Yes," said Anita and leaned her head back. "Venice stinks."

Sophie eyed her closely. "You've been in a gondola with someone before, haven't you?"

"Yes."

"Were you happy?"

"No."

"Then it doesn't count." She slipped an arm around her shoulder. The old gondolier gave a toothless smile.

"You're showing your daughter Venice, Signora?"

"Yes," said Anita slowly, without moving. "I'm showing my daughter Venice." Sophie giggled and dug her fingernails into Anita's shoulder.

"Life goes on," said the gondolier, and looked up into the sky over their heads, the old eyes foggy with memory.

Dusky green light on the water, shadows of the bridges, the oar dipping gently, gliding, gliding . . .

Sophie took her cushion and laid it in the bottom of the gondola, stretched out full length on it, her head on Anita's feet, and watched the bridges' dark arches go past, then once more a narrow strip of sky between old roofs—and another few yards of bridge—darkness—and then soft light again.

"Beautiful," said Sophie and sighed happily. "Beautiful." After a short while she added, still with that dreamy smile on her face: "Do you know I tried to kill myself?"

"Really?"

"You don't believe me?"

"Certainly."

"I wasn't far off."

"Far enough, or you wouldn't be here."

Sophie raised her arm and let it hang over the side, trailing her fingertips in the water.

"I went to the swimming baths one day," she said slowly and casually, as though nothing was further from her mind than trying to convince Anita. "There's no water in the pool on Saturday afternoons, they fill it up again on Mondays. I told the doorkeeper I'd left my bathing cap, then I climbed up to the ten-meter board."

Another bridge, and soothing darkness. Anita looked down at the girl at her feet, watched the shadow creep across the white face, and across the strands of red hair.

"And why didn't you jump?"

Darkness again, comforting. "I was afraid to." And quickly, before the bright light returned: "I wanted to get back at you."

They were in the sun again, she could feel the heat in her cheeks, just as she had as a child.

But Anita's voice came, unruffled: "We all do that; I wanted to get back at your father. I've been into the kitchen, at night, and taken the breadknife from the drawer, found the spot where I could feel my heart beating, and put the point of the knife against it—"

"The breadknife?"

"Why not? An innocent knife, it hadn't shed anyone's blood. Besides, I knew the whole time it was a game, it even helped me to sleep. But one has to play it properly, *almost* to the bitter end. You did the same, you climbed those steps up to the diving board, ten meters up. Did you look down when you got there?"

"I dream about it quite often, and in the dream I jump."

"You'll be free of it in time."

Sophie reached behind her, fumbled the air till she found Anita's knee, then rested her hand on it and closed her eyes. She could tell through her eyelids whether they were gliding under bridges or emerging into the open. Light—dark—light—and the soft, soft dipping of the oar.

"Papa says one must remain absolutely free. There's nothing worse in life than being dependent, he says."

"Does he."

"Meaning things like love, or other things too?"

"Everything."

"But I adore being dependent on you. If you weren't here, if you wouldn't let me love you, well then, I'd be free, as Papa wants me to be—and so unhappy."

"Your father is a man shaken by fear, though he doesn't know it."

Sophie opened her eyes. Papa, shaken by fear?

"But—does it take courage to be dependent?"

"One has to stand up for something. Take a risk if needs be, or else life isn't worth living."

The small white face at the bottom of the gondola relaxed, the eyes searched for Anita's face, upward and behind. "We both live by risk, don't we, Anita?" And after a little while she said so softly, as if it weren't really important that Anita should hear it, "I've always known I'm like Papa. Shaken by fear."

"What are you afraid of?"

"That I'm bound hand and foot, with ropes, and that I'm dependent—and that I like it."

Anita touched the small hand which was still clutching her knee.

"Don't be afraid, I won't let you down. However, later on, you've got to be on your guard. Your father, by the way, is by no means invulnerable. If something attacked him from behind, say, he'd collapse like a row of ninepins, precisely because he thinks he is so safe."

"How does one go about being on one's guard, Anita?"

"It's only a question of being aware. It means you'll watch out quite automatically."

"I'll never love anyone else as much as you."

"That's perfectly possible."

The gondolier drew the oar in, sat down, took off his straw hat and wiped the sweat from his forehead. He tilted his gray head to one side and gazed at the pretty young woman with the grave, narrow face, and at the little girl's hand, resting so tenderly on her knee.

"Your daughter loves you, Signora."

Anita nodded, and slowly stroked the hand on her knee.

"*Ecco.* That's the truth."

.

That first night already saw a fundamental change. Sophie didn't wait for Anita's arm to pull her close, it was she, Sophie, who led the dance, and Anita who followed. It simply turned out that way, it wasn't planned. Anita lay in her arms, and the small, surprisingly strong hands held her and protected her.

By the light of the street lamp Anita saw that Sophie's eyes were wide open, staring at the ceiling. She waited, but the girl said nothing. Anita lay in silence, feeling suddenly insecure, dependent. How soon! How soon!

"What are you thinking, Sophie?"

"Who were you here in Venice with?"

"My first husband."

Sophie relaxed her hold, pulled back to peer into Anita's face.

"You've been married before?"

"What's so strange about that?"

"I—" She faltered, shook her head. "It's just that I can't imagine it. You and Papa, yes. But another man! Who was he? Was it a long time ago?"

"I was eighteen years old, but much younger than you. I wasn't just young, I was ignorant, and there were many things I had no talent for. Love, for instance, and sensuality. One learns, with time, but some people are born with it, they simply *know*, they know *how*, and you're one of those people."

Instead of answering, Sophie began to rock her gently back and forth, as if cradling a child.

"Tell me about it."

"He was a friend of my father's. I used to sit on his knee when I was a child, and he'd say: 'You'll marry me one day, won't you?' 'Of course,' I said. His second wife was still alive in those days, and I knew her well and it didn't mean anything. Then she died, and I was sitting on his knee again, and he was saying: 'You see? We'll be married soon.' And I said, 'Of course,' because I didn't know what else to say. Two years later I left school and went with him to the registry office, as if it were still part of the school curriculum. And now you'll want to know what my parents had to say, won't you? He was a very rich man. They probably just said: 'Of course.'"

"Where is he? Is he still alive?"

Anita shifted, and Sophie let go of her. She rolled onto her back and looked up at the ceiling.

"Yes, he's still alive. He had two bad heart attacks, and can't move. He has to lie in bed at home, and be looked after. All around the clock."

"Do you go and see him?"

"Yes."

"Now I know where you go when you disappear sometimes, and no one knows where you are."

"He likes me to come. I sit at his bedside, and talk. *He* did the talking once, all of it. Now it's my turn. And I often think: I had an easier time of it, in the old days. He can't answer, he just looks at me, but from his eyes I can more or less tell what he's thinking."

"Poor darling!" said Sophie gently and opened her arms.

Chapter 2   In the early morning, long before Sophie was awake, Anita sometimes dressed and went out. She had begun to sleep badly, all of a sudden, and for no more than a few hours at a time; even then she dozed more than slept.

She took the same route every time, to the Rialto, then across the Lateran Canal to the *scrigno d'oro*, the "gold casket," as the Venetians called the church of Santa Maria dei Miracoli. Wedged between ugly and envious houses, it glowed like a gem, small, and smaller still inside, where the ancient wood and faded marble were lit by the faint candlelight. The same old women were always there at matins, shrunken figures dressed in black, all of them elderly, misshapen, and contentedly griefstricken. Anita waited until they rose like a flock of crows and left the church, and she was alone at last, on the hard pew. Now He can concentrate on me, she thought, perhaps I interest Him. Anyway, I like to pretend I'm talking to Him, just as the old women do, and I always begin with a carefully illuminated capital letter. In for a penny . . .

I wonder if He remembers me. Of course He does, to Him time doesn't mean a thing. Whereas, to me! An eternity ago I sat here next to Rudolf. He dragged me into so many churches, but this was the only one I liked. Later he once admitted it was his favorite too. And here I am again, fifteen years later, sitting here—what are fifteen years to these walls! People have been sitting here for five *hundred* years, pouring out their hearts to Him, bringing Him their complaints. I won't trouble Him with complaints, I just want a word of advice. He knows what's been happening, I don't have to tell Him. That's the best thing about consulting Him, there's no need for long explanations, He already knows. I don't have to explain about Johannes, or about Sophie, or about myself. Perhaps He can explain it all to *me*. Or at least give me some indication of what's going to happen next, because I honestly don't know.

Perhaps He's even got a sense of humor—or is that blasphemy? Though why? A sense of humor's a good thing to have, and He's supposed to be the embodiment of all things good—so: He's got a sense of humor. He's going to need one, when it comes to my situation. Here I am, a woman with all sorts of experiences behind me, and now I've got a lover, who is a thirteen-year-old girl. My stepdaughter. That's a laugh, isn't it? And now, how does it go on, so that we don't all end up crying? *I love my stepdaughter*, loved her from the word go. First in *one* way, then in another, but without the first one disappearing, d'You understand? All of it "love." Put to a different use, that's all. *Never abused.*

I admit I can't see a way out; that's why I'm here, talking to You. I don't claim to want the best for everyone, I don't! I want to save Sophie, somehow, and I want to save myself. Johannes can go to hell. So, *da capo:* what's going to happen when we get back to Berlin?

·

143

When she returned to the hotel, Sophie would be waiting for her downstairs in the dining room. She never asked her where she'd been.

They visited none of the churches, none of the museums, just walked hand in hand around the city, over the bridges, or passed beneath them in a gondola. Sometimes they ate ice cream at one of the small cafés on the Piazza. There was no shortage of ice cream, there had been ice cream right through the war, they were proudly informed.

They stayed for three weeks, and soon forgot they were in Venice, it could just as well have been somewhere else, somewhere without gondolas and ice cream.

Night after night they lay in each other's arms, Anita wide awake. I want to enjoy it, she thought, I want to savor it. Guilt? You can't force yourself to feel guilty, you either do or you don't. All the same, I think I shall be punished. Guilty, then, after all? No, that doesn't qualify as proof. One gets punished for one's virtues too. I shall be punished because it has to do with love, and that's always lethal.

One night before she fell asleep, Sophie murmured: "What'll happen to us, when we're back in Berlin?"

The reply was a long time in coming. "Anita, did you hear me?"

"I'm thinking. Do you know what they were called, the men who used to rule Venice?"

"The doges."

"But you don't know about their oath."

"You're not answering me."

"I am. When you swear an oath, you promise to do this or that, whatever it is, don't you? But the Venetians were cleverer than that: the doge of Venice had to swear *not* to do this or that. They knew, the old Venetians, that it's easier to abstain from doing harm than it is to do good. Rudolf told me that. I think I can swear to you that I won't lie to you, I won't betray you, and I won't abandon you. Does that satisfy you?"

"But—do you think you'll always love me?"

After a moment's hesitation: "Yes. Perhaps not in the same way. The same goes for you, you'll love me—only differently."

"Anita! I'll always love you—I'll love you more and more—"

"No, not *more*. Differently."

She refused to go on talking, and Sophie cried herself to sleep. Next morning she had to promise Anita never to mention love again.

Chapter 3

On the day of their departure Anita got up even earlier than usual and went to the church of Santa Maria dei Miracoli. That night she had hardly slept at all, and heard the many church towers strike almost every hour, and had counted with them. Yet she didn't feel tired; she felt herself walking spring-heeled down the dark lanes, and jumping up the steps onto the bridges as though her feet had no weight at all to carry. It couldn't be later than five o'clock, the church would probably still be shut. Never mind. She'd go back to the Rialto and sit on the railings of the bridge.

But the old, low wooden door in the main portal was open. Perfect. Inside it was as good as pitch dark, with only three candles burning in one niche. She felt her way—lucky she knew it so well—along the pews to her usual place. She wanted to make it easier for Him, so that He'd always know where to find her. Today is Your last chance, she thought, if You've got anything to tell me, make it now, before the black crows flock in for mass. Pointless. He isn't going to speak to me, He knows I don't believe in Him. Pity. He speaks to the crows. . . .

She heard a sound behind her. The crows. This early? She turned to look—no, no one had come in. But now that her eyes had become used to the darkness she could see, right at the back, two seated figures. The candles threw a weak, wavering light over the pair, with their dark coats. Men? Yes, two men, the first she had seen in this church. Both wore slouch hats pulled low over their faces. One of them, she could now make out, had a white, pointed beard, and the other—did he have a beard too? She screwed up her eyes to see. Yes he did, a black beard. They looked somehow alike, the pair of them, probably because they were so similarly dressed. Pilgrims, maybe. Father and son? Perhaps it was they who had lit the candles.

She turned back toward the altar. I'm leaving today, she thought. Am I sad? I don't know. I don't seem to be able to feel anything clearly. Very odd. I'm not tired, I'm not hungry, I don't want to stay here, I don't want to go home—

Behind her the men were talking to each other, in low voices. But in the silence she could hear them, if she listened hard. One had just said: "There is no new thing under the sun. Is there anything of which it may be said, this is new?"

She turned her head, curious to know which of the two had just spoken, the older or the younger man, but it was too dark to tell. Now the other one answered: "What is crooked cannot be made straight." That's the younger voice, thought Anita. The two men sat once more in silence, unmoving. It must be a father and son on a pilgrimage, she thought, and turned back to the altar.

They were speaking again, behind her. "To every thing there is a season," said the old man. Anita turned around and looked at the dark figures. What were they doing here so early? Fulfilling a vow? "And a time to every purpose under heaven," continued the same voice, and the other said: "Yes. A time to embrace, and a time to refrain from embracing."

Now she could see the old man quite clearly, nodding as he whispered: "Better is the end of a thing than the beginning."

That's true, she thought, that's the only thing that matters: the end. The little door in the main portal creaked, she turned to look, and saw the first of the old women enter, then the next; one after the other they headed for the font, a dozen shadowy faces under the black scarves, curtsying, whispering, giggling; some had brought candles, set them up and lit them. Their dusky, flickering gleam brightened the dark church, and now, Anita thought, now I'm really curious. What do they look like, those two at the back there. She turned once more to them—but they had left.

The priest came down the center aisle, and she stood up quickly and went out.

Outside the church she looked around for the men, but they were already gone. Slowly she walked to the Lateran Canal, and sat down on a bench. It's cold and damp here, she thought, but it doesn't matter. Just then the church towers struck six; the dark water before her grew slowly paler. Her thoughts were still with the two men— strange to find two Germans sitting there, in the early morning, in Santa Maria dei Miracoli. Or hadn't they been speaking German?

Had they said it all in Italian? She tried to replay their words in her head, shutting her eyes. Was it *Meglio la fine di una cosa anziche dell'inizio* or "Better the end of a thing than the beginning"—the last word, had it been "beginning" or *inizio*? The more she struggled to remember, the more elusive the memory. Anyway, she thought, whether a person says *meglio* or "better," it's the same to me; she spoke Italian as fluently as German. Her grandmother, *la nonna*, had been Italian. Genoese. Never learned German, only ever spoke to her in Italian, from childhood on. And she had lived with them, her room next to Anita's, till she died, the first dead person she ever saw. Aged sixteen. *La nonna, cara nonna.* Perhaps the men *had* been Italians after all.

She stood up and walked slowly back to the hotel.

Chapter 4

Once again the long journey back to Berlin. They sat opposite each other, in silence. From time to time they looked at each other and smiled, one as if to say, "Don't worry, trust me," the other answering, "I know, I know."

Anita left her book unopened in her lap and looked out of the window. Positively weird, thought Sophie, the way she can sit there hour after hour, as if she weren't really seeing the landscape outside but something far more beautiful; and she leafed through her magazines as quietly as possible, so as not to disturb her. She didn't find the silence at all oppressive, was filled to the brim with a wonderful feeling of protectedness. She thought she knew why Anita said so little and gazed out of the window, so utterly withdrawn, even long after darkness had fallen: Anita was planning what she would do, what she would say, when they got back to Berlin, probably word for word. "I shall never lie to you, never betray you, never abandon you." Never betray—that could only mean never betray their love, which must, which *could* only grow, and deepen, unhindered. How? That, then, was what Anita was busy working on, the "how."

Shortly before they arrived, Sophie leaned forward and touched her arm. She started, returning from a long way away, and smiled at Sophie.

"Will you tell me now what we're going to do, when we're at home?"

Anita made no reply. She stroked the hand that lay on her arm, raised it to her face, and kissed it with such gentleness, with such unprecedented tenderness, that Sophie felt there was no more need for words, Anita had clearly got it all thought out.

As the train drew in, wheezing, she could already see Berglund on the platform, towering above the crowd—and felt a sharp pain in her stomach.

"There's Papa."

Anita glanced out of the window, nodded, stood up slowly and stretched like a contented cat after a long sleep. Sophie's last doubts vanished, and she leaned out of the window, waving vigorously.

Berglund hugged them both, the same quick friendly hug—and behind him, grinning shyly, stood Peelke. Good Lord—Peelke! Sophie put her hands on his shoulders, and might even have kissed him if he hadn't leaned so stiffly back. He quickly gathered up the suitcases and followed them.

"Peelke! You're limping."

"I'm a chauffeur these days, Fräulein Sophie."

"He had a bullet in his thigh," said Berglund. "They persuaded him to become a driver. He's our chauffeur now, drives me to the office every day."

Papa's old Daimler was waiting for them outside the station. Peelke stowed away the luggage and limped, with dignity, to the driver's seat.

"You've opened the office again, Papa?"

"In a manner of speaking. Nothing's working yet, we're short of everything, and anyway I'd really like to wait for Gerste—though I don't even know if he's alive. They put him on the missing list two years ago, but hundreds of them are coming home every day. I need Gerste to make sense of the paperwork—it's maddening, I could be doing business, I've had inquiries already, via Switzerland. The Americans who've stayed at home think they might be able to buy valuable objects here in Germany—cheap. And they're right, too."

He was silent for a moment, and noticed that Anita was sitting staring ahead.

"Well—how was Venice? Did you get some rest? You both look well, especially you, Sophie—you've grown."

"Have I, Papa?"

"You're going to have to get used to school again. You might even need some extra tuition."

"I won't, Papa, I promise, you'll see. I feel so, so strong. I'll manage all right."

"Good. Good. It was a success, then, your holiday in Venice." He left a tiny pause, gave Sophie a sideways glance. "Did you do the rounds, see everything, churches, museums, all that sort of thing?"

Sophie hesitated. Anita didn't consider herself addressed.

"We—we mostly wanted to stay outside, the weather was so lovely."

He nodded. "I've never had a passion for museums, myself, but I thought Anita would probably drag you around a few."

Anita softly shook her head.

"No? So much the better."

Nothing more was said, till the car drew up outside the house in the Ruemelangstrasse.

"Dahde!"

"You're tall, Sophie."

"Oh, Dahde—"

She hugged the old woman, and for the first time dared to pull back the Petsche and kiss her dark, wrinkled cheek, this also for the first time, for the Dahde had always discouraged physical demonstrations of affection. But in the last three weeks everything had changed, Sophie hadn't merely grown taller, she entered a room differently, she stood differently, spoke differently, the words no longer tumbling out on top of one another.

"Dahde, you're getting smaller every day."

"Yes."

"Are you sick? Have you got pains anywhere?"

The Dahde shook her head, but her voice rasped more hoarsely than before. "I am as healthy as Allah wishes me to be."

Turhan came into the room, and Sophie hugged him, looking up enviously at him.

"You're even taller than I am."

"I'm two years older, after all."

"I always forget."

Now I know how he's going to look, later on, thought Sophie, even taller, even narrower, like a paper pattern. As if he had a dimension missing. People will say how handsome he is—but, all the same, too weak and pale. People will also say he's stupid, and that he certainly isn't. Only—only what? What was missing? Body was missing; substance. Juice.

He sat down on a stool beside the Dahde's chair, took her hand and stroked it. As time went by everything changed; the Dahde had never allowed this small gesture of affection. She looked from one to the other, murmured: "Allah be praised."

Anita opened the door. The Dahde heaved laboriously to her feet and turned her huge eyes toward her. With her, it was never only a movement of the pupils when she looked at one; there was a taking off, and a landing afresh.

Anita stretched out her hand toward her, but the Dahde fell back a step, bowed, and only then took Anita's hand. Sophie and Turhan looked at each other. The Dahde had never bowed to anyone before, except to Papa, and that not for a long time now. Did Anita realize? She said to Sophie: "Tell her I'm glad to see her. Tell her I'm particularly glad to see her."

Sophie said a few words, and the Dahde nodded.

"Tell her to please sit down again."

But the Dahde remained standing.

Anita turned to Turhan, who was waiting patiently to see whether she would notice him.

"How are you, Turhan?"

He kissed her hand, without an answer; she expected none, and left the room.

It grew dark, and Sophie lit the oil lamp. After dinner, she thought, that's when she'll speak to Papa. Perhaps they'll call me in to join them.

The Dahde was staring at the closed door.

"What has happened to her?" she asked suddenly, without taking her eyes off the door. Sophie looked at her, not understanding. "What ails her?" said the Dahde once more.

"Anita? Nothing, Dahde, nothing." But the old woman continued to stare at the door.

"She's sick," she said, finally, and sat down again in her chair.

"No she isn't, Dahde, she's not sick, on the contrary, she's—we had a lovely time—"

The Dahde turned her glowing, timeless eyes on her, and all at once Sophie felt sinful and guilt-laden, and lost. She looked at Turhan, pleadingly, for help.

"Turhan, tell her Anita's fine—I haven't done anything, I swear I haven't—"

Turhan sat down again on the stool, at the Dahde's feet, but when he reached for her hand, she pulled it away from him. He still tried to take it.

"What's wrong with Anita, Dahde? What makes you think she's sick?"

But the old woman only shook her head impatiently, and looked at the corner where her prayer mat stood in a roll, then drew the veil back down across her face.

Turhan stood up at once, and Sophie too knew that they had to leave the room now.

.

Peelke waited on them at dinner, limping from chair to chair. The wound in his thigh, and his stay in the military hospital in Alsace, was the sole topic during dinner. Sophie stole glances at Anita. Nonsense, she wasn't sick, she showed a healthy appetite. She didn't say much, but her expression was lively and interested; though perhaps not altogether in Peelke's passion play—he had hung on the barbed wire, spitted, for two hours and more—but evidently engrossed in *something*. No trace of pain or unease in her eyes; they were cloudless, peaceful. Because she's found the answer, thought Sophie, she's getting ready to tell Papa about it, and not just tell him about "it" but tell him in a way that will make him understand and not be angry, not with me and not with her. She smiled at her across the table, and Anita smiled back. Sophie sighed happily and decided to try and make some contribution to the conversation. So she told Papa about the cruel pigeons in St. Mark's Square.

"Pigeons? Cruel?"

"Yes, Papa. Anita saw them peck a sick pigeon to death, didn't you, Anita?"

All eyes turned to Anita. Even Peelke stopped, cheeseboard in hand.

"Oh yes," said Anita, almost dreamily. "They're wicked creatures, pigeons."

Berglund gave his wife a quick sidelong glance and changed the subject back to Peelke's injury.

Oh, for the meal to end! To get it over with, get up at last! But Papa was eating cheese, Edam cheese. There was no cheese in Germany, he'd brought it back from Rotterdam the week before. Sophie shut her eyes and clenched her fists to control the frenzied impatience in her head.

At last. Anita stood up, everyone stood up. But instead of strolling off, as Sophie expected, toward the drawing room, she walked firmly to the hallway door, turned and gave a friendly, vague nod: "Goodnight."

Sophie leaned against her chair and stared open-mouthed at the door as it shut behind Anita.

"I'm having coffee at the club," said Berglund. "Go to bed, Sophie, you look quite drained. Aren't you tired after that long journey?"

Tired! That was it—of course: Anita was *tired*. She'd been amazed at how Anita never seemed to want to sleep, right through the journey. Certainly not during the day; but even at night, when the train stopped in a station and the clatter suddenly ceased, waking Sophie, and she had peeped over the edge of her bunk, down at Anita, she'd been lying there staring ahead, eyes wide open, arms folded across her chest, not at all like someone who'd just woken up.

Of course. Anita was dying to *sleep*.

Papa put his coat on, in the hall.

"Goodnight, Sophie."

"Goodnight, Papa."

She stood outside her bedroom door, upstairs, for a moment, then couldn't resist the few more steps along to Anita's door. No sound from inside. She raised both fists. If only she could pound against this door, this abominable, accursed door! She'd never want to live in this house, because of this door, or else she'd smash it down herself, with a big ax, and have another one put in, with different paneling, different grooves, different notches. . . .

No point in trying to see if the door was locked, not even very carefully. She knew it was locked.

.

November dawn, dark and foggy, misery to get up at seven o'clock in the morning. She packed her bag—no satchel anymore, a proper schoolbag. Grown-up.

Papa was right, she'd fallen a long way behind, these last three weeks in Venice. She'd never once opened the books she'd taken with her, and Anita hadn't prompted her.

"Tell us a bit about Venice, Sophie," said the teacher. "I'm sure you had a good look round. Come up here and give us a little lecture on it."

Friendly, expectant eyes behind a thick pair of glasses looked down at her from the rostrum; below it, twenty girls' faces, lazy, sanctimonious, vaguely curious.

"Well?"

Sophie stood up. The only thing that came to mind were the pigeons.

"I—I'd like to think about it, please, perhaps tomorrow I could—"

Very well. Tomorrow. A short essay on Venice. It was generally felt that Sophie was bursting with health, but still, it seemed, couldn't concentrate properly, in fact didn't even listen properly.

"I—I seem to have lost a lot of ground—perhaps I need some extra tuition—"

.

On the way home everything to do with school vanished. One simple issue remained: to get things out into the open, with Papa. And get Anita's door unlocked. She'd simply take away her key, in case Anita should decide to keep her out because of the Dahde or Turhan. It was nobody's business but hers and Anita's. Papa's too, perhaps, but that was going to be dealt with today. By now Anita had had enough time to catch up on sleep. To her surprise, Sophie felt anger rising up inside her. Against whom?

Frau Glaubitz opened the door. Was Anita there? Yes. Was Papa? No.

"Frau Berglund has been crying." This in a whisper.

Aha. They'd already talked, then. And it hadn't gone so easily. Why not, though? He had his girl in Belgium, he had no right to forbid Anita *her* love. And the fact that it involved her, Sophie, and not some strange man—well, that kept it in the family, as it were; Papa had a sense of humor, after all!

"Frau Berglund went out very early. When she came back later I could see she'd been crying."

Sophie turned on the landing.

"When did Papa go out?"

"After breakfast, as usual. To the office."

Sophie's mind raced. Anita out "very early," Papa after breakfast— perhaps they'd had a quick discussion *before* breakfast. . . .

She rushed up the stairs, didn't even stop to put down her coat and bag, ran to Anita's door and knocked. Locked. "It's me." Footsteps. The door opened.

"Was it awful, Anita?"

Anita looked dazed, seemed not to understand. Sophie grabbed her hand, pulled her toward the two small chairs beside the window, and sat down opposite her. She waited, forced herself to look down at the floor so that Anita wouldn't see her eyes, wouldn't see the impatience and that strange anger that refused to dissolve. Keep calm, let *her* talk, it wouldn't be long now.

But it *was* too long.

"Well? What did he say?"

"Who?" Anita's eyes were half closed.

"Who? Papa, of course."

"I haven't seen your father today."

"*What?*" Sophie just let fly. "You haven't spoken to him at all?"

"No."

"Why were you crying, then?"

"Rudolf's dead."

"Who?"

"Rudolf. My first husband."

Sophie took a deep breath. Someone was dead. Rudolf. What did that matter? Hold your tongue, shut up and let *her* talk. Keep calm!

"I went over there this morning, I wanted to tell him about Venice, about Santa Maria dei Miracoli—"

"About what?"

"And his housekeeper told me he was dead. Just . . . gone, shortly after we left. Quite suddenly. The night nurse was sitting in his room, knitting. When she started a new row, she looked over at him—and he was dead."

Sophie said nothing. Couldn't even manage "My God," couldn't reach for her hand. That terrible anger seemed to choke her, wouldn't go away.

"And it was important for me to see him," said Anita, as if needing to justify herself. "I wanted to tell him about our church, and what happened—"

"What church?"

"He'd have been interested. He'd have known exactly—and now it's too late. It would have been so important for me," she said again, like a student who'd missed a lecture.

"Anita—I don't know what you're talking about. What would have been important? What church?"

Anita's eyes were dry, only the thick lashes still glinted wetly.

"You don't know the church."

"When are you going to talk to Papa?"

"Tonight, after dinner. I've *got* to talk to him tonight." With unexpected emphasis.

"Anita!" All at once she was able to take her hand, kiss it, make sympathetic noises. "Oh, Anita! Poor—what was his name? Rudolf? Poor Rudolf! Oh, I'm so sorry. And you wanted to see him one more time...."

.

In the afternoon she even managed to concentrate on her homework, fill in exercise books, make geographical drawings, and suddenly remembered the promised piece on Venice. She crept down to the drawing room—no need to creep, Turhan was out doing gym, the Dahde wasn't to be seen, and Anita had gone to the cemetery to look for Rudolf's grave.

Papa didn't have many books, and most of those were about antique furniture, vases, carpets, china, paintings—stop! There was one on Venetian paintings.

Upstairs she copied out some useful bits: where which painting hung, where which statue stood, and which ceiling had this or that fresco painted on it. That should do; she'd learn the Italian names off by heart and then produce a drone of Tintoretto-Guardi-Canaletto-Donatello ...

She heard the sound of the front door, rushed out of her room and looked. Downstairs Anita took off a black coat Sophie had never seen her wear before, shook it—was it raining?—and hung it in the cloakroom. Then she slowly climbed the stairs, her eyes lowered.

Better leave her alone right now. Sophie was moving furtively back to stand in the doorway of her room when she heard another door open: the Dahde came out into the corridor. By chance? Or had she been waiting for Anita? Sophie retreated a few more steps, but left her door open.

The Dahde met Anita on the landing and rasped urgently at her, but when Anita only stared at her uncomprehendingly, she turned and abruptly hauled Sophie out of her room as though she'd known all the time that she was lurking there.

"Tell her to come with me."

"Anita—you're to go with the Dahde."

"Now? Why?"

"I don't know. Dahde, shouldn't I come too?"

"No."

"But you need me to translate!"

"Stay here."

Shortly afterward the two women left the house, Anita once more wearing the wet black coat, the Dahde wrapped in a heavy shawl against the rain, with her veil over her face.

In the Koenigsplatz the Dahde took Anita's hand and led her to the Siegesallee, turning right, to the first group of statues. In the center, dwarfing the figures on either side, towered Albrecht the Bear, the dripping cross in his right hand. The curved bench behind him, where the Dahde usually sat, was dripping too; the devotions would have to be brief. She pulled Anita up the three steps, so that her face was at the same height as the pedestal.

Anita knew that the Dahde regarded the marble statues in the Siegesallee as tribal gods—neither Sophie nor Turhan had ever tried to talk her out of the idea—but nobody knew why this one was her favorite god. Now she suddenly thought she understood: the gigantic figure was the only one holding aloft a cross, and the cross, that much the Dahde knew, was the symbol of the Christian religion. This, then, must be the god-in-chief: Albrecht the Bear.

The Dahde pulled back her veil, raised her face, and basked for a moment in the raindrops falling on her face. Then she made for the marble chainmail of the defiantly outstretched left foot, planted a kiss on the slippery big toe, turned to Anita and signaled her to do the same. Anita hesitated. The Dahde growled and opened her mouth in a wide grin of encouragement. She's hardly got a tooth left! thought Anita, bending obediently over the foot of the Bear. Behind her, the Dahde started to hum, let her veil fall down, swaying back and forth in the pouring rain. I mustn't interrupt her, thought Anita, she's in her own Santa Maria dei Miracoli. But when she saw that the old woman was trembling with cold, and wet through, she decided to cut the ritual short. Not a soul in sight, only a hackney cab trotting slowly along the other side of the Siegesallee. Anita called and waved. Please let it be an empty one, Albrecht, old bear! The cab stopped. The driver leaned forward—was that two women over by Albrecht, in the pouring rain, one of them rocking, the other waving?

On the way home in the cab the Dahde began to cough, and had to pull back her veil to breathe. When they arrived, soon afterward, the cab driver caught sight of her face. "Jesus, Mary and Joseph," he said, and forgot to count his tip.

Dinner was silent, and soon over. Berglund made no effort to get a conversation going, he'd clearly had enough of that. Turhan never raised his eyes from his plate; Anita sat smiling dreamily, gazing into space.

At the end of the meal she rose and turned to her husband, the same gentle smile on her face.

"Johannes, shall we take coffee together in the drawing room?"

Berglund had other plans in mind and was about to cry off. The smile, this serene, detached smile, disconcerted him and, at the same time, seemed to guarantee a painless quarter of an hour. It wouldn't be too late to escape, afterward.

Sophie grabbed a book and sat in her room, facing the door. Just wait, wait calmly. *Read* the book. When she found she'd read the same page four times in a row, she left her room and stood listening in the corridor. Silence from downstairs. Silence from Turhan's room. A noise, behind the Dahde's door: coughing. Better than nothing; Sophie knocked and went in.

"Dahde, have you caught cold?"

A shake of the head.

"Dahde, how did it go, at lunchtime?" Sophie knew, of course, where the two women had been; the Dahde always went straight to the Bear if anyone at home was sick, and she had said Anita was sick.

Nodding. Sophie sighed. The Stone of Knowledge came to mind and she smiled, remembering. It was hard work living with a stone, knowledge or no knowledge.

"She is sick," said the Dahde suddenly, and was at once seized by a fit of coughing.

"*You're* sick."

Sophie rummaged in the cupboard till she found what she was looking for. The Dahde's first small parcel had recently arrived from Turkey, with the same old sweet-smelling medicinal herbs. She put the kettle on the little stove in the corner and lit the gas.

"Which herbs, Dahde?"

Without looking, the old woman fingered through the small linen pouches and brought one out.

"How many spoonfuls?"

The Dahde raised two fingers.

There it was, easy as pie. Overthrow, putsch, new regime: now Sophie was cooking for the Dahde.

She knew it, and savored the moment, feeling the Dahde's eyes on her back. There must come a particular moment in one's life, she thought, when one finally feels grown up, for good and all; it doesn't have to be a grand moment, nothing out of the ordinary need happen, it might feel just like this—the way I'm feeling now, while *I* cook for the Dahde. Is there anything that could still cut me down to size and plunge me back into childhood . . . the conference downstairs, for example, right at this minute? No, I'm a match for that. Let Papa shout. What can he do to me? Show me the front door? Throw Anita out? So much the better. No one can keep us apart.

The kettle boiled. Hurrah, she thought, turning down the gas and shaking the herbs into the water, that's exactly how *I* feel: boiling over with strength and love and anger and gallop. . . .

She poured the boiling, drowsy-smelling drink into a cup and brought it to the Dahde. The old woman drank obediently and looked up at the girl, standing very erect and very still, as if she were listening for something. The red hair fell over her shoulders in long, thick, belligerent strands, and the white face they framed did nothing to soften the effect. The Dahde sipped the brew, never taking her eyes off Sophie's face, without speaking, in the half-darkness she loved. One oil lamp burned in a corner of the room.

Turhan came in.

"The Dahde isn't well," said Sophie and sat down on his stool. He found himself a place on the floor and put his head against the old woman's knees. Abruptly he began to sing: "A crow accompanied me out of the ci-i-ty, flying ever and again around my head . . ." Schubert; nothing had changed.

The Dahde eased back in her chair, the dark old face at peace.

After the song was finished, they sat for a while without moving. It is a good long time by now, Sophie thought, that Anita has been talking to Papa downstairs.

"Sing another song, Turhan, but don't make it a sad one."

He shook his head. "Goodnight, Dahde." He stroked her knee, nodded at Sophie and left the room.

Waiting. How much longer? She jumped up and hurried to the door. The old woman's voice reached her just in time.

"Sophie—all misfortunes are part of Allah's design."

"Leave me alone, Dahde."

Outside in the corridor. Still silence from downstairs—or was that Papa's voice? She sat down on the top step, listening. Yes, Papa's voice, but not angry, not even arguing, more—could it be—*pleading*?

Arms folded around her knees, she sat and waited on the stairs. Why not simply storm into the drawing room and cry: "I can't hold out any longer, I've got to be here. It's about *me*, isn't it?"

Not quite true: it wasn't about her, not *only* about her. . . .

Downstairs, the drawing-room door opened, and her stomach went cold. Papa stood in the doorway.

"Sophie!" Then he saw her, and lowered his voice. "Come down here."

As she went into the room, Anita stood up and walked slowly past her out of the door. She didn't hesitate for a moment, but smiled at Sophie as she went past, friendly and affectionate, but oddly neutral.

Sophie followed her with her eyes until the door closed behind her. Only then did she turn around to face her father. Berglund stood in the middle of the room, legs apart, arms folded, his head bowed a little way and his eyes fixed on Sophie. She had never seen him look like that. Was it possible that Papa was ill at ease, that he was nervous?

He said nothing, and she stood, waiting.

"Sit down, Sophie. Just give me a moment or two longer. Don't ask me anything yet."

She sank into the huge armchair, watched him as he stood there rocking back and forth on his heels, watched him go to the desk and take a cigar out of the box, cut it, light it, inhale deeply, then come back slowly to his armchair, smoking, not looking at her.

"I don't quite know how to explain this to you, Sophie. I imagine you don't really know anything about it—so be patient with me, will you?"

"Don't know anything about what, Papa?"

He drew on his cigar, and gazed at it as if wondering what sort of an object it was.

"Has Anita told you about the church?"

"About which church?"

"Good God—about the church where she saw the men."

"Which men?"

"I thought so. You know nothing."

"Men?"

Berglund put down his cigar and looked hard at Sophie. Her eyes were wide open, her lips trembled.

"Sophie! What's the matter with you?"

"Which men, Papa?" Suddenly a child, begging, holding nothing back. He decided not to press the point. Not now, at any rate. Perhaps later, but not now. He forced himself to speak softly. "Listen to me, Sophie, and don't interrupt me, all right?" She nodded violently, as if she had the shivers. "Anita tells me she had a—an encounter, in a church in Venice—dear God, I couldn't quite get the hang of it, myself. Two men, she says, pilgrims, father and son. I didn't gather how she came to meet them, but she mentioned some of the things they said, these two, and I don't know, but they seemed familiar to me. That is, I had the feeling that I'd heard it all somewhere before, but where? It doesn't matter, at least not for the moment. What matters is, Sophie—" He stopped and looked closely at her. "Notice I'm speaking to you as I would to an adult, and you must behave like one too, even if it's very hard for you."

"Papa?" Breathed, barely audible.

"Anita wants to go back to this church."

"Back to Venice?"

"Yes. Right away."

"How—how d'you mean, Papa?"

"She's going back to Venice tomorrow."

She gave a sharp cry, a single sound before she stifled it again.

"Papa, will you let me go with her? Please, Papa, please! I've *got* to go with her—I can't just stay here on my own."

"Sophie, if it were up to me, I'd let you go, even though it's utter madness. All that traveling—when you've only just got back! However, I can fully understand that you want to stay with her." He didn't look at her while he said it; the cigar occupied his full attention. Then he turned to her again. "But—"

"Papa?" She had barely moved her lips, anticipating the answer.

"She says she needs to travel alone. And she doesn't know when she'll be coming back."

Sophie sat motionless for a long moment, then jumped to her feet. But he was ready for it and seized her by the arm.

"When you speak to her now, Sophie, remember one thing: Anita is—she's not really listening, she can't hear you at the moment, d'you understand? She's disappeared into whatever it is she found there, and you must leave her be. Don't pester her, d'you hear?"

She tore herself free, and he let her go.

.

The door was not locked—she was expected, then. She burst into the room as if about to set fire to it. Anita stood with her back to the window, the narrow, calm face turned toward her. Sophie had rushed up the stairs so fast that she was still gasping for breath, couldn't form the words.

"Is it true?"

Anita nodded, her eyes inexorable. Sophie ran at her, a battering ram charging at a fortress wall. She shouted, hoarse with rage, grabbing hold of her, pouring out incoherent words, shaking her. Anita offered no resistance, kept her eyes tightly shut.

"You don't want me—why?—what men?—you swore you'd never leave me—"

"I'm not leaving you, Sophie."

A whisper, but Sophie heard it, stopped at once, panting: "You're taking me with you?"

"No."

Sophie raised both fists and struck out. Anita fell to the floor; blood trickled slowly from her mouth, where her teeth had bitten into her lower lip. Sophie stood over her, arms hanging by her side, looking down at her.

The door flew open. Berglund pushed her aside and lifted Anita up. He carried her to the bed, put her carefully down, took the handkerchief from his breast pocket and wiped the blood from her mouth and chin. Sophie came a step closer, watching. Anita opened her eyes.

"It doesn't hurt, Johannes." The voice shook a little, but the tone was quite calm. "Thank you." She sat up and took the handkerchief from him, held it to her mouth. Sophie turned to go.

"Stay here, Sophie, come and sit by me."

Berglund got up and made room for her. She approached hesitantly, sat as far away as she could, on the edge of the bed.

"I'm leaving tomorrow, Sophie. I must go back. You wouldn't understand why, even if I explained it to you. If Rudolf were still alive—I might have been able to stay, at least for a while." She spoke laboriously; the lip was swelling up. "I've got to try to find the men again, the two men I saw in Santa Maria dei Miracoli. They might still be there. Perhaps the verger will know where to find them. I've got to talk to them. That's why I don't know when I'll be coming back. I'm not leaving you, Sophie, you're with me every minute of the day. But I have to go away now—for a while, I have no choice. If I had to stay here, in the end I might not love you anymore."

Sophie got up and walked to the door. "I'm not allowed to come with you," she said hoarsely, and when no answer came, she left the room.

.

For the first time she locked her door, without knowing against whom, she simply felt a need to turn the lock. And had to open up again almost at once. Papa. He sat beside her on the bed.

"Listen to me," he said, and his face suddenly brightened. "There are moments in life when one has to make a clean break. I'm going to make one for you, right now, because if you stay here waiting for the post every day, you'll go under. And that really would be a pity. You must get away. Far away. It helps, you'll see. There's an old friend of mine in London, an old classmate, I'm sure he's still a friend—if he's alive. I'll send a telegram tomorrow, ask him how long it'll be till they'll let a young girl visit England. A month or two, I daresay, while they fish all the mines out of the Channel. In the meantime I'll drive with you to Antwerp. No, you don't have to see Keitje if you don't want to. There's a family I know, called van Fliet. They have two daughters, older than you, it should be just right. And a son. Recovering from mustard gas. I'll notify your school in the morning. We'll go off together, you and I. You need to be doing something, d'you understand? We've never been on a journey together—it'll be fun, you'll see. And as for Anita—let her go, tomorrow. If you take my advice: don't see her again. It's pointless, it only leaves more scars. Don't reproach yourself for having hit her. It doesn't hurt—she told you—and that's true. Such things don't hurt. They don't hurt *her*. Only you. Don't think about it anymore. Sleep now. I'm going to bring you a whiskey and a sleeping pill. Let Anita leave in the morning. We're leaving, too."

BOOK V

Chapter 1
London.

Thinking back to these first days, later, when London had become her town, Sophie couldn't believe it was one and the same place. It had been threatening then, blackish-gray, utterly alien. She had clung to Miss Whiting's hand, which was no less alien, but more hospitable. Had Sophie really looked at her, even once, she would have liked the wispy white hair—so feathery it danced in every breeze—and the row of dreadfully even porcelain teeth that smiled at her. But she didn't yet see anything. People, places, things came and went without her noticing. The four months in Antwerp had achieved nothing, except that she now ate quite normally, most of the time. When she left Berlin, fasting seemed the most natural thing—why force herself to choke on every bite? She felt only thirst, drank a lot of water, simply wanted to sit quietly somewhere on her own, not have to pay attention or answer any questions.

Papa had understood this and soon had given up trying to draw her out. She was aware of it, felt relieved and grateful—and at the same time even more impoverished. He had delivered her at the van Fliets like a tightly bound parcel and warned everyone not to try to unwrap her. She'd do it herself, he'd said, all in good time.

Then he'd gone off to his Keitje, and turned up briefly, a couple of times, before returning to Berlin. Sophie didn't know what he'd given as a reason for her state, nor did she care, as long as it had the desired effect. She was left alone, no one insisted, no one asked, the food was there. If she didn't touch it, it disappeared again. After a few days she began to take a spoonful or two. No comment from the family. Gradually she got used to eating again.

Only one clear memory remained of the months with the van Fliets: the day that Jan, the mustard-gas victim, showed her his leg burns. Why he did it remained a mystery—perhaps he wanted to shock her, or rouse her to sympathy, or perhaps he had less therapeutic motives. At any rate, he limped past her in his dressing gown, along the corridor toward the bathroom, as he had dozens of times before, only this time he suddenly turned around and asked her if she had ever seen mustard-gas scars. Then he drew back his dressing gown. His legs were like two birch trees, white with black gouges in them. The skin was still fitted for their earlier size, and hung off his calves in limp folds. He gave her time, and she studied them thoroughly. "Thank you," she said eventually. He let the dressing gown fall again, and limped off.

The incident roused no sympathy, but it stuck in her memory. Afterward she had the feeling she'd slept through her four months there, she couldn't even remember the name or face of the van Fliet girl she'd shared a room with.

Then London. And Miss Whiting, who had fetched her from Antwerp, at Papa's bidding. She only spoke English, which was all to the good, since for the time being no answers were expected of her and she could go on letting her mind doze and dawdle. How long, whether it was weeks or months, she couldn't tell, but one morning Papa was standing at her bedhead in Miss Whiting's little flat in Half Moon Street, by Green Park, saying it was spring, and she must wake up now.

While she got dressed, she asked herself how the sleeping princess had really felt about the kiss with which the handsome prince had brought her back to life. Perhaps she would rather have gone on sleeping, behind her hedge of thorns.

They took a walk in Green Park, beside the duckpond, and Papa brought her news of home. Everything as it always was. The Dahde? Coughing. Peelke, Frau Glaubitz, Gerhard—much as ever. Turhan? Hm. Turhan was a problem, and he, Papa, had decided to take him away from school at Easter, after the yearly exams. What was one to do with a boy who wasn't good at anything, except possibly music, and not even good enough at that? Oh yes—he took a letter out of his pocket. For Sophie. From Turhan. "Read it at home, or right away, as you wish." She put it in her coat pocket, forgot it.

They walked for a while, side by side, without speaking. Papa was clearly pondering something and abruptly steered toward an empty bench by the waterside, beneath a weeping willow.

"I think I *will* tell you about it, Sophie. I had misgivings, at first, but it seems to me you've come to your senses—and, who knows, it may even do you good. Well now, tell me, have you ever asked yourself what it all meant, that business with the two men in the church, in Venice? Haven't you?" He fell silent, boring holes in the sandy ground with his stick. "Didn't it ever occur to you that—that Anita wasn't entirely normal, all of a sudden?"

Sophie followed the stick with her eyes and counted the holes, reached eleven, then twelve, still wasn't quite sure what he meant. Not entirely "normal"? If only a hedge of thorns would grow up around *her*!

"When I first left you with the van Fliets in Antwerp, I returned to Berlin to speak to a psychiatrist. Do you know what a psychiatrist is? Good. A friend of old Schweikart's, a bit dotty, but then they all are. They spend all day dealing with mad people, and in the end no one can establish the dividing line—if there is one. Anita's a perfect example. Who's to say which side of the line she is? Anyway, I told the fellow, the psychiatrist, about Anita's encounter in the church— remember? The pilgrims, father and son? And I read out to him what they're supposed to have said; I'd written it all down the night she told me, because it seemed—odd, in some way. I was only on the second line when he interrupted me and said: 'That's from Ecclesiastes.' Do you know what that is, Sophie—Ecclesiastes?"

He put his stick across his knees and looked searchingly at her. She stopped counting the holes backward.

"Yes, Papa, it's something from the Bible."

"Quite right. Good for you. *I* didn't know. It seemed familiar, that was all. 'They're proverbs,' he said, 'famous Old Testament proverbs, often taken as texts, for sermons, and for book titles.' Of course! School, Bible classes! Then I told the man the whole business. I also told him about—you and Anita." He wasn't looking at her, his stick was once more busy boring holes in the sand. "In the end he said something like: 'Your wife is suffering from a guilt complex, and has taken refuge in religion. The two men, the pilgrims, are of course God the Father and Jesus, and what they were supposedly saying was what she could remember—without knowing it, of course —from school lessons, because that is what she wants to hear, and it brings her comfort.' That's more or less what he said. He also said it might be dangerous to just leave her be, she could get more and more trapped in it and end up in some sort of religious mania." For a while he sat without speaking, hoping Sophie would say something, but nothing came.

He sighed, and began afresh: "I phoned the Hotel Fenice—one can do that now, it costs a fortune—but she wasn't there any longer. My Italian isn't very good, but I understood this much: she was now staying with the porter's sister. Do you know who that is?"

Sophie shook her head, and then, racking her brain, suddenly burst out: "It's the woman Anita used to fetch our food from, bread and eggs and honey."

"That's the one. I know because I went there."

At once there was fear in Sophie's eyes.

"You went there?"

"I thought I owed it to her. I mean, someone had to make the effort." He gave a deep sigh. "It was thoroughly inconvenient, but in the end I came across a number of interesting items there, not too expensive, so it wasn't all in vain, financially, I mean. Anyway, I got to the Fenice, and the porter took me to his sister. I'm not particularly squeamish—but that shook me, I can tell you. Rats! Rats—everywhere, running past you down the corridor. Anita was in bed when I arrived, although it was lunchtime. The porter's sister—great big fat woman—led me to her. A tiny room, the bed was clean enough, but otherwise . . . a single shuttered window—the entire place was nothing more than the domestic quarters of the palazzo next door. She wasn't exactly overjoyed to see me standing there, looking at her on the bed. She refused to explain anything, said something about the hotel being 'too expensive'—utter nonsense, I'd given her all the dollars she needed. Besides, I'd sent her a whole lot of documents—she's the sole heir to her first husband's estate, including, among other things, a handsome account in Switzerland. No, all she wanted was to stay there with the fat woman, among the rats. There was nothing I could do, I felt a fool for having come all that way. The porter told me she goes to that church every morning. Whether she's found the men again, I don't know. But before I left I had a word with the porter—a few dollars, you know, and it's surprising how intelligent people can become. So I told him to keep an eye on Anita, or rather to make sure his sister warned him of anything untoward in her behavior, and to inform the doctor at once. I had the address of an Italian psychiatrist, Bolognini by name, quite a sensible man. My Italian wasn't really up to it, but by the time I left him he'd got a rough idea what it was all about. Anyway, I gave his address to the porter. There was nothing more I could do, you understand that, don't you?"

Sophie nodded. She had understood every word of it, she could remember every single word Papa had said, and on top of it all, her mind was back in Venice again, something she had strictly forbidden herself. But there she was once more, at the Hotel Fenice, there was the porter—and Anita—and she could take it. At least, so far.

"So I left again, Sophie. I heard nothing for five or six weeks. Then suddenly a letter arrived from this doctor, Bolognini. I had it translated at once. They'd had to—you must be expecting this by now, you can imagine, can't you, what happened?" But her chalk-white face alarmed him, and he wished he hadn't begun. "They'd had to take her to the psychiatric clinic, Sophie. There was no alternative."

"Why? What had she done?" A breathless, stifled cry.

"She'd started to bless everyone. Even the rats in the corridor. She blessed them too. And the fat woman began to worry—"

"But why? She wasn't doing any harm, why—"

"Because when the doctor spoke to her, she wasn't entirely rational. She claimed she was a wandering preacher, and spoke a lot of stuff no one could understand. Besides, she hadn't slept for days, had hardly eaten anything, and looked dreadful ... don't cry, Sophie, it's all much better now, I should have told you right from the start, she's really very much better. She knows who she is and where she is. I gather it's a beautiful house, not like a clinic at all, just with bars on the windows. She's eating again, and sleeping a little, which was the most important thing, and the nurses are all very fond of her. The doctor too, he's really taken with her, he says she'll be perfectly all right again. She's been there two months now and he's just written to say she needs to stay another two. And she doesn't want to leave, either; I've spoken to her once on the telephone. She didn't say much, but when I asked if she'd rather come home she said no, very firmly, and that she was quite happy there. You see?"

.

Sophie asked herself what would happen if she were suddenly to walk into Anita's room. Would Anita recognize her? Or would she perhaps take her for a rat and bless her? And what would she do then? Giggle, and run quickly from the room—or stay and hide in a corner where she could watch her secretly? Once there had been a girl in her class, just for one day, much older than the others, lumpish, with a runny nose and a silly open mouth. In the break somebody had given her a pencil and said: "Better stick that up your nose or it'll run away!" And everyone had screamed with laughter, Sophie too of course, but, what was strange, so had the new girl. She'd accepted the pencil and laughed aloud with them, and suddenly it hadn't been so funny any more.

Madhouse. Nurses. The Dahde had been right after all, and Anita *had* been sick. It had not been a betrayal then, Anita had not just abandoned her, she was sick. And in a creepy sort of way . . .

Step by step she backed away, until invisible as well as visible bars separated them.

Papa and Miss Whiting accompanied her to a so-called finishing school for young ladies at St. Leonards, a small town on the South Coast. Sophie was the youngest, and was regularly at the bottom of the class. Her English wasn't good enough, and her general education lacking. But a few weeks after Papa's departure she noticed that when she woke up in the morning the black cloth had lifted slightly and that there was strong, salt sea air all around her. No more than that—but it was at least something that didn't actually hurt, and she hung onto this first timid hint of well-being, suppressed the longing for the protective thorns and asked herself for the first time in many months whether life was perhaps, after all, not entirely evil. It was still a shaky, precarious notion, but it was June, and the sea was growing warm. The sea, swimming, diving—she suddenly heard herself shouting and actually laughing like the others. And as they were all drying themselves on the beach afterward, one of them, a French girl from Rouen, said to her: "Well, well, you're human after all."

Then she found she had an appetite again, at last, real hunger, she wanted to *eat*, almost as before. In the weeks that followed she often found herself thinking: now I'm doing this or that again for the first time. I'm feeling, thinking this or that again for the first time, I'm running for the first time—I'm galloping!

They slept three to a room. Three was the "safe" number, it put a brake on possible shenanigans. Sophie shared with Danielle, the girl from Rouen, and Jeannie, a Scot from Edinburgh. One night when Jeannie was in the infirmary with mumps, the French girl's voice came suddenly out of the darkness.

"Sophie? Are you still awake?"

No encouragement from the bed opposite, but that was only to be expected; the German girl had always been completely unapproachable. Noiselessly, barefoot, Danielle crossed the linoleum floor to Sophie's bed and squatted on the end of it.

"What happened with your stepmother? Come on, tell."

Silence. Not a peaceful or a reflective silence, but one so charged that even the cocky French girl was taken aback. She got up, made to go, turned again.

"Sorry," she whispered. "Sorry, if it's something that—I only asked because we'd all really like to know—"

"What?" Like a whiplash. Danielle, frightened and bewildered, didn't dare to move and get back to her bed.

"*What?*" Fiercely demanding now, and threatening.

Danielle suddenly remembered that this German girl was, after all, two years younger than she was, and that the Germans had lost the war.

"Well, we've been told that your mother's dead and that you've got a nasty stepmother—"

"I've got *what?*"

The sudden rustling told Danielle that Sophie had sat up, and she found her legs, taking one huge jump back into her bed. There she crouched and rekindled her courage.

"What the hell is the matter? It's happened to people before."

Silence. Then more rustling; she hoped it meant that the German girl was lying down again. She was a real menace!

"Who told you that, about my stepmother?" Still tense.

"Well, right at the beginning, when you first came, we were told—I think it was the old girl who brought you, she told us about it, something to do with your stepmother, and we were all to leave you alone, because your mother was dead, and all that. Isn't it true, then, about your stepmother?"

"No."

.

This nocturnal exchange pushed her back behind the prickly hedge again, though not altogether. She peeked out between the branches, went for solitary walks and one day came to the conclusion that the story of the dead mother and nasty stepmother was perhaps quite a useful one: people were friendly but no one made any further attempts to get closer.

Until the afternoon with Mr. Goodenday. Physics, chemistry and biology were his subjects, and Sophie was particularly bad at all three. One day, after class, he called her up onto the podium. It was a lovely day, why didn't they make a little expedition together, to Hastings perhaps. They could see the spot where William the Conqueror had landed in 1066—she was interested in history, wasn't she? Well then: this afternoon at two o'clock.

At first they strolled in silence along the stony beach. His sparse gray hair flapped in the strong wind, he was trying to say something, but his Adam's apple merely wobbled up and down above his stiff collar. Sophie was wearing her heavy winter coat against the cold and the wind, with her long red hair tucked under a cap. He simply couldn't find the right opening words, and began to wonder whether the whole thing was worth the trouble. Miss Newman, the principal, had raised the subject of Sophie Berglund at a staff meeting the previous week, and suggested that someone should "do something" about the girl. Her father had written to ask whether she had "thawed out" at all. The answer, of course, was no. But now it was perhaps time to have a try. Which of the members of staff would be prepared to take this on? No one rushed in; the girl was a bit too strange. Interesting perhaps, but not exactly likable. Then, hesitantly, Goodenday had offered to help. He found her likable.

"Up there—see the walls, and the tower? That's all that's left of the battle. When you think that it decided all our fates . . . "

He paused.

"Just imagine, they landed here, a few dozen ships, the men wading through the water in their heavy armor. They had to hurry, because the Saxon king—do you know his name?"

"Harold."

"That's right. He'd got the news at once, of course. It took place right here—right where we're standing—a couple of hundred Frenchmen, on foreign soil. Amazing to think of it, isn't it?"

Sophie nodded, looking around. A wide, grayish-yellow stretch of beach, bare, no more than a dune or two. The wind roared, seemed to come from all directions; they were struggling to make headway even without armor. Only the little seabirds ran freely to and fro, darting around them and only dodging Sophie's shoes at the very last moment.

"It must have been just like this," the teacher's voice crackled through the wind in separate, choleric explosions, "the same stony beach, the same raging wind. What can they have been thinking as they sat down and dried themselves and started to polish their swords and lances! Godforsaken alien land—they must have been scared stiff."

Sophie looked out across the sea. In the distance, not very far away, there was France, and a train to Paris or Berlin—or Venice. . . .

Goodenday decided on a frontal assault.

"You're a sort of foreign soldier here yourself, aren't you? Polishing your armor and preparing for an attack from all sides. But there's no one hiding behind the dunes now, you know, we're all thoroughly well disposed toward you and would like to get to know you better, if you'll let us. What do you say? Do you still feel like an intruder, still feel strange?"

"Not strange, no."

"Lonely, then?"

She looked at the ground, sent pebbles flying in all directions with the tip of her shoe. He watched her with a certain puzzlement. Was it still the childish refusal to behave obligingly, or was it already a premature self-containment, defying all attempts to make contact with her, leaving one oddly disconcerted? If it suited her to ignore a question, she simply ignored it. He decided he would, in turn, ignore her rebuff.

"It isn't good for you to cut yourself off like this, Sophie. Have you ever noticed what sort of animal cuts itself off from the herd? A sick animal."

She looked at him, and her mouth twisted into a half-pitying, half-ironic smile. It didn't fit her face, still that of a child under the woolly cap.

"Are we herd animals?"

"Yes. All of us."

She shrugged.

"Perhaps I *am* sick."

"No you're not, you're perfectly healthy. You may have had a hard time of it, an unhappy childhood perhaps—"

"Oh no!" she shouted against the wind. "I had a happy childhood."

"So did I," he said unexpectedly, and wondered why on earth he was confiding in her. "Things became harder later on, but that's often the way it is, everything has its price."

She didn't consider this worth an answer, raised her head and looked at the sky. Huge, white towering clouds chased headlong across it. Sophie's cap flew off her head and rolled away over the stones. Goodenday ran after it while she stood still, watching him try to save it from the eagerly snatching waves. Soon it was bobbing out to sea, attended by a pair of uninterested seagulls.

He returned, breathless, raising his arms in a gesture of apology.

"Doesn't matter," Sophie signaled, her long red hair raging in Medusa strands around her head. Like a young witch, thought the teacher; in the Middle Ages they'd have burned her at the stake.

"I understand you've had—misunderstandings, with your stepmother?"

The sentence was largely lost in the howling wind, but she heard "misunderstanding" and "stepmother," and her yellow eyes studied him appraisingly, then turned back to the seagulls, among whom the cap was slowly sinking.

"Are seagulls a kind of pigeon?"

"They're not even related. Why?"

"Are they cruel too?"

"Cruel? I don't understand—"

The wind eased off a little, as if to give poor old Goodenday a break.

"My stepmother was like a pigeon. Tender and cruel."

Goodenday stood bewildered.

"In what way?" he shouted above a new onslaught of wind.

"Gone," said Sophie, and pointed at the seagulls. "My cap has drowned, they haven't saved it. They never bother."

But he wouldn't be sidetracked.

"Is that why you're here with us, Sophie, because you didn't get on with your stepmother?"

She nodded, closed her eyes and let the wind tug at her hair and lash her face.

The teacher refused to give up; he'd need more than this when he reported to the staff meeting.

"Did she—hit you?" he ventured.

"I hit *her*."

He stared at her, and took a deep breath.

"What about your father? Couldn't he do anything?"

She shook her head. All of a sudden the wind dropped abruptly, and the thick red hair, exhausted from its wild dance, fell on either side of her pale features. In the sudden silence she heard herself say, much too loud: "She's gone. He sent her away."

"But then everything's all right!" he cried with exaggerated cheerfulness, took a step nearer to her, suppressed a desire to stroke her hair. "When you go home, the bad memories will have disappeared, you can return to your happy childhood—"

"I'm not a child anymore."

On the way home neither of them spoke. Goodenday felt he'd at least gone some way toward fulfilling his task, even if he hadn't managed to get any closer to the girl. Perhaps it was better that way. She was dangerous, the little witch, she might easily hit out.

The wind had died down at last, leaving a cold, dry air in its wake. Sophie shivered and dug her hands into her coat pockets, suddenly found herself touching something stiff and papery, and pulled it out. A letter—Turhan's letter! My God, the one Papa had given her, in Green Park, in London, almost a year ago!

Back to the dormitory after a brief farewell to Goodenday; no smile—but nonetheless, not without a certain feeling of goodwill toward him. Just like Miss Newman at the end of term, when she bids one a gracious farewell, thought the teacher, and decided to check whether Sophie was really only fifteen years old.

She huddled in her bed, warming her frozen limbs. Then opened Turhan's letter.

Dear Sophie,

Can you help me? Papa wants me to leave school at Easter and start work in his office. School's been my only refuge—music lessons twice a week. They're what I've been living for. I know I don't have enough talent to be a musician, but I'd be perfectly happy to give piano lessons. It would be quite enough for me. That and the Dahde, while she's still there. Perhaps, when she *isn't* anymore—I might go to Istanbul. I don't know. I'm not sure I've got the guts. But I can't face Papa's office. Talk to him for me. I can't, you know that. Imagine me sitting there, with Papa walking in and out! Apparently, Gerste's come back from a Russian prisoner-of-war camp; he's not yet supposed to work, he's got a head wound, but his mother says he can still do sums. *I* can't—even without a head wound. Do something, I beg you—the Dahde's tried, she told Papa it would kill me, but of course he didn't understand her. She even dragged him to Albrecht the Bear, and he got really angry with her, the first time ever. He didn't understand any of it. Do something, Sophie!

Turhan

She tore up the letter. Too late. Too late to do anything now. Her stomach ached with shame. What must Turhan think of her? She'd better write to him at once, explain—

And what good would that do? He'd been stuck there in Papa's office for ages now, suffering like a dog, eight hours a day, every day—or had he got used to it? Never. Perhaps Gerste was back now and Turhan was having to bring him coffee and lay out the documents. Gerste. Hard to conjure him up in memory; he'd always seemed to blend into the wall he worked next to, just as bland and gray. Dimly, Sophie recalled colorless hair parted in the center, on a thin, egg-shaped skull. A skull that now had a hole in it. Strange to think it hadn't cracked open altogether.

And now Turhan was working under him. Was there any point at all in writing *now*, to Turhan? Anita could have helped. But where was she? No hope of tracking her down. Still at the clinic? Or back with the fat woman among the rats? And every morning at that church again—

For a moment, on the beach, she'd been tempted to shout the whole story, over the wind, right into the face of that well-meaning, respectable old boy, if only to see his Adam's apple dance up and down.

Just as well she hadn't. She'd never tell a soul about it, not a soul.

 *Chapter 2*

"Except you, Brother. No one else. You're the first person I've told about Anita. The true story, that is. My husband? He knows nothing about it. I wouldn't have had any fun unraveling it all, for him to see. My first husband didn't know anything about it either. It would have amused *him*, though. That's why I never told him. You see, Brother, there are things in my life that make even *my* sense of humor blench. You're the only one who knows the whole story."

178

Eleven o'clock at night. The fourth since her admission, and the young doctor had been sitting at her bedside for an hour. She had been given two more shots of morphine during the day, that was as much as they could do for her. She utterly refused to let herself be X-rayed again. The first time, she had fainted in the dark room and since she wasn't strapped to the stretcher, fallen sideways off it, onto the floor. When other kinds of treatment were suggested, the caved-in chest and ravaged face produced astonishingly robust language. Operation? A single glare from her wide-open yellow eyes drove the surgeon out of the room. And her husband wouldn't give permission to do anything, without her consent.

Just morphine, then. His, Karanogliu's, night reports were positive: the patient slept most of the time, and when awake lay quietly. No pain. At peace.

Sometimes she spoke quite distinctly, though softly, and he could make out long passages word for word. Then suddenly the sense would get lost, and she was only mumbling.

He reached for his book and adjusted the lamp. But before he could open the pages she had begun to speak again, forcing him to shut the book.

There were also pauses when she rested her eyes on him, search-ingly, expecting him to offer something, ask a question at least, to show that he cared.

"Did you ever see her again—Anita, I mean?"

She closed her eyes, moaned softly.

"Are you in pain? Do you want me to—"

Her head moved, just a fraction.

"I'm still all right," she breathed. "One moment—I'll be right back—" Like someone slipping out of the room to catch a breath of fresh air.

He waited patiently, without reaching for his book, although she was a long time coming back.

"Have you ever had something awful happen to you, Brother? Something really dreadful?"

"I don't know—yes, perhaps it was the sort of thing you mean."

"Tell me."

"I watched my grandfather's left arm being dragged under the sawmill. The button at his cuff had been undone, and the shirt hang-ing down—I shouted, but there was nothing anyone could do, it happened much too fast. I watched the two big blades cut the arm off at the shoulder, as easily and smoothly as cutting cloth. Only the sound was different, a sort of scraping, grinding sound—in the one second before Grandfather screamed." He was silent for a moment. "I still steer clear of amputations, even now."

"Did it kill him?"

"No. They sewed him up again. And he went to the taverna and bought everyone a round of drinks. Told everyone who'd listen all the gory details, including the ones he couldn't possibly have remembered—he'd passed out almost at once, of course. But I was the one who saw it all. I can still see it now, the busy way the blades chopped and ground, as though they were pleased to have finally caught a nice solid morsel—"

He stopped, angry with himself. That he, as a doctor, should be unable to resist the gruesome details! But the old woman's face showed neither disgust nor horror.

"And he lived . . . " she murmured.

"Another sixteen years."

She nodded. Yes, yes, that must have been a horrible experience. It qualified all right.

"One day a telegram came from Papa." How seamlessly she moved from the Greek taverna back to the girls' boarding school on the English Channel! "The Dahde was very ill, I was to come at once. I packed only essentials, and amused myself by scattering a few crumbs from the Thousand and One Nights among the girls standing around me, who were naturally curious to know who 'the Dahde' was. I assumed I'd be coming back to St. Leonards, I'd got used to it during my three years there, spoke English well now, and didn't especially want to go back to the house in Ruemelangstrasse, but I couldn't leave the Dahde to die alone. 'Very ill' clearly meant 'dying.'

"That same evening I took the boat from Dover to Ostend, and then the train. I had two hours to fill at Cologne, and I visited the cathedral. Very beautiful, Brother, very dark, a great big cavern, but cozy all the same. It still had the old windows. I sat down somewhere in one of the pews, it was early in the morning, hardly anyone there. It smelled of morning Mass. For a moment Anita and her pilgrims came to mind—I pushed them away, and thought about the Dahde. Strange to think of her dying, like other people; she'd never grown older, she'd been old as long as I could remember, a piece of our domestic furnishings, an old, locked chest from Papa's oriental store-rooms. You loved the chest, it belonged to the house. Why had no one ever told her that? I'd make up for it now: '*Seni seviyorum*, Dahde.' "

Peelke stood waiting on the platform. Alone. Not a good sign.

"Is she still alive, Peelke?"

"Who, Fräulein Sophie?"

"For God's sake, Peelke—the Dahde!"

"Yes, Fräulein Sophie."

He took my suitcase to the car, keeping his face averted. Or was that my imagination? Probably, but something stopped me asking how Papa and the others were. I sat next to him in front. He didn't ask how the journey had been, either, and just gazed stonily ahead. Once, when we'd stopped at a red light, I asked him straight out: "Come on, Peelke, what's happened? Why don't you tell me, man?"

The lights changed, and he drove on.

"We're almost there, Fräulein Sophie."

Fear began to knot up my stomach as we turned into Ruemelang-strasse. The car stopped.

"Peelke! *Tell* me—" But he behaved as if he hadn't heard me, limped hastily to the gate, rang, limped back and hid his head in the trunk of the car.

I reached for the round iron handle of the gate and looked up at the house. Above me the heavy front door opened slowly—and Anita stood in the entrance.

Up the steps. I was now taller than she was, looking down at her. Her tanned face was emaciated and her eyes even more deeply sunken than before.

"The Dahde?" I whispered.

She shook her head and placed both her hands around my face. It was a loving gesture, but her fingers held my cheeks and temples in a painfully firm grip.

"Sophie—get a hold of whatever courage and willpower you've got and tell yourself: I *won't* crack, I can live through this. That's what I'm demanding of you. D'you hear me?"

We were still standing in the front doorway, it was as if Anita were barring my way until I'd done what she asked. And Peelke was still standing down by the gate, with my suitcase; it seemed he knew that certain things had to be sorted out up there, before I and my luggage were allowed in.

"What—" was all I managed to say, and didn't even try to escape Anita's racking hold on my temples. It helped, though it hurt; it held me together.

"Turhan," said Anita, without taking her eyes from mine. "He's dead." She gave me a moment's grace before continuing: "He hanged himself. The Dahde found him."

Don't take your hands away, I thought, hold me tight.

"Come," she said.

She released me, and led me into the house. Behind us I heard Peelke limping up the front steps.

.

The first word I managed was: "Dahde?"

"She's asleep. The doctor gave her an injection; she was too weak to fight him off."

Only then: "Papa?"

"Upstairs, in the bedroom. He's waiting for you. But I think I ought to prepare you—" I could only use my eyes to plead: say it! But she had to wring each word out of herself.

"I have to tell you why Turhan—died."

I sat in the chair in front of Papa's desk and followed her with my eyes to make sure she couldn't escape. She walked back and forth, from one corner of the drawing room to the other. Now she was at the window, turning her back to me.

"You know that Turhan was working in your father's office?"

The letter! The letter! I *should* have answered, no matter when.

Another silence. Anita had to summon her strength. She stared out of the window: autumn garden, dead leaves, asters. I saw a large crow hopping all alone around the lawn. I'll never forget this crow, I thought, I'll remember it, every time I think of Turhan—

"You probably also know he wasn't very happy there."

He had never written to me again, but I'd been able to guess it from Papa's letters.

"When did you last hear from your father?"

"A month ago."

"A letter?"

"Yes."

"Did he mention—no, it's all happened since then."

"What?"

"Sophie—remember what I told you at the door. You haven't forgotten?"

"No." I don't know if I was audible, but she turned and looked me in the face.

"At first your father put Turhan to work in the cataloguing department, and sent him to the art museum every day, to the bibliography section, but Turhan took walks in the Tiergarten instead. Your father came across him there, feeding the swans on the lake. So he put him in Gerste's charge—you know Gerste's back again?—at the office, to learn bookkeeping. This was about two months ago, I'm not quite sure, I got here only last night." From Venice, I thought. Another pause. Again she paced the room with long, heavy strides, then stopped some way off, not looking at me. "Two weeks ago—your father says—there was some money missing from the petty cash. Gerste didn't say anything at first, he thought he'd made a mistake. But two days ago, there were eighty-five marks missing. So he had to report it. Your father says it couldn't have been anyone else, no one else had the key to the cash box. He called Turhan in right away—"

"What did he say? Anita, *please!*"

"Your father says he didn't deny it."

"What?"

"He just shook his head, and didn't say a word."

I got up, and had to hold onto the desk. My breath was coming in such gasps that I couldn't manage more than a few words at a time.

"Never! D'you understand? Turhan would never have stolen money—never! I'll—I'll kill you, if you say he'd have—"

"*I'm* not saying he did, Sophie."

I ran outside and up the stairs.

"Papa!" Before I'd even reached the door.

I didn't knock, just broke straight in. He was standing in the middle of the room, legs apart, arms crossed, silhouetted against the fading light, shapeless, immense.

I shut the door behind me, had to lean against it for support. He started to speak at once.

"You half brother is—was—a thief." He wobbled slightly, spread his legs a little wider and stood firm. Only when he began to talk again and the words came out oddly stuck together did it occur to me that he was drunk. I'd never seen anyone drunk, but that was what it had to be. "At least he was ashamed of it. That's something. About all he could manage."

"Papa!"

"What are you shouting for? Because he went and hanged himself in sheer funk—is that to his credit? Are we supposed to mourn for him? Is he a loss? Only for the Dahde, and she's dying. That's another one of his achievements. Don't tell me you'll *miss* him! What was he to you? Nothing." And again: "Nothing." A roar. "Or are you going to tell me it would have been better if he *hadn't*? How would you have looked him in the face? Would you have shaken his hand and later counted the money in your purse?"

"Papa!"

He took a step toward me, but still left enough room between us, room to breathe.

"Yes. I drank a bit last night—so what—I haven't lost my senses, not for a moment. Of course it wasn't exactly pleasant, seeing him lying there, of course it was—it was—" He made a wide gesture, as if describing something huge and round. "But then I realized it was better like this. And you'll see it that way too, if you've got any sense. No false emotion! You won't see him anymore, that's all there is to it. Cheer up. It'll kill the Dahde. And a good thing too. The quicker the better. Don't know if it's her fault he turned out—the way he did. Perhaps—his mother—" Without turning, he called imperiously over his shoulder: "Hey, Georg! What was her name?"

I dragged my eyes away from him, and saw Georg Wertheimer sitting in the corner, motionless, staring at the floor. "Amina," he said, without lifting his head.

A single word, spoken softly, but the colossus tottered as if he'd been struck. Wertheimer got up and went over to him. He was almost a head shorter, had once been slim and athletic but now had a paunch and a neck crisscrossed with wrinkles, like a turtle's. He was in his shirtsleeves, waistcoat unbuttoned, eyes staring with tiredness. He put an arm around Papa's shoulders and led him to bed, without a struggle, as though they both knew the time had come.

I was still standing by the door, watching Papa be stretched out, unresisting, on the bed, watching him reach automatically for the brandy on the bedside table, and Georg Wertheimer push it beyond his grasp and, instead, fold his friend's hands on his chest, as if he were dead. Papa's head fell to one side, the red-gray hair falling across his forehead, his eyes shut.

"You go now, Sophie," said the little man, pulling up an armchair beside his friend's bed and stretching out on it as if it were a sofa. His eyes closed.

"Go now," he repeated.

"The Dahde—" I whispered, but Wertheimer shook his head, without opening his eyes.

"Don't disturb her."

.

"Fräulein Sophie!"

Frau Glaubitz stood on the landing below, dressed in black. Even the hair in her bun, once gray, shone jet black; eyes and nostrils, in contrast, were red with crying and wiping.

"How is your—"

"He's asleep."

"Oh, that is good. Frau—Frau—I'm sorry, Fräulein Sophie, but I can never remember Frau Berglund's new name—"

I stopped dead.

"New name?"

"She's got married again, didn't you know that?" I opened the drawing-room door. There was no one to be seen. "She's in the guest-room, Fräulein Sophie. My God, how you've grown!"

I did an about-turn, then turned back again; it was the dyed black hair that did it.

"Frau Glaubitz—how are you?"

The old woman threw her arms around me and burst into loud, unrestrained sobs, out of keeping with the silent house.

I held out for a while, then freed myself from her clinging arms and stroked her bowed head cautiously, as though the color might come off on my hands.

"It will pass, Frau Glaubitz," I heard myself say, but she shook her head.

"I shall not live to see it pass, Fräulein Sophie." Grief had given her a certain dignity. "Nor shall I *let* it pass. I shall think of it every day." She straightened up and vigorously wiped her eyes and nose. "I don't believe it, Fräulein Sophie, and you know what I mean—I don't believe it." And in the full flood of her grief she added, mouth pinched in anger: "Just let him throw me out—your father—I don't care. I don't believe it."

I turned to go, was grabbed by the arm and pulled back again: "Do *you* believe it?" There were tears in her eyes, and a determination I had never seen there. "I don't know—" I meant to answer, but instead I said, firmly: "I don't either."

.

I found Anita sitting at the little desk in the guestroom, writing. As I came in she pointed at the armchair by the window, without looking up. It was already almost dark, but I could make out Gerhard, pushing the wheelbarrow toward the greenhouse.

"I'm writing to my husband, Sophie, I've nearly finished. Just wait a moment."

I watched Gerhard carry flowerpots into the greenhouse, heard him whistling loudly, cheerfully. Did he know? Did it affect him at all? Perhaps his aversion to all nondwarfish things was so deeply ingrained it even gave him pleasure to see others crushed by grief, till they were smaller than he was.

I turned around and watched Anita writing. Saying what? "I'm sitting here with my former love, and I feel—"

What did she feel for me?

And I? What did I feel? Nothing, if I was honest.

She carefully folded the letter, wrote the address in bold, firm letters on the envelope, and looked at it for a moment before she spoke.

"You probably know that I married again last year. Or rather, someone married *me*, and I'm glad he did. Without the pressure on me, I don't think I would have had the courage. Your father told you, didn't he, that I was in a clinic? And no doubt why." She hesitated, looked at the letter in her hand. "The professor there, he . . . sorted me out completely. And then he married me. I'm called Bolognini now." She cradled the letter between her palms and stroked it. "He let me come here, after your father phoned the clinic yesterday morning. I was even allowed to come alone, although Lorenzo knew perfectly well what was waiting for me here. He thought I could cope with it all now, and that I owed it to you to be here when you arrived. He knows, of course."

She put the letter back on the desk and turned to me, but I saw that one hand was still lying on it as though she couldn't quite tear herself away.

"I don't know whether the Dahde will wake up again. I was upstairs with her while you were with your father. It's hard to say whether she's breathing or not. I hope she doesn't wake up."

"Why not?" I stammered. "I want to speak to her again—she's *my* Dahde too—"

"She found Turhan, she cut him down. He'd locked himself in his room, after your father had spoken to him, and wouldn't let her in. She sat on the floor outside his room—that's where Frau Glaubitz found her when she brought her up her supper. The Dahde has spent the last few weeks entirely in bed, but somehow she had managed to get up and reach Turhan's door. Frau Glaubitz wanted to take her back to her room, but she frightened her off, and spent the whole night there, on the floor. Your father heard her praying. He couldn't get anywhere with her either, and didn't dare take hold of her, the way she was looking at him. He said he had the feeling she'd throttle him. In the end, she must have fallen alseep. When she woke up in the morning and tried the door again, it was unlocked—and that was how she found him. He'd used his dressing-gown cord. Then she went to your father's room and put the cord in his hands."

Chapter 3

"Brother? Sometimes I can see you sitting there, when you're not here at all."

"I'm here."

Strange, the way you hardly notice someone living right beside you—then he's gone and it leaves you in shreds. I sat beside the Dahde's bed that night, and thought I couldn't go on living, not without Turhan. Before, he'd have come in and sung a Schubert song and gone out again, and I'd have hardly noticed. Now, now, now I needed him, needed to talk to him, to tell him everything about Anita, and about his own death, too. Needed to cry with him about his death. We could have talked to the Dahde together—and now he wasn't there any more. He'd made off.

The Dahde—she was very cold, when I felt her hands. Already dead, perhaps. Her eyes were open wide, but I don't know whether she saw me or not—though they were looking at me. I spoke once or twice, but she made no response, just looked at me. Once I thought she blinked.

Later Anita came in and said she was dead, but her eyes went on looking at me till Anita closed them.

Turhan's funeral, next day—I can hardly remember anything about it, I was suddenly dog-tired. Papa didn't want me to come, but I went all the same. Wearing a bright summer dress—my things were all still in St. Leonards—and a dark veil over my head. People stared at me, but the veil was like a shield.

When I woke up, in my old room, it was all over. Turhan in the black box in the Weissensee cemetery, the Dahde in her long shroud on the way to Constantinople, Anita back in Venice as Signora Bolognini—all erased. So much the better. If any of the three had still been there, I would have begun to lament. One needs an audience to lament properly, and all I had was Frau Glaubitz, who wasn't worth the trouble.

Papa I only saw at mealtimes, and always in Georg Wertheimer's company. Though not for long. A month after Turhan's death he stopped reaching for the brandy, and Georg was released from duty. So now we ate alone, Papa and I. No question of my going back to England. Who could he have talked to about Turhan? Because that was what he wanted to do, Brother, day in, day out. He couldn't dredge up enough details of Turhan's office life. Sometimes he brought Gerste along, for dinner, who prompted him tactfully, reminding him of one or another of Turhan's misdeeds—and then looked unhappily at me, begging silently for forgiveness; he obviously hated to do that sort of thing, but he knew such discussions did Papa good, for Turhan's sins of omission suddenly took on other dimensions when one thought of their end result.

I was a coward. Only once did I dare ask whether perhaps a third party—the charwoman or someone like that—whether there wasn't a faint possibility that—

"Then why do you think he hanged himself?" asked Papa ruthlessly. Gerste closed his eyes.

I would have had one or two theories to offer, mere guesses, but I didn't dare. The pale-blue discs swam threateningly on his reddened eyeballs—soon his voice would take on the ghastly calm that frightened me so, and I would have to flee to my room.

.

And so it went on for a year. Don't ask me how I spent the time. Officially I went to the Berlitz school to keep my English from getting rusty. Apart from that all I can remember is that I bought a dog, a big black poodle called August who bit Gerhard in the calf whenever he had the chance.

At one point a letter arrived from Anita. I read it so often, I still know it by heart. One doesn't forget those early things. "Dear Sophie, forgive me for having left while you were still asleep. I could feel the broken, forked thoughts starting again in my head, the ones that follow each other too fast, and I had to get away. Whatever I'd managed to scratch together in the way of sanity, I'd offered you during the bad days; there was no more left. I had to get back to my husband and stock up again. Now I'm so well I've started to help Lorenzo at the hospital. With the disturbed children. I'm good at it, I know the long climb they're crawling up. One of the girls reminds me of you, she's got red hair too, and needs love. I'm really very happy. Except for the idea that when you think back, about us, it isn't with love. Tell me, and tell me the truth. It's important. Anita."

.

She coughed, pressing both fists against her breastbone. He stood up at once and bent over her, and she raised a hand to stroke his face.

"You're always taken in, Brother," she whispered. "I just need to cough a bit, that's all—it hurts a little, but it's worth it—and you're right there at once. No, don't go away, sit by the bed again and give me your hand." She coughed again, doubled up, twisted, gasping for breath. He carefully raised her head and poured a little liquid into her, from a tube that led to a glass on the bedtable.

"Ask me something," she whispered hoarsely.

"What did you write back to her?"

"I didn't." Her breath still came in short jolts, but the eyes glittered again. "She said 'the truth'—and I'd have had to answer: when I think about 'us,' I feel full of shame, I feel—sick." She said nothing for a moment, gazed past him. "Then came a letter from her husband, in bad English. It went something like this: 'Dear Sophie, I take the liberty of calling you this because I share my wife's feelings

189

toward you, as indeed all her feelings. Write her a few lines. One should never forgo an opportunity to give with a good heart and open hand while one can. Lorenzo Bolognini.'

"When this letter arrived, I was already much further on—further away, that is. And that's what I most needed then, distance, a clean break, clear skies. And then I did write to her. Briefly. Just that I thought about her, about us, with love. Still a lie, at the time. It took years and years before it became true." Her eyes flickered suddenly, clouding, and she tugged at his white coat. "Give me another one—please, a little one. I can feel something—something bad on the way, and there is one thing I want to tell you—and I'm afraid I'm going to start moaning and groaning any moment—"

He went into the bathroom, returned with the syringe, drew back the sheet and sank the needle into her thigh with a short, firm stab. She had lost even more weight during these last three days, and was now being fed intravenously, while she slept. It was risky; if she happened to wake up on her own, she'd pull the tube out of the vein and fling the whole apparatus to the floor.

A few minutes later she was already breathing more regularly, groaning only very softly now, eyes closed, motionless.

"Wait," she whispered. "I'll be with you in a moment."

He sat on the edge of the bed and took her hand, no more than an envelope of skin stretched tight across the bones. He marveled that it weighed anything at all, perhaps it was the freckles, scattered here and there across the whiteness.

She opened her eyes. Not a trace of exhaustion, they positively glowed with eagerness and enterprise. Witchcraft, he thought, the morphine worked so quickly on her, and so powerfully.

.

That year, Brother, that empty, desperate year after Turhan's death, something quite extraordinary happened: I met my mother. That made you open your eyes, didn't it? You'd forgotten her, hadn't you, that silly thing with the corset and the feather hat! In my book this chapter is called "Yasmin's Return" and it begins with a telephone call. There was a lady on the line, Peelke announced, but he couldn't gather her name. Our phone conversation went something like this:

"Sophie?"

"Yes? Who's that speaking?"

"Madame Yasmin Berglund Karabey."

"*Who?*"

At which point she said loudly and coarsely in perfect German: "I'm your mother, you silly cow."

You see—now you're laughing, Brother. I had to laugh myself, at the time, it was too absurd, and I liked the fact that she was so matter-of-fact about it, not trying to make it an emotional event. She gave me her phone number, at the Hotel Adlon, no less, Unter den Linden; would I like to drop by and see her? I hung up, and stood there laughing aloud like an idiot. "I'm your mother . . . "

Papa didn't laugh at all when I told him that evening.

"That's all I needed now. Go and see her, if you must—do what you like as long as you keep me out of it." And then he said suddenly: "Are you curious?"

Of course I was curious. I went around the very next day. But she wouldn't let me come up to her room, I was to wait downstairs in the foyer. So I sat down and waited. Nothing but English all around me, spoken with an American accent, women with lots of makeup and all with short hair. Mine too was short now, and waved with curling irons. I saw myself in the distance in one of the wall mirrors, and found myself quite beautiful. *She* was obviously making herself look beautiful too, upstairs, because I had to wait a long time.

Clever of her, I thought, to choose the foyer for our meeting, surrounded by people. Tears of joy unwanted. So much the better.

The lift doors opened and shut again and again, people kept pouring out. Perhaps she was already in the foyer—how was I to recognize her? How was she to recognize *me*? She'd never even seen a photograph of me, and all *I* had to go on was the wasp waist and the feather hat.

How old was she now? My birthday was two days away, I'd be nineteen, making her thirty-six or so. I kept watch for a single woman of early middle age. Here was one now, very beautiful, slender, black-haired—hesitating, looking around. I stood up, hesitating too, I smiled, and she smiled—but at someone behind me, a matching gentleman. Pity, I'd have settled for her.

Then there she was. Yasmin. Without any doubt. As soon as she stepped out of the lift and started to look around, she reminded me—of me. She stood still, and studied people one after the other till her gaze fell on me. No doubt in her mind either.

"Just as I thought: red hair," she said, in place of hello. "Shall we have some coffee?"

And without waiting for an answer, she turned and led the way to the tearoom. I followed, making a quick inventory: a good deal shorter than I, plump, very well dressed, wonderful golden skin. This last I had noticed first and with envy, because of my freckles.

We sat opposite each other and carefully avoided any appraising glance. But what I glimpsed I liked.

"I'm on my way through," she said, and I was amazed at her fluent German. "I'm going to visit friends in Paris. How is your father?"

"Thank you, he's well."

That was the end of that subject. I dreaded the next question. She would surely ask about Turhan—but the waiter saved me with the cake trolley, and she deliberated a long time before selecting two slices.

"I'm too fat," she said, "but I can't resist."

I couldn't get anything down. Everything always traveled directly to my stomach, which was either frozen with fear or full of glowing coals of joy or tied up in knots of apprehension.

She asked the usual questions, what did I do, was I already engaged, all in a calm and straightforward manner. I told her about England, safe, neutral territory. She listened, munching away. Did she so much as know of Anita's existence? Probably not. Finally I got around to my poodle, August, and that was it, the cupboard was bare. What could one say to a woman, a complete stranger, but who could well claim a right to intimacy? *Could*, but didn't. She, in turn, produced no charming little memories from my babyhood, discovered no "similarities," never once so much as touched my hand. All the same she was interested, genuinely so, to judge by her eyes and voice, a particularly cozy, affectionate voice.

She finished the last of her coffee and looked at me reflectively before saying, with perfect calm: "Don't worry, I'm not going to ask about Turhan."

"How do you know—" I stammered.

"The Turkish ambassador wrote to us. All it said in our newspapers was that my late father had lost his grandson. Does one know why he did it? Was there a reason?"

And I answered, "Yes," as if it were a matter of course.

Hardly anyone knew about the money missing from the cash box, and the subsequent conversation between Papa and Turhan. Friends and relatives—even Aunt Vera—had accepted it as "adolescent depression" or a "temporary aberration." That was the official version. And here I sat, in the tearoom of the Hotel Adlon, unhesitatingly telling this strange woman that Turhan was a thief. However, I omitted to mention the letter, his last letter to me. We weren't ready for that yet.

She listened without interrupting, without any questions, looked down at her empty plate, and blinked vigorously, a nervous tic, as I later found out. When I came to the end, she sat in silence for a long while.

"Oh God," she murmured at last. "Poor Dahde. I'm glad my father didn't live to know about it." Then she raised her eyes and gave me a searching look, the first really searching one. "Do you feel guilty?"

"I? Why should I?"

"You weren't there, and he could have done with you."

"But I didn't know anything about it."

"Exactly. One feels guilty *because* one didn't know, and also because one's still alive and the other person's dead."

I couldn't even nod, she was so absolutely, so devastatingly right. After a while she hailed the waiter, paid and got up. "I think that'll do, for this time," she said, and headed back toward the foyer. "If we're to be friends we've got to take it slowly, and not overdo things."

She came with me to the front door, waved to a taxi. "Turkish embassy, please. Can I drop you at home?"

"I'll walk, it isn't far from here."

"Of course." She smiled, her features oddly twisted, and her eyelids twitched. "I'd forgotten. I'm leaving for Paris tomorrow. I'll get in touch, when I'm back. Goodbye, Sophie."

She climbed in, and waved, once.

Chapter 4

She would have liked to tell someone about this encounter. But whom? None of her female friends were close enough to her, and all Berglund had growled that evening was: "Well? Did she clasp you to the maternal bosom?" And when Sophie said no, he'd nodded, pleased.

"You don't need a mother. Sometimes one is better off without. I didn't have one either."

"What about the woman with the red hair—the painting in the drawing room—isn't that your mother?"

"I suppose so," he said. "Because of the red hair."

"Why's she hanging in the drawing room?"

"Because of the red hair."

.

Later, lying in bed, she caught herself telling Yasmin about Richard Junghans. Richard, her first "boyfriend"; girls now had a "boyfriend" rather than a fiancé. Richard was twenty, a student, looked good, and it was fun cuddling and kissing in his car. The problem was: how far should it go? Where to stop—at the waist? The dropped waistline was coming into fashion. . . . She would have liked to discuss all that with Yasmin, much rather with her than with her giggling girlfriends, none of whom told the truth anyway. Yasmin— strange, she was already sure—would have given her a definite answer, perhaps even an amusing one. The more she thought back and replayed the hour in the Hotel Adlon, the more she liked her. "And she's my mother," she said aloud in the darkness, as if in answer to a challenge. Next time she'd tell her—what, exactly? Well, that she was really pleased she'd been given a mother for her birthday.

Perhaps one day she'd be able to tell her what no one knew about, the thing that still haunted her: the letter, Turhan's letter, the unheard cry for help.

A year ago next Monday he had died, and the Dahde two days later. She would buy two wreaths, one to put on Turhan's grave at Weissensee, the other at the feet of Albrecht the Bear.

.

But the wreaths were never bought.

On Monday morning, while she was gathering her English books for the Berlitz school, the phone rang: Papa's new secretary, a Fräulein von Siebrich, of impoverished noble Prussian stock. The old girl whispered, hoarse with agitation, Sophie must come at once, take a taxi, quickly, quickly—

Sophie broke in, shouting: "Papa?"

No, no, not Herr Berglund, no, no, but please come quickly, Herr Wertheimer was already on the way.

Sophie shouted again: "What's happened? *Tell* me, for goodness sake!"

Impossible—on the telephone—please come at once—

And she hung up.

When Sophie arrived, there was a police car at the door. Fräulein von Siebrich was waiting in the corridor upstairs, outside the office. Even on good days she had a silent grievance written on her thin face, and a permanent sob in her voice.

"Don't go in, Fräulein Sophie," she whispered, two hectic red spots on her cheeks. Sophie pushed her aside. Everything in the room had been turned upside down, pamphlets, invoices, ledgers, art books lying all over the floor. Two men in ordinary clothes, but surely police officers, were burrowing and sorting and examining. The inner door to Berglund's private office was shut.

"Come, Fräulein Sophie, I'll explain it all to you." A hand knotted with arthritis—but surprisingly deft when it came to typing, so Papa said—pulled her out into the corridor again and into the little washroom by the toilet, shutting the door as softly as if she were doing something forbidden.

"Well?"

"Herr Gerstenkorn has gone," whispered the old girl, and her eyes goggled like an owl's, behind her glasses.

"What do you mean, gone?"

Fräulein von Siebrich took a deep breath and held it as though about to dive, then whispered in Sophie's ear: "He didn't come in this morning, I thought perhaps he was sick—" She ran out of air and had to breathe in again. "'I called him at home and his mother said he'd left last night, Herr Berglund had given him two weeks' leave—"

Sophie pushed her back impatiently.

"Why are you whispering? No one can hear us."

But the old fräulein clapped her hand over her own mouth—the whole business made her twitch with anguish.

"'Then what?"

"Then your father arrived. He *hadn't* given him leave at all!"

"And?"

"Your father went straight to the safe—" She could barely form the words. "It was empty! Completely empty, Fräulein Sophie! There was a note, that's all, I didn't see what was written on it, but your

195

father—he read it and went quite white, I thought he was going to pass out. I quickly brought a chair—he didn't say a word, just stared at the note. I said: 'Herr Berglund! Herr Berglund!' But he didn't hear me. Then he told me to ring Herr Wertheimer—"

"Is he here?"

"He's inside, with your father. He said I should tell you what had happened, but would you please wait till he came to fetch you."

Sophie went out into the corridor and peered into the office. The men were still rummaging, the door to Papa's inner sanctum was still shut. Back to the washroom.

"Was there a lot of money in the safe?"

The owl eyes widened. "Nearly sixty thousand marks, Fräulein Sophie. The American gentleman, the one from San Francisco, he paid in dollars yesterday morning, and Herr Naegeli brought the first installment on the Louis XVI writing desk, in Swiss francs! Your father was going to take it all to the bank today—"

Sophie shook her head. The old girl got quite upset.

"It's true, Fräulein Sophie, it's true! I was there! I wrote out the receipts myself."

Sophie wasn't listening. Papa—white in the face, propped up by the little scarecrow here, because of a sum of money? Never. Not even Gerste's betrayal would have had this effect on him. He would have cursed and raged, but it wouldn't have struck him down.

"What are they doing in there, those men?"

"They're looking for forged entries. One of them is inside with your father—"

That one came at this moment out of her father's room and spoke briefly with his men, before leaving. Behind him Georg Wertheimer. He saw Sophie in the corridor and beckoned to her, and she followed him to the little lift that ran from the office to the showrooms below. They waited in silence while the old contraption creaked its way up. Just as they were about to get in, a trembling voice came from the office doorway.

"Oh, please! Excuse me—I'm Frau Gerstenkorn, his mother." She got no further, held onto the door frame, and looked around for help, a little woman with a crumpled face and ragged gray hair, out of breath, eyes full of tears.

Sophie looked at Wertheimer. The policemen, too, raised their heads expectantly.

196

"A glass of water, please, Fräulein von Siebrich," said Wertheimer, and led the old woman to a chair. The policemen turned back to their work.

"Oh God," whispered Frau Gerstenkorn, gazing at the shambles around her. She swallowed convulsively. "My son—believe me, the head injury—he wasn't the same when he came back—he wasn't the same—"

Sophie took the glass of water from the secretary's hand and held it to Frau Gerstenkorn's mouth. Obediently she took a few sips, and gazed up at Sophie.

"Oh!" she said in a trembling, barely intelligible voice. "Are you Fräulein Sophie? My son talked about you so often—he loved you—" she broke into silent, hopeless sobs.

"I didn't know," murmured Sophie, and bit her lip.

"Take Frau Gerstenkorn home," said Wertheimer to the secretary, and opened the door to the lift.

During their journey down he stayed obstinately silent and stared at the floor.

The shop below was shut, and half in darkness, not a soul to be seen. Wertheimer let himself fall heavily on a heap of carpets as though his legs couldn't have carried him for another second, elbows propped up on his knees, both fists pressed to his forehead. Sophie grabbed one of the oriental leather stools and sat down opposite him.

"Georg—what did the note say?"

He slowly raised his head, looked at her for a moment, and closed his eyes.

" 'With love from Turhan'—in Gerste's handwriting."

Chapter 5

None of Berglund's usual sources of comfort were any use this time, neither Georg nor the brandy.

Early one morning he stood at Sophie's bed, shaking her awake, wearing hat and overcoat and carrying a suitcase.

"I'm going away, Sophie. When I look at the corridor up here, with all those doors—I've got to get away. Georg will look after the business. If it doesn't work out, I'll sell it, I don't give a damn. You know what I always say: when the water comes up to *here*—get out fast. Remember that. You and I, we're not unalike in many ways, so watch out when things begin to crowd you." For a moment he looked down at her wide-open, bewildered eyes and sat down on the side of the bed. "I'm sunk." He bowed his head, and she dared not touch him. "I'll let you know where I'll be. Don't know yet myself."

He leaned down over her, kissed her hair and left.

Sophie got dressed mechanically, stared at her Berlitz books, and pushed them aside. She sat down to breakfast in the drawing room, August beside her, and drank her coffee. They both looked out of the window and watched Gerhard working on the rosebushes that loomed over him. August growled softly, hating Gerhard even through the window, and she stroked his thick woolly head.

Papa's gone, she thought. Now what am I supposed to do, pretend he *hasn't*? Simply go on living here with Peelke and Frau Glaubitz and the dwarf—or should I go away myself, somewhere, just with August—

The phone. She heard Peelke answering in the kitchen. He limped in.

"It's that lady again, I can't catch her name—"

In one bound Sophie was at the phone. Yasmin—rescue line—escape—sanctuary—

May she come to the Adlon? Right away?

This time she was allowed up to her room. Yasmin, in a housecoat, was at her dressing table when she saw Sophie come in, and stood up at once.

"What's happened? Tell me."

Sophie would have liked to burst into tears, but they wouldn't come. They would have made it easier to explain things. But her arms came up of their own accord and went around Yasmin's neck.

"Tell me, Sophie."

Where to start? With Turhan? With Papa? With Anita, even?

"I'm all alone," she said at last. "I've only got the dog."

.

She spent the day with Yasmin, and walked slowly home in the late afternoon. From there she rang Georg Wertheimer.

"Georg?—Sophie. You probably know Papa's gone. I don't want to stay here. . . . No, I can't go back to St. Leonards because of August.

You can't bring dogs into England. . . . Yes he does, Georg, he means a lot to me. I'm going to stay here in Berlin and live with my mother —Yasmin—yes. She's here. She's going to rent an apartment, and I'm going to live with her."

.

She packed that evening. Frau Glaubitz helped her, quietly crying. "Of course I understand, Fräulein Sophie, but what's going to happen to *us*?"

Wertheimer came by later, and they sat downstairs in the drawing room talking about money. Sophie was to say how much she needed a month. How would she know? Everything had always been paid for her, there had always been someone to hand her what she needed, Anita, or Papa, or the house matron in England. No one had ever told her: "No, you can't, that's too expensive."

Wertheimer shook his head. "You've got to learn how to handle money, Sophie. Your father probably meant to wait until you came of age, but now you'll have to learn a little earlier, that's all. Other young people have known that sort of thing since childhood, but in your family everything was always different. Besides, you spent three years in England, our worst years here, you only know by hearsay what it was like after the war. And you were lucky, too, your father was one of the few who didn't lose out as a result of the war and inflation, because his stock in trade, antiques, never fell in value. Have you ever thought about what it's been like for other people? I lost everything, every penny, and your father had to help me back onto my feet with my law practice. *He* could afford to run this house all through the war. With the servants! But now—" He studied her. How much of a blow could she take? "He'll never go back to running the business the way he did before; he says so, and I believe him. His enthusiasm, his joy in it, they're gone, along with your brother. I've found someone who knows the trade well enough, but your father isn't easy to replace, and I'm afraid the business is bound to go downhill. It might last a few more years, but that's all."

"You don't think Papa might eventually want to—"

The little man shook his head. "Something else has come into his life, something which used to play only a small part in it. But now I'm afraid it's going to become more and more important."

Sophie looked at him, waiting for him to go on. He hesitated, then decided he owed it to her.

"This woman in Antwerp—"

"Keitje?"

"Yes. She's a gambler. A compulsive gambler. Chemin de fer and baccarat—that's what she lives for, otherwise your father would have married her long ago. He accompanied her to gambling clubs in Antwerp, but he didn't play much himself. It wasn't the sort of thing he wanted in his life—you know how he hates to be dependent. But now he wants to turn his life inside out, and I fear he'll need something like this. Not something solid and real, he's had his fill of that, it's what he wants to break with, d'you understand? He needs something with enough excitement to blot out everything else, and I think he'll be playing for high stakes, to make it work."

Sophie looked at him, without answering, but he knew she'd understood him, and understood *it*, at once, intuitively—and he was suddenly worried for her.

"Let me know where you're living," he said, once more matter-of-fact. "I'll tell your father you're not living here anymore. Perhaps he'll want to sell the house. Don't worry, I'll see to Frau Glaubitz and Peelke and Gerhard. If you take my advice, start to learn about money. It won't do any harm to make an effort to save some. I'll provide you with five hundred marks a month, that should see you through. By the way—you ought to find yourself a job."

.

But what kind of job? Sophie racked her brains, while she helped Yasmin furnish a flat in Olivaerplatz. Meanwhile she lived in the Adlon, in a small room opposite Yasmin's.

Leaving Ruemelangstrasse had not been that easy. She had wandered for a long time from room to room, and August had pressed tight against her, whining softly, as if afraid of ghosts.

She had spent even longer upstairs in her room, gazing out of the window as so many times before. How many? Hundreds and hundreds of times, nose and forehead pressed against the panes. First as a child, low down by the sill, peering excitedly: were the roses in bloom, the strawberries ripe, had it snowed during the night? Later growing up the windowpanes, staring lazily out or frantically waiting for something—and finally hour after hour in utter misery, listening for the sound of Anita's door, still looking out but seeing nothing.

The big bedroom next door—first Anita's, then Papa's—one quick look in, and so savage a kick at the hated door that she nearly fell over and August barked in alarm. Past Turhan's door without stopping or looking in. Coward, she thought, and crept on toward the Dahde's. Her "kitchen" was bare. The few things she had owned, the prayer mat, the bowls, her pots and pans, had all been sent back to Constantinople ("Istanbul" now) with her, on Papa's orders.

Saying goodbye to Frau Glaubitz. Tears, but not too many, since she would still be within reach, as Georg Wertheimer's new housekeeper. Peelke kissed her hand, formal and dignified. Georg had found him a job as department manager at Horch's, the automobile company. I'm so glad, Peelke, all the very best! And to you, Fräulein Sophie.

And Gerhard. He was waiting by the steps, outside the house. Beside him stood a dwarfess, even smaller than he was, snub-nosed and doll-faced. Gerhard glowed. Next month they were going to be married, yes indeed. He and Fräulein Beluka here had got a contract with the Krone Circus—he did a somersault by way of proof, without interrupting his speech—he would earn good money, and he and Fräulein Beluka here—as if on cue she did a somersault too, only backward—would live in a caravan.

Speechless, Sophie shook their hands. She had trouble holding back August, driven to a frenzy by the sight of *two* dwarfs and the somersaults. They both waved and ran off laughing like two children, hand in hand.

Sophie stood watching them until they had turned the corner. She couldn't remember Gerhard *ever* laughing, not once. Now that he was leaving, he laughed. She'd never particularly liked him—why did she suddenly mind?

.

Two months later they moved into the flat in Olivaerplatz. By now they knew each other quite well. What Sophie liked about Yasmin was her self-containment, and her matter-of-factness. She still couldn't bring herself to call her Mother. It'll come, she thought, in time, but it never did. She was content that Yasmin was fond of her without longing for any deep kinship with her. She was accepted and even appreciated as she was—except for her red hair. This Yasmin clearly hated. It was the color, she insisted, nothing to do with memories of her father. But Sophie knew better.

The flat was large, big enough for two people to live their own lives independent of each other. To Yasmin's mind Sophie was a grownup, at twenty, and answerable for herself. She never probed, even when she could see that Sophie was longing to be asked. That would already have contained an element of risk, and she was never going to let a red-haired person get too close to her.

Money was not at issue; valuable furniture, expensive antiques, arrived, as if according to local custom. She was obviously well off, but never spoke about it. Presumably, as her father's favorite daughter, she had been the main heir. Nevertheless Sophie insisted on paying one hundred and fifty of her five hundred marks, for bed and board, and Yasmin accepted it. It was no more than fair.

No comment was passed on the fact that Sophie's main interest was in the boyfriend of the moment. Or that she brought them to the flat. But why did she insist on introducing every one of these young men, these Richards and Ludwigs and Hans-Joachims?

"Sophie—can't you keep to your room when you've got visitors? I don't really have to get to know your friends, as long as you like them, that's all that matters."

"But I want to know if *you* like them. I mean, I might stay with one of them."

"As long as it's 'might,' there's no danger."

Sophie sulked. "How can one be sure that one is sure? How does one tell? Did you know right away, with Papa?"

Sophie found herself staring into a suddenly drained face and hostile, frozen eyes. Is it possible, thought Yasmin, does she really not know what happened then? Did she never ask? The Dahde could have told her. Did she never miss me? Probably not. Her father's daughter, emotionally impoverished. But then—I didn't miss *her* either, I was even afraid of ever meeting her, afraid she'd remind me of her father. Thank God I don't hate her; I like her, but she's utterly foreign to me. *I* can't tell her how it was with her father. Too late. And still too dangerous, for me. There'll never be a real bond. My fault. Why did I come at all? Curiosity, pure and stupid.

After a while she said with her usual calm: "No one can spell it out for you, it takes everyone in different ways. You'll find out all by yourself one day."

·

That day was already marked—though she didn't know it—in Sophie's diary, on her desk: Tuesday eleven o'clock. Martensen photo, Uhlandstrasse 48. Georg Wertheimer had reminded her about Papa's birthday.

"I think your father could do with a nicely framed photograph of you, on his bedside table."

"Are you in touch with him, Georg?"

"Now and again."

"Why does he never call me? Why doesn't he answer my letters?"

"Perhaps if you were living somewhere else—but don't worry, Sophie, you stay where you are, it's a good arrangement. Your father doesn't have a lot to offer, at the moment."

"Is he ill? Couldn't I go and see him, if he's—"

"Don't do that. He's all right—physically, that is."

"Is he drinking?"

"Yes."

"And—gambling?"

"Yes. Stay where you are. You still haven't got a job?"

"I'm looking, Georg."

"Learn shorthand and typing."

"What?"

"Think about it. Meanwhile I'll make an appointment with Martensen for you. He makes the best portraits in Berlin, especially when it comes to women. A bit too prettified, but your father won't mind that. I'll let you know when and where."

.

Tuesday, eleven o'clock. Sophie in a white, pleated skirt, and a white blouse. She'd rung up earlier to find out what to wear, and a female voice had answered.

"One moment, please, I'll ask Herr Martensen."

Then a man's voice, somewhat bored and not even bothering to say hello.

"How old are you, Fräulein—um—Berglund?"

"Twenty."

"What type?"

"Stunning."

The man at the other end laughed. "I mean are you blond or brunette?"

"Fire-engine red."

"That comes out dark in the photograph. Wear something white. Something simple."

The female voice turned out to belong to a pretty, fair-haired girl who opened the door to her and led her to the waiting room. Shortly, Herr Martensen appeared.

"I usually leave my clients waiting for a bit, that way they get impatient and there's some expression on their face. But I was curious about you. A redhead, all right. How d'you do—come into the studio."

A large, darkened room, virtually unfurnished. Lights on stands and a variety of chairs. He picked out a stool.

"I want no contours behind your head, just the blank wall."

She sat with her hands folded in her lap, looked this way and that at his command. The blond girl helped move the lights back and forth. After a while he sent her out and worked on his own.

Despite his instructions, she tried to get a look at him. The lights blinded her and made him a shadowy figure, a tall, thin silhouette, that was all she could make out. And dark hair, that much she knew for certain.

When she left Uhlandstrasse 48 an hour later—and then only because the next client had been waiting so long that she had more expression in her face than Martensen could use—Sophie knew several other things. For instance, that she was definitely going to accept his invitation to dinner, although she'd only murmured, "Well —perhaps." The blonde had helped her into her coat and tonelessly said goodbye. Aha. *That* was the situation, then. Too bad.

He picked her up at the flat that evening and was presented to Yasmin. As they said their goodbyes, Sophie said suddenly: "I'll be home early." And wondered, as they went down the stairs, why she'd been so willing to put the brakes on herself.

They climbed into Martensen's sports car, a black Auburn-Cord. Papa would have said: too conspicuous, but that matched its owner. Martensen was—apart from Papa—the most conspicuous man she had ever seen. Any resemblance to Papa? None. Quite the contrary, yet they had a similar effect.

He sat down behind the wheel, but instead of driving off he leaned across and without taking hold of her or touching her, he kissed her. No effort, she met him halfway.

They drove to the Restaurant Horcher, where he was greeted with enthusiasm and led to "his" table. He ordered the food and the wine for both of them. She had learned to drink wine at Ruemelangstrasse "so that some fellow doesn't come along one day and think he can make you drunk and then—! I used to do it myself, with respectable girls. An old trick."

When the wine arrived, they clinked glasses.

"Dimitrios," he said. "Dimi. And you?"

"Sophie."

"To us, Sophie. Will you marry me?"

"Why are you called Dimitrios?"

"A last relic. My father was a Serbian count, an illegitimate son of Kaiserin Elizabeth of Austria. Cheers."

Sophie laughed. A Hapsburg, from the wrong side of the blanket—why not? She'd take his word for it.

When they climbed into the low black car again, after the meal, he kissed her the same way as before, just by leaning over to her side, and then asked her whether she'd come home with him.

"No."

"Why not? We're going to get married."

"That's why not," she said, and kissed him again. He leaned back again and studied her.

"For the love of God—you're not by any chance a virgin?"

She nodded gravely, and gave a smile he didn't understand at first, then misinterpreted.

"You almost had me fooled."

On the way back to the Olivaerplatz she put her head on his shoulder, and he rubbed his cheek in her hair.

"There's something I've got to do, tomorrow—" he said in a low voice.

"I know. What's your assistant's name?"

"Marie. Who told you—"

"It'll be painful," she said. "Do it nicely." He nodded, silently. "My father never could." She added reflectively, "His women never recovered."

.

In the flat she found Yasmin in the sitting room, playing patience.

"Already home? It's barely eleven o'clock," she remarked, turning up a card.

"I told you I'd be home early."

Yasmin nodded vaguely and tried the next card. Sophie waited to see if she wasn't going to ask her something after all, then walked slowly to her bedroom, undressed, and returned to the sitting room in her dressing gown.

"Yasmin—did you like him?"

"No."

She wasn't altogether unprepared for this, having caught a look Yasmin had thrown at Dimi. Was it possible he had the same effect on *her* too, as Papa? Was that why her aversion was so instantaneous?

"I want to marry him."

"What's stopping you?"

Sophie sat down beside her on the floor and put her head against Yasmin's knee. "It would have been so nice if you'd liked him."

Yasmin raised a hand but couldn't quite bring herself to stroke the red hair.

"I'm glad it would have meant something to you—*very* glad. And I'm going to tell you why I don't like him." Sophie raised her head. Was she actually going to admit it? "There's a word in your language which doesn't exist in mine, and even in French or in English you need half a sentence to arrive at the same meaning. But in German it is just a single, short word: *Güte*. It is somewhere between plain, elementary goodness and an awareness of the true priorities in life. That man has none of it. Believe me."

Like Papa, thought Sophie. No, that wasn't fair. Papa wasn't entirely without goodness, not entirely *without*—and that was, probably, not good enough. Perhaps it was downright fatal.

"Is that really so important?"

"It's the only thing that matters," said Yasmin, and fitted two cards to one pile.

Sophie gave a sigh. More than likely Dimi didn't have it, was stuck halfway, like Papa. So what? She wasn't ever going to be at his mercy, she was different from Yasmin, wanted different things from a man. Dimi wasn't there to protect her or sympathize with her or comfort her, he was there to excite her. As he did now. And always would—if such a thing was possible. Well, she'd find out. Besides, all this goodness and awareness stuff, that was something to do with age, wasn't it? Did Yasmin have it? Without a doubt. Did she, Sophie?

Chapter 6 The fifth night.
Once, on his return to her room, when he cautiously opened the door in case she had fallen asleep, she stretched out both hands toward him, full of excitement.

"Come quickly—I've just got to the bit you've been waiting for all this time. You have, haven't you?"

It was growing lighter, and he put out the nightlight. A faint reddish glow outlined his hair and his profile against the darkness of the room, and the spectacles gleamed faintly.

"I've no idea what you're talking about."

She giggled, laughed, coughed, all at once.

"Put your hand on my chest, up here, below the neck, then it'll stop hurting."

"Do you need—"

"No, no, I'm still all right. Be quiet. I'm too worked up, because—well, you'll see!" She forced herself to breathe more calmly. "Just give me a second longer—hold on. . . . There now: you see, we had to wait until my twenty-first birthday to get married, Dimi and I, or have I already mentioned that? Papa refused permission. He didn't answer my letters, but he said on the phone to Georg Wertheimer that the photo Dimi had taken of me was nice, but that that was no reason to go and marry the fellow. I must be off my head. *He'd* done enough mischief himself, in that department, enough was enough. A full year to have a good think. One day I'd be grateful to him.

"And during that year of the good think—it happened: the thing you've been wanting to ask me about for so long." She closed her eyes for a moment, then suddenly gave him a serious, almost anxious look. "I don't know, Brother—now that we've got there, I feel quite sick all of a sudden . . ."

"Don't force yourself," he said, though by now he felt definitely curious. "You can tell me some other time."

"No, no. Now! I mustn't leave it out and put it in later; this is where it fits in. I can't dodge it. So: one evening, when I was waiting

for Dimi at home—we were going to go to the theater—I suddenly
got a sharp pain in my belly, so strong I had to bend double. Here!"
She found the place on the bedcovers, spread flat across the bed as if
there were no body underneath. "A stabbing pain, just in that spot.
I'd had it before, though never like that, but Dimi and I always had
something marvelous planned, there was never time to worry about
it or to go to the doctor. But now, *there* it was, impossible to ignore.
I felt awful, was violently sick, and Yasmin called the doctor. Straight
off to the hospital and on the operating table within the hour. Burst
appendix, peritonitis, the whole works—you've already guessed what
I'm about to tell you, haven't you?"

He nodded, smiled like a conspirator, and she gave something like
a gleeful whoop.

"If only you knew how much I love you, Brother! You don't believe me, of course; you think: poor old thing, there she is, babbling
away—"

She closed her eyes, and when she opened them again they were
full of tears. "To be so lucky, to be given this, now! These long,
miraculous nights—and even the days, while you aren't there and I
pretend I'm asleep so that no one will come in and worry me while
I'm writing, even then you're always there, in the chair that's waiting
for you, till it's dark."

He stroked the bedcovers, and murmured: "I know. I know."

.

Well now—we were at the Diakonissen hospital, where I woke up
from the anesthetic and began to scream, and someone gave me an
injection and it stopped me screaming, and now I lay quietly,
happily; I liked everything around me, my room, the nurses, the
doctor, everything was simply beautiful.

And so it went for the next ten days. I moaned, was given
morphine—and sailed away on calm seas, all pain dissolved, every
gap filled, saturated, released, with just one wish: to stay like that.

Then the wound slowly healed and hardly hurt anymore. No more
injections. For a few days I managed to extort one here and there by
my convincing groans, but then it stopped completely. By strict
order of the surgeon, who took one look at my scar—and another one
at me. And not a friendly one.

At night I couldn't sleep in spite of sleeping pills, threw myself
around the bed, rang my emergency bell incessantly, howled and

whined—in vain. No injections, just idiotic little sedatives, which I spat back into the nurse's face. It was a dreadful week, Brother. I had no idea what had happened to me, never imagined in a hundred years that my desperate state, the awful storm raging inside me, the pains I felt but couldn't describe—that these were all withdrawal symptoms. And quite mild ones, too, after only two weeks of morphine.

Gradually the torment lessened, I became calmer, slept again at night, managed to sit up during the day. Dimi came every evening, Yasmin always in the morning. Georg Wertheimer visited me—Papa had been on the verge of taking the train to come and see me, but the surgeon had reassured him on the phone: a few more days and I'd be able to go home.

And then it happened. The night before I left the hospital. Dimi had just gone home, I'd put out the light and was about to go to sleep. Suddenly the door opened and quickly shut again. A white coat stood in the room.

"Psst!" whispered a hoarse, male voice. "Not a sound. Or I'll bash your face in." The coat slipped silently over to my bed. "Keep quiet and you'll get something nice." He leant over me, I couldn't see anything, but I heard him right above me, breathing heavily. "But it's only for good girls, understand?"

I felt as if paralyzed, could only whisper: "Please don't! Please—please—I've just had an operation."

He grinned silently, and I caught the sudden glitter of his teeth.

"What—what do you want?"

"Shut up," he said softly and threateningly, and glanced around at the door. "Yes and no is all I want to hear from you. And only when you're asked."

He sat on the bed. "That's it," he whispered. "Keep it nice and quiet." And he lit a cigarette. I had a second's glimpse of his face, young, the chin too long, the cheekbones prominent, hollow cheeks, sagging skin under the eyes.

He was silent for a few moments, drawing strongly on the cigarette. Suddenly he said in a completely different voice: "Well, Fräulein—I can get the stuff for you."

"What stuff?" I stammered.

He grinned again and said it was no secret, around the ward, how I'd reacted to morphine. So, if I wanted some more . . . This last in what was virtually a helpless mumble. I breathed more calmly again.

"You take morphine yourself?"

He nodded and glanced at the door again.

Come on, then. Yes or no.

And that was it, Brother. I bought a little packet off him, and a syringe, and he showed me how to do it, sticking the needle into his own thigh right through his trousers.

"If you need some, ring me and we'll meet somewhere. Sorry I was so rough, before, but I had to keep you quiet. My name's Wächter. I'd rather you didn't write down my number, but you'll remember it easily enough: oh-oh-too-too."

He vanished as silently as he had come, and I sat upright in my bed, holding the packet and the syringe, which scared me, lying there in my hand, a long, cool, sinister, stream-lined thing.

.

She stopped, exhausted, and closed her eyes.

"And you went ahead and injected yourself that very night, didn't you? Why? You didn't need it anymore."

"For the hell of it," she whispered. "To see if I had the nerve. And also because I didn't believe I'd be able to make it work. I made it work, Brother, and how! At the very first try I floated happily off again, didn't sleep a wink, just lay there, drowsily ecstatic, all night. Next morning I hid it all carefully in the new handbag Dimi had just bought for me, a big one, made of crocodile skin, with lots of room and a separate, sealed-off inner pocket, just as if he'd had my needs in mind. That bag and I were inseparable for years, no matter how often it clashed with what I was wearing. 'My Dimi gave it to me,' I would say, and people thought it rather touching.

"At first I didn't shoot up much, but it did the trick, I was instantly elated and even became quite witty, which I'm not, ordinarily. I slept with Dimi, as soon as I was on my feet again, and he discovered that I really was a virgin—don't look at me like that, Brother, from his point of view I *was*. He was appalled, at first—it wasn't quite the thing in 1926—then rather pleased. I was full of surprises, he said.

"We got married on the morning of my twenty-first birthday. Papa had arrived a few days earlier, to look Dimi over. And I looked *him* over: almost white-haired now, with a paunch, and heavy bags under the eyes. 'What do you expect,' he said. 'I'm fifty-six, and the last few years have counted double, believe me.' Then he gave me a check, and said: 'Good luck, you'll need it.' And left at once, so as not to run into Yasmin."

"Didn't he notice anything?"

"About me? Perhaps he just thought it was the excitement. That's what Yasmin thought. 'You've changed a lot,' she said once. 'Do you drink, when you're with Dimi?'"

"No, I drank very little, but I *had* changed, though that had nothing to do with Dimi and my happiness.

"Sometimes I heard my own voice in the gondola in Venice: 'Anita —I'm afraid I am "enslaved" and I *like* it!' And her answer: 'It's only a question of being aware. . . . Later, of course, you must be on your guard.' I had not been on my guard. On my nighttable or under my arm sat a crocodile. And not a soul knew, not even Yasmin, with whom I had shared a flat.

"Our relationship, of course, wasn't the same anymore, quite apart from the fact that I'd spent entire nights away from our flat. Not that she ever commented on that, but I knew what she thought. She was old-fashioned-Turkish on that subject to the end of her days. But our life together wasn't working out anyway; something fragmentary, unrealized, and 'failed' was in the air. We had not become mother and daughter, we both knew it, and were both trying not to let it show."

She studied the young man.

"What's your mother like, Brother? Why does that embarrass you? I've often noticed that people get embarrassed when you ask about their mothers. Tongue-tied, without knowing why. Perhaps because one was a part of her, once. One feels responsible, as if it were the other way round, as if one had given birth to *her*. When it's a question of one's father, or brother or sister, there's no such shyness."

He took off his glasses and polished them carefully.

"You see? Same with you. You wish I hadn't asked."

"My mother," said the young man, putting his glasses on, "is a peasant woman. She's not unlike your Dahde, except that she speaks Greek, of course. But she can't read or write. She lives as in the Middle Ages. By the Bible."

"Do you love her? Don't polish your glasses again, they're quite clean."

"If she fell ill, I'd go home at once and look after her."

"But you don't miss her." He said nothing. "You see, you just can't bring yourself to admit it, because you feel guilty. I never felt that way toward Yasmin. As for the nine months I spent inside her, I might as well have been stuck in a flowerpot. We were just two women, one of them young, the other older—" She stopped, and chewed her lower lip. "I admit she did a lot for me. She had *Güte*—remember that stuff she once explained to me about elementary goodness and awareness of the right priorities? I obviously had neither. Only once was I able to do something for *her*—much later on."

The last words were barely audible. Her large yellow eyes stared past him at the window, suddenly disconsolate, as if outside she saw something lonely, godforsaken.

BOOK VI

Chapter 1

Later, whenever Sophie was asked about her first marriage, the same scene always came promptly to mind: sitting in a shoeshop, Leiser's in the Tauentzienstrasse, with mountains of boxes and tissue paper on either side of her. She'd wanted to buy a pair of shoes, and Dimi had come along. Three salesgirls ran breathlessly to and fro with more and more boxes; he had already bought a dozen pairs, and it still wasn't enough.

"Dimi, I beg you—"

"Bring me this pair in a dark blue, would you, Fräulein?"

"I've already got a dark-blue pair!"

"One can't have enough dark-blue pairs. Isn't there something a darker blue than that, Fräulein? Dark blue with a green hue, not a reddish one, d'you understand?"

"Oh yes, sir," she breathed. "I understand." Before she could make it even clearer to him how well she'd understood, one of the other girls dislodged her and held a pair of sports shoes under his nose.

"What about these, sir? The leather! Just smell it," she piped, only to be dethroned by number three, who rushed up with two pairs of gilded sandals.

"Why, both pairs, Fräulein, naturally. Try them on."

"Dimi—!"

No one listened. The salesgirls, as if hypnotized by this man and his appetite, knelt before him, offering him their leather idols, and raising and lowering Sophie's feet like a doll's.

She gave up. Tears ran down her cheeks, but no one looked at her face, only her feet.

After selecting seventeen pairs, Dimi had had his fill and strode triumphantly to the cashier's desk, surrounded by three salesgirls in a trance.

Sophie was still sitting on her chair, one foot in a satin slipper, the other in a brown brogue. She groped in her handbag for a handkerchief—in her big, beautiful crocodile bag, and something cool touched her hand through the inner partition. She got up and asked where the toilet was.

She returned shortly, relaxed, and smiling at her husband.

"You see—you'll love all these beautiful shoes. You *need* them."

"I do, Dimi, I do."

.

The entire house, No. 48 Uhlandstrasse, belonged to Dimi. So he said. He didn't mention the mortgages, and it was a while before she found out about them. Downstairs there was his studio, leading to a bachelor flat next to it. On the first floor, a three-room flat which he'd previously rented out, and above, extensive storerooms. During the think-it-over year he redecorated the flat, and Sophie was allowed to watch. She'd thought she knew something about antiques, but that was beginner's stuff to Dimi. Colors and shapes, the exquisite and at the same time the simple, those were the things he cared about, and he never tired in his search for the exactly right. Sophie was amazed.

She was also amazed when, shortly before the wedding, he asked without the slightest embarrassment whether her father would guarantee her a monthly income. No, said Georg Wertheimer, with a dirty look.

Yasmin quickly guessed the reason for Sophie's downcast face, on her return from Georg's office. For her there was nothing disreputable about Dimi's question, a marriage was a business deal, someone had to pay, either the father or the groom. If both refused, a third party had to be found, that was the custom. She gave Sophie a check for twenty thousand marks and shrugged off her clamorous thanks, with surprise. This money went toward the decorating of the apartment, and also paid for several other items which Dimi didn't specify in detail. "Commitments."

Papa's check covered the wedding and Sophie's wardrobe—chosen by Dimi—and left enough for two dozen silk shirts, English sports jackets and French cravats for the bridegroom.

"It's good that he thinks big," said Yasmin. "It's his best quality. Men who think small never get anywhere."

"But he gets into debt! Papa always said one should live within one's means."

"It'll come, with time. How old is he?"

"Thirty-one."

"Already? Well then—in a few years' time you'll have to curb him."

.

Curb? Dimi? She suspected it was better to indulge him. In one respect she found this quite easy, and her adaptability and inventiveness delighted him. He once mentioned that his first and in some respects most satisfying affair had been with a manicurist. The girl in question hadn't even been especially attractive, but she had insisted on always giving him a manicure beforehand, and it had had an astounding effect.

That evening Sophie suddenly announced that she had to go out for a short time but that someone would be paying him a visit. Dimi, startled but intrigued, promised to wait and sit in the armchair she designated. Shortly afterward came a knock at the door. "Come in." Sophie appeared in a white smock, with a box under her arm, and curtsied.

"Good evening, sir, I'm from the Hotel Adlon. I believe you requested a manicure. Where can I get some warm water?"

"Over there in the bathroom, Fräulein."

She came back with a little dish of water and balanced it carefully on the left arm of the chair.

"Please dip your left hand, I always begin with the right. I hope that's to your satisfaction, sir?"

"Thank you, Fräulein."

She sat down beside him on a stool and unpacked the box, scissors, nail file, tissues, creams, the lot. "May I have your right hand, sir?"

He slowly raised his hand and placed it on her knee, lightly, but she felt it was burning her through the smock. She looked up, and their eyes met for a moment. Then she began to file his nails, and studied his strong brown fingers attentively.

"Everything to your satisfaction, sir?"

"Yes, Fräulein. You're obviously an expert."

"I'm a professional, sir. The left hand, please, and dip the right."

They concentrated on the matter at hand, discreetly and politely. While she dried his right hand, the left landed gently on her knee.

"Do you have many customers, Fräulein?"

"Enough, sir. My services don't come cheap."

"Am I wrong, Fräulein, or have you got nothing on beneath your smock?"

"You're very observant. Left hand, please."

"Are you always available?"

"I'll leave you my phone number, it isn't in the book. Nail varnish, sir, or just a polishing?"

"Just the polishing, please, but carefully, will you."

"Leave it to me, sir. Nothing will be left unpolished."

She brought a small white leather pad out of the box and began to polish his nails. At one moment she happened to look up and into his eyes, and the manicure came to an abrupt end. The bedroom was too far away, but there was a sofa in the sitting room.

•

He had been meant to be a violinist, he told her, and had shown talent, but not enough; all that remained was a passion for music, and they went to concerts, or to the opera, several times a week. Apart from Turhan's a capella Schubert songs there had been virtually no music at Ruemelangstrasse. It meant little to Papa, and Anita had no ear for music. Sophie's ignorance appalled Dimi, but he soon discovered that her ear was perfect and that she learned quickly and enthusiastically. "I've deflowered you twice," he said. "The second time at the Philharmonic."

Each day was an event, every single one a revelation—or was it just, perhaps, that little bit of "stuff" she was shooting? Nonsense, it was Dimi who made her feel high all day. She always had to check and confirm that he was really there, within reach, right under her feet in the studio, at her disposal, hers alone. And while he was at work, and she would walk alone through the streets on a fine summer day, she felt so gloriously young, so invincible, so immeasurably blessed, that she thought her shoes must surely be leaving footprints in the asphalt.

•

In the mornings she'd lie in, in her yellow bedroom ("Yellow, so that the sun shines even when it's raining"), lolling about, hearing August barking downstairs. (One thing she had forfeited was the dog. When she got back from the hospital, he wouldn't come near her; he pressed close to Dimi's legs, had become his dog.) Dimi would already be at work, developing plates, sifting them out, making copies, receiving his first client at nine o'clock. Instead of blond Marie there was dark-haired Susanne with slightly protruding teeth, who fell for him within a week, although she had a husband and two children at home. Sophie noticed, and found it perfectly natural, it was so easy to love Dimi. He was never moody, never unapproachable (unlike

Papa, in all things and forever her standard). Nothing ever bored him, he went at everything with the same newfound delight, as long as it was uncomplicated and, above all, healthy. He was so aggressively healthy himself, he said, that he simply couldn't understand illness and always had a secret feeling that the sick were just *pretending*, weren't they? He guiltily confessed to her that he had almost stopped loving her during her four weeks in the hospital. She had suddenly become completely different, quite alien, unrecognizable. Thank God she had got well just in time. He was laughing as he said it, but Sophie knew she would have to put an end to the stuff lurking in the inner pocket of her handbag. And quickly.

.

Once a month it was oh-oh-too-too on the phone, and a meeting with Wächter in Moabit, a notoriously squalid suburb of Berlin. She bought the packets one at a time in the hope that each would be the last. Wächter, disappointed, raised the price relentlessly.

"What's the matter?" He eyed her spitefully. "No cash? Or no guts?"

On the way home in the taxi she always left waiting for her outside the café, she swore every time: as of Monday—finished.

.

On her twenty-fifth birthday Dimi left the bedroom even earlier than usual. Still fast asleep, Sophie didn't hear him come back in, didn't feel him spread something light and soft across her, slowly and carefully. Then he tiptoed out of the room.

Downstairs, Susanne was taking the covers off the lights.

"Is your wife awake? I've brought her a few carnations."

He beckoned her over.

"Come—I want to show you something."

She followed him up the stairs, and he opened the bedroom door a crack. "Can you see—on the bed—"

"The blanket?"

"It's a mink coat. I want her to wake up beneath it."

He pushed her aside and peered in. Sophie sneezed; the mink had tickled her nose. He quickly stepped inside and shut the door.

Susanne went slowly down the stairs. A wave of envy rose up in her, and she closed her eyes in pain. "What's it got to do with me," she whispered, and began to look for a vase, for the carnations.

.

The mink was the morning surprise. The afternoon surprise in-volved a drive to the Grunewaldsee and a walk through the woods, Sophie in her mink, since she wouldn't be parted from it, despite the spring sunshine. When they came to a fenced-in clearing, Dimi put two fingers in his mouth and whistled. In the distance, in the shadow of a group of pine trees, something moved and then stepped out into the light, ears pricked, its chestnut coat polished and glittering in the sun.

"Oh God," sighed Sophie. "He's beautiful."

"That's Katrina. She's yours, because she's the color of your hair."

The mare snorted, and ambled over. Dimi brought sugar from his pocket, and Katrina bared her wide lips and took it from his out-stretched palm. She let herself be stroked, nodding vigorously and pawing the ground.

"Now, *you* give her some—she already knows me, we've been out together a few times. She's got to get used to *you*."

Not without misgivings, Sophie held out a couple of sugar cubes, under the horse's pale-pink muzzle. Katrina ignored her hand and snuffled at Dimi's face.

"I don't know—" she said hesitantly. "I don't think horses like me. We used to ride along the beach in England, and my horse always tried to squeeze me up against the breakwater and knock me off."

"Hired horses—lazy and spiteful, all of them. Just wait till you're sitting on Katrina, and you'll know the difference."

The difference was that Katrina managed to throw Sophie the very first time she rode her. She had gone out with the riding teacher, but Katrina had galloped away as if possessed, made straight for a large oak tree, and only ducked aside at the last moment. Sophie was hurled from the saddle and lay motionless on the ground. When the teacher tried to lift her up, she moaned and pointed at her left leg, bent askew between knee and ankle, in the grass, as if it didn't belong to her. There was no way of bandaging it, all he could do was give her aspirin, stretch her out in his car, and drive her back to town. On the journey she moaned incessantly and, halfway back, vomited up the aspirin.

.

The riding school had informed Dimi. He was standing outside the front door when they arrived, and carried her up to the bedroom where his own doctor was already waiting, an energetic young fellow called Fritsche. Susanne had canceled all appointments. She stood helplessly in the studio among the dead lamps, not daring to speak to Dimi, who sat with his face buried in his hands.

Dr. Fritsche came down the stairs, and Dimi jumped up.

"It's the shinbone, isn't it?"

"I've got to take your wife to the hospital, Martensen—I can't set it without an anesthetic." He went to the telephone, called for an ambulance, and turned back to Dimi.

"Which hospital should she go to?"

"The Diakonissen, she's been there before."

Dr. Fritsche shook his head. "Your wife tells me she doesn't want to go back there."

"But why not? She liked it there."

Upstairs Sophie could be heard, half sobbing, half screaming. He looked angrily at the doctor.

"Haven't you got anything, something to stop the pain, while we're waiting? Haven't you even given her an injection?"

Dr. Fritsche looked at him, then turned to Susanne. "Fräulein—would you mind leaving us for a moment?"

Susanne ran hurriedly to the door. The doctor waited till it had closed behind her.

"Martensen," he said quietly, "don't you know? I can't give your wife an injection, and at any rate, I'd rather try and manage without it—" He stopped, and gave a sigh, and stared into Dimi's tense, unsuspecting face. "Don't you know your wife is a morphine addict? Haven't you ever noticed the puncture marks on her thighs?"

Chapter 2 When Sophie woke from the anesthetic, at the Westend hospital, Yasmin was sitting by her bed. Not Dimi. Yasmin.

She closed her eyes. The pain in her left leg threatened to engulf her. She groaned and flung her head from side to side. Yasmin left the room, and returned with Dr. Fritsche.

"There," she said threateningly and pointed to the bed. "Are you going to leave her like that? Are you a doctor or a monster?"

"I can't square it with my conscience—giving more of the drug to an addict."

"I'm her mother, and I'm telling you this is *not* the moment to wean her off it."

Sophie was given morphine for four days, and then taken home in an ambulance, at her urgent request and to Fritsche's relief. She hadn't seen Dimi once during these four days, but the night nurse told her that he'd come the first night. What she didn't tell her patient was the way he'd stood over the bed, strangely stiff, and leaning away as if to avoid a bad smell from the pillows.

She hadn't tried to phone him, she knew Dr. Fritsche had seen her thighs. . . . In the late afternoon, the day she got home, she heard him slowly climb the stairs from the studio to their apartment. He sat by her bed and took her hand, which lay limply in his. She tried to catch his eyes, but he gazed obstinately at the floor. Tears constricted her throat, and she swallowed desperately to keep them at bay.

"Dimi—I'll give it up—you'll see!"

Absently, he stroked her hand.

"I don't know what's going to happen, Sophie. The thought that you—it makes me feel quite sick. I'm sorry to have to say it, but it's better that you know."

"And if I stop, Dimi? If I stop?"

"I don't know. I don't know how much there'll be left."

He came every day after work and sat by her bed for half an hour. It was the moment she waited for all day, listening to every sound, her despair growing. No question of cutting out the morphine, even for a day. On the contrary, she needed to take more of it to seem cheerful, and she let Wächter secretly enter the house. It was three packets at a time now.

"Do you realize what you've done?" she whispered hoarsely as he grinned at her. He shook his head.

"The way I see it, I'm your benefactor. You're a born sucker for the stuff, you're lucky to have me."

Yasmin came every day.

"Your marriage is kaput," she said. "There are worse things. You'll marry again, you're still young."

"*You* didn't—and you were a lot younger."

"I was too young, and it broke me. You'll never break. But right now you've got to get free of this drug."

"Yes," said Sophie. But she couldn't think how.

.

One day, as Yasmin was leaving, she turned back in the doorway.

"Your husband's having an affair. It's better for you to know."

Sophie lay still for a long time, then reached for the crocodile bag.

That evening she asked him about it when he came into the room, and he made no attempt at denial. "Pity," was all he said, "I wanted to tell you myself. But only when you were back on your feet. Your mother happened to see us together—"

"Susanne?"

He nodded. "It's not important, doesn't mean a thing to me. She knows."

Sophie said nothing. The crocodile bag had done its duty, she'd reached the pitch where nothing mattered. Poor Susanne. She even managed a little smile, saying: "Will this happen often now?"

"Probably."

She sat up and reached for his hand. "Dimi—do what you like, but, please, just one thing: don't take them to concerts—please! Promise me." Her eyes pleaded, her cheeks were flushed with urgency.

He had to laugh, and stroked her hand, which clasped his. Almost as before, thought Sophie. Then he glanced sadly at her, no doubt with the same thought.

"I promise."

.

In the weeks that followed Sophie tried day after day to ignore or suppress the longing for the injection. At first she thought that all she needed was to use her full willpower and the crocodile bag would be flung onto the rubbish heap. The full willpower lasted a couple of hours, before surrendering. Then *iron* will was pressed into service. And caved in shortly afterward. She hadn't counted on the pain, thought it was mere coincidence that her head was throbbing and that she felt a pressure ready to burst inside her. At the same time she fought not to cry out in panic, for Dimi would hear her, in the studio downstairs. The crocodile bag, quickly! Try again tomorrow.

. . . But as the daily backslidings began to mount up, her courage gradually disappeared, and with it all pretense of a will of her own. Who could she turn to? Only Dimi, Fritsche, and Yasmin knew. She was ashamed to talk to Dimi, and afraid of Fritsche. That left Yasmin, who, for her part, turned to her friends at the Turkish embassy, for advice.

"You must go to a clinic for a few weeks. There are some that specialize in it."

In an institution? For weeks on end? That would certainly cut the last threads that held her marriage together even if she succeeded. He still came home to eat most evenings, they still went for a drive in the Auburn-Cord on Sundays, or listened to music; there was still hope, though the tender intimacy and above all the laughter had disappeared. Sometimes he went out late at night, and Sophie didn't ask questions. She had no right to.

Even more than from the threat to her love, she suffered from the devastating rebuff her own will had dealt her. The claustrophobic terror of the cage, the prison, she was in kept pace with the sense of well-being the injections brought. Something had to happen, someone had to help her. Papa? Georg Wertheimer said he was now living in Baden-Baden with Keitje, within reach of a casino. It was as if he suspected something and had written her off. Worse still, though, was the prospect—coming closer!—of writing herself off.

The day came when somebody mentioned to her on the phone that she had seen Dimi at the Philharmonic the night before.

"I know," said Sophie, though she didn't, and added automatically: "I had toothache, I had to give my ticket to my cousin."

"Ah yes. The blond lady he was with."

She put her clenched fists to her face, sobbing, trembling, beginning to spiral down into the abyss, from which only the crocodile bag could save her.

•

Next morning she got up early and went into the sitting room. Dimi sat at the breakfast table, by the window. The winter sunshine fell across the table with its pretty Rosenthal china, which they'd looked for and found together. "Essential," he'd said then, "first thing in the morning, to start us off in the right mood."

He was just about to place an egg in its little cup, looked up in surprise and raised himself a little way from his chair, smiling at her. She sat down opposite him. He picked up the egg spoon, then put it down again. She clearly had something to ask him; one couldn't possibly devote one's attention to an egg.

"Why didn't you take me with you, the night before last? You know I love Kreisler."

He said nothing, thinking what a pity it was that he'd had to go and break his promise.

"Dimi—did you take someone else to the concert?" Quietly and without reproach, just to establish the facts.

A pity. A pity. In the wave of remorse that overcame him, and ashamed of the mess he'd got himself into, he groped involuntarily for the spoon, just for something to do, and beheaded the egg.

"Do you *have* to eat it when I'm talking to you?"

The spoon, with the little egg crown in it, hovered in midair— should he return to the egg with it, like a coward, or bravely put it on the plate?

"I thought I could trust you, it was the one thing I asked you to do for me."

Dreadful of me, he thought, deciding to save the sliver of egg from its exposed position by quickly eating it. Then he put the spoon down and braced himself for the coming storm. Instead, Sophie's hands came up to her face. Tears ran down between her fingers and dripped onto the tablecloth.

Had she already stuck the needle into herself today? The thought unnerved him so much that he reached for the spoon and attacked the egg again.

Sophie wiped away her tears. Her heart was pounding so strongly that she could feel the rhythmic throbbing in her head and throat at the same time. I'll *say* it, she thought. If I don't, I'll despise myself for the rest of my life. *Say* it. Now. *Ask* him—perhaps he'll say no—

"Dimi, would you—would you rather I moved out?"

Half the contents of the egg was still there. She stared at the remaining yolk cupped in gentle white and thought, as she had at Turhan's death, watching the crow hopping across the lawn: I'll never forget this half-finished egg, or the spoon, or his head bowed over it—

The spoon dipped twice more into the shell, and then returned to the plate; the head lifted, and the eyes looked calmly at her.

"Yes," he said. "I think that would be best."

Chapter 3

And she *hadn't* injected herself that morning. A big mistake, though past redeeming now. It took a double dose of the stuff to enable her to get out her luggage and pack, quite calmly, one piece after another.

Downstairs, August barked. *His* dog, nothing to do with her any more. From time to time she heard Dimi's voice, but the stuff kept faith with her and she didn't once stop to listen, just kept going, back and forth, carefully stacking and folding.

At lunchtime she rang the bell at Olivaerplatz, and put down her suitcases in the hall.

"Don't worry—I'm not moving in."

"Do you want something to eat?"

Sophie shook her head. Yasmin had some coffee brought for her. She herself sat down to a plate of shashlik.

"I'm getting fat," she said as she chewed. "Like all Eastern women. Mind you, you're too thin, you hardly eat a thing." She put her fork down for a moment. "Was it awful?"

Sophie told her.

"Remember," said her mother, mopping up the sauce with a piece of bread, "remember what I said to you about *Güte*. He hasn't got any, your Dimi, that's why he's no great loss. One can't even grieve, that's the pity of it. Why don't you go into the clinic now and try their treatment? Now's the right moment."

"Now's the wrong moment, I *need* the stuff. For the first time, really."

Yasmin immersed herself in a chocolate mousse. When she was finished she carefully wiped her mouth with a damask napkin, and looked at her daughter.

"You're making it easy for yourself. You refuse to suffer the way you ought to. But in time you'll pay for it, you'll see. You'll have to be rid of it one day, I'm sure you know that. I suppose you'll double

your ration, from today. But it's right now, when you're in real
trouble, that you should fight fire with fire. An old saying—with a lot
of sense. If your head aches, pinch your arm, and you won't feel the
headache anymore."

"I haven't got the strength, even to pinch myself."

"Don't be so feeble," said Yasmin, not without tenderness. "Well
then: what are you going to do?"

"Can you help me find somewhere to live? Somewhere small, I
haven't got any money. Then I'll have to get a job. Could you see me
through the next three months? I don't want to take anything from
Dimi."

"He hasn't got anything," said Yasmin calmly. "He's come twice to
sponge off me."

Sophie had to laugh. Besides, it did her good to picture Dimi as a
supplicant.

"I'm all in favor of your living alone. Never fall twice into the same
rut. I'll give you three hundred marks a month, until you're self-
sufficient."

"But—"

"I know. It's not enough to cover your 'ration.' But you're the kind
who only makes the worst of it, if others make life easy for you."

She had a choice: either live decently, with tiny rations—or in
squalor but with big enough doses to keep the longing for Dimi at
bay. It wasn't a hard decision, there was really no choice at all. She
took a furnished room behind Nollendorfplatz for sixty marks a
month. Perhaps Georg Wertheimer would—

He didn't even let her finish.

"Not a penny. I won't even mention it to your father, it would only
upset him, and he's not well at present. I've finally liquidated the
business, and he'll have to cut down now himself."

"Cut down? What about his gambling?"

"That's his problem. And your problem is your problem."

.

Nollendorfplatz. Her room was at the back, with the underground
trains emerging from their tunnel and rumbling past every twenty
minutes. There was no wardrobe, just a sort of partition with a curtain across it, so she never unpacked her better clothes. She didn't
like the landlady, or her son. Once, as she passed his room, the door
was open and she saw, over the bed, two crossed daggers with a

swastika flag above them, and beneath them a picture of the man with the forelock and the mustache. "Disreputable-looking individual," Papa had called him, when he had begun to "put on airs" a few years earlier. Now Sophie's daily paper, the *Berliner Tageblatt*, had a lot to say about him. She read it every day from end to end, and not just the classified ads. She couldn't sleep, often spent half the night at the window, brooding and crying. The trains, hurtling past, marked the passage of time, and she became almost fond of them. But the last one went by at two A.M., and then there were six long hours before breakfast coffee and the full syringe.

Wächter noticed, of course. Suddenly no taxi anymore; and for the first time she spat angrily at him: "If you don't drop your price I'll find somebody else."

"You just try," he grinned, but for once he paid for her coffee. "Hubby smelled something and threw you out, did he? Why don't you get a job?"

"Where? What sort of job?" she snarled. "Aren't there enough unemployed people looking for work?" Her jaws were clamped tightly together, the hand with the cup trembled.

"You're not from the moon, girl, you must be able to do *something—*"

"Nothing!" she screamed suddenly. The handful of seedy customers turned around to look, and the barman stepped out from behind the bar. It was routine. If she was going to have a fit, better throw her out. "I can't do anything! I haven't learned anything!" she yelled once more, piercingly. The barman advanced toward her—but she had already let her head sink to the dirty marble tabletop, sobbing, and he returned to the bar, reassured. Wächter fingered his long chin and calmly eyed the red hair and the heaving shoulders.

"Stop it, you silly cow, it's not the end of the world; you can have today's for free, all right? You speak well, you've seen something of the world, haven't you? Why don't you write it down, instead of howling? My brother's a journalist, writes about football—it's all he knows about, but he earns more than I do at the hospital."

·

She wrote a piece about Venice, and another about Hastings. She preferred the one on Venice, although it had little to say about the art treasures and only mentioned the architecture in passing. The whole thing was presented as a dream of the past, dreamed by a young girl lying stretched out in the bottom of a gondola, gliding through the water. The Dahde came into it a good deal, and Turhan, but no one else. The one about Hastings was rather pedantic by comparison, but perhaps it was a good idea to send in two contrasting pieces.

Yasmin volunteered the money for the rented typewriter, and Sophie typed with one finger, then with two, constantly having to start again because of mistakes.

One evening, late, her door opened. She hadn't heard anyone knock. The landlady's son stood in the doorway.

"Number one, Fräulein, don't type at night, I'm trying to sleep. Number two, why don't you learn to type properly, eh? One click every few seconds, it's enough to drive you mad. What are you typing, anyway?"

"An article."

"For a paper? I know someone that works on a paper." He went back to his room and returned with a newspaper printed in heavy type. "Here. Have a read of this. What are you writing about, then?"

"About Venice."

"Venice—that's in Italy, isn't it? Might be the sort of thing. Good bloke, Mussolini. You can read about him in there. When you've finished your typing, let me have it, they might be interested. Good night."

She closed the typewriter and took the newspaper to read in bed. *Der Völkische Beobachter*—that was *their* newspaper, wasn't it, the one with the banner headlines underlined in red. Toilet paper, Papa had called it. But could she afford to be choosy?

.

Yasmin paid—once again without remonstrating—for her shorthand-cum-typing course, had in fact been quite prepared to pay for private lessons, but Sophie refused. The time for special treatment was gone.

She plunged with a real frenzy into these oversubscribed classes, in shabby classrooms, surrounded by hundreds of pupils, who were mostly younger than she, and learned faster. Nonetheless a few weeks later she was able to type out both articles, slowly but without mistakes, and give them to "the son." In exchange he brought her a book from his room.

"Give it at least a quick read, or you won't stand a chance at the *Völkische*. You *are* Aryan, I suppose?"

"I'm what?"

"Read the book. Then you'll know."

After a few days she gave him back *Mein Kampf*, feeling rather shaken.

"Well? D'you know now?"

"Yes."

"And are you Aryan all right?"

"Yes."

.

But there she had a surprise coming.

When she told Yasmin over lunch that she might be going to work for the *Völkische Beobachter*, her mother stopped eating.

"You can't go there—you're not Aryan."

Sophie stared at her, openmouthed. "How d'you mean? Why aren't I?"

"Because I'm half Jewish. My mother came from Haifa. Your father may never have known, it didn't really matter then."

A few days later, when "the son" proudly informed her that she was summoned to the *Völkische*, something could perhaps be made out of her little effort on Venice, as long as she left out the black woman and made the whole thing a little more interesting politically, she lied to him that she'd already sold the article.

"Really? Who to?"

"The *Berliner Tageblatt*."

"The Jewish rag? I see—I might have known, with that red hair!" He left the room, slamming the door, before she could tell him that she owed that particular trait to her Aryan father. Next morning the landlady asked her to leave. She took it stoically, had already started to look for another room.

She sent copies of her article to every one of the newspapers in Berlin. The first answering letter came from Ullstein Verlag, Kochstrasse 22–26, Kreuzberg. Her first rejection? Thank you for your manuscript, unfortunately we—etcetera? She had the crocodile bag ready and waiting on the table before tearing open the envelope: Ten o'clock next Monday at the editor's office. Signature illegible.

She put the handbag away and for the first time opened the suit-

case with her good clothes in it. Brought out a black outfit from
Knieze, and a white blouse. Took both to Yasmin's, to iron; and went
there on Monday morning, early, to wash her hair and get made up.
The final touch: Papa's last present, a pair of earrings, two large,
cream-colored pearls.

"Why wear *them*?" asked Yasmin.

"To impress the editor," said Sophie grimly.

.

The bus set her down at the corner of Wilhelmstrasse and Kochstrasse. No. 22–26, an enormous, imposing building, eight stories
high. With a trembling hand, she held out her letter.

"Frau Mewes," said the porter, studying his book.

"Is that the editor?"

"That's it. Frau Mewes. Fourth floor, then to your left. Name's on
the door."

Frau Mewes waved a hand with long, dark-red fingernails in greeting, without looking up. "With you in a moment," she said, signing a
pile of documents on her desk. Sophie sat down and studied her.
Straight, white hair around a young face, white blouse and skirt—
Frau Mewes looked like a determined, enterprising seagull. She
signed the last piece of paper and put it aside.

"How d'you do, Frau—or is it Fräulein Martensen?"

"Frau. How d'you do."

The Seagull studied her, taking her time.

"Yes," she said at last. "Still very young. That's what I thought
when I read your pieces. Twenty-two? Twenty-three?"

"Twenty-five."

"Aha. Well—I liked them both, each in its own way. What I liked
best of all was that you didn't try to lecture people about Venice, city
of the arts, or the battle of Hastings, 1066. You carefully left all that
out. Cunning."

"That wasn't why."

"No? Why, then?"

"Ignorance."

The Seagull laughed. "So much the better. If you invented the
whole thing from scratch—"

"I've been to Venice and Hastings. I just wasn't interested in all
the historical business."

"Aha," said Frau Mewes. She always said it, when she wanted to gain time. "What were you doing there? Were you on holiday?"

"A sort of quarantine," said Sophie, and wondered why she'd confided this.

"Did you need a little break, from home?"

"I spent three years in England," said Sophie stiffly, changing tone.

"Aha. Then you speak good English. Can you type? Shorthand?"

"Only sixty words a minute."

"That'll do. I think we could use you in the English section. You'd be reading English newspapers and cataloguing articles according to topics of international interest, or specific German interest, or simply finding revealing and unusual items about English life—I have a feeling you've got a nose for the unusual, that is, to judge by your gondola dream. The nurse—what was she called, again?"

"Dahde," said Sophie.

"That's right—I liked her best of all. You must tell me more about her. Yours is the rare case where one wants to know *more*, for instance about this Dahde, and Turhan. It's usually the opposite. Do they exist, those two?"

"They're dead."

"Aha." A pause. "But if you're going to tell us about them, you've got to give us a clear picture. You know, a newspaper article has to lay it on more thickly than, say, a book. An article is short, the reader doesn't have a lot of time or patience, but he still wants to be caught up and get something out of it, while reading in the underground or on the bus, d'you understand?"

"I'll have a go."

"Good. Here are your pieces with my comments. Work on them a bit, all right? I think we might be able to find a place for the one on Venice next Sunday, in our serial section. Meanwhile I'll introduce you to our business manager, he'll want your details, name, age, and so on. I get the feeling you've never worked in an editor's office before—"

"I've never worked anywhere before."

"Don't tell him that, will you, or you'll get the minimum wage. How much were you expecting, anyway?"

"I don't know."

"Do you have to live off it? Or is this just to keep you busy?"

"I have to live off it and—buy some things as well."

"Three hundred a month?"

"I can't manage on that."

"My dear girl!" exclaimed the Seagull. "You don't seem to understand. Three hundred is often enough for a family man with children." She had got up, and her eyes, though not unfriendly, were firm and final. Sophie also got up, reaching for her handbag. "You'll have to learn to do without *that* sort of thing!" said the Seagull, eyeing the crocodile skin. Sophie giggled inwardly, and headed for the door.

The Seagull followed, offering her hand. "Well then—to our future collaboration," she said in a slightly strangled voice and clasped Sophie's hand.

"Thank you." And, finding that the woman didn't let go of her hand, Sophie said again: "Many thanks—goodbye."

A second later she found herself in the Seagull's arms. She tried to free herself, but the white wings held her tight, and she had to struggle not to completely surrender her mouth. The Seagull kiss lasted for what seemed an eternity. Finally she was released and able to steady herself and clear her head. Ping—something had hit the floor. An earring! The pearl had broken from its setting under the Seagull's onslaught and was rolling along the parquet floor.

"Oh God," said the Seagull.

"Doesn't matter." Sophie caught the pearl and slipped it into her bag, using the time to recover.

"Frau Mewes—it's not really my line, that sort of thing. I'm sorry, I hope you won't hold it against me."

"Hold it against you? Are you mad? You mean—you're *not* queer? That's odd, I'm hardly ever wrong." Once again the birdlike eyes peered hard at her.

"Should I . . . *not* go and see the business manager, now?"

"Why not, for goodness sake?" said the Seagull in astonishment. "What on earth do you think of me?"

Sophie bent forward and kissed her on the cheek.

"Thank you."

Chapter 4 Just before eight o'clock in the evening, on Sophie's fifth day in the hospital, Lutz was walking up and down the empty corridor. The lift door opened, and Dr. Karanogliu emerged.

"Excuse me, Doctor—"

"Yes?" Then he recognized the man; Sophie's husband. "Herr Reinhold, isn't it?"

"Could you spare me a few minutes?"

At the far end of the corridor stood a couple of wicker chairs, and a table with old magazines, to accommodate relatives and friends who had, on occasion, to be abruptly ushered from the sickroom. When the nurse subsequently left the room, carrying a discreetly covered basin, they slipped back in again. Visiting time was long since over for the night, and the wicker chairs had each been set at the same angle to the table, correct, primed for inspection, and the tattered old magazines full of completed crossword puzzles had been carefully stacked as if brand-new.

"What can I do for you, Herr Reinhold?" He made it sound as if he had unlimited time at his disposal, but he was nervously fingering the little apparatus in his coat pocket. Sophie was waiting for him. Any moment she could raise the roof—

"I won't ask you how my wife's coming along, Doctor. I know. I just want to know why she won't see me. I come here from the office twice a day, it's a long way, once during lunch hour and again at six o'clock."

"What sort of work do you do—if you don't mind me asking?"

"I'm a music reviewer for the *Süddeutsche*. Not their number-one critic, of course. Number two or three, as it were. I have to go out most evenings, to cover some concert that number one doesn't find interesting enough. The sister tells me that my wife only talks at night, and then solely to you. She's only once paid me the slightest attention—that was when she wanted something for her 'book.' What does she mean by that, Doctor?"

"Your wife is on morphine." Lutz's face betrayed nothing. "She's in a twilight zone where she can't clearly distinguish whether she's talking or writing the book she apparently always wanted to write. She's using me as a kind of catalyst—"

"And as father confessor?"

The young doctor hesitated. This man, Sophie's husband, had really rather a remarkable face beneath the stubbly beard and the long, uncombed locks hanging low over his forehead. The eyes fixed him with a gaze at once melancholy and scornful.

"Please don't forget, she only tells me disconnected bits, Herr Reinhold. Somehow, in the wanderings of her mind, she thinks she's spending all day writing her chapters, which I mysteriously get to read. There's no logic to it. I'm only there at night."

"Ought *I* to stay up with her one night?"

"I don't know—it's very tiring, if you have to work all next day."

"It's Saturday today, I'm not working tomorrow."

His coat pocket began to buzz, and on the panel in the corridor light flashed by his number, and by No. 384.

"That's your wife. You go in—I'll wait here."

Lutz grabbed his crumpled checked cap and put it on his head before disappearing into Room 384.

I should have gone in with him, thought the doctor, then she might have restrained herself and let him stay a bit—

His thoughts got no further. The door to Room 384 burst open and Lutz stumbled out as if given a sharp kick from behind. He was still wearing the hat, which looked even more battered than before, and closed the door with artificial calmness, knowing he was being watched. He took a deep breath and marched back to the wicker chairs, sat down, took off his hat and patted it into shape.

"It belongs to my friend," he said, stroking it. "It's a sort of talisman, for me. When I've got something difficult to do, he lends it to me, but it's not infallible—as you just saw."

"Does your wife need me?"

"Yes. Yes, of course. She wants to write some more."

As if on cue the buzzing noise came from his pocket. Let her wait, thought the doctor.

"You're looking very pale, Herr Reinhold. Why don't you sit here and rest for a moment? Shall I order you a taxi?"

But Lutz was already on his feet, and putting on his hat.

"I'm all right now. Just a little anemic, that's all. My friend is waiting for me downstairs. He's got a car."

235

Incessant buzzing from his pocket. The doctor brought out the small apparatus, pressed a button and switched Sophie off.

"Go to her, Doctor. And thank you for everything you're doing for her. They'll know where to find me at the office. I won't come any more—unless you send word."

.

"Has he gone?"

He sat down on the chair, and for a moment even thought of taking out his book.

"What's the matter, Brother? Are you angry with me? I ought to be angry with *you*! The door opens—at last. And what comes marching in? Lutz. How could you allow it? I've got no time to be nice anymore, don't you understand that? Every minute counts."

He sat on the edge of her bed and took her hand, as always, and she pressed it to her cheek, as always.

"What exactly is the matter between you and your husband?"

"You'll find out. I haven't got there yet." She was silent for a moment, frowning. "Was he alone or was my nephew with him?"

"He said a friend was waiting for him downstairs."

"My nephew. That's what I call him—I have no nephews. Nice boy. Looks after Lutz. Brother! Brother! We're wasting so much time. Where were we—we'd met the Seagull, hadn't we? The Seagull was my salvation, you must have gathered that, and not only because of the three hundred marks a month. I urgently needed two things: work, demanding, tiring work, and a friend, a girl my own age. She was ten years older, but as young as a spring chicken. She was a lesbian, of course—but then again she wasn't. She lunged for whatever attracted her, and the best thing about her was the completely ungrudging way she took a rebuff. She was utterly generous, noble even, there's no other word for it. And when someone misunderstood her chivalry, and exploited it, she was always rather amazed, no more than that, never bitter or vindictive—why are you giving me that strange look, Brother, what's the matter?"

"But you yourself—you were a—"

"Lesbian? Not at all. What makes you think that?"

"But—your stepmother—after all, you—"

"Anita?" She said nothing for a short while. "Yes," she said at last, reflectively. "When you tell that sort of thing, of course, it's labeled 'queer.' But it was something utterly different between Anita and me, it was a completely pure love, the sort that goes the whole way. If she'd been a humpback I wouldn't have noticed it, or maybe I would have cherished her all the more. Children have no real grasp of beauty as such, and I didn't love Anita because she was beautiful but because she was Anita. And also—though naturally I only realized it much later—because Papa had paved the way for me. I *was* Papa, inasmuch as I could be; it wasn't till much later that he gradually began to lose his grip on me. And never completely, not to this day." She was breathing with a struggle, wheezing. "Now I'm back to Papa —absurd. At the time he was being well looked after in Baden-Baden, with his Keitje—*there* was a woman! Where am I—I'm losing the thread, Brother—"

"You were telling about the Seagull, and your work."

"Yes. Yes." But she was still fighting to breathe, and had to take her hand from his, to press both fists against her chest. Without waiting any longer he went into the bathroom and returned with the syringe.

"Thank you," she breathed, her eyes closed. This time it took several minutes, while he watched her closely and put his ear to her chest, before she opened her eyes again. But not with the radiance that always amazed him; they looked feverish, and full of fear.

"So little time," she whispered. "And still so much to write. I'll never manage it, Brother."

"Yes, you will. I'll give you another one whenever you need it. This was just a small one."

A lie, but it worked. The promise was enough; her face relaxed, her eyes rested, and her hand found its way back into his.

.

The Seagull even hit upon a place for me to live. In her house, in a decent neighborhood. That suddenly became important, you know, I couldn't have gone on living behind Nollendorfplatz. Suddenly the streets were full of trucks carrying men with armbands—they weren't allowed to wear uniforms yet—brawling and shouting for the "Reds" to come out, and when they found any there were shots, and blood on the walls, and people ran into doorways and hid, and pretended they hadn't seen anything. Early every morning I took the bus to Kochstrasse, and there were already long dole queues on the pavements. Everyone in the bus craned their necks and gawked, and we were glad when the bus moved on, but each of us was wondering where in God's name all this would end. In my little top-floor flat, however—two pretty, unfurnished attic rooms with sloping walls—I could play deaf and dumb. At the office, of course, there were violent arguments every day, precisely because we were "Jew-ridden," as the phrase went. One group shouting "Alarmists! Defeatists! Merchants of doom!" and the other "Blind fools! Take off your blinkers!" Both insisting they had a responsibility toward their readers. But none of them, Brother, not even the most pessimistic of them, not one of them foresaw what would happen—or how fast.

Yasmin was so pleased about my job at the newspaper that she bought me a bed. More than that I wouldn't allow. I was saving up, and every week purchased something secondhand, a chair, a table, a cupboard, nothing fancy, only serviceable pieces, and every one filled me with pride. If I'd been able to give Wächter up—at least he kept his word and didn't raise the price any further—I could have gone a cut above the merely serviceable, but every so often it was still oh-oh-too-too.

The Seagull soon noticed, of course, with her sharp bird's eyes. And she raised the roof. Back and forth she stormed in my attic till the people living below started banging on their ceiling with a broom. I was a criminal, I was evil, a filthy, depraved creature, she was going to throw me out at once, I could go and blow my brains out for all she cared, in the gutter, in public toilets, anywhere as long as she was rid of this obscenity.

I cowered in a corner, on the floor, and never said a word. The tornado raged way above me, and meant nothing. I saw the Seagull's face, grotesquely contorted, but she shouted in a foreign language, one I didn't understand; I'd just had my shot, I was at peace, blissfully at peace. If only she'd stop and I could make some coffee.

At last she fell exhausted into my only chair and began to cry. I brought her a handkerchief and gazed curiously at her.

"I'm sorry," she said, and vigorously blew her nose. "I really don't know what came over me. I must be very fond of you, and the thought that you're about to kill yourself, at the age of twenty-five—"

I listened attentively, understood none of it. Kill myself? What nonsense. I was fine, getting better every day. Admittedly I took two fixes a day now, but I hardly ever wailed for Dimi any more, did my work at the office well, even with enthusiasm—what more did she want?

I made the coffee, in my tiny kitchen, and she came and stood in the doorway.

"Listen to me—you've got to have treatment."

"I'm not going into a hospital."

"We'll do it right here, in your own room. And I'll help you, I'll find out exactly how it's done. You'll see—we'll make it. All you need is goodwill."

I remembered my own attempts, the full will and the iron one. Now it was the turn of the *good* one. Fine by me.

.

The Seagull was in a frenzy to start the cure at once, while I kept finding reasons to put it off. I'd only just started at the office, only been there three months—how could I suddenly take a few days off, perhaps even a week? "Leave it to me," said the Seagull. "I'm your boss. I'm sending you to London—officially. There's no time to lose. I have an appointment with a doctor tomorrow, and he's going to tell me exactly what to do."

.

I waited peacefully for her in my attic room, had just had a fix. Not even the Seagull's furrowed brow, as she came in, could disturb my perfect serenity. She accepted a Cognac, but wouldn't sit down, and paced back and forth.

"It's more complicated than I thought. And it takes at least three weeks—"

"Then don't let's do it, Frau Mewes. Or we could leave it till some other time, when it's more convenient, during the holidays—"

She stopped in front of me and twirled the glass, threateningly. "*Now*, or—"

"Or?" I asked cheerfully.

"Or I'll report you tomorrow, as a drug addict."

It was a hefty blow, and not even my wonder weapon could shield me from it.

"Well then?"

"Frau Mewes—"

"Yes or no?"

She meant it. Shit.

.

Next day I left for London—officially. No one knew the truth except Yasmin, who was to watch over me during the day, while the

Seagull was at work. At first meeting they understood one another perfectly, and were soon on first-name terms. The Seagull was called Alice, with the emphasis on the second syllable. Aleece would come at six every evening, to relieve Yasmin and spend the night with me in the attic. On the sofa in my sitting room.

"Don't worry," she said with a meaningful bird-glance. "It's the cure we're concerned with now, and nothing else. Besides—I don't want to scare you, but it isn't going to be a cakewalk. Tonight you had your last full dose. Tomorrow it's going to be halved. And halved again next week. Then halved again. Then none at all."

Later she admitted to me that the doctor had held out little hope. "It requires extraordinary determination and fortitude," he warned her, "of the patient, because of the pain, and of you, because you have to watch and not give in. *Yours* is the harder task." He had given her Eudokal and Pantopon pills, by way of sedatives, and declared himself ready to come at any time, and inject Somnifen or Luminal to enable me to sleep.

Ah, Brother—you know what it's like, of course. Even today it's almost impossible to kick the habit, except under hospital conditions, and now there are far stronger painkillers available. But at the beginning of the thirties, people were still fairly helpless.

The Seagull and Yasmin were partly prepared for it. But they thought it wiser not to tell me too much, except: "Yes, yes, Sophie—that's how it is at this stage, be patient, you'll just have to put up with it." And panic and rage convulsed me as strongly as the physical pain.

The first few days were surprisingly easy, and the Seagull glowed, and Yasmin praised me. My room was full of books, magazines, the radio blaring all the time. Yasmin bought dozens of records, tirelessly cranked up the gramophone, played my favorite operas, my favorite symphonies, and took no notice of my irritability and occasional outbursts. At night the Seagull left the door open between my bedroom and the sitting room; the keys had vanished, even to the bathroom, and the front door was locked.

On the fifth day it started. The pain, the freezing cold, and violent attacks of the shivers. Yasmin fed me with Pantopon to keep me quiet, but I yelled and cursed her through chattering teeth. She put me in a hot bath, almost scalding me—that helped a bit. She rang up the Seagull at Ullstein's, and spoke the agreed codeword: "Frau Mewes? Your niece has caught a heavy cold." And the Seagull flew home at once. I screamed and cursed them both, amazed to discover what a range of filthy curses I had on tap.

And then the first, dreadful, sleepless night. Sleepless for the Seagull too, of course. When Yasmin rang the front doorbell in the morning to relieve her, I watched her reeling sleepily toward the door. Here was my chance. I waited till she finally managed to get the key into the lock, and opened the door, then I jumped on her, as I was, in my nightdress, pushed her out of the way, and tried to get past Yasmin and out into the stairwell. But Yasmin stood like a rock, and the Seagull seized me from behind, clapping a hand across my mouth so that I couldn't scream.

The doctor came and injected me full of sedatives, while Yasmin and the Seagull held me by the arms and legs. I tried to spit in his face, but I couldn't, my mouth was completely dry. Then I did sleep for an hour or two, woke up with every limb in pain and shaking with cold as if I were plugged into an electrical circuit. Yasmin carried me once more to a hot bath—I passed out—she pulled my head out of the water—I came to again—struck out blindly, drenching her from head to foot—screamed for all I was worth. The people in the flat below banged on the ceiling again, then threatened to call the police—the Seagull came, speechless with exhaustion, bringing the doctor and the injection of Luminal. But this time it wore off after only half an hour.

Yasmin had gone, we were alone. I fell to my knees before the chair where the Seagull lay, shattered, and cried, begged, threatened —till she gave in. Fetched the syringe from her handbag; and I jabbed it into my arm through the nightdress, right there, kneeling on the floor. I hugged her knees, lay my head against them, the agonizing pressure, the pain, the cold—all gone.

"You poor child," was all she said. Then she stood up, took her coat and handbag and went to the door. But she didn't make it, fell, as she was, onto the sofa, and lay motionless. Whereas I was newborn, pain-free and blissful, looking for something to do, I felt so well, but my legs wouldn't even carry me to my clothes. I dragged myself on all fours to the telephone. What was the time, anyway? Two in the morning. Never mind. I rang up Yasmin. She answered at once, her sleepy voice fraught with anxiety.

"Yasmin? No more pain—everything's all right again—I'm so happy—"

She hung up.

I decided to take no notice. I woke up only on the rare occasions when something punched me really hard. Then I came to for a short time and looked around me in amazement. And around me, Brother, were nothing less than the first years of the Third Reich.

Chapter 5

In 1934 the publishing house of Ullstein was "brought into line," in other words all the non-Aryan "elements" were to be eliminated. Sophie, being one-quarter Jewish, was examined at great length by the inspectors into racial probity. She had two first-rate Aryan grandparents to declare, on the Berglund side, an unmentionable Jewish grandmother from Haifa, and a questionable (since he was of uncertain category) Turkish grandfather, Mustafa Karabey. The committee at first postponed their decision, they had to find out whether a Turkish Muslim could be classified as Aryan or not. It turned out he *could*, Sophie was benevolently informed, he was a Caucasian, and she could henceforth regard herself as an Aryan, and continue to sit on public benches. She must, however, give up all hope of joining the Party.

That evening she went to see the Seagull.

"Alice, I'm going to emigrate to England. They can stick the job at Ullstein's."

"That's exactly how I feel," said the Seagull and tore up the four birth certificates of her impeccably Aryan grandparents from Bremen. "I'm coming with you. Perhaps they could use me at Balthus Books in London, I've done business with them for years." She fell silent, and took a sip of Cognac. "The trouble is—" She hesitated, couldn't bring herself to say it.

"Oh, *that's* all right." Sophie oozed imperturbability, newly injected confidence. "One can get the stuff over there too, it's only a question of making the right contacts. I'm meeting Wächter tomorrow, he'll probably know some, his kind are always in touch, internationally."

"You belong to 'his kind' too, you do realize that, don't you?"

Sophie left the room, shrugging her shoulders. Why pick on her, when she was in such a good mood!

Next day, a couple of errors showed up in her calculations. The first error was Yasmin; over lunch she made it clear that she was staying in Germany. The Nazis were really no worse than the last Turkish sultan had been, and, like him, they would pass. No need for panic. Her friends at the Turkish embassy had told her all would be all right. And England—with that climate—what a dreadful thought! And she'd no intention of going back to Turkey.

"But you're not safe here, you're half Jewish."

"For that matter, I'm half Muslim. All this nonsense has nothing to do with me."

"It has—you've got a German passport."

"The embassy will protect me."

.

Error number two was Wächter. He failed to turn up at their usual Moabit rendezvous. He'd answered oh-oh-too-too the day before, and promised to bring her an extra-large supply. She waited over an hour at her usual table, in the café, struck by how empty the place was. Everything seemed to have changed lately, different kinds of people seemed to be sitting in the restaurants, different kinds of people swaggering through the streets—or was it just that they were so conspicuous in their brown uniforms and black boots? There were no SA uniforms here in the café, but the old familiar faces had all gone. She went over to the counter. The barman sat alone in the corner, motionless.

"Excuse me—you know the gentleman I sometimes sit here with—" He made no sign, neither yes or no, just looked at her. "Perhaps he left a message for me?" A shake of the head. "I'd like to make a phone call."

The man's eyes drifted slowly, as if half asleep, around the room. Without looking at her and hardly moving his lips, he whispered: "They picked him up this morning. Clear off. Don't come back. Don't ring up."

She walked out of the place like someone half stunned by an up-

percut, not feeling the pain yet but not sure of his feet, either. Out-side she stumbled and held onto a lamp post. A man approached—
"Hello there, girlie?"—and she ran across the street, amazed to find her feet working after all.

At home she totted up her remaining vials of morphine. She'd been getting extravagant recently, had sometimes injected three a day, but had saved up extra cash for Wächter—

Down the stairs to the Seagull. Who chewed one of her white strands of hair for a while, before committing herself.

"What you're asking of me is of course out of the question. But—"

"Yes?" Why was she shouting, she'd only just had a fix, why was she shaking, breaking into a sweat, why was her breath coming in gasps? The Seagull looked away.

"I know someone. Had to throw him out, a few years ago. He used to work in the photography department; one of his colleagues in-formed on him. He had a wife, and a father to keep. I got him a job at Agfa, and vouched for him myself. He must have become more careful, because he's still there now."

"Alice!"

"Stop it, I can't stand this hysterical yelling." The Seagull struck her own forehead with the flat of her hand, but spoke quite calmly. "That *I* should have come to this! Middleman in the drug world. Do you really understand what it is you're doing?"

Sophie fell to her knees on the floor, her hands covering her face, rocking back and forth in muffled, ragged sobs. The Seagull stood up abruptly.

"Get out of here."

Two days later she appeared in Sophie's attic.

"Here you are," she said, and handed her a slip of paper, without looking at her. "That's his address. He knows."

Sophie didn't dare thank her, clasping the piece of paper between her palms, which she raised as if in prayer.

"How much money have you got?"

"Eight hundred and fifty marks."

"Will that last you for a while?" Sophie nodded silently. "Now listen to me: I'm going to London tomorrow. See what's up at Bal-thus Books, for me, and possibly also for you. The labor permit is the biggest problem—England is crammed with refugees, and people are beginning to resent it. Here's your ticket to London. Put it somewhere safe. As soon as I know anything, I'll wire you, then you can come over."

.

The new "contact" was called Heinrich Bosse, a short, stringy man with a bald head and a gray, taciturn face. He was a good deal cheaper than Wächter, and she was wiser now—no taxi. She went on foot, wearing her oldest clothes.

He had brought along a small package, and she at once hurried off to the toilets, strolling calmly back a little later, to the corner table in the little fish restaurant in Halensee, not far from the Kurfürstendamm, which now replaced Moabit. She sat opposite him, and the light caught her hair from behind, giving her a red halo. She smiled at him, carefree, buoyant, light as a feather. He didn't smile back, eyed her with watery, suspicious eyes.

"I'm doing this for Frau Mewes. How much do you need?"

"As much as you can get."

He glanced at her pale, eager young face and the red halo around it—and looked away. Till now his own sources had been reliable, he said in a tight, low voice. The Nazis followed every trail—except the one that Goering used, which led to Sweden. He twisted his mouth into a smile. His, Bosse's, wife was Swedish, like Goering's first wife; one of his sources was a relative of the first Mrs. Goering, a distant relative; still, it worked.

"You're in clover then," said Sophie enviously.

"In clover?" he repeated, and suddenly his look was full of hatred. "Why do you take the stuff, anyway? Are you crazy? Some sort of imbecile?"

"Well, *you* take it."

"I've got a punctured lung, every breath is—" He left the sentence unfinished, as if it wasn't worth his while. "But you! You don't have to, but you do, because it's made easy for you."

"Easy?" hissed Sophie, the yellow eyes glittering. "How would you know what I've been through—"

He didn't let her finish, got up to go, then leaned once more across the table and whispered: "You've got no idea, have you—and it's none of my business, I'm doing it for you because of Frau Mewes.

245

But I'll tell you this—if you don't stop soon, you'll find yourself lying in a corner one day like a flea-ridden old rat, and there won't be a soul to help you to your feet, you can depend on that."

He left before she could find an answer, and, anyway, there wasn't one. She sat for a while, her trembling hands stroking the crocodile bag, now taut and full.

·

The Seagull had left, without saying goodbye, but Sophie didn't worry. She knew by now that normal friendly relations were a thing of the past. Either people didn't "know" and had to remain strangers, or became accomplices like Yasmin and the Seagull, gritting their teeth—but steadfast. She began to pack her belongings. A telegram from England could come any moment, and then—on her way. Did her new Swedish nightingale perhaps build nests in England, too?

She plucked up the courage to ask Herr Bosse, at their next rendezvous, since he was less aggressive this time, merely indifferent and matter-of-fact. He shook his head: no, he had no contacts in England. Oh God. Did that mean she would have to stay in Germany? She rang the Seagull once, and cautiously hinted at her dilemma. To which the Seagull said calmly: "Die in a Nazi gutter, then, it's all you deserve." And hung up.

It resolved the dilemma. If she was going to die in the gutter, she could do that just as well in England. For the time being there was no reason to change her plans. Until now a little hole had always opened, at the last minute, for her to slip through.

She went on working at Ullstein's, doing overtime so as to stockpile the vials. What else was there to be done? Of the few acquaintances she had, most had emigrated, whether Jews or not. She hardly missed them. The "stuff" had placed her in a sort of glass box, and there were only purely functional openings to the outside world; only the voices she *needed* rang out loud and clear, the rest mumbled somewhere outside.

·

Georg Wertheimer rang up one morning. Papa had suffered a mild stroke the month before—no, no cause for alarm, now he was home again, and would be glad of a visit from her. With a loud report the walls of her glass box shattered, she quickly fixed another rendezvous in Halensee, then took the next train.

246

Chapter 6

Baden-Baden. Change at Stuttgart. It was getting dark by the time she arrived. Papa's address didn't sound good, it wasn't a hotel, but a *"Pension* for Distinguished Guests from Home and Abroad" in a narrow lane behind the marketplace. She left her suitcase downstairs with a grimy woman in the kitchen and made her way along a dark corridor, on the ground floor. Herr Berglund couldn't manage stairs, last room on the left, Fräulein.

He was sitting in a wheelchair, by the window.

"Papa?"

The big snow-white head turned slowly around to her, the mouth tried to smile, but only one corner went up, the other drooped in slack folds of skin. Even the eye seemed to hang at a slight angle, deeply shadowed by an anxious lid. The other half of the face was normal, and its eye frosty.

"Pretend I've just been to the dentist, that often leaves one with a crooked expression like this, doesn't it, and later on it comes back to life again. That's how it is with me at the moment. Give it a few weeks. Sit down."

Sophie took off her coat, sat down beside him and took his hand.

"Why didn't you let me know at once?"

"I didn't know whether I was going to pull through. Deathbed scenes in the hospital—not my sort of thing. The stroke was on the right side, thank God, it means the left is affected, the right still works. I can even write, if I could think of anyone to write to." He read the question in her face. "Keitje? In the casino, where else."

"But you need someone to look after you, Papa."

"The casino doesn't open till six in the evening. There's a nurse who comes and fumbles around, ghastly woman, I'm glad to be rid of her for a few days, she's on holiday. That's why I phoned Georg, to ask you. . . . Besides, I've got books and a radio, but I don't turn it on much, in case I have *another* stroke. Have you *heard* the fellow? At his Party rallies?"

"I'm leaving, Papa, I'm going to England."

"So Georg told me. Good for you." A long pause. She squeezed his hand and felt the answering squeeze. "Let's have no tears, Sophie. I'm glad you're getting out, even if it means I won't see you again. No tears, girl, I can't stand it. What's happened to your looks? You're only—what?—twenty-seven, twenty-eight? D'you drink? Then I don't understand. Pity. You look older. You've shrunk. Too thin, of course. Take the cap off."

She knew what he wanted, and held out her head to him like a dog to be stroked. He stretched out his good hand, and let the red strands glide through his fingers.

"What's wrong with you—have you got a boyfriend?"

"No." He looked sharply at her. "Nor a girlfriend, Papa, at least not in *that* sense."

"You ought to divorce that Yugoslavian gigolo of yours. Something else might turn up. You still mooning around after him?"

"No, Papa. We're already divorced."

"Good. The first time I saw you with him, I was afraid he had you by the nose. Never let yourself become dependent on anyone, promise me that."

"I promise, Papa."

He eyed her, gave a crooked smile.

"You're lying. Like all women."

She raised her head and looked him in the face. "Anita once said you weren't bulletproof yourself, Papa."

"Did she say that? Well, well."

"She said that if something came at you from behind and you weren't ready for it, it would knock you out quite easily."

He turned his head and looked out of the window. It was pitch dark outside. He nodded. "Turhan. That—came from behind."

"Papa, this business about not being dependent—it isn't *possible*. And if you're always on your guard and being careful, you don't live."

"I don't know," he said slowly, "why I suddenly think of my father so often. Certainly not for pleasure. One or two things—I told you, didn't I, for instance, that he had to break in my mother's new shoes, d'you remember?"

"And sometimes he'd fall over." She laughed, then fell silent, frightened, as he slowly turned his eyes toward her.

"When she died, they laid her out in the drawing room with

candles and flowers around her. He crept in, carrying something under his arm; I couldn't see what it was. Then he came out and *I* crept in, I wanted to know what it was that he meant her to take to the grave. I couldn't find anything, but her head lay higher than it had before. I reached under the white satin pillow—felt something hard. A pair of high-heeled shoes! At that moment the front doorbell rang, it must have been the undertakers come to nail the coffin down and take it away, so I only had a few seconds to make up my mind." He stopped. Sophie waited, but he was looking out of the window again, had forgotten her.

"You left the shoes there, Papa?"

"Do you know, I often feel them pressing into me. Just now, for instance, as you came in. Here, at the back of my neck." He leaned his head back, twisting it from side to side. "Not that I believe in an afterlife, can't stand all that metaphysical twaddle, but I feel something digging into me, right here, as if the heels were pressing into my neck."

"Dimi taught me how to give a massage, Papa—"

"Massage won't help. And it's all utter nonsense, anyway. Why should they dig into *me*? After all, the whole thing was between him and her, nothing to do with me. And she was a wicked woman, believe me, I can feel it in *me*, how wicked she was. Enough of that, now, I don't know why I mentioned it. But there's something you could do for me—"

"Whatever you want, Papa, if you only knew, how much I'd love to—"

"Ever been to a gambling casino? No?" The good half of the face drooped in disappointment, till it almost resembled the lifeless one. "Well then, it'll have to be roulette, and I'll try to fill you in somehow. You go into the big room with the long tables covered in green baize. You'll find they've got numbers written on them. The highest is thirty-six. Sit as near to it as you can, and don't do a thing till the last six numbers have *failed* to come up twelve times in a row, d'you understand?"

"Where do they come from, Papa?"

"Idiot," he grumbled. "The little ball on the turntable lands by a number, and they call it out. So you listen carefully and be sure to notice whether any of the last six, that's from thirty to thirty-six, get called out. If they do, you start counting. And if none of these numbers have recurred for twelve turns in a row, then there's a good chance one of them will, and you put the money on the next turn. Open the cupboard over there. At the bottom, right at the back, the mountaineering boots—bring them here. Are they still stuffed with paper? Good. Take it all out, all that newspaper stuff—carefully now! Slowly!"

The last balls of newspaper were extracted, and, behind them, a roll of banknotes.

"Count them. There should be roughly ten thousand. My last ten thousand, Keitje's confiscated the rest. I'm not allowed to gamble anymore. *She* does, though. She even wins, sometimes. When all's said and done, she's no fool. She doesn't let me play the devil with her, and you know women haven't had too good a time with me, except—"

"Except for Amina. I know, Papa. What was it about her? What did she have that was so special?"

"Nothing. Apart from her youth—and perhaps a certain indolence that pleased me. My romantic vein dries up fast, and then all that's left is the question: is she of use or isn't she? Keitje *is*."

"I know you better than that, you're not that coldblooded."

"Sophie, listen to me: I want one last fling! *You* go and play for me. Ten times. At the desk get yourself ten one-thousand-mark chips, sit down at the table and wait, the way I told you. Put on a single one-thousand chip at a time. Hang onto your winnings. Only play with whatever you've got there in your hand. Then go back to your hotel —you can't spend the night here. Come back tomorrow evening, after six, and bring me the money."

·

It was nine o'clock by the time she reached the casino, and she was tired. Tired and full of anxiety should she let Papa down. His last bit of money! Well, not exactly a "bit"—ten thousand marks.

She left her suitcase at a little hotel not far from Papa's *pension* behind the market square. Who knows, perhaps she'd be moving into the Grand Hotel later tonight; Papa would surely give her some portion of his winnings.

The commissionaire looked at her with some suspicion as she climbed the broad steps to the entrance, both arms folded stiffly across her chest like an Egyptian Ushapti. Under the left arm a large crocodile bag jutted out, while the right arm crossed over the left, to

protect the precious bag, for tonight it contained three irreplace-
ables: the usual one in its inside compartment, the ticket to London,
and Papa's last bankroll.

The room with the two green tables was only half full; Hitler had
no liking for gambling casinos and the place survived only from day
to day. She found herself a chair at one end, right beside the last six
numbers, and looked around. There were two croupiers, a young one
with pomaded black hair, holding a rake, and an older one standing
behind him. The red-white-and-black turntable, the little ball, the
men and women sitting round the table, their faces, their hands, the
chips—nothing escaped his fixed, cold stare.

Sophie learned quickly, got used to the clatter of the ball, the
young croupier's voice calling out the winning number, and the
lightning, snakelike movements of the rake, greedily gathering in
the chips, or pushing them contemptuously at the winner. She started
to count, the way Papa had said. Now and again one of the last six
came up, and she started again from scratch, but so far there hadn't
been a run of twelve without them. *"Mesdames, Messieurs, faites vos
jeux! . . . Rien ne va plus."* After half an hour she felt as blasé as a
veteran—and she still hadn't placed a single one of her precious
chips onto the green cloth in front of her.

Suddenly she was conscious of being scrutinized, from the other
side of the table. Behind and looming above a fat, pearl-encrusted
lady rose a tall woman in a black woolen dress, with a heavy-boned,
powerful build, long neck, and ruddy features, not at all in character
with the casino, more in place in a rowing boat, at the helm, or
casting nets. A pair of colorless eyes stared hard at her, and as Sophie
met them, she thought they became faintly threatening.

"Rien ne va plus! Numero vingt-six." Sophie automatically added
one more to her score. Eight—or did that make it nine, in a row? The
woman's eyes drilled into her—perhaps she wanted her place? But
there were still a few empty chairs at the table! *"Rien ne va plus!
Numero neuf."* And then it hit her all of a sudden: the woman was
Keitje, and she had recognized Sophie by her resemblance to Papa.
The hell with Keitje, number nineteen had just come up, that meant
just one more number under thirty and she could place a bet. Her
hands trembled—shouldn't she quickly go to the toilet and inject
some courage? Too late. Number three had been announced. The
great moment had arrived: the last six hadn't come up, twelve times

in a row. Go! If only the woman over there would clear off! Casually, and as if it was just a last-minute whim, she pushed the first of her ten chips onto the green baize cloth. There it swam, all alone on the *Six derniers*. Sophie's hands were shaking so much she had to hide them under the table. *Rien ne va plus!* The rattle of the ball, first skipping eagerly, then a weary clatter, then silence. "*Numero vingt.*" The greedy rake shot out and grabbed her lonely thousand. Bye-bye . . .

She began to count again, and raised her eyes defiantly to the Belgian woman's. They were no longer threatening, they smirked with undisguised amusement. Sophie lost count, clamped her fists down on either side of her little pile of chips. The tall woman didn't budge.

She lost the next three thousand, and the woman had suddenly vanished. Thank God. Still plenty of chances—she could still win it all back on one turn; one lucky go would bring in six thousand!

"Stop that," said a gruff voice, right behind her. "Give the rest to me, I'll place it sensibly for him. At chemin de fer. Roulette is a kindergarten game."

Sophie didn't turn around. I've got to keep count! she thought desperately—where had it got to? Six, or eight, or what? Aloud she said, over her shoulder: "What do you want? I don't understand—"

"I can't bear to watch you throw his money down the drain."

"Who are you, anyway? What right have you got to tell me what to do with my money!"

"It's not your money. And you don't know what you're doing. Come on, give it to me."

"Kindly go away, or I'll—"

"You'll what?"

Sophie said nothing, and in her fury and embarrassment pushed another thousand onto the table, only to see it whisked away a few seconds later. A husky laugh came from behind her—then silence. She cautiously turned her head. Keitje was gone.

An hour later Sophie was broke. "Skint" as they used to say at school. Skint! she thought on the way to the toilet, and returned gaily singing: Skint! Skint! I'm skint all right—yoohoo—

"I'd say you were off your head," remarked the gruff voice, and Keitje towered over her. "Come on, let's have a drink, it's on me."

"One moment," said Sophie and went to the cashier's desk.

"You're not going to chuck *more* money away!" Keitje blocked her path. "You're even more pigheaded than your father."

"Out of the way," said Sophie and pushed past her. "Mademoiselle —could you give me cash for this ticket to London? I think it's worth four hundred marks."

"Are you completely crackers?" Keitje rasped in her ear.

The girl examined the second-class ticket.

"*Rien*," she said contemptuously.

.

Sophie drank a Cointreau, Keitje a double Scotch. They sat at the bar of the casino, eyeing each other carefully, from head to foot. Keitje wasn't too bad, seen from close to; there wasn't much in the way of softness about her, but the overall effect wasn't as coarse as it had seemed at first sight.

"You seem in pretty good spirits for somebody who's just gambled away their sick father's last savings," said Keitje pleasantly. "Or don't you give a damn?"

She didn't. Thanks to the crocodile and the Cointreau.

"Where had he hidden it?" Sophie shook her head. "Never mind. Doesn't really matter." They sat in silence. "Cheers," said Keitje and they clinked their glasses, then sat in silence again. "If you want my advice, clear off. Save him a painful scene. *I'll* tell him. Don't worry, I'll do it nicely, I'll tell him you were even prepared to hock your ticket to London."

Sophie bowed her head. Tears of love for Papa, and for herself, fell into her glass.

"You see—that's the sort of thing we want to spare him, don't we?"

Sophie nodded, a little too vigorously, and nearly fell off the bar stool. Morphine plus alcohol was a stunning mixture, and a new one.

"In any case," said Keitje, raising Sophie's face and wiping the tears away with her rough hand, and adding a friendly wink, "as far as his little hidey-hole is concerned, where he kept the ten thousand —I bet it's not the only one. And I'll eat my hat if that was his *last* ten thousand—so relax."

.

At the station in Berlin next afternoon she didn't even have enough money left for a taxi. She got on a bus and went to the travel agency,

253

where she cashed in her London ticket without any trouble. She wired the Seagull: "S.O.S. Sophie." And headed for Yasmin's. Over dinner she told the story of her visit to Papa and the events in the casino—omitting Keitje. Yasmin listened attentively, chewing, and finally nodded as if to say: ah well, that's life.

When the lemon mousse arrived, Sophie decided that the moment had come and tentatively probed the subject of money. She struck bedrock. Not a penny. She was welcome to come for meals whenever she was hungry, even for breakfast. On foot.

During the next two days she sold all her possessions, right down to the bed. Her earrings and one or two gold knick-knacks. She cleared, in all, some three thousand marks. Then she phoned Bosse and took an empty suitcase to the Halensee fish restaurant. He brought a suitcase too, but his was full. They exchanged them in silence, and the three thousand marks changed hands, too. Many thanks, Herr Bosse, and bye-bye.

Apart from meals at Yasmin's, she stayed in her attic, lying waiting on the bed, dreaming. The Seagull would come, of that she was sure. They all fall into my snare, she thought, Anita, the cruel dove, Alice, the faithful Seagull. . . .

Who indeed arrived three days later.

Even before she'd taken off her hat and coat, Sophie had confessed everything—including the cashed-in ticket—in a single, rash, un-broken torrent of words. The Seagull was prepared for the worst, but even so she now had to sit down hastily on the bed.

"Skint!" sang Sophie. "I'm totally, hopelessly, one hundred percent skint."

The Seagull looked around the bare rooms. "You've got nothing left," she said tonelessly, "nothing at all."

"Except this," cried Sophie and brought out Bosse's suitcase. "Full up, right to the top."

For her part the Seagull brought good news, though she was now in no mood to celebrate. She had got a contract with Balthus, to translate German books and make herself generally useful. She knew, of course, that it wasn't a real job but an act of kindness; the main thing was, though, that this time she would be returning to England *with* a labor permit.

254

"Hurrah!" shouted Sophie and danced around on the naked floor-boards till the people below used their broom again.

"But *you*'ll have to come on a visitor's permit," said the Seagull sadly. "And I don't know what I'll be able to do for you over there. You've got no skills, no qualifications—"

"I'm your friend!" cried Sophie and kissed her on the cheek. "You'll need one there, in that cold country."

.

In the next few weeks she worked with energy and stamina to help the Seagull sell her possessions. There were now special agencies ready to relieve emigrants of their "valuables" at cheap rates, and convert the proceeds into a few small pieces of jewelry, which in due course might fetch enough to keep them for the first few months in England. One was not allowed to take cash out of the country.

At last they were ready. They sat in the naked apartment among their suitcases, and studied the map. The Seagull's ancient Mercedes-Benz cabriolet was to carry them across the border, so as to avoid the strict customs procedure on the railways.

"We'll be crossing into Belgium between Aachen and Mastricht," said the Seagull, looking at her three suitcases and Sophie's two—plus the black one, Bosse's suitcase. "We may as well abandon the old machine there. Let's just hope it gets us there."

"Can't you use it in England?"

"In the first place, it's too expensive, and in the second—" She took a breath before going on. "In the second place we can't afford to risk two border crossings in it. The Belgians are usually pretty sloppy, we stand a good chance there, but the English might give a car like ours a close inspection."

"And why shouldn't they give it—" Sophie broke off, realizing. The Bosse suitcase! Full up to the top. "Where are we going to hide it?"

"I don't know yet. I'll think of somewhere."

.

They said goodbye to Yasmin, but to no one else. She stood in the hall, at seven in the morning, in her pink dressing gown, squeezed the Seagull's hand and stroked Sophie's cheek.

"Good luck."

"Yasmin—you can still change your mind! There's a Turkish embassy in London too."

"Yes. Yes, I suppose so. Send me your address." And finally the ancient oriental blessing: "Go in good health—return in good health."

From the window she looked down at the Olivaerplatz, and watched Sophie climb into the front seat beside the Seagull. The hood was down, the back seat filled with coats and suitcases. Suddenly she opened the window and called: *"Seni sev-iyorum!"*—I love you—not really loud enough to be heard, but in the early-morning stillness, as they shut the car doors and just before the Seagull pressed the starting button, the *Seni sev-iyorum* reached Sophie's ear like a faint puff of wind. She whipped round, thinking automatically: Dahde!—then realized and looked up at the window. Yasmin raised a hand, and Sophie wanted to call back *"Seni sev-iyorum!"* because it had never been said between them—but the engine started, the car moved off, and she could only wave, until they reached the corner.

Chapter 7 During the journey they avoided drawing each other's attention to the beauties of the countryside. These magnificent meadows in yellow-white bloom, these pine woods, old farmsteads, church spires—would they ever see them again? They drove westward in silence, without hurrying, the Seagull deliberately choosing country lanes. And now, quietly sitting there, hour after hour, they began to grasp what leaving meant. Emigration: blind man's buff. Emigrant: a first offender.

The Seagull had the worst of it, for on top of her apprehensions for the future, she was frantic with worry about the immediate peril ahead of them. Better not tell Sophie, or she would spend the entire journey in fear and trembling; when the moment came, she would most probably keep her nerve. The problem was the Bosse suitcase. It lay on the back seat next to two other, larger ones. *If* they were searched, they would certainly start with the trunk and might forgo the rest of the luggage. She had told Sophie about the Belgian and the English customs, but her real terror was about the German side of the border. *That*'s where the heat would be on, *that*'s where they were really on the prowl. There were too many suitcases in the car for a mere holiday, five of them, plus the ominous little black one. It wasn't hard to guess that they were emigrating—and they did *not* have an authorization! All their luggage would be opened, and then—

"Why are you groaning?" asked Sophie.

On the first day they reached Hanover, then Dortmund, where they spent the night, and on to Cologne the next day.

"Oh!" cried Sophie. "Do drive past the cathedral, I'd love to go in once more and sit for five minutes."

"D'you have to?"

"The last time I was there, the Dahde was still alive—what's the matter, Alice? You look quite ill!"

"I've got a headache."

"Then come into the cathedral with me, it's nice and dark and cool inside."

The Seagull stopped the car at the cathedral square without answering. "I'll wait for you here. But don't be long." She followed her with her eyes, till she vanished through the great doorway. The crocodile bag under her arm. Of course. In the cathedral it was nice and dark. . . .

.

Then Aachen, and only a couple of miles to go, to the Belgian border. The Seagull drove even more slowly, wiping the sweat from her forehead with the back of her hand.

"What *is* it—don't you feel well?"

"Oh, shut up," growled the Seagull, and dawdled through a small town called Vaals. Somewhere here there was a border post. She drove at a snail's pace, looking round. It was about three in the afternoon, not a soul to be seen, even the dogs were dozing in the shade. A young man in SS uniform emerged from a bar, his back to them, and strolled down the street, into the distance.

"Whatever happens now, Sophie—keep your mouth shut, understood?"

"But why—" She got no further, for the Seagull was driving after the young SS man, and catching up with him. "Are you mad?" whispered Sophie.

Now they'd reached him, and were at eye level.

"Oh, excuse me—"

The young man stopped and saluted, hand to his cap. "Heil Hitler."

"Heil Hitler," smiled the Seagull. He looked at Sophie.

" 'l Hitler," she mumbled.

"Could you possibly tell us where the border crossing is?" burbled the Seagull.

"You turn left at the end here, then take the first right past the town hall, and keep going—"

"Thank you so much. Right at the end here, then left at the town hall—"

"No, no, *gnädige Frau*, you've got it the wrong way around!" The Seagull giggled foolishly, and the other one just sat there with her mouth open. Women! he thought. Nothing between the ears but they drive a Mercedes! The redhead was pretty.

"I think I'd better show you," he said. "Otherwise you'll be going around in circles."

"Oh, but that *is* kind of you," warbled the Seagull. "Is there room in the back? We can take the little black suitcase in front—"

"No need," said the SS man, opening the door. "I'll take it on my lap, it can't be *that* heavy." He lifted the Bosse suitcase, and grimaced. "Hello—what have you got in here—stones?"

He squeezed into the back seat and lay the suitcase flat across his knees. Sophie swallowed and closed her eyes.

"Right first time," laughed the Seagull. "Stones. Precious ones, nothing but rubies and emeralds. All right there?" she added solicitously. "Not too uncomfortable?"

"Not at all, *gnädige Frau*, my knees aren't *that* feeble." The Seagull doubled up with laughter. "Off we go then—straight on, then left at the bottom—"

Shortly afterward they reached the German customs post, recognizable from afar by the huge swastika-blazoned flags. Two uniformed officials stood by the barrier. They clicked their heels and saluted when they saw the young SS man.

"Here we are then," he said, opening the car door, climbing out, and carefully replacing the Bosse suitcase on the seat. "Everything back in place again. *Bon voyage*, ladies!" He saluted, dismissing the Seagull's thanks with a friendly smile—the redhead was certainly pretty but not exactly a ball of fire—nodded to the customs men and walked off.

The Seagull took her passport out of her handbag, and nudged

Sophie, who was sitting bolt upright and staring after the SS man, to do the same.

"It's all right, ladies, perfectly all right—many thanks—have a good journey!" They fell over each other with eager respectfulness, and wouldn't even glance at their passports.

"Bye!" The Seagull casually waved two fingers in the air and pressed down hard on the accelerator. The car shot forward, Sophie's head hit the seat back, and she came to.

"Good God!"

BOOK VII

Chapter 1 The bookshop Sophie was searching for was in the High Street in Hastings, not far from the promenade. She'd been given the address that afternoon in St. Leonards, when she visited her old school. The principal, Miss Newman, was still there, and several other familiar faces appeared for staff tea, with milk and thinly sliced cucumber sandwiches, as always. Sophie was the guest of honor; everyone seemed pleased in the undemonstrative Anglo-Saxon manner to see her again. And Mr. Goodenday? Had he left the school? Miss Newman's eyes turned into round pools: yes, indeed he had. He had come into a substantial inheritance, wasn't it marvelous. Was positively well off now and had bought a large bookshop in Hastings. Why didn't Sophie drop in on him there, he'd be ever so pleased. No, no, said Sophie, why bother him.

But on the way back, when her bus stopped at Hastings, she'd suddenly got off, stood undecided in the bus shelter, then headed slowly up the High Street. It was just before six, the shop was still open, its windows brightly lit, three huge windows full of books. Sophie stood for a few moments, transfixed. Inside, the shelves glowed with hundreds of volumes in brightly colored dust covers, and half a dozen employees served a considerable number of customers, who were searching and ordering and paying.

The cash register tinkled discreetly; there was muffled conversation; the aura of literature imposed a respectful tone. I'd like to stay here for a bit, thought Sophie, and sat on a chair and looked around her. All these faces, old, young, they were all here with a definite, gratifying purpose, all of them absorbed, anchored, knowing where they belonged, what they were doing here, especially the younger, poorer ones, just "taking a quick look" at some book. She had never felt so utterly shipwrecked.

"Can I help you, Miss?"

"Could I have a word with Mr. Goodenday?"

"Who shall I say it is?"

"Sophie Berglund."

The salesgirl disappeared and returned a few moments later with Goodenday, running in front of her.

"No! I don't believe it."

263

Outstretched hands, almost an embrace. Employees and customers watched curiously, and he looked around, embarrassed, beckoned to her and hurried to his office, glancing back a couple of times to make sure she was following him.

Maybe it was the beautiful old desk he sat behind with such ease, legs casually crossed, and the splendid, solemn room with its paneled walls that gave him such a different impact. Thinking back, she remembered a rather shabby elderly man with thinning gray hair and trousers too short—now he wore an elegant suede jacket over a silk shirt, and his eyes, once so jumpy, inspected her calmly.

"What brings you here, Sophie? I may still call you Sophie?"

"I wanted to see my old school—nostalgia and curiosity, professional curiosity—I'm doing some work for Balthus Books."

"Balthus? Who for, the old boy, or his son?"

"The son." Take a chance.

"Are you writing a book?"

"A book? No. Articles—on travel . . . and politics . . ."

"For Johnny Balthus? I thought he only went in for the belletristic."

"Oh yes?" she said, since she couldn't think of anything better.

"Are you just . . . passing through, in England, that is?"

"Not really, Mr. Goodenday. I've emigrated."

"Ah. I hadn't realized you were Jewish."

"Nor had I."

They both laughed like old comrades in arms. When she said goodbye he held onto her hand for a moment. "Do you remember our walk along the beach? And . . . are things better now?"

"Much better. Thank you. Goodbye then, Mr. Goodenday."

The shop was empty now; a salesgirl locked up behind her. She slowly walked down the High Street, and past the bus stop, across the promenade, to the beach. Here, by the sea, on the gray-and-white pebbles, she suddenly saw him again as he then was: shifting from foot to foot, a ragged old crane, trying awkwardly to make her talk about her wicked stepmother, and then vainly chasing after her cap.

She sat down. The stones were still warm, it had been a hot day. The beach was all but deserted, a few people folding the last deck chairs, a couple of children still swimming in the calm, dark sea, calling out to each other.

No rush to get back to London, to her room in the cheap boarding-house. Anything unfamiliar helped. Better to sit here on the beach than lie on her bed, listening to the radio. It distracted her from the stranglehold and the longing and the wretched fury. That was why she'd come down to St. Leonards today, it made a change, even if she didn't really care a hoot about the place. The same with the visit to Goodenday, anything to break the journey, to put off getting home—because she had no more stuff left for tonight. The Seagull gave her only two a day, and they simply weren't enough. Christ—here we go again—goddam Seagull—goddam to hell—help me, someone, I just can't go on—I can't go on—enough—I'm ready—I'll go into the water—now—as soon as the children have gone.

She watched them wading out of the sea, laughing, chasing each other down the beach. Piss off, you little brats, go home! All I have to do is swim far out—I'm looking forward to it—bugger off home, damn you—you *have* a home—bugger off!

A crunching on the stones behind her. Footsteps. Coming nearer. She sat up stiffly, stared out across the sea, motionless.

The person stood beside her. Probably some man. If he says one word, I'll take a stone and smash his face in—

"Sophie," said Mr. Goodenday, and sat down. "I thought so."

.

There was a decent meal to be had at a pub called the Norman. Goodenday insisted she try the claret, famous in the town. "There now, you see, you've got a bit of color in your face. The wine's doing you good." Sophie downed her third glass. If only he knew how *much* good! On her budget alcohol was out of the question. The Seagull earned twelve pounds a week and gave Sophie four pounds ten; today she had contributed a little extra for the bus fare.

Goodenday ordered another bottle. And when that too was empty, Sophie was ready to answer his questions. He had, of course, spotted the lie about young Balthus. But why particularly Balthus? Sophie explained about the Seagull.

"How long have you been here, then?"

"Six months."

"And why haven't you got a job?"

No labor permit. And no prospect of getting one, either.

"I see."

He ordered coffee, and saw how her hand shook as she reached for her cup. "Sophie, just now, on the beach—was that a bad moment?"

"I must go soon," she said. "My bus—"

He rang her up next morning, at her boardinghouse. He was coming to London at the weekend, would she keep Saturday evening free for him?

Why not? Another distraction; and the weekends were always the worst time, for the Seagull was there all day to be pestered for more vials and, in consequence, locked herself in, or ran out on her. She had the Bosse suitcase under strictest supervision. Sophie never asked how many vials were left. At the end of the Bosse supply there was always "the way out." The Seagull knew it, and it gave her the strength to resist Sophie's onslaughts.

They met at Prunier's restaurant, in St. James Street; Sophie didn't want Goodenday to see the cheap boardinghouse where she and the Seagull lived. Her black Knieze outfit with the white blouse was timelessly flattering, as were the glances from neighboring tables.

He judged it nicely; there was much he wanted to know about her, so he started out by talking about himself. After the first bottle of wine, listening became easier, she rarely lost the thread. Also because of his way of tackling serious matters as though they'd happened to somebody else. The snails whose insides he was exploring occupied his full attention while he described how his first wife had died in a motor accident twenty years earlier, how his wealthy father-in-law had seen him as nothing more than a coldblooded opportunist, and how, after many years of stubborn silence, this same man had died leaving a will which began: "I name my son-in-law Alan Goodenday as my sole heir, because I was mistaken about him."

How she could listen! Goodenday marveled. Those amber-colored eyes and that look of utter concentration! She was indeed concentrating as hard as she could, but mainly on what in God's name she was going to offer by way of a life's history when *her* turn came. He gazed at her, enraptured. What a beautiful creature, and so reserved and shy, cardinal virtues in his eyes; she obviously still found it hard to talk about herself. How very nice. Tactfully he started to question her, and received precise and utterly untruthful answers. How was her father? Very well indeed. Splendid. And—had there ever been another stepmother? Oh no, Papa was living quietly retired, devoted to his rose garden. And she, Sophie, had she never thought of marrying? She was just about to deny Dimi, when she remembered in the nick of time that the name on her identity card was Sophie Martensen. Well—as a matter of fact, yes, she had been married, only briefly, a youthful mistake, not exactly a happy memory, long past, thank you, the sole is really excellent. No, there was nothing else to report, except that she had worked at Ullstein Verlag in Berlin and been thrown out on her ear for racial reasons. There.

"And now?"

"My visitor's permit is good for a year."

"And then?"

She shrugged her shoulders and smiled. That was the English way, and should go down all right. Brave little woman.

It went down even better than she had hoped. He stretched out his hand and laid it on hers.

"Sophie, would it surprise you very much if I were to confess to—to—"

To what? After the second bottle of wine nothing would have surprised her. Since she didn't take her hand away, he found the courage to complete the sentence: ". . . to having fallen in love with you?" Both hands lay calmly on the tablecloth, one on top of the other, and he proceeded passionately: "Even all that time ago, on the beach, I—of course I couldn't say anything then. But now that I'm in a position to—"

.

When she arrived home, around midnight, she had a proposal in the bag. The Seagull was still up, and said: "Aha."

Chapter 2 But next morning, before she caught her bus on the way to Balthus, she knocked at Sophie's door. Sophie was still in bed, staring at the ceiling, her hands crossed behind her head.

"I've been thinking," said the Seagull hesitantly, "how are you going to do it? Can you sleep with a man—without wanting to?"

Sophie focused her gaze on the figure by the door. A few minutes ago, she had had her fix, and the stuff was beginning to work, not the ideal moment to be asked leading questions.

"Somehow," she murmured vaguely, "somehow—I'll manage."

She avoided thinking of the wedding night. It had to be dark, that much she knew. The puncture marks in her arms and legs were crowding together in rashes, and one or another always oozed pus. Usually it was the Seagull who solved all problems—but not this time, unless she, Sophie–Isolde, found a way, à la Wagner, of substituting the Seagull–Brangäne in Mr. Goodenday–King Marke's bed. She burst out laughing at the very thought, and the Seagull stared at her.

"You think it's funny?"

.

Goodenday said they were too old for a long engagement, and Sophie wholeheartedly agreed. She knew there could not be many more vials left in the Bosse suitcase. Eleventh-hour rescue! Neither the Seagull nor Sophie said it in so many words, but both were thinking the same: there would be plenty of money, and with money, contacts might be arranged. . . .

All the Seagull said was: "I'm getting to be just as amoral as you are."

"I can't afford morals," murmured Sophie.

"The man deserves to be liked."

"I like him."

"I'm afraid he loves you," said the Seagull with a sigh. Sophie nodded. Everything would be so much easier, if he had not fallen so much in love with her. She had never considered that possibility, when she had said yes over the excellent sole meunière at Prunier's. After all, he was by now—well, how old *was* he, for the love of God? She had never asked, one didn't ask that kind of thing, but in those long-ago days at St. Leonards, he must have been at least—what? Late thirties? And that was fifteen years ago! She had of course assumed, considering his age, that she could count on fulfilling her marital duties in a leisurely now-and-then way, but the passionately longing embraces on which he embarked whenever he saw a chance made her fear the worst. How long could she continue being coy?

With one eye dry and happy (Bosse suitcase) and the other wet and worried (looming wedding night), she watched Goodenday's preparations for the great day, observed with a mixture of involuntary emotion and awful foreboding the way in which he conferred with the various authorities, looking flushed and full of pride. He never saw—or perhaps he misunderstood—the looks the officials gave first him and then her, whenever he introduced her as his future bride. She was now nearly twenty-nine, but looked younger, particularly at certain times of the day, after having "fortified" herself.

Or *did* he catch on?

They stood one night in front of the door to her boardinghouse, and he covered the palm of her hands with kisses, pressed his forehead and his eyes to them, like a playful dog.

"Sophie—what would you say, if I had my hair dyed a bit? Very discreetly, of course," he added hastily.

She left him one hand to hide in, and with the other stroked his thin gray hair. It hadn't changed, hadn't become any grayer or thinner since the day they had taken their walk on the beach, when it had danced so madly in the wind.

"Why not? If it gives you pleasure."

But next day at luncheon at Prunier's—by now their habitual haunt—she did get a shock, when a gentleman with bootblack hair suddenly sat down at her table, imploring her with tensely apprehensive eyes to give her blessing.

"Astonishing," was all she managed to utter.

He smiled, relieved, but needed further confirmation.

"It isn't too much? I mean, too black? I mean, too youthful?"

Youthful it certainly was not. It looked as if he had less hair all of a sudden, and what there was shone as if it had been varnished. What the hell, thought Sophie, one doesn't see it in the dark.

"It really suits you." And, to elaborate a bit more: "Did you used to have hair like that?"

"Not really. I've never looked like this in my life. My hair was always the colorless sort, they never knew how to describe it in my passport." He put his glasses on and looked at his reflection in a faraway mirror on the wall of the restaurant. "I don't really recognize myself, but if *you* like it . . ."

"I like it," said Sophie, and he squeezed her hand under the table.

.

Early in the morning, on the wedding day, the Seagull went to Sophie's room and handed her the Bosse suitcase without a word. It felt light, much too light. Sophie hadn't the courage to open it. Later, later . . .

·

At Caxton Hall registry office, Sophie and the Seagull met Goodenday's best man, a whitehaired professor of archaeology at Cambridge, with whom he had shared rooms in their student days. Sophie wore her Knieze outfit with the white blouse, her red hair rolled up in the new pageboy hairstyle. The Seagull was entirely in white.

The professor was probably a little hard of hearing, for he warmly shook the Seagull's hand and offered her his congratulations and blessings for her future wedded bliss. Goodenday, aghast, cut him short and once more introduced Sophie as his bride, which mortified the poor man to such an extent that he wanted to leave at once, having turned out the worst and not the best man.

Sophie laughed and reassured him, but Goodenday—Alan, as she now had to call him—was pale with shock. She took his hand and tried to smile him back into his usual equanimity, but even later, in front of the registrar, his voice was still hoarse and hardly audible.

While the bridegroom filled out the various forms, Sophie happened to glance at the professor. His eyes were gazing at her full of dismay and then got stuck at his old friend's new black hair. She pinched her palms as hard as she could, not to burst out laughing. In honor of the day, she had donated an extra ration to herself and thought Caxton Hall, the professor, Alan, the Seagull and herself all killingly funny.

Later, at the Savoy Hotel, where the formal wedding lunch was held, the professor downed a couple of stiff martinis and found his tongue again. Alan, too, took one, and so did the Seagull. Sophie drank only orange juice—she wanted to keep her head clear. *After* lunch would come her most important happening of the day: a visit to the Home Office, Aliens section. With her wedding certificate still wet from the registry, she filled out the necessary papers. Within two weeks she would have a British passport!

The professor was rather taken aback by these, as he put it, rather precipitous measures on their wedding day, but Goodenday—Alan, as she reminded herself—smiled indulgently: of course she wanted to exchange her dreary gray alien's identity card at once for a splendid dark-blue English passport! Then they could go off on a honeymoon, to Spain perhaps. While she was writing, he put his arm around her waist.

"Everything's all right, you're my wife now."

I'm English now, thought Sophie, and signed, for the first time, Sophie Goodenday.

.

And then, inevitably, she had to foot the bill. But why didn't the extra vial help? Rigidly, like a deep-frozen fish, she lay naked in Goodenday's arms, eyes wide open with panic and horror.

"I don't understand," he said, when he could trust his voice again. "Explain to me—"

She didn't answer, couldn't, her teeth were chattering too hard. All of a sudden she had begun to shake violently, trying in vain to steady herself by hanging onto the bedstead. What's the matter with me? she thought desperately. Why am I flopping about like this—

"Are you ill?"

No answer, only clamped jaws, and quivering limbs. He wrapped her in as many blankets as he could find, put on his pajamas and sat, freezing, on the edge of the bed. Gradually the spasm subsided, and she lay like a corpse, her eyes shut, made no protest as he switched on the bedside lamp.

"Sophie—say something! Shall I call the doctor?"

She shook her head and whispered without opening her eyes: "I must sleep. Tomorrow morning—I'll tell you—tomorrow."

He got up and put on the suit that had been specially made for the great day, wrapped himself in his coat, lay down beside her and did his best to get some sleep. She never moved, all night.

In the morning she told him. He'd have found out, one way or another, as Dimi had. In the middle of her confession he got up, went to the window, and stared down at the Thames, at the barges passing quietly up and down. She was silent for a moment, watching his back, and giving him time. He was still standing at the window, long after she had finished. When he turns around, she thought, he'll ask me if I married him because of *that*—or because of the passport. I like the man. I'll lie.

But he didn't ask her. He left the window, and put on his hat and coat, while she watched him numbly.

"Have you injected yourself today?" Without looking at her, the dry, factual tone of Mr. Goodenday in chemistry class.

"Yes."

"Then wait here for me. I'll be as quick as I can, but it may be two hours or so before I'm back." He went to the telephone and pulled the cord out of the wall. "I'm afraid I'll have to lock you in. Don't be alarmed. Trust me." He looked once, quickly, into her terrified eyes, and left the room.

She sank back onto the bed. Now he's going to the Home Office to have my passport canceled—and then to the police. Drug addiction and marriage under false pretenses. Jump out of the window? Don't really want to. Must be the stuff. She was still flooded with it, and unable to think straight. Later, perhaps, she'd jump.

.

But "later" turned out to be the beginning of the end, or rather of the starting point, for Goodenday didn't return alone. Next to him, by Sophie's bed, stood a tall man with a sharp eagle's nose and a mustache. Scotland Yard? No, Dr. Hartley, medical superintendent of a private clinic in Wimpole Street, one with a special ward devoted to drug cures.

"Hallo, there, Mrs. Goodenday," he said in a hearty voice. Sophie looked without a word from one to the other. "How many vials have you got left?"

Slowly, as if she had shackles around her feet, she got up and brought the Bosse suitcase. It seemed to weigh a ton. Together they counted the vials. There would have been enough for about six more weeks.

"Right," said Hartley in the same hearty tone, and emptied the precious contents into his Gladstone bag. "Here's the form you have to sign. It says that you're entering my clinic of your own free will—"

"Free will?" yelled Sophie.

"And that you'll remain there till I pronounce you cured."

The empty Bosse suitcase flew in a wild arc through the air, and Sophie hurled herself at Goodenday, hammering with her fists at his chest: "You said 'Trust me'!"

"That's right," said Goodenday. She pushed him aside and ran to the window, struck out with all her strength—it smashed, leaving a splinter sticking sideways from her fist. Screaming, and half unconscious with pain and rage, she tried to tear out one of the splintered panes of glass with her other hand, but by that time they'd caught her.

.

"What you're doing to yourself is a great deal worse than what's waiting for you at my clinic, you know," said the doctor calmly, as he bandaged her hand after removing the splinter. She was whimpering, eyes shut, stammering incoherent syllables, but the frenzy was over, and Goodenday cautiously relaxed his hold on her. "Lucky it was the left hand," said Hartley, and smiled at her as if she'd just allowed herself a little prank. "You can still sign with your right. Here." He passed her the form and put his fountain pen between her fingers.

Chapter 3

"It wasn't that different from the first time, Brother. Except that I had strangers around me instead of Yasmin and the Seagull, to call jailers and murderers. In the few years that had gone by since my first attempt, they knew a little more about it, and you know yourself how much 'a little' can mean in medicine. But above all, this time I knew what was in store for me, didn't expect early results and didn't wear myself out in fury and shock. 'There'll be three bad weeks, here's a calendar, I give one to all my patients. Cross the days off one by one, in the fourth week you'll turn the corner. Don't you think it's worth fighting for three miserable weeks—for your life?'

"And the battle began. At once, and ferociously, with racking pains in every limb, and the dreadful cold. I was kept semiconscious up to eight hours in a regulated hot bath and at night in electrically heated sheets. They watched me every second of the day, even in the toilet; for hours, with angelic patience, they spooned food into me. I yelled, as I had the first time, probably louder, since it relieved the torment, and now all barriers were down. When you are that deeply humiliated, you want above all to justify the treatment. On the worst days, during the second week, they gave me ether, and for a while I was gloriously out—but all too rarely, because I was too weak, so weak I couldn't yell anymore. I knew how badly things stood by the way Hartley came and looked down at me every few hours. Wächter

273

had been right, I was a 'natural,' physiologically prone to addiction, and the morphine that had homed in on me so unerringly fought to stay put, like a cat on its back.

"Once, Hartley demanded a cigarette for me, and put it between my lips himself. 'Smoke!' I had never smoked before, inhaled, coughed, choked, drew on it a few more times—and it provided a brief distraction. On other occasions I remember being given a few drops of brandy. Small measures, but each one pushed me forward a few inches at a time.

"And then—I hadn't been able to cross off the days anymore, not for some time now, had no idea how many had gone past—one morning it was as if the blood was somehow running differently in my veins, I can't put it any other way; I felt a very, very faint hope lapping back and forth inside me. The following night, I slept a little and managed to take a bit of food. And Hartley came and sat down by my bed.

"'Well then! Hats off and hurrah and congratulations. It's the twenty-third day. Things'll start to look up now, and quickly. Go on, cry if you like, it means you've heard me.'

"They carried me to the scales. I had lost over thirty pounds. Skin and bone. Exactly as I am now, Brother, the only difference is—"

She stopped, smiled, waved the thought away with her hand and went on. "Incredible, the way the pains began to ease over the next few days, and how the cold vanished altogether. I started to eat three meals a day, that is, I was fed, because I couldn't move a finger. When I no longer needed the hot bath, I began to shovel in food, couldn't get enough of it. They left me six sandwiches by the bed at night, and I still ate three helpings of breakfast. Only the weakness remained. It was fully two weeks before I could hobble about the room, on the nurse's arm. Then they let me see a mirror: a ghastly white moonface stared back at me, eyes sunk in dark hollows, mouth slack. But my arms and legs were free of holes, no more running sores, the skin was smooth again, and for the first time in years I wore a short-sleeved nightdress.

"Every morning Hartley dropped in for a few minutes 'to enjoy the sight of me' as he put it. I was now allowed visitors. Two people had rung up every day, he said. 'Your husband, of course, and a Mrs. Mewes. Whom would you like to see first?'

"'Mrs. Mewes, please.'

"He looked at me for a moment, gave his instructions, and the

Seagull came fluttering over, within the hour. She fell around my neck, without a word.

" 'How do I look? Be honest.'

" 'I've seen you looking better.'

"We laughed with some sobs in between, till she said firmly: 'You nearly went under, but you were dragged out by the hair, at the last minute. We'll never speak about it again, do you hear? Never. Over and done with.'

.

"The last act was set in Hartley's study, the morning I went to say goodbye. He was placing a large log on the fire in his grate.

" 'In your honor,' he said. 'This is my private auto-da-fé. All sorts of cartons and boxes have been burned here, handbags, knapsacks, folders, tin cans—containers of every kind imaginable. It stinks to high heaven all day long, but it's my favorite smell. There!' He pointed at his desk. On it, sullen and brooding in its black cassock, stood the Bosse suitcase. 'One, two . . . and into the fire!'

"I picked it up—it felt light as a feather—then slowly and with a last shudder of awe I pushed it onto the blazing logs.

"Which it smothered at once. I turned to Hartley in alarm, and he took my hand. 'Watch, this is the exciting part. Who'll win, the black devil or the cleansing fire?'

" 'Has it ever happened—that—that—' I suddenly imagined that my chances of survival were at stake, and I felt my skin creep.

" 'That the fire goes out? It's happened. But my chimney draws well, it's as obstinate as I am.' His eyes never left the fire. The thick blocks of wood were frantically hissing and spitting, and wisps of foul-smelling smoke filled the room.

" 'Do you ever play the oracle game with your auto-da-fé, doctor?' I ventured to ask, since he was staring so fixedly into the smoldering fireplace. He nodded.

" 'One hangs on to the most primitive things at times.'

"A loud bang—the smoke cleared for an instant—and the black thing burst apart, pale-green sulfurous flames licking all around the leather.

" 'Quite a stink, eh?' cried Hartley cheerfully. 'Soon we'll get the orange ones, then the good hot red ones, and then the monster will be done for. We've won. The oracle says you will never succumb again. Congratulations—and give my regards to your husband.'

275

"To my husband. . . . That hurdle was still looming ahead of me, Brother. He had rung up every day, but hadn't once come to see me. I had no idea what he felt for me—anger, affection, desire, pity, or nothing at all."

She closed her eyes, and was silent for such a long time that he thought she'd fallen asleep, and was just about to get off the side of her bed.

"No, stay here, please, I had to do a bit of thinking, that's all. About the English. I'd often heard it said that many English couples lived side by side without ever knowing, or ever asking, what they felt about each other or if they felt anything at all. I'd never really believed it. One of those national jokes, I thought, a political carica-ture. And suddenly there *I* was, Brother, in that very situation, *I* suddenly had a muzzle on, didn't dare or didn't want to know, or ask. I crept back to Mr. Goodenday, to Hastings, to his house and his bookshop, and to this day I don't know what went through his mind when I got there, when I was standing before him once again. He didn't ask what it had been like, or whether I was still . . . or not anymore . . . or never again . . . nothing, not a word. I followed him into the house, he showed me my room, without crossing its thresh-old. Ever. I don't think it was my fault, I was so deeply in his debt, it was for *him* to bend the knee. And that he couldn't. Too proud, too reserved, too deeply hurt, who the hell knows, too small a man."

"I know," said the young doctor. "You can't win, it's a sort of bottleneck. My godfather paid for my medical studies, and then, on top of that, he married my mother when his wife died, and he was good to her, we were no longer poor. But I stayed away from home, I didn't know what to say to him, whatever I said would be too little— or perhaps too much. *He* should have released me."

Her eyes searched his face. "I know exactly what you looked like when you were a boy. You always wore glasses, didn't you? You have the kind of face that needs glasses."

He nodded and stroked her hand in silence, and it suddenly turned over and gripped his. "Now comes a bad, bad bit, Brother—"

"Don't forget," he said, "you're writing a book. You're only the narrator, don't get too involved. Stay behind your typewriter and think of nice turns of phrase."

She stared at him, outraged, and then, gradually, reconsidered. "That's right. I'm the narrator. I'm safe." A pause. "Well—the next

chapter is called: 'In the Balthus Canteen.' New page. The Seagull
rang up, had to see me right away, wouldn't say why, sounded altogether too cheery on the phone, I was quite angry with her. I went
up to London next day, and we met in the canteen at Balthus. She
had a proper job there at last, similar to the one she'd had at Ullstein.
I saw her draw up in her new little car, with the hood down; she
looked bright and breezy, white hair flying in the wind. But I could
see at once that something was wrong. She didn't dally, placed two
letters on the table before me, one from the Turkish consulate in
Berlin, the other in an unfamiliar handwriting, with no address on
the back. Both opened, even though they were addressed to me, at
our former joint address.

" 'No, I'm not in the least ashamed!' she said belligerently. 'I won't
allow anyone to write to you things that might upset you, without
my knowing, because—because you might start again . . .'

" 'No,' I said. 'That's over. Over and done with. Can't you smell
that?'

" 'Then read them,' she said. 'But give me your hand.'

"I read, and she held my hand throughout. The Turkish consulate
in Berlin informed me in somewhat unorthodox English that Yasmin
had been arrested. During the *Kristallnacht*—do you know what that
was, Brother, the *Kristallnacht*? When they made their first orga-
nized attack on the Jews? Good, then I don't have to explain it to
you. That night she had hidden her Jewish grocer and his wife in her
flat. The letter ended with a sentence which I remember. 'We are
making every effort to certify where she is being blockaded and will
never relax until our investigation has met with advantage.' Well, it
was I who never relaxed, who, from that moment onward, could not
go calmly about my business or sit about, somewhere, at ease—until
the war broke out, two years later. Then I gave up on her. That
sounds bad, doesn't it, Brother, but in wartime you learn to amputate
things."

"And the other letter?"

"From Keitje. The Seagull had deliberated for a while whether to
give me both letters at the same time. They'd arrived by the same
post, as it happened. In the end she decided that one blow might
help to deaden the other. Better than drinking one sorrow to the
dregs, and then, a few days later, having to drink from the same
cup all over again.

" 'Dear Sophie, your father died last night. I won't pretend to you that he died in his sleep. He had another stroke and lived a whole day after it. I was glad for him when it was over. Be glad for him, too. All the best, Keitje.'

"I stayed close to the Seagull that day. First I sat around her office, then she took me home with her. She'd rented a small mews house, as befitted her name, tiny, but a house all to herself after all. She made up a bed for me, on the sofa in the sitting room, and phoned Mr. Goodenday. I would be going back to Hastings tomorrow, I'd had a violent attack of toothache.

"Correct. Now I knew where I was, at last: at the dentist. And he was drilling. Without Novocaine.

"My private cemetery grew, Brother. The Dahde lay there, and Turhan, and Papa—and I prepared a place for Yasmin."

Chapter 4

On the 3rd of September 1939, everyone in England seemed to know where they belonged, and they listened to the radio to be told what to do. This enabled them to behave with—apart from a certain amount of excitement—a sense of collective confidence. Whether they were lugging their gasmasks around with them (soon to be abandoned), joining the armed forces or queuing for their ration books, fortifying their cellars or sending their children to safety in America, they all reacted with a common, reassuring sense of national emergency which nonetheless left room for the all-important touch of individuality. A newspaper proclaimed: "Hitler Occupies Warsaw. Welsh Pastor Succeeds in Breeding Completely Green Mouse."

The Seagull, however, stood at her window watching the crowds hurrying through the street, all, apparently, with a fixity of purpose, and wondered what to do with herself. She remained outside, didn't belong. Not that anybody was unfriendly, but no one knew what to advise her. Balthus Books vouched for her absolute loyalty, but she still had to endure a humiliating interview at the Home Office, Aliens Department, recognizable from afar by a queue hundreds of troubled faces long.

"You're not Jewish," they established, knitting their brows. "What are you doing here? Go back to Germany." "By all means," said the Seagull. "With handcuffs on. Never of my own free will." They were impressed and released her, though subject to the law regarding aliens: no journeys beyond a radius of twenty miles without police permission, or even a single night away from home; no radio. There were newspapers, after all.

Sophie had no such problems, she was Mrs. Goodenday. But whenever anyone addressed her as that, she felt as if she'd unlawfully bought an English passport like the French tarts at Piccadilly Circus, who quickly married any pair of trousers they could get hold of, so they wouldn't be deported.

She wrote to the Turkish embassy in Berlin, and gave her new name and address, though without any real hope, just in case. And then suddenly a letter from the Red Cross arrived, in telegram language and without a signature: "Frau Yasmin Berglund in Ravensbrueck labor camp."

"Well, that's good," said Goodenday. Good? Didn't he know that labor camp meant concentration camp? Oh, really? Well, better than dead, wasn't it.

Sophie restrained herself, swallowing hard. What did he know of Germany? To him Hitler was the German head of state. Before, it had been the Kaiser—not exactly a bundle of charm either. Now it was Hitler. And he hinted that perhaps the Foreign Office had "boobed" a bit, the fellow might have been quite useful. In what way? As a bulwark against the Russians, what else?

Mr. Goodenday. She never thought of him as Alan, he remained Mr. Goodenday, and once or twice she even addressed him as such. (He pretended not to have noticed; perhaps he found it right and proper.) She saw little of him, for he now worked right through his lunch hour at the bookshop, to compensate for the employees who'd been called up, but even their short dinners together were hard going. He sat opposite her, spoke only about what was absolutely necessary, never asked her anything, always polite but full of buried resentment under thick layers of Anglo-Saxon taboo against unburdening oneself and clearing the air. While Sophie never lifted her eyes from her plate and racked her brain for the right kind of words to make it clear to him that she knew and understood, that she was grateful, that she was now without morphine but also without self-confidence—dear God, didn't he see how reduced she was, how chastened and how cold. . . .

But perhaps the worst was the waiting for a single but deadly moment, which occurred after dinner, while coffee was being served. He would get his cigarette case out of his pocket—that wasn't it, why shouldn't he smoke?—and would offer it to her, night after night, always with the same politely questioning expression on his face. And when she would shake her head—during the first few weeks she had added: "No, thank you, I never smoke"—he would hesitate for a second, lift his eyebrows in surprise as if to say: "No cigarette? Really!" to be followed by a slight incline of the head which meant: "Ah well, then I'll have to smoke on my own and can only hope it isn't too troublesome to you."

Her nerves were still in a sorry state, or rather, she could not get rid of the feeling that in the clinic the top layer of her skin had somehow been peeled off her body and that the next layer wasn't yet ready to be aired. If Goodenday had asked her how she spent her days, she could only have answered: "I'm doing nothing, absolutely nothing, I must wait until my skin has solidified."

In the spring of 1940, however, when the uncouth German head of state began to gobble up France, Goodenday thought that the fellow had gone too far, and all of a sudden there were neutral topics of conversation during their evening meal. They found a certain pleasure in seeing eye to eye, and there was something like a burgeoning fondness between them.

Sophie scratched at her skin and decided it was now weatherproof. Soon I'll have freckles again, she thought, and took the train to London to visit the Seagull, who wasn't allowed to move outside her radius of twenty miles.

"*Do* something, for the love of God, Sophie. I'm not allowed to, but *you* can. Why don't you enlist as an ambulance driver or as a canteen worker at the Red Cross—*do* something."

On her return she talked to Goodenday, and he looked at her thoughtfully and for the first time without the guardedness in his eyes that had stymied them for so long. "If you really want to work, why don't you help me in the shop? All I've got is two ancient females who can't even lift the books out of their crates."

She smiled at him and gave a deep sigh.

"I would love that. It would mean that I could at long last—" But he wouldn't let her finish, got up quickly.

"I shall report to the Hastings Home Guard," he said at the door. "My old gun from the last war must be somewhere around the house."

He found it and cleaned it and presented arms in front of the large mirror in the hall. Sophie watched him standing stiffly at attention in the twilight, staring at himself with an expression of resolute defiance, yet she didn't think him funny. When he saw her, he dropped the gun. "Must have a haircut," he murmured and went out quickly. His hair had already been back to its own mousy gray when Sophie returned from the hospital. He had the black shaved off and had worn a cap for several weeks, even inside the bookstore. From now on he paraded on the common where one used to play cricket on Sundays, while Sophie worked eight hours a day in the bookstore, carrying mountains of books from the warehouse to the sorting room. It looked as if he appreciated her efforts, and when she fell into bed at night, dog-tired, she thought she was really starting to pay back her heavy load of gratitude toward him. Even the nightly cigarette ritual didn't worry her any more.

.

In the summer of 1940 Mr. Goodenday turned positively jolly. Threat of invasion! Perhaps "the fellow" had a sense of history and would land, like the late William the Conqueror, at Hastings! That really would be something. When the first bombs fell on London, and one or two bombers whizzed overhead on their way there, Goodenday gazed longingly at the skies.

One night Sophie looked out of the window and watched him patrolling the beach in the moonlight, part of his Home Guard duties. Now and then he stopped and stared out to sea. He had taken off his cap, and his gray hair flapped free in the night wind. The ill-fitting uniform made him look like the science master once again. He sat down on the stones, not far from the spot where he had found her, that day. And sat for a long time. He'll soon have something to tell me, thought Sophie.

Early in 1941, he came out with it. "I'm only fifty-six, after all, even if my lungs aren't A-one—they could probably fit me in somewhere, I *was* a major. . . . Perhaps overseas. Warmer climate. Australia, India, somewhere like that—I know a few people from the old days, at the Commonwealth Office."

After a week in London he returned in high excitement. Burma! An administrative job only—still, across the Indian Ocean on a destroyer!

"I'll keep the shop going," said Sophie. "I can manage."

"It's not worth it with the shortage of paper and the few books being published. Besides, it's dangerous here, on the South Coast. But—I've got a proposition for you." It had been a long time since they'd talked with such interest in each other. "D'you think you might enjoy working at the Propaganda Ministry? I've put a word in for you."

Not only Sophie but the Seagull, too, landed at M.I.5. She could have moved into the little mews house with her, but remembered in time Yasmin's dictum about not falling into old ruts, and took a furnished room within striking distance of Whitehall.

She left Goodenday's house as if she'd been a boarder there. His sailing orders for Burma arrived so quickly that they'd had no time to capitalize on their newly revived relationship, or even to grieve at their parting. Goodbye, Mr. Goodenday, she thought as she stood in the doorway waving at his departing car. I gave you a rotten deal. You deserved better. Sorry.

.

It was hard work, at M.I.5. Sophie and the Seagull sifted, classified and translated Wehrmacht reports and German radio commentaries, occasionally quite interesting but for the most part routine work. German-born employees were naturally kept away from anything of real significance.

In the basement there was a large air-raid shelter, and night-shift workers were under strict orders to report there when the sirens began to wail. If, however, you were on day shift, you could spend the night at home in bed during the alarm and keep your fingers crossed. But in the summer of '43 the attacks were so frequent and so violent that Sophie got used to installing herself in a neighboring cellar as soon as it grew dark, taking with her a pillow and a detective story. The Seagull strapped a Home Guard helmet on her head and lay down to sleep under her heavy oak kitchen table; just as safe, she said.

At the beginning of August, Sophie was put on night shift for a week. When she left the M.I.5. basement shelter after the all clear early one morning, the general devastation seemed more harrowing than ever before. Fires everywhere, the streets littered with craters. The air throbbed with the crackle of the flames, the hissing of the fire hoses, the deafening incomprehensible lowing of hundreds of mega-phones, the occasional all-too-familiar scream. It should have been light for some time already but the heavy smoke from the smoldering buildings formed an impenetrable shroud between the houses and kept the daylight out. She helped set up oil lamps around the craters on her way home, so that the ambulances could at least get through, drank a cup of tea with one of the salvage teams and wandered home, dropping with fatigue. Well, well, her house was still stand-ing. The one next door had no windowpanes left. Before climbing into bed, she phoned the Seagull, as they each did when one or the other of them was on night duty. No answer. Most likely she hadn't been able to close an eye all night and was fast asleep now, under-neath her kitchen table.

At nine o'clock a call woke her, from M.I.5. "Mrs. Goodenday? Mrs. Mewes hasn't got in yet, and we can't get an answer from her phone number—"

Sophie was downstairs in minutes. A passing taximan took pity on the expression on her face and brought her to Chelsea. The street where the Seagull lived was roped off. Sophie ran, and could already see a knot of people gathered around Alice's house, a familiar, unmis-takable kind of knot, moving, working, one next to the other, digging and shoveling. "Something's happened over there," one said, seeing that kind of knot, and quickly turned one's head away.

The Seagull's little house was no more than a pile of rubble. Direct hit. Neighbors recognized Sophie and made room for her.

"Was she inside, Miss—or was she out, perhaps?"

Sophie muttered hoarsely that Mrs. Mewes wasn't *allowed* to be out. . . .

Someone brought her a cup of tea, stroked her face. "You can never tell, she might not have been able to get home, during the raid. Happened with my auntie, we dug and dug—and she wasn't even under it."

"You go home," said the air-raid warden in charge. "We'll call you if we find anything. Word of honor."

She didn't move. It was a familiar response; they let her be. One of

283

the men brought out a cardboard box on the end of his shovel. "Eggs!
A couple of them unbroken—would you believe it. Must have been
the kitchen, here. How many rooms did this place have, Miss—d'you
know where her bedroom was?"

Sophie didn't answer. She had sunk to her knees, staring at a spot
not far from where the egg box had emerged. Out of the plaster and
the debris stuck something bright red. The man followed her gaze,
and at once tried to block Sophie's view with his back.

But she had recognized the Seagull's hand by the red fingernails.
She slumped forward, and the man gathered her up and carried her
to the emergency hut, stretched her out on a pair of hastily drawn-up
chairs. She opened her eyes as the approaching ambulance siren
grew louder.

"Perhaps she's still alive."

"Perhaps," said the uniformed nurse who sat next to her. She'd
seen stranger things than that before now, she added.

Sophie sat up and looked through the open door of the hut. A body
was being placed on a stretcher. She ran out, kneeled beside it. No
one pulled her away; the woman was virtually unmarked, there
would be no screams of horror.

"She's dead." The man laid his hand on Sophie's shoulder. "The
table there protected her from the falling masonry—it's hardly damaged, you can see—but the explosion made her lungs cave in. It
happens instantly, she couldn't have felt a thing."

He bent down and picked small pieces of plaster off the face. The
Seagull appeared, peaceful, eyes closed, the beautiful white hair dark-
gray with debris.

"An old lady," he said.

"No," whispered Sophie. "Quite young."

"Your mother?"

"No."

They let her climb into the ambulance and sit beside the Seagull
till they reached the hospital. Then they took her away from her.

Chapter 5 Weeks? Months? How long was it since the Seagull had disappeared? Sophie rose punctually every morning, went to M.I.5., did her work as before. During the days she could blot out the hand with its red fingernails jutting from the debris as if to say goodbye. But at night, when Sophie got back to her room, the hand was there. Away, out of the room—anywhere, didn't matter where, usually the M.I.5. canteen. There she sat down beside people she hardly knew, drank herself into life, had a short joyless affair with a colleague.

One day she fell and caught a long wooden splinter in her knee. They carried her to the first-aid, where the nurse on duty, bored and leafing through a magazine, was glad of something to do.

"Don't worry," she said cheerfully, "I'll just give you a little jab of morphine, and then I can cut the whole thing out and you won't even know I'm doing it."

"No morphine," whispered Sophie between clenched teeth.

"Allergic, are you? Well then, I'll give you a local anesthetic—"

Sophie violently shook her head.

"Not that either? Well, what am I to give you?"

"Nothing," Sophie groaned, barely audible. "I mustn't. I mustn't have anything at all."

The nurse was slow on the uptake. "Why on earth not?"

"I'm a junkie. Not even an aspirin—for five years—" She got no further, passed out with the pain and shock. The horrified nurse used the opportunity to extract the splinter with a pair of tweezers.

Sophie came to while she was still being bandaged, but kept her eyes closed and talked to the Seagull: That was for you, Alice, okay?

The first "good" day, despite the pain, the first day when the hand never appeared, the first day she didn't feel so utterly godforsaken. She'd proved to herself that she, Sophie, was still there.

.

One morning they asked her if she could sing. Sing? She was taken to a room with a piano in it. A young man sat playing and humming a tune from *Oklahoma*. He raised up an inch off the piano stool, murmured, "Lutz Reinhold," and went on playing and humming, till he got to the end of "I'm just a girl who can't say no . . . "

"Do you know it?"

"Yes."

"Here are the words in German." He pushed a piece of paper across the piano at her. "All right?"

He played four bars of introduction, but the red-haired girl missed the cue.

"Why didn't you come in?"

"I don't know how to."

What *had* they sent him this time? That pale, uncommunicative face—and the "girl who can't say no"! Plain silly. But something stopped him from sending her away.

"How about the 'Lorelei,' then?"

He played and sang the first verse, waiting for her to join in, but she simply stood listening.

"Well?" he said impatiently and took his hands off the keyboard.

Suddenly she began to sing the second verse, unaccompanied. *"Die schoenste Jungfrau sitzet . . . "* Her voice was a young girl's voice. Good God, he thought, she *is* the Lorelei with her "golden hair"! Careful now—dangerous rocks . . .

.

Sophie's home from then onward, till the end of the war, was a place called Bletchley. A few streets, a couple of churches, one pub —the others were all closed—one cinema. A dreary hole. A little way outside the town stood a long two-story building of the kind you'd pass without even noticing it. But ideally suited to its purpose. There were several such buildings in the district, all answerable to Woburn Abbey, one of the headquarters of the OSS, the American Secret Service broadcasting web.

The staff of the subsidiary units was kept deliberately small, so as not to attract attention, and no one wore uniform. In Sophie's building there were three other female colleagues, a Czech, an Austrian and another German girl, all equally fluent in English and German. Lutz Reinhold, American by birth, sergeant by rank, carried sole responsibility for the selection and the quality of the program, which was supposed to seduce the German audience into secret and highly dangerous listening. It consisted of a potpourri of Allied communiqués, jazz, general entertainment, and "personal messages": the names of real prisoners of war attached to fictitious messages to their relatives at home. Every day all this was carefully rehearsed and recorded, and taken by Reinhold in the evening to Woburn Abbey, where it was played to the section commander. This individual, known as the Beard, bullied Lutz mercilessly, day in day out, and made him feel that if they lost the war it was *his* fault.

Sophie had her own room, her American salary was twice as much as she'd been getting at M.I.5., PX goods were on sale in the basement of the building—a paradise, compared to the rest of wartime Britain, if only she'd been able to take it in.

The other girls liked her, since she was neither a talented performer nor did she show any interest in Lutz Reinhold, the cock of the walk. Thank God for him, young, sturdy, and appetizing, for the evenings were long and tedious. All one could do was to trot to the pub in Bletchley, listen to the nine-o'clock news, eat a cheese sandwich with PX butter and go to bed with Lutz. He was quite impartial, they all got their turn.

One evening he asked Sophie if she would carry his scripts while he took the tapes out to the car. Here we go, she thought, and waited in the car in front of Woburn Abbey while he went inside to be bawled out by the Beard; my turn now.

He emerged from the blackout like a ghost, his face still crestfallen from the drubbing he'd received, sat down behind the wheel and lit a cigarette. "There," he said, and exhaled deeply. "That's got *that* over —let's go and have some fun."

He spoke in German, in a heavy and funny drawl, and she laughed politely. "I'm really from Leipzig," he went on, "a real old Saxon, didn't you know?"

He drove briskly past Bletchley, without explanation, and on to Winslow, the next village, to the Rose and Crown—indistinguishable from the Bletchley pub, except that here they were alone. He had brought along some Spam from the PX, cigarettes for the landlord and nylons for his wife. Which was how they ended up alone in the alcove with three asters in a vase on the table.

The other girls must have been given the same routine, she thought, and till now it had always worked. Of course he'd also brought a bottle of Scotch. "Your health, Lorelei." She nodded and sipped.

The old routine continued over dinner: mutual journeys of discovery, who-where-and-what information. Why not just show our passports and get it over with? she thought and quickly drank another glass to drown her hostility and be able to listen to his case history with proper attention. Goodness gracious me, born in Kentucky by mistake, what a lark, a seven-month child, still trying to catch up, ha ha. Quite what his mother was doing in Kentucky she had somehow missed, and by now he was already deep in mid-description of his father, who seemed to have had something to do with leather. In Leipzig. Pray God he doesn't ask about *my* father. Or my mother. Hold on a minute! Why ever not? Earn a little sympathy.

"My mother's in Ravensbrueck."

"Mine's dead." One up on Ravensbrueck, dead is dead. "She died when I was twelve."

Hard to compete with that. Sympathy was called for.

"Twelve! That must have been pretty grim, losing her at that age." She thought of Anita, though there was really no connection, but the Scotch had done its duty, and suffering humanity had her by the throat.

"Even harder for Jonathan, my brother. He was only five. He killed himself, later."

That did it; cut right through the Scotch.

"Why did your brother kill himself?"

"Nobody knows."

"How old was he?"

"Seventeen."

Turhan had been nineteen.

"Tell me about it."

He told her briefly about the night, the twelve hours in the zoo, and the shooting in front of the gorilla's cage. After a short silence she said: "My brother killed himself too."

"Does anyone know—"

"Yes," she interrupted quickly, and in a way that forbade further questions.

"It comes to the same thing," he said after a while. "I mean, in the end, at the last moment, it's always for the same reason."

She nodded, and began to eat the Spam.

"Have *you* ever been tempted?"

"Yes."

"Me too."

They laughed, as if they'd both shared the same beautiful experience. He refilled their glasses; the bottle was already half empty.

"I've got a problem," he said boldly. "I'm really queer."

"What do you mean by 'really'?"

"I have affairs with women, but my only real love was a man."

"Why not?" she said calmly, and helped herself to some mashed potatoes.

"You wouldn't call that a problem?"

"*Was* it, when you loved the man?"

"No."

"Find yourself another one."

"I don't really want to." He raised his glass, but didn't drink, and gazed longingly at her over the rim. "Do you know—I believe I could fall very much in love with you."

"Then you'd really have a problem."

"Why? Do you love someone else? Your husband?"

"My husband?"

"Well—Mr. Goodenday."

"Ah—yes." How far away he was, much farther away than Burma.

"You don't? Then I've got no problem!" He emptied his glass in one go. "Just give me a week or two . . . "

"You've *got* a problem. I was a morphine addict, for years."

He looked at her, dismayed, like a child who'd been good and yet had his bar of chocolate taken away. "And—now?"

"Now I'm cured, as they call it."

It had clearly thrown him, and he said nothing. Tentatively he examined her face, to see if there were any traces left. "I don't know anything about—that sort of thing. I only know it's not very pleasant—" He stopped, hoping she would agree, not knowing she was quietly seething. (Not very pleasant! Mealy-mouthed idiot.) "Can it start up again?"

"It can. But it won't." Her voice could get quite rough.

"Then why is it a problem?"

"It's *your* problem, if you fall in love with someone who's capable of it."

She could be quite unnerving, the Lorelei, with those strange eyes in her white, triangular face.

"I don't want to know about it. I just feel sure that—" He hesitated.

"That what?"

"That you're a good person."

Touching, his desperate seriousness. And why the hell wasn't she touched? I must wake up, she told herself, I must feel something again—there's another hedge growing up around me. I'll act as if I do feel something, and perhaps it'll come, in time.

·

To his surprise she let him into her room that very night. When they'd got back to Bletchley, he'd only asked lightly, purely protocol, whether he could have a last drink with her.

"Come up, if you like. And come in." She had nothing to offer him by way of a drink, and didn't even bother to turn off the light. *He* did. She gave him far more than he could have expected the first night, but he couldn't entirely rid himself of the feeling that her passion remained cold. He was the hapless sailor in his skiff on the river Rhine, gazing up at the Lorelei on the rock—despite the fact that the Lorelei was lying in bed right next to him.

He said the usual things: "How beautiful you are!"

"Yes," she said.

After a while he said: "Why did you let me come up with you? Do you find me attractive?"

"I don't know yet."

·

Throughout next day's rehearsals, she behaved as if nothing had happened, never gave him a single stolen glance. Their absence the night before had set the cat among the pigeons, but now the other girls began to wonder if anything had actually taken place. The Goodenday woman was a prude, and as cold as a polar bear's snout.

But the next few days confirmed their worst suspicions: it *had* taken place, and it was continuing to take place, in her room, all night and every night.

An anonymous letter found its way to the Beard: the female employees of the American Forces Network could not be expected to give of their best to the war effort in such a lewd, immoral atmosphere.

At which the Beard, after the evening's routine dressing-down, waved Lutz back for more.

"What the hell are you up to down there in Bletchley, Reinhold?

Can't you do it without everybody knowing? Is it the redhead you're—"

"Yes, sir."

"Nothing special, is she?"

"Oh, yes, sir."

"I *mean* at singing, Reinhold."

"Oh, I see, sir."

The Beard had to laugh, and Lutz lost his head.

"We're getting married, sir."

This was news not only to the Beard but to Sophie. Lutz was afraid she'd laugh in his face, but instead she eyed him thoughtfully.

"How old are you?"

"Twenty-seven next month."

"Eleven years younger."

"Doesn't worry me, far from it," he said, and hugged her. "Does it worry you?"

If I loved him, thought Sophie, it *would* worry me.

.

She wrote to Goodenday in Burma, and he answered by return: she was welcome to begin proceedings whenever she wanted, he was living with an Indonesian woman who could be made the official grounds for divorce, as he planned to marry her anyway, the climate was simply spendid.

She sat with his letter in her lap, gazing out of her window at the rain-soaked gray-brown fields. Whatever would the Seagull have said, if she could have told her she was going to marry Lutz Reinhold? Aha, she would have said.

And why am I doing it? Nobody's forcing me, what do I want with this nice young man? Trying to squeeze some feeling out of myself, without even knowing if there's any left? They used to brim over— Papa! Anita! Dimi! And—in a different way—the Seagull! I didn't have to jog myself, to squeeze it out. Could it all have gone up in smoke at the auto-da-fé—and then, later, the last flickering of the flame stamped out in the rubble around the red fingernails? Did that sort of thing happen?

Lutz. Suppose for a moment he didn't come back tonight. An accident. Killed. Would I miss him? Yes. Oh yes! But wouldn't I also be—relieved? God, I don't know. Perhaps.

Stalemate.

Yet, there was something that might tip the scales. Not the fact
that I like sleeping with him—that's replaceable—but the exultation
in his voice, night after night, saying: "At last! At last! You've made
me break out, I'm free, I'm like other men, I *love* a woman." Not bad,
to listen to that sort of thing in the darkness.

.

The Beard gave them three days' leave as a wedding present, and
they drove straight from the registry office to the station. Eight hours
in an overcrowded compartment on their way to Torquay, where
people could walk in the sun on the beach. There were palm trees,
too, it was said.

But when they finally arrived at Torquay and clambered out of the
compartment with a sigh of relief, they were greeted by an ear-
splitting roar of aircraft engines and machine-gun fire, and blown
straight back into the compartment. A squadron of Messerschmitts
was bombing the station.

Their hotel yawned, huge and emptied by the war. The guests
were half a dozen of what looked like other honeymoon couples,
mostly in uniform, and, like them, holding hands and searching for
palm trees. If there were any they stayed out of sight, as it poured all
day and every day with rain. Sophie and Lutz spent the three days in
the frozen splendor of the deserted reception rooms, gazing out at
the stormy gray sea. Sometimes they glanced at each other, thinking:
we're on our honeymoon! And laughed.

They were never bored with each other, certainly not at night, and
for daytime use they discovered at least one new and inexhaustible
common interest: music. Lutz knew considerably more about it than
even Dimi, and succeeded in making her like some modern music,
too. He was delighted—as Dimi had once been—to find her such a
quick learner. While Sophie, eager as always to hunt down the weak
points in her armory, thought: Perhaps *that*'s it! I learn fast, *too* fast,
and I reach a high plateau, where I stand and look around me—and I
don't feel I've made any real progress. . . .

Life was good with Lutz. It was easy to live with someone who
was so obviously happy, who thought that he'd glued his shaky com-
ponents together for all time. If only he didn't look so ludicrously
young! With his wavy hair and snub nose, he looked like a twenty-
year-old. Sophie, on the other hand, had found her first gray hair,

during their honeymoon, and on that very day the hotel maid had called out: "Mrs. Reinhold—your son's waiting for you downstairs."

She nodded, off guard. Should she have answered: "That's not my son, you silly cow, that's my husband!"?

Slowly, she walked down the wide staircase. In the foyer Lutz came toward her, beaming.

"Do you know what they just told me? 'Your mother'll be down in a moment.' Come along, then—Mum."

He opened his arms and she fell into them, laughing with relief.

BOOK VIII

Chapter 1

The front doorbell rang in the flat. Lutz looked at the clock: half past five—who could it be? Karlheinz, his friend, never came before seven.

Who the hell was it, then?

He pushed Othello, the cat, off his lap, and quickly emptied the glass on the table before him. Then he got up, angrily, and with an effort. Why didn't they leave him alone, this time of day was his and his alone. Time to relax and recover for the eight-o'clock performance. What he did between leaving the office and doing his nightly stint was his business.

First turn off the radio. Pity, a good concert, Stravinsky.

The doorbell went again, longer this time.

"All right! All right!" He shuffled to the door, in one slipper, couldn't find the other one, probably under the sofa. He groped unsuccessfully for the light switch in the hall, called: "Who is it?" A man's voice answered, but he couldn't catch what he said, and opened the door. A young man, middle height, glasses, the face somehow familiar.

"Yes?"

"My name is Karanogliu, Dr. Karanogliu, do you remember me? I look after your wife, that is, I'm on night duty—no, no!" he interrupted himself quickly, seeing the fear in Lutz's eyes. "Nothing's happened, it's all right, I just wanted to look you up, because—" He hesitated, would have liked to leave, the man hardly looked welcoming.

"Come on in," said Lutz, and led his visitor through the dark hallway into the sitting room. "Sit down." He hobbled into the kitchen and came back with a second glass. "*There* it is!" He chased Othello off his other slipper and carefully put it on his naked foot. "You'll have to excuse me." He made a vague gesture which included the slippers, the lonely bottle, the wet stains on the table, and the sad, dilapidated look of the room. "I've just had a bath. The cleaning woman didn't come today, I don't know why." The cat jumped up onto his lap, and he began to stroke it absent-mindedly. "I don't like cats," he murmured. "Do you?"

"Yes. Yes, I do."

"Would you like a glass of sherry?" Without waiting for an answer, he filled the second glass and pushed it across the table. "Not very good quality. Sorry. Cheers."

The young doctor took a sip. What am I doing here? he thought, I'm intruding and the sherry is undrinkable. Knock it back and leave.

His host seemed to have forgotten about him. He stared ahead, an elderly child's face beneath gray-brown curls, his naked belly protruding, one hand vainly searching for a button to close the gap in the old cardigan. Only the cat, purring happily, glistened with well-being.

"Herr Reinhold, you said you wouldn't come to the hospital again, unless I sent word. Well, I'm here—bringing you word." He smiled encouragingly, but Lutz stared coldly back. "I'm off duty for the next three days, which means there'll be a nurse sitting by your wife's bed, and for periods of time no one at all." He left a pause, giving Lutz a chance to offer his services unprompted, but the man only pushed the glass farther toward him.

"Drink it, now you're here. Miserable bloody sherry, but you get used to it, and quantity's all that matters to me. I'm not an alcoholic, but you'd be right in thinking: Her husband drinks, poor Sophie. What's your name—your first name?"

"Kostas."

"Cheers, Father Confessor Costas. To Sophie's book!"

"Herr Reinhold, there are moments when sick people urgently need to get things off their chest and you just have to listen, whether you want to or not. You automatically forget it all afterward. Though, in your wife's case—" Lutz's eyes were suddenly full of interest.

"Different in my wife's case, eh?" he said dryly. "What did you say your name was?"

"Kostas. I have to admit, Herr Reinhold—"

"Lutz. Call me Lutz. I bet you know more about me than I do myself, don't you?"

"Herr Reinhold, your wife will get a shock when she finds a strange face at her bedside tonight, someone who knows nothing about her, and I wouldn't be sure—"

"That she'll survive it? She's tougher than you think. And now she's got something to hang onto."

"I don't understand—"

"You! She's hanging onto *you*." He laughed. The doctor looked down, but went on obstinately: "I can't be there tonight, don't you understand? You're her husband, you're allowed to—"

"Well, doesn't that beat everything!" cried Lutz in sudden cheerfulness. "The old bag o' bones has done it again—you're in love, man!"

"No." The eyes behind the glasses gazed unblinkingly at him. "But it's got something to do with love, you're right."

"Kostas, my friend, you are naive—Sophie doesn't want to tell *me* her next chapters. I know them anyway, only too well. It's *you* she wants to tell, *you* she wants there gaping with the wonder of it all. How far has she got? Has all been confessed?"

"Your wife had just finished telling me how you got married, during the war, and how happy you were."

Lutz scratched Othello behind the ears. "Is that what she said?"

"Why—isn't it true?"

"Oh yes."

"To judge by what I've heard so far, these years with you must have been among her happiest. I can't understand how it could go wrong. You weren't just lovers, you were friends, too."

"Did she say that?"

"Yes," Kostas lied, but it was worth it for the look the man gave him. After a while Lutz spoke without lifting his eyes from Othello. "Do you know who Yasmin was?"

"Your wife's mother."

The head shot up. "No, man. *My* mother!"

"*Your* mother? I don't understand—"

"Don't you know the story of how we found her again? You don't? Well then, I'll tell you a chapter from Sophie's book, one that'll take your breath away. And afterward you won't have to ask again why it all went wrong, as you put it. Come on, drink up, even if you don't like it." He emptied the last of the bottle into the doctor's glass, till it overflowed. "Sorry. Empty now anyway, I'll get another one."

He returned from the kitchen with a whiskey bottle, and angrily dismissed the young man's gesture of protest. "What's it matter, who cares what it is, as long as it's something. Anyway—here goes: end of the war, right? Everything at sixes and sevens, no one knowing where to go or what to do. No more Armed Forces Network, obviously, but I had a new job, not a bad one either: sorting out the prisoners of war, sheep to the right, goats to the left.

299

"We were still living in Bletchley, in two little rooms. London was a wilderness, they were just starting to clear the rubble, you couldn't find anywhere to live, or to eat, everything was still rationed. But life was good, that's how I remember it. We were—yes, I'll use the word 'happy' without throwing up. And in the middle of it all—a letter from the Turkish embassy in Paris: they had Yasmin there! We flew over at once—I was still able to pull strings via my old boss, the Beard—and, you know, I was even more excited than Sophie. She was glad, obviously, but a bit apprehensive, we'd met a few concentration camp survivors and every one of 'em was different from the other. One or two seemed fairly normal, but some wouldn't speak a word, others laughed all the time, I remember one who winced every time a door was shut. Quite a few had no teeth left. I hadn't known Yasmin before, so it was easier for me, but Sophie was shit-scared, unusual for her.

"On the flight over she was very quiet, and we both had a brandy at the airport. Then we phoned the embassy, to give Yasmin a chance to prepare. When we got there, she came through the door, a fat, white-haired woman, smiling, hugging Sophie and then me. She hugged me! Right away." He paused for a moment. The cat rubbed its head against his hand, but without effect. "Anyway, Yasmin and I . . . from the moment we met she was my mother, and I was her son—she often told me so. Sophie remained a bit on the outside, looking at us in surprise. Rather put out, too. Not that she was jealous, she didn't love either of us enough for that." He began to stroke the cat again and leaned back, shutting his eyes, as if reluctant to abandon the memory of this first meeting.

"I wanted to take Yasmin back to England with us, at once, but she was determined not to be a burden to us. 'First find somewhere *yourselves.*' All things considered she had been lucky, no one had beaten her or ill-treated her, thanks to the Turkish embassy, for the Nazis didn't wish to antagonize the Turks. She was so fat only because her belly was distended by hunger, she said, and she would soon get her figure back, but she stayed the same size. 'You're round all over, there isn't a straight line or an angle on you. You look like an egg,' said Sophie. The name stuck, and she didn't mind.

"I think I must have got on Sophie's nerves in my enthusiasm for Yasmin. It had never entered my mind that I needed a mother. But I did."

"Of course," said the doctor. "Only natural, in your case."

"Well, well," said Lutz. "So she's told you about that, too, has she? So much the better, I don't have to explain to you why I found myself writing to Yasmin every day, why I missed her so much. I had no idea why, I was convinced that I loved *Sophie* in Yasmin or the other way around. Balls. Queers love their mamas, and that was all there was to it, as we know now, you and I—Sophie already knew it then. But, as I say, she wasn't at all jealous, she just—didn't know how it would work out, the three of us under one roof. As it turned out, I received a good offer from Munich, through the Beard of course, with his finger in every pie. I was to be music critic for one of the newly founded newspapers, just what I'd always dreamed of. I flew to Munich, signed a contract, and started looking for an apartment. I was all go, in those days. Apartment houses hadn't begun to be built yet, but they were planning one in the Ottostrasse, and we put our name down for a flat. A big, brand-new flat with a sitting room and two bedrooms. Ours would look out on what must have once been a fine garden, with a stone lion standing all alone on a low, crumbling wall, surrounded by weeds—simply beautiful. Just right for us, and when I say us, I mean Sophie, Yasmin and me." He fell silent, staring into his glass. Othello stood up and rubbed himself against Lutz's chin. "Bloody bore they are, cats. They don't give a damn whether you like them or not."

"And was that a mistake, then? Your mother-in-law moving in with you?"

"Mother-in-law? Ah yes. No, that was no mistake, on the contrary, it worked very well. For a long time. The best years of all for me, and for Sophie too, I think. Her most peaceful years, at any rate, and that means a good deal in her case. She got used to Munich, made our flat look quite beautiful, we were able to buy a car and the three of us would drive out into the country on the weekends, to the mountains or to one of the many lakes. It was Yasmin, of course, who made it all so special, she was so—so—I don't know how to describe it to you—and so pretty to look at with her white hair and golden skin, always dressed in Easter-egg colors, pink and pale blue, and smelling of her strange Turkish herbs—it was a joy to come home, every day." He forgot his dislike of the cat and pressed it tight against him. Othello immediately stopped purring and showed his claws.

"Gradually, all around us—the great German economic miracle;

and in our little flat another kind of miracle: a mother and daughter who didn't belong together but who could *live* together all the same. Mind you, through *me*, and only through me. I was their filling station, refueling both of them, supplying them with what they needed: a bit of clowning, fooling around, you know, some primitive fun, which I once had on tap—can you imagine that? There were never any tensions, and that was all due to me, since deep down, they were suspicious of each other, and tricky by nature. But all that relaxed after a while and they got on really well, even if Sophie's feelings toward Yasmin were never as intense as mine. I simply drowned her in tenderness, something she had never known in all her life. It made Sophie laugh, and she said she would call our chapter "The Egg and Her Lover," in the book she always said she'd write one day." He stared at the table and started to mop up the wet stains with the sleeves of his cardigan.

The doctor, leaning across, put his hand lightly on his arm. "But if it all worked so well, what happened? Can you explain it to me? Three perfectly rational, intelligent, grown-up people—"

"Patience, man. First I've got to make you understand what it was we *had*." He suddenly laughed, shaking his head. "We even had a child—well, nearly. It sort of dangled before my eyes, if you don't mind my saying so, and was already blueprinted onto our future. Just imagine, one day Sophie told me she was pregnant, as we were walking arm in arm after dinner in the English Garden Park. I stopped dead in my tracks, while she walked on as if nothing had happened. I ran after her, grabbed hold of her, stared her in the face. 'A baby?' She nodded, and gave a little off-guard smile, as if she too thought the idea adventurous, to say the least. 'Don't forget, I'm forty-three,' she said. 'Never mind' I cried. 'That doesn't matter, it's just—' 'Just what?' 'I was thinking . . . what do you do with a baby in a small flat, if you want to listen to Bartok?' At that she stood still and laughed so loud that people turned and stared at us. Then she hugged me and said: 'You're the dearest, silliest man I've ever met.' She said those words, Doctor."

"And the baby?"

"She lost it. In the third month. I think we were both rather relieved, and not only because of Bartok. Yasmin, however, was sad, she still had the old oriental longing for continuity. And then it was forgotten. Just as well." He fell silent, stroked the cat, stared vacantly at the opposite wall.

"You were going to tell me how it was, that—"

"I'm putting it off, as you've noticed, dear Father Confessor, because—what was it you said just now? Three rational, intelligent, grown-up people, wasn't that what you called us? And then along comes something so trivial, so banal, and rips everything apart. If it had been a great passion, at least, but to jump into bed with a Herr Soldien, of two floors below! You know the routine, I certainly do, I've been through it often enough myself: hurry, hurry, darling, not much time today, curtains closed, clothes pulled off, quick wrestle in the sheets, discreet glance at the wristwatch: God, I must be off! Fasten the bra, open up the curtains, where on earth are my shoes? Stocking seams all crooked—who cares? Bye-bye darling, it was wonderful, ring you tomorrow as soon as he's gone. Blow a kiss, shut the door, straighten your hat and climb two flights of stairs, slightly out of breath. That's the form, isn't it? You must have had a dose of this at one time or another, am I right?

"But my Sophie! I still don't know how it came about, I've never asked her. Yasmin told me, when it was already in full swing. She expected me to take 'appropriate measures.' Don't forget, where she came from Sophie would have been stoned, without further ado, certainly in the days of Yasmin's youth. I can only tell you, Kostas, that *my* measures were a disaster. It was clear at once that I couldn't handle the situation. I was too green and too young really, thirty-four, I'd just come by a new mother—and I loved being a nursling. Sophie was forty-five and she held the whip hand in our relationship, because—because I—"

"Because you weren't sure of your sexuality."

Lutz smiled grimly. "But I didn't know that at the time. I nearly burst with jealousy, made a dreadful scene, screamed, pulled her hair, did God knows what. She remained completely silent till I'd finished. Then she said: 'Did Yasmin tell you?' And from that moment it was all over between them. Of course, Yasmin took it out on her much more effectively than I could, because she never lost her temper, but she told Sophie in so many words that she didn't deserve me. Sorry to have to say such a thing about myself, but that's what she said. Also, that Sophie was her father's true daughter and that

303

she didn't deserve to have anyone offer her his life, and the like. Sophie was white with rage, and ran out of the flat. 'Let her go,' said Yasmin. 'She's going to Herr Soldien. He's got an ex-wife and two children to keep, and no steady job. Sit back and wait.' Sophie came in late. I could see she'd been crying, and tried to take her in my arms, I was so longing to forgive her! But she wouldn't let me."

"Herr Reinhold, your wife has a man's attitude to these things."

"But *I* don't—that's the trouble. *I'm* not a real man, perhaps that's why I couldn't cope. She promised me it was all over, but she was lying. All the same, I wouldn't call her an untruthful person. She lied like a child, to make things easier for herself. The meetings with Soldien went on, though not as frequently, and I knew about it, every time, from Yasmin. Our telephone had an extension in every room, Yasmin simply picked up the receiver in her room and listened in, when Sophie spoke to Soldien. Then she told *me*. After all, I was her son! She suffered for me and threw stones *for* me, d'you understand? And every time I made such a dreadful scene with Sophie that in the end it just wasn't worth her while. Either that, or the thing went sour of its own accord. She stopped phoning him, and disappearing without notice. That's to say, she now disappeared regularly, but we knew where she went, and I checked on her, and Yasmin checked on her, and it all tallied: an old lady was teaching her to play bridge.

"I couldn't really object, although I hate card games—mindless, time-abusing nonsense—but Yasmin said Sophie had to have *something*, so I kept my mouth shut and paid for the very expensive lessons. Also, it was good that she spent less time in the flat, because I couldn't straighten things out between Sophie and Yasmin, however hard I tried. Not that they quarreled, you couldn't quarrel with Yasmin, but they were happier when they didn't have to see each other. Each was furiously disappointed in the other, and they were suddenly mother and daughter, chips off the same unyielding block."

His glass was empty. So was the bottle.

"Sorry," he murmured, and disappeared into the kitchen. Came back with a half-empty bottle of Campari.

"Listen, Kolja—"

"Kostas."

"Listen, do you think you could make me a good cup of coffee, later on? Right now I need another drop of something, to—well, to tell you what's coming. But later on I've got to cover a concert at the Residenz or somewhere . . . oh well, maybe I just won't bother." He slumped heavily into the old armchair and brushed Othello off his lap before the cat could make itself comfortable. "Not now," he told the animal, with a frown and an upraised finger while Othello gazed at him expectantly. "I can't be doing with you now." He fell back, gripping the arms of the chair, and stared into the doctor's face. "I don't envy you *your* bloody job, either. I'd rather listen to second-rate musicians, any day."

"Why?" said the doctor, dumbfounded. "What have I done?"

"Nothing to do with *you*, it's that whole damn, gibbering hospital nightmare. I *hate* it." He gestured violently, almost fell out of the chair. "Down! Down!" he mumbled sternly to himself as if admonishing a fractious dog. "Calm down. Got to concentrate or I won't be able to sort it all out properly. Now: one morning Yasmin couldn't get out of bed and the doctor came. Circulation collapse. She had to stay strictly in bed, not even put her feet on the ground. Imagine what that did to our life, in that little flat: an old woman suddenly bedridden, Sophie having to wash her and put her on a chamberpot, and myself, rushing home every evening between office hours and the next concert, to make sure that everything was all right. It wasn't all right, I tell you. Yasmin tried to get up, fell over, was in pain and didn't tell anyone, but when the doctor saw her he insisted she should go to the hospital to be looked after properly. And as he said that, he looked at Sophie. . . .

"And Sophie—well, you can guess. She'd done all that was necessary, carefully, punctually, but without love. Which is unbearable, if you can't do anything for yourself. You can either be lovingly looked after at home, or stay at a hospital and *pay* for proper care. Anything midway between the two is torture. So Yasmin went into the hospital, was nursed efficiently and didn't have to worry about what the nurses felt. She came to like it there very much and got better, and the day came when they said she would have to go home soon, and remain in bed there. They needed her hospital bed for other, acute cases. Yasmin was reduced to pleading and begging—I think for the first time in her life. Anything, not to have to go back to our flat and once again be utterly dependent on Sophie. Don't get me wrong, Doctor: Sophie had done her duty by Yasmin, and more than her duty. She had sat up all night with her, had cooked special food for her, carried trays, laundered sheets, given up her bridge lessons without complaint; and later, when Yasmin was in the hospital, she visited her every single day, brought grapes and magazines and chocolate. But—without love, Doctor, as I say. One day, as she sat beside the bed, the nurse told her she would have to take her mother home, by the end of the week at the latest. Sophie nodded, she'd been expecting it. But no sooner had the woman left the room than Yasmin seized her hand—Sophie told me all this afterward—and said lovingly, *lovingly*, Kostas, for the first time in ages, or perhaps even the first time ever: 'Sophie, my child, I want you to do something for me. I'm not coming home, under any circumstances. You understand that, don't you? I'll only ruin your lives. You'd feel the same way, if you were in my position. Help me. Bring me something, so that I can die. I'm an old woman, and I've had enough.' "

"Oh no," said the young doctor, hardly audible.

"Oh yes, Doctor, oh yes! Sophie found a man—nothing to do with the hospital. He'd been a doctor once, but he had a Nazi past, something to do with euthanasia and those so-called clinics, you know the ones I mean. It turned out that he still had some potassium cyanide capsules, from the war, the ones thousands of SS men carried around with them, and all the others who had something to hide. She bought a few off him. 'Might come in handy some other time,' she said. And the next day she took Yasmin one. She had a last try, she told me, and I believe her. She said: 'Egg—be reasonable! Come back to us, you've got a son now, what will Lutz do without you?' She didn't say, what will *I* do without you, she was too honest for that, she's not untruthful, as I say, and anyway Yasmin would have known she was pretending. Instead, she put her arms around her—this too for the first time in ages—kissed her and said: 'You're a good daughter, Sophie, and I thank you with all my heart. God bless you.' Sophie fled from the room.

"That very evening, late, the hospital rang up. It happened to be me that answered. Regretfully, they had to inform us that Yasmin had died. 'What?' I shouted. 'That's impossible! I saw her only a few hours ago, and she was perfectly all right!' Sophie came running out of the kitchen and grabbed the receiver from me. She was white in the face, trembling so much she could hardly hold it to her ear. 'Heart failure?' she stammered. 'Yes—yes, of course—' I pushed her aside, yelled into the phone, God knows what I said, I'd beat up the doctors, I'd sue the hospital for negligence—meanwhile I had to hold Sophie at bay, while she tried to tear the receiver away from me. All the same I managed to make out something of what they were saying, at the other end: they had brought Yasmin her supper, and she had eaten it all, and talked to the nurse, feeling perfectly all right, just a little hot, and she'd asked the nurse to open the window. Later on, when the night nurse came on duty, she'd found her lying there. Of course, if we wanted a postmortem, they'd oblige."

" 'Postmortem?' I said.

"At that, Sophie shoved me aside with all her might, seized the phone and turned her back on me.

" 'This is her daughter speaking,' she said imperiously. 'I do not with to have a postmortem examination. My mother was a Muslim. Any kind of tampering with her body would be sacrilegious.'

"For the last few words she turned around and looked at me, eyes wide open and glowing like coals.

"Sacrilege. I hadn't thought of that. I heard her go on to say, crisply: 'Thank you. We'll come right away.'

"I broke down, I fell into this chair, and cried and cried, I don't know how long. Sophie sat where you're sitting, without a word, until I calmed down at last. Then she took my hand, held it very tightly and said: 'Before we drive to the hospital, there's something I've got to tell you . . .' "

Chapter 2   When he got home from his visit to Lutz he found a note pushed under the door of his room in the staff quarters. "Dr. K. please ring Ward 5c." The head-physician's secretary answered. Could the doctor spare five minutes of his off-duty time?

He took the lift to the top floor, where the administrative offices were to be found. No need to try to find out from the secretary what it was about, he already knew.

"Would you mind telling me, my dear colleague," said the head physician, "what's going on in Room 384? We'll be forced to take some drastic action—the other patients are losing sleep. Can you explain to me why the patient in question gets in such a state when you're not on duty?"

"The patient—is laboring under the impression that she's writing a book, and that I read her daily chapters."

"Writing a book? She's under heavy sedation, morphine, unless I'm mistaken."

He avoided the older man's eyes. "In her case it produces this hallucinatory state."

"Young man," said the head physician, "I'm beginning to wonder whether your concern for the patient hasn't gone a bit too far."

"I'm prepared to defer my leave for a week."

"That appears to be the only solution. At least for the time being. Perhaps you could manage to wean the patient off your presence. How you do that is your affair. But *do* it. Let there be no mistake about that."

He took the lift down to the third floor, hurried along the corridor, and not a moment too soon; in the distance, he could already hear Sophie's frenzied shrieking, and a few anguished noises in between, from another female voice. He ran past the open door of the ward-room, glimpsed two nurses and an attendant out of the corner of his eye, heard them break off their conversation as they saw him rush past. Footsteps behind him. One of the women hurrying after him.

"Doctor!" It was the matron. He stopped, reluctantly, and she caught up with him. "Thank goodness you're here. We're having trouble with Number 384. She thinks Sister Baerbel is the Italian woman—"

"What Italian woman?"

"An Italian woman came this afternoon, during visiting hours, and insisted on seeing Frau Reinhold. I told her that you'd strictly forbidden any visits, but somehow she managed to slip in—Sister Baerbel found her in the room and threw her out at once. But when she went back to the patient, it all started. She won't let her come near her bed—"

The shrieking rang out again, and he turned and left the matron standing.

Sophie had somehow raised herself halfway up, her hair damp and tangled around her flushed face. She was wheezing for breath, spit running from her mouth. In one hand she held her bedside clock, and

waved it threateningly. Seeing him in the doorway, she croaked:
"The bitch! The rotten bitch! If she comes any closer, I'll—I'll—"

The nurse was cowering in the farthest corner of the room. She
was a young girl, with a round, peasant face under her lopsided
cap.

"I don't know what to do, Doctor," she sobbed, "I only wanted
to—"

"Out!" growled Sophie and waved the clock again. It slipped from
her shaking hand and crashed to the floor; splinters of glass and
pieces of metal flew in all directions.

"Never mind, I'll take care of it." He moved toward the nurse.

"Don't touch her!" Sophie screeched. She tried to pull back the
covers and throw herself out of bed, but instead collapsed to one
side, hitting her forehead on the bedside table.

"Oh God," whimpered the nurse and hid her face in her hands. He
put his arm around her shoulders and led her to the door. "Tell them
not to send anyone in here, Sister Baerbel, I'll deal with it." He
smiled at her. "I'll take over your duty hours tonight, all right?" And
shut the door behind her.

Sophie still lay where she'd fallen, forehead on the table, one long
emaciated arm brushing the floor. He pulled her upright, lay her
back on the pillows; she was conscious, though trembling all over,
eyes partly shut, a faint rattling in her throat. He brought a towel,
moistened it, dabbed the lump on her forehead, wiped the spittle
from her chin and neck. Then he read the chart at the end of the
bed: the last injection had been three hours ago. He prepared another one, in the bathroom, dispensed it at once, then started to
gather up the scattered fragments of the clock. Pity, it was an old
one, with a beautifully incised face, now lying in pieces alongside the
twisted golden hands. The casing had Arabic letters engraved on it.

"It was my grandfather's," came a whisper from the bed.

He placed the casing and the hands on the bedside table, and
silently continued picking up the remaining shards of glass. Then he
sat himself in his chair, folded his hands in his lap, and gazed at the
ceiling. The fitful, rattling breath slowly eased. After a while it had
become almost inaudible, and he looked at her. Her eyes were open
now, the dry, cracked lips moving incessantly. He pulled out a
bedside-table drawer, found a tube of vaseline and rubbed some on

her lips. When he felt them close, kissing his finger, he drew back, and turned the lamp so that it hit neither his face nor hers. Then he sat back in his chair again. And closed his eyes.

"Forgive me." It came so softly he could hardly hear it. "Say you forgive me."

"Say that to Sister Baerbel tomorrow, not to me."

"To whom? Come nearer, Brother, don't make it so hard for me, I can't speak that loudly."

"You managed to, before."

"I had to scream or she wouldn't have left. Don't you understand?"

"Who is the Italian woman?"

She looked at him in surprise. "You mean you don't know? Oh! Oh dear! Of course you don't know about her—I haven't got there yet, have I. She'll show up any minute, she's already waiting in the wings —just one more chapter. But this chapter . . . I've been putting it off . . . I'm afraid of this chapter, Brother . . ." She covered her face with her hands, lay motionless for a long time.

"What did she want from you, this woman?"

Her hands fell away from her face. "Imagine, Brother, I opened my eyes—and there she was! There, at the foot of the bed, staring at me without a word, just staring. I thought it was a nightmare, and I quickly closed my eyes, but when I opened them again, she was standing *here*, right next to me, she'd put on a white cap and she was trying to—"

"That was Sister Baerbel, she was trying to take your pulse."

But Sophie wasn't listening. "She's one of the cruel doves," she whispered. "She came to see if I was already lame . . . but I'm not afraid of her. It's you I'm afraid of! You see, this next chapter, it's got something terrible in it, but I've got to write it or the book's a lie. Come a little nearer. I'll have to whisper it. I did something very bad—"

"I think—" he said slowly, "I think you've already told me. I've already read the chapter."

She stared at him, then narrowed her eyes and squinted as if trying to see into a thick mist. Then she said softly, every syllable distinct: "About—Yasmin? You've read it?"

"Yes," he said calmly. "Don't you remember?"

Her eyes still studied him suspiciously. "You mean I've already written it? Have I really? And here I am, torturing myself, and you've already read it! The entire chapter? Right to the end?"

"You mean about bringing her the capsule?"

His eyes, behind the glasses, looked steadfastly into hers, which relaxed, slowly, and then closed in blissful exhaustion. "Oh—how wonderful," she whispered. "You know all about it, and you still love me." He didn't respond quickly enough, and her eyes opened at once in anxiety. "Don't you?" He nodded. "That's what I need. You don't know how badly, because, from that day onward, Lutz stopped loving me. An outcast, a leper, that's what I became. He looked after me, but he didn't want to touch me anymore, and I suddenly realized that I needed his love. I'd always seen our marriage as a solid, simple structure, without much in the way of fancy decoration, and with his love as the cement. Now it crashed to the ground—no, that's not right, it didn't crash, it crumbled. Every day you could hear it crackle and rip inside the walls. The facade's still there. Pity," she said softly.

The doctor sat in silence, thinking of what Lutz had told him. There was something about the story of the capsule that didn't quite add up.

"Mind you," he said casually, and began to stroke her hand, speaking apparently out of merely professional interest, nothing more, "cyanide capsules leave a sickly smell when they're opened. A bitter-almond smell, very distinctive. I don't really understand why the hospital staff didn't notice it, when they went into your mother's room."

She shook her head, slowly and feebly. "Don't forget, Yasmin had been in concentration camp, they knew about that sort of thing there. She told the nurse it was too hot and would she open the window. When the night nurse arrived, two hours later, the smell was gone."

"I see," he conceded. "That was well thought out. Cover the traces."

"Yasmin was no fool." She smiled faintly. "Well now—there's still Umberto to tell you about, and I'll have to do it carefully. Perhaps you'll laugh, who knows. That might not be a bad thing for the last chapter in the book! But first—will you comb my hair? So I look my best for it, not like a bald old parrot. My comb is in the drawer, on the right. Lift me up a little."

He held her around the shoulders and her head sank onto his arm, while he carefully combed the thin red strands. They were snow-white at the roots, and it moved him so much that he put down the comb and stroked her head. She lay quite still until he let her sink back onto the pillows.

"You look quite beautiful now," he said.

She nodded seriously. "Good. It's important. When I took the trouble, I could still look beautiful. For instance, all those days when I walked down Theatinerstrasse—and into that house. There was a drugstore on the ground floor . . ."

Chapter 3

. . . and on the third floor, a bridge club, with what she was looking forward to: noise, bustle, a bit of fun, a bit of excitement.

For now Lutz spoke to her only when he absolutely had to. He had had a mother, she could have still been living with them here in their flat, in her pink bed, in her pink nightdress, smiling when he came home, perhaps for months and months. Sophie realized that Yasmin had been more important to him than she.

How to spend the time? What to *do?* Go to museums? Beautiful things hurt and made it worse. Do something *useful*. She bought toys and went to a home for "problem" children. The first child they handed her, a bouncing three-year-old, punched her cheerfully in the face, while the matron exclaimed: "But, Waldi, you mustn't hit your nice new auntie—"

The small fist carried a knockout punch. She reeled, and fled.

Walks were better. Motion. She walked and walked, not in the parks, where spring blossom was spreading, but through the street, the uglier the better, until she was exhausted; and, one day, found herself standing outside a cinema, already open, it seemed, at this hour, midday. Who went to the cinema at this time of day? No one, apart from her. She sat in a back row. A small cinema, a peaceful, sunny film in a strange language. She didn't bother to read the subtitles. There were fields and a peasant girl, to whom something was happening, the usual thing, no doubt.

Shortly afterward the usual thing happened to Sophie—so to speak, for a hand suddenly appeared on her knee. She hadn't noticed that two young men had sat down beside her. Usually she was up to handling that sort of situation without difficulty, but this time the groping hand felt like a branding iron. She screamed—the hand instantly withdrew—and a narrow flashlight beam advanced toward them, with the usherette dimly visible behind.

"This man's molesting me," said Sophie hoarsely.

"Just looking for my umbrella," the young man bleated.

But he hadn't got one, as the flashlight soon revealed. They moved off, tittering. Sophie remained, trembling, trying to get a hold on herself. Where on earth am I, she thought, what's happened to me, I'm Sophie Berglund, where's the Dahde, where's Papa, where's Turhan, where's Anita, where's the sailing boat . . .

The usherette sat down beside her. In the darkness Sophie saw a profile made up of a series of soft hollows and several chins, and immediately beneath them a bosom like a carton. Sophie recognized her as the woman who had sold her the ticket, at the box office outside. She smelled of a cheap, pleasant flower perfume, and her close presence did Sophie so much good that she could feel goose pimples rising on her arm, not the cold, frightened variety, but the kind that prickle sleepily when someone plays old favorites on the piano.

The woman gazed intently at the screen. "Now comes my favorite bit," she said under her breath. Things on the screen had taken their natural course and the peasant girl was now sitting under a cherry tree in full blossom, nursing a baby.

"Isn't that beautiful?" said the usherette.

Sophie thought of the first time she'd seen her Aunt Vera nursing her baby. "Is the coffee in the other bag?" she'd asked.

The usherette glanced at her. "I always get people like you at the first showing. On their last legs, some of them. Would you like a cup of coffee?" She disappeared and came back shortly with two steaming cups. On the screen above them the peasant girl was once again pushed onto her back in the flowering meadow, this time by another chap.

"Don't look," said the woman. "Sugar? It's a Swedish film, it goes on and on like that."

Sophie drank from the sweet-smelling steaming cup and felt the intolerable pressure in her head ease. A cup of hot coffee in a small dark room, brightly colored images and incomprehensible sounds, demanding nothing of her yet giving the impression that something was happening. And at her side the comforting presence of a stranger.

"My mother is dead," she said suddenly.

"Oh dear," said the woman.

"I killed her."

"That's what one always thinks," said the usherette. "Your mother's fine. She's asleep. So's mine, thank the Lord."

"Anyone here?" came a voice. "Anyone selling tickets?"

"Coming!" The woman disappeared, and Sophie slowly finished her coffee.

Chapter 4 Downstairs, outside the drugstore in Theatinerstrasse, a sign showed an elegant female hand holding a set of playing cards. Underneath it read: "BRIDGE CLUB BIANCAMANO, 3rd floor."

At first sight she didn't like the place. Probably because of the woman who sat by the door, on a little dais, as though to get a good look at everyone's cards. She scrutinized Sophie out of tiny, dark eyes, hard pressed by tautly upholstered, bulging cheeks. The crow-black hair was pulled back into a knot, painfully tight, as if she wanted to punish it. She gave Sophie a form to fill in, and informed her that she had four children and that she and her husband did their best. Meanwhile the little piggy eyes darted back and forth between Sophie and the cardplayers. Nothing was going to escape her, it was her kingdom, entrance fee five marks a day, stake ten pfennigs a point. (Oh dear, thought Sophie. Expensive!) Herr Biancamano would choose her partners, once he knew how good she was. One hand would be sufficient. He was never wrong.

The room was like a classroom, with a counter along one wall bearing the coffee machine, the cups, and a vase of artificial roses. Sophie counted eight tables, each fully occupied. Entirely by women. At one table, the only exception: Herr Biancamano. His spouse not only took the money but kept an eye out for impending quarrels, for instance, one of the members turning on a partner who had made the wrong bid or played the wrong card. Then she hurriedly clambered off the dais and whispered in her husband's ear, at which his eyes lit up as if it was a special treat, and he would soothe or separate the partners in question. But it rarely came to this. The ladies, for the most part, merely threatened their partners with an upraised finger: "Really, my dear! Really!"

From her stool at the counter, Sophie looked around. None of the women were under forty, most were in their fifties. They all looked somehow similar, as though they were distantly related, but that was only their uniformly stiff posture, their arms held at the same angle, necks outstretched, chins forward, clothes and hair dolled up as if for a lover's rendezvous.

What she liked was the spirit of utter concentration. All eyes—mostly behind glasses—on the cards. No chit-chat. Even those who were playing dummy for a hand sat erect and followed their partner's game with Argus eyes. Best of all she liked the sounds, an entire score of low-keyed, absorbed noises that hovered like a cloud over each table. Some were humming in a daze, others tootled or whistled disapprovingly or clucked to themselves in frenzied concentration—she could hardly wait to join in.

When Herr Biancamano stood up, he proved to be half a head shorter than Sophie. He had the same straight black hair as his wife, but not the squashed piggy eyes. His were large and slightly moist, and quite beautiful. His suit hugged his strapping frame as if glued to it, and Sophie wondered if he was wearing a corset.

She was to take his seat, and play a hand while he sat watching behind her on a stool—he gave a moistly tender smile—so that he could assess her game. He sat very close behind her, so close that his firm thigh accidentally stroked hers. "*Scusi*, Signora." Another tender smile. Sophie turned her head—yes, piggy-eyes had noticed.

She was lucky. A good hand. Her partner, a blonde with her hair piled high, deposited her cards on the table, suit by suit, with a graceful flourish, earning a moistly admiring glance from Biancamano. Sophie made every one of the tricks. Herr Biancamano, delighted, showed his white teeth, but asked to see her play one more hand, and this time she had bad cards. She tried to salvage what she could, but Herr Biancamano had to intervene a couple of times. He reached forward with one hand to hold her cards, and around her with the other hand to pick out the one he favored. It was virtually an embrace, though it lasted barely a few seconds. Later he told her it had been as if an electric shock had passed through him. The other three players noticed nothing. They weren't playing bridge as a distraction, or for fun, they were here to scheme, to risk, delude and dare. It was less a pastime than a showdown.

Despite the electric shock several weeks passed before he rang Sophie up for the first time, and then only to tell her the club was closed that day, his wife was unwell. A blank day. She felt at a loss, completely thrown.

.

Since Yasmin's death Lutz had been sleeping in her room, in the pink bed. He wore a black armband and listened to music only when his work obliged him to.

One evening he failed to come home immediately after the concert, as he usually did. Sophie kept his dinner warm and waited. It had never happened before, Lutz was normally reluctant to go out at night, and she began to worry. A packet of cigarettes lay on the table, one of his, already opened. She took one out and lit it, the first she'd ever smoked. Quite pleasant. It passed the time. Why hadn't she done it before? She took another, then gradually smoked her way through the whole packet, and fell asleep on the sofa.

The sound of the key in the front door woke her up. Lutz danced and staggered his way down the hall, put his head in at the sitting-room door and cried: "Aha! The red devil's still up." He turned around and called out. "Come on in, Herbie, she won't bite." Behind him appeared, hesitantly, a blond head, a boy of no more than twenty.

" 'Scuse me," he mumbled, disconcerted, and stayed in the doorway.

"Come on in. It's my home, isn't it, Sophie?"

"It's your home, Lutz."

"I want Herbie to move in here," he said, holding onto the wardrobe.

"Good idea," said Sophie. "Where's he going to sleep?" She got up and went to the door into Yasmin's room. "In here?"

Lutz shuffled after her and looked over her shoulder at the bed with its pink coverlet, and the lace-edged pillow where her head used to lie. "No," he said darkly. "I sleep in here, nobody else. He can spend the night on the sofa."

"Fine," said Sophie. "Sleep well, Herbie." And went to her room.

Next morning the boy had gone. She found a little note on the kitchen table. "Most awfully sorry. Herbie."

The door to Yasmin's room was still shut. She set about making coffee and boiling a couple of eggs. Lutz appeared in the kitchen doorway, wearing nothing but his pajama jacket, buttoned up the wrong way, his hair hanging down across his face as if to hide behind.

"Morning," said Sophie, and poured some milk into the jug. He looked around.

"Where is he?"

"Gone."

He sat at the kitchen table and propped up his head with both hands.

"D'you know what I did yesterday?"

"I can guess."

"And?"

"And what?"

"What have you got to say?"

She set a plate and a cup in front of him and stroked his head.

"If you find it helps, then I've got nothing to say."

He stared somberly up at her, through the tangle of hair.

"You don't care?"

"I want you to do whatever you find helps."

He held onto her skirt and hid his face in it. She stood, letting him cry. At last he wiped the hair from his forehead and looked up at her, out of swollen, red eyes.

"Why did you do it, Sophie? Why? Why?"

"If it had been you she'd begged, what would you have done?"

"I don't know."

"Of course you do, and you're glad you were spared it, because you're—" She looked tenderly at him. "You're a bit of a coward. And because you know it, you'd like to punish *me*. I understand that, and I'm still fond of you, but I don't respect you."

"Because of Herbie?"

"Don't be silly, he seems a nice young man."

"What do you want me to do, Sophie?"

"Don't fool yourself, and don't hide from yourself. If you want to go back to young men, then do it without getting drunk."

"I'd like to come back to *you*."

She shook her head. "You can't, and you don't really want to, either. It's just your muddled sense of propriety that wants to."

Now he was crying again, softly and despairingly.

She stretched out a hand and stroked his damp face. "You know, I think that sooner or later it would have come to this, even if Yasmin hadn't died."

He stopped crying and gave her a glance full of hatred.

"In other words: I was never a real man with you."

"What do you mean, 'a real man'? Who *is*? Even if such a thing existed, what a dull beast he'd be! You and I and everybody else, we've all got both sexes within us, day in day out, don't you know that?"

She left him to warm the milk, poured the coffee into the pot, put toast and marmalade on the table. He followed her with his eyes.

"All right," he said sullenly. "If you say so. I see it all rather differently—but if you say so . . ." He mused, frowning, and closed his eyes as if over a knotty problem.

She spread butter on her piece of toast, opened the jar of marmalade, and let him be.

"Sophie—" he said at last. "I need your help—it's not so easy for me, everything's caving in. I need something to cling to." She nodded. "You know, that boy, the one yesterday—he made it easy for me, I mean it wasn't nearly as awful as I was afraid it would be."

"You were lucky."

"I—" He stopped, grinning in sheer embarrassment. "Sophie— what was he *called*, the boy last night?"

"Herbie."

"Yes, but Herbie what? Sophie, how am I going to find him again?"

Chapter 5

He didn't find Herbie again, but he found a Friedrich, who was also quite nice, though he never brought him to the flat. I'm free now, thought Sophie. Or you could call it godforsaken. I drift, I live without a compass—except for Theatinerstrasse, 3rd floor, five o'clock sharp.

One day Herr Biancamano rang her. Would she meet him in the English Gardens, at nine o'clock that evening?

"What for?"

"I'd like to show you a lilac bush, Signora, you've never seen a lilac bush like this one." And he told her how to get there; he seemed to know the way well.

She found it without any trouble. Beneath two large, intertwined lilac trees stood a bench, and on it Herr Biancamano was waiting. The bench was rather high, and his short legs didn't quite reach the ground, but apart from that everything was just the way it should be: twilight, the lilac releasing wave after wave of perfume, forcing one to breathe in deeply, and in the end a little dizzily.

The opening moves were awkward. They sat next to each other in silence, breathing in and out. Herr Biancamano then informed her that he had found an after-shave lotion that smelled of lilac. Would she like to convince herself? And he pushed his smooth, newly shaven cheek under her nose. What now, thought Sophie, am I supposed to fall into his arms?

Immediately afterward she was able to confirm that his after-shave did smell of lilac blossom, and that he did not wear a corset. His firm little body was built like an hourglass, with a proper waist.

She was at once plunged into a kiss of astoundingly long duration, so that she was seriously gasping for air, at which he seemed proud. The entire setting—the summer evening, the lilac bush, the never-ending kisses—all reminded her of the days of her first "experiences," aged eighteen. The Richards and Ludwigs and Hans-Joachims of those days—the same mixture of boy scout and devil of a fellow, the same clumsy, exploring hands during endless kisses. The memories moved her, but at the same time they struck her as funny and she suddenly laughed out loud, at which he quickly let go of her and removed his hand.

"*Scusi*, Signora."

Sorry. For now they sat in silence, though still very close to each other, under the lilac umbrella, staring into the growing darkness.

At last: "May I, Signora?"

She bit back on the laugh. "*Yes!* Herr Biancamano."

This time he bent her backward, as in a silent film, one hand supporting her spine, the other the back of her head. We're in operetta land, thought Sophie, I'm the queen of the gypsies. . . .

319

Her breath gave out again. "Enough," she gasped, and pushed him off with all her might. "Herr Biancamano—I'm a married woman." Let's see how he took that.

He released her at once, and even the taut little thighs inched away along the bench.

"Didn't you know?"

"I thought, perhaps the Signora was no longer quite so happy with her husband, and that now . . . with the spring . . ."

"Herr Biancamano—" He slowly turned his head toward her. Those eyes, those moist eyes! "You like consoling people?"

"Yes, Signora," he said with modest dignity.

"What is your Christian name?"

"Umberto."

"And here, under this lilac tree, you console the ladies of your bridge club, Umberto?"

"Yes, Signora. One can't live off bridge alone."

.

Lilac trees stay in bloom a long time, and Sophie's patience was soon exhausted.

"My husband is in Vienna, at the festival," she said one evening during a breathing space. No reaction from Umberto, who merely plunged into the next round. "He won't be back till the end of the week," Sophie gasped when she returned to the surface.

"Really," he said.

"Umberto . . . is this bench as far as you go, in consoling your ladies?"

"*Sì*, Signora."

"Do you mean you've never slept with any of them?"

"*Mai*, Signora, never." Almost affronted.

"Why not?"

"That's what my wife—la Pina—is there for."

A rebuff? She would entice him to Ottostrasse, that very day.

Easier said than done, for every time Umberto stuck closely to his time-honored routine: outside her door he kissed her hand, and left. That evening, she just managed to catch him by the tightly fastened belt on his coat, and dragged him into the hallway. It was pitch dark, but she didn't turn on the light until the elevator came, to give him time to collect himself. As they swept silently upward, she had three different views of him in the lift mirrors. He looked a bit green, but perhaps that was only the lighting.

Later, in the bedroom, she couldn't stop wondering how the four *bambini* had come into the world. The man was virtually still a virgin. His life seemed to be strictly compartmentalized: tender caresses on the bench, and marital duty in bed. At the first he was a master, at the second a mere beginner.

"Umberto, tell me about yourself."

He sat up and thought hard. Words were not his strong suit. Suddenly his face lit up, and he pointed at the window, arm outstretched. Out in the yard, in the faint light from the flats above, stood the stone lion that Lutz had liked so much when he had first taken the flat. He still perched on his old, crumbling bit of wall, and the weeds now reached up to his belly. His right paw was held high as if in protest—or was he by origin a Nazi lion, giving the Hitler salute?

"*Ecco*," said Umberto. "*Ecco*," he repeated and sighed from the depths of his soul. "That's me—in the middle of a rubbish dump."

A lion? Nice, that he saw himself that way, but what did he mean by rubbish dump? It came out gradually, reluctantly: the bridge club was the rubbish dump. He had been meant for better things, had been the youngest officer in his regiment, dashing, unafraid, Umberto Leone he had been dubbed. Then after the war—back to Lecce, the small southern Italian town he had been born in. Suddenly no uniform, no job, no money. And then—la Pina.

"Why?" Sophie wanted to know. Had he fallen in love?

Amore? He gazed out at the lion again. Four *bambini* . . .

"What's she like, your Pina?"

"*Brava*." She loved her papa, her mamma and the *bambini*, and she did her duty. In the bedroom too. And when she fell pregnant, they were both pleased; for months they wouldn't have to have anything to do with each other.

"Dear God," said Sophie.

"Rubbish dump," he said darkly, still staring at the lion.

Virgin soil. Wonderful prospects opened up before Sophie's eyes.

Next morning she went to the hairdresser and had her hair dyed. There were many white strands in it now, if you had a good look at it. Then she strolled, whistling, to Theatinerstrasse.

But the extra-cheerful "Good afternoon" stuck in her throat, when she saw la Pina. The piggy eyes didn't dart around as usual, they stuck fast, as if glued on, under reddened, swollen lids. And stared at her. She felt the blood rush to her cheeks, as if caught redhanded by the Dahde. Surely he hadn't told her?

"Five marks, please."

She didn't dare place the coin in the outstretched palm, quickly dropped it in the till instead, and fled toward the card tables.

Umberto sat her—deliberately?—with her back to the entrance. But for two hours she could feel the look from Pina's swollen eyes, drilling into the nape of her neck.

Chapter 6

"Who's the fat little chap with the pointed shoes?" asked Lutz one evening.

"I know several people with pointed shoes," said Sophie and reached for the cigarettes. Where could Lutz have seen them? Didn't matter.

"I see," he said, pain showing in his eyes. "You're smoking too much."

Two to three packets a day now. So soon, thought Sophie, what a lust for addiction I have inside me!

The new passion for cigarettes helped, when she was waiting for the phone to ring. Waiting tore at her nerves, and she had to wait for Umberto's call, every day. And by two phones, one in Ottostrasse, and the other in a furnished room in Wurzerstrasse.

At first she hadn't been at all sure that her seductive arts were having the right effect on Umberto. He was certainly involved, heart and soul, but with a bad conscience; as though they were black arts that she was practicing on him.

All the more it surprised and excited her when she found that, without asking her, he had rented the room in Wurzerstrasse, when Lutz came back from Vienna. He called it a *pied-à-terre*, despite the fact that their *pieds* were rarely on the *terre* and almost entirely on the bed.

Did Pina know?

Of course; he had no secrets from his wife.

"I don't understand," she said, stunned. "Your wife *knows* about this place?"

"Of course," he repeated, with that same modest and impregnable dignity that, each time, took her breath away. "We do the accounts every Saturday. On Monday she takes the money to the savings bank. Now there's a hundred and fifteen marks fifty less. Wurzerstrasse is expensive."

"Umberto, don't tell me your wife doesn't care whether I— whether we—" She ended up actually stammering. And I'll be fifty-seven in September, she thought.

He admitted that, right at the beginning, there had been certain upsets, and the *bambini* had waked up and come into the bedroom, howling. Pina had had her hands full just getting them back to bed. They had undressed in silence, and then, in the dark, "the right words suddenly came to me. Everything has its good side, I don't have to bother her anymore, now that I've got *you.* Why are you looking at me like that? Would you have liked it better if she'd scratched my eyes out?"

A thousand times better. To be seen by Mrs. Pig-Eyes as an understudy for her marital duties, as a kind of baby sitter for Umberto so that she, Pina, could go out and see Italian films with her women friends!

That first day of shame had been redundant. She had thought of herself as *maîtresse-en-titre*—but now she was suddenly under *contract* as Miss Adultery! The realization came near to spoiling Wurzerstrasse for her.

.

She usually got there before him, and lay on the bed in a lilac-colored negligee—a tender allusion—preparing herself for the entry of her lion. A lion indeed, certainly in the majestic gesture of dismissal with which he met her every attempt to influence his personal appearance. The gleaming silk ties with their matching pocket handkerchiefs, the black-and-white shoes, the gold-braided dressing gown —he would never give them up. It was not his taste but hers that needed educating; hers was—*scusi*, Sophie, *mio tesoro*—dull.

He even went one small but significant step further by insinuating that perhaps "in her day" it had been different. . . .

And her lion—how old was he? Thirty-six. But the situation was quite different from the one with Lutz. The lion was still a "learner," she was still the guide, but how fast he clambered in pursuit, taking peak after peak by storm!

.

The room in Wurzerstrasse turned the little escapade into a full-blown affair, and reactions were quick to follow. First, from Lutz.

"Sophie, this little fat fellow of yours . . . you're not serious about him, are you?"

"What do you mean by 'serious'?"

"Sophie! He's not your type."

"And what exactly *is* my type, according to you? That large shaggy-headed butcher boy you said goodbye to so tenderly last night, outside the front door, is that *your* type?"

"Sophie—do you think of Yasmin now and then?"

"Why?"

"I think of her every day, and I tell her about everything, including the butcher boy, as you call him, who happens to play second violin at the opera house. So far she's understood it all, but I can't believe she'd be too pleased about your—well, about this fellow."

"I'm sure she wouldn't."

"I can't bear to see you do it," he said in a low voice, his eyes on the table. "You live way below your standards. And—that dyed hair of yours! It's all right at night, but in the daylight! I'll bring you a mirror—d'you want to see?"

"Thank you. I know."

"Sophie—do you *have* to?"

"Yes!" she suddenly shouted at him.

A different reaction from the bridge club. Which became hostile territory, overnight. La Pina had circulated the news, and the ladies of the rubbish dump reacted as one. The bench under the lilac tree was known to most of them, and felt to be wholly acceptable. But a rented room! That was no way to treat a wife with four *bambini*.

Umberto was concerned for her. "Wouldn't you rather stay away? Doesn't it upset you?"

"Does it upset *you*?"

"I'm a man," said the Lion. "Nothing upsets me."

I must be one too, thought Sophie, I actually enjoy it. The first silent duel was daily fought at the entrance, with la Pina of the no-longer-swollen eyes. La Pina of the spiteful eyes. All right, Mrs. Pig-Eyes, thought Sophie and dropped her previously polite "Good

324

afternoon," made a point of having a five-mark piece ready, so she could go past without being held up.

The rubbish-dump battalion awaited, inside, with its thirty pairs of piercing eyes, watching her remove her hat and coat. All activity ceased, cards, pencils, pads, frozen in midair till Sophie, with her red head held high, reached Umberto. "Good afternoon, Herr Biancamano, where am I sitting today?"

Her appointed partners didn't dare grumble—what could they have said?—but they gave her no more than a mumbled "Afternoon." Once, one of them rose ostentatiously to her feet, as Sophie sat down at her table, to announce that she had a sudden headache and was going home. The other two gazed up at her uncertainly, not quite sure whether they too had sudden headaches—it was after all far and away the best club in town. . . .

"A headache?" said Sophie. "I'm sure Herr Biancamano's got some aspirin, haven't you, Umberto?"

There it was. Out in the open. She'd called him Umberto.

It hit the lady with the headache so hard she had to sit down again. The rest, no less overcome, began to bid distractedly.

"Two spades."

"I thought you said two hearts?"

"I couldn't have said hearts! Two spades."

"Aha. Two spades—I—ah—pass."

The lady in question had a very good hand, and should never have passed, but the cards were a blur before her eyes, and she simply *had* to pass.

Not so Sophie, who won the bidding with three clubs and promptly lost trick after trick.

No "Really, my dear" this time. Sophie's partner bellowed with rage: "Frau Reinhold! Not even a beginner would have made such an almighty mess. Club, you said! *Clubs!*"

"Clubs" resounded around the room, blowing a fuse at every table. Pina appeared not to have heard. Umberto, on the far side of the room, looked up anxiously, but Sophie gave him a cheery wave. Shameless old trollop!

When it came to open hostility the rubbish-dump ladies were no match for her. But Pina's look, as she left the club, troubled her. There was no grief left in it, only hatred and a touch of sly forbearance which Sophie found unsettling.

Besides which she was now losing about thirty marks a day, for lack of concentration. Lutz paid up without a word of protest.

She tried to save on other things, giving up their cleaning woman and doing the work herself. After three days Lutz said: "It's all right, I'll do it." From then on the flat was kept reasonably clean. She allowed herself almost nothing on food. Just cigarettes, which were far from cheap, though.

.

The lilac tree in the English Gardens was in bloom again. She sometimes visited it on her own, in the evening light, and took deep breaths of its perfume. The huge clusters of blossom hung all around and down over the bench, as before. What was missing was the laughter of her operetta courtship. Where had that got to? But she couldn't complain, they still had Wurzerstrasse.

It was Umberto who complained. She was getting thinner and thinner, and when one reached a certain age (did he know how old she was? He couldn't!), then, Sophie, *tesoro*, it was better to be a little overweight, like Italian women, otherwise . . .

Otherwise what?

He wouldn't specify.

.

Lutz told her they were going to have to give up the flat. Higher rent, heavier expenses, he couldn't manage anymore. Not a word about the money gambled away every day. Or the cigarettes. Did he suspect? Had he guessed that she now sometimes stole them? She went as usual to her favorite shops, where she was known and liked, and it never occurred to them to search her shopping bag. The first time she'd done it, and reached the pavement, shaking with fright, the shopkeeper had come hurrying out to ask her to come back inside and sit down for a moment, she didn't look at all well. She followed him back into the little supermarket, and let his wife bring her a chair and a cup of coffee. The stolen packet smoldered in her shopping bag.

Gradually, she learned to do it without a qualm. See what I'm up to now, Dahde! "Down with your pants"? Not on your life.

.

She lay on the bed in Wurzerstrasse, waiting, raised an arm up to the light, gazed at it through the lilac negligee. Both were wearing thin, the arm and the chiffon.

She reached for the hand mirror, held it above her. Still far from lame, this pigeon, she thought, not yet ready to be pecked at. I can see Papa in my eyes, though his were blue, a cold blue. Are mine cold? Hard to tell, looking so lovingly into the mirror. I like my face, still white and triangular, and the red hair snaking around it. This is how Umberto sees me when he's on top of me, but I don't believe he ever really looks at me.

She put down the mirror. Baden-Baden came to her mind, Papa at the window with the blanket across his knees, and she could hear herself ask: "What was it that was so special about Amina?" And his answer: "Nothing—apart from her youth. Nothing, really."

And what was so special about Umberto? She had long since ceased to find his lilac-Romeo act preposterous, as she once had—that is, it still was and would always be preposterous, only it didn't worry her anymore, and *that* was the alarming part.

The door opened.

"*Adorata* Sophia *mia*." He knelt beside her and, eyes closed, she inhaled the waves of lilac-water after-shave.

.

Lutz found them a cheap and dreadful flat in Schwabing. "You'll make it beautiful," he said. "You've got a gift for it, you can make anything beautiful."

Did she have that gift? Once, perhaps. She let the moving men put down the furniture wherever they saw fit, and watched indifferently from an armchair. That day Lutz made the first attempt to get her to see a doctor. Out of the question.

.

Every so often someone new joined the club, and a regular would leave. On her first day there the newcomer would be as friendly toward Sophie as toward the others, but by next day she had already been "informed" and joined the hostile ranks. Sophie had now been Miss Adultery for almost three years, but the rubbish-dump ladies' hatred hadn't diminished with time. They must enjoy it as much as I do, thought Sophie, and besides, the name of the game may be bridge but it isn't about making bridges, it's a bloody battlefield where people are cut off and quietly butchered according to the rules. And if all sorts of private grievances should find an outlet here, so much the better. Like boxers working themselves up into a rage against their opponents before the fight; it all helps.

327

And for three years now, for more than a thousand days, she hadn't exchanged a single word with Pina. As though by telepathic consent, they had agreed to deaf-and-dumbness. Not even the sum that Sophie owed every evening was spoken aloud. Pina wrote the figure on a slip of paper and pushed it across the table to Sophie. Sophie read it and paid up.

One day she couldn't read the hastily scribbled figure, and pushed the slip of paper back, without a word. Once more the paper crossed the table, this time inscribed in the huge, thick strokes one uses for the almost-blind.

Next evening Sophie put her glasses on, before reading the figure —and caught a look from the pig eyes. The old hatred was still lurking, but she thought she could make out something else as well: a whiff of pity. Sophie almost hit her.

Lutz again suggested—and this time he wasn't to be easily put off—that she go to the doctor: "You look dreadful!" Sophie smiled. Lutz brought up his heavy artillery: how long did she expect to go on being attractive to "people," at twenty pounds below her normal weight?

"Shut up. I'm not going." But she said it gently, for Lutz had just brought her a kitten, which she'd named Othello. It was a gift from Lutz's new friend Karl-Heinz, a music student. Sometimes the three of them went out for the evening, Sophie in the middle, Lutz and Karl-Heinz on either arm. She always introduced the young man as her nephew, and all three treated it as a capital joke.

"You'll soon have a whole new family," said Lutz. "All nephews."

Not a bad idea, thought Sophie, anything to escape the memories of my own family: Papa's lopsided face and his "I want one last fling, Sophie," the crow forever hopping across the lawn whenever she thought of Turhan—and last of all Yasmin and the small round cardboard box, with the capsule in it. Whereas to be surrounded by half a dozen adoring young men, all grateful to her for not only handing over Lutz without a protest but actually serving them coffee and cakes at home—in return for which they brought *her* flowers or kittens—what could be nicer?

·

One day at the bridge club a young blond woman appeared and applied for membership. Everyone looked up from her cards in surprise. At Biancamano's, young women were few and far between.

That evening, when Sophie paid, she felt a gaze of such burning intensity on her bent forehead that she took off her glasses and looked up. For the first time, la Pina's stare contained no hatred; the little raisin eyes glittered with unalloyed delight.

Next day the blonde returned and played her trial hand. Umberto sat behind her, just as he had with Sophie, and held her cards—*scusi,* Signorina!

Her name was Fräulein Hoffe, Eva Hoffe, and she was assigned to Sophie's table. She played even worse than Sophie, and lost every hand. Since she hadn't yet been "informed," they fell into conversation during the coffee break, and got on so well that, when the session was over, they went and had a drink together in a bar next door, where Fräulein Hoffe enlightened Sophie as to her personal circumstances: she was single, determinedly so, keen on her job as personal assistant at a firm of architects, with a good chance of promotion if she played her cards right—literally, as it happened, because her boss was a bridge fanatic. And wouldn't it be a good idea if she herself mastered the game? He might be in need of a fourth one day. . . .

An ambitious girl. Well, why not? Sophie felt benevolent after her dry martini. And resolved to volunteer some information about herself.

"Fräulein Hoffe, I ought to explain about Herr Biancamano and myself: we've been having an affair for the last four years."

The young woman put down her drink and looked at her in surprise and confusion. "But why—I'm afraid I don't quite understand . . ."

Sophie smiled. "I just wanted to beat the rubbish-dump ladies to it. For once."

"I beg your pardon?"

"You'll find out tomorrow. I wanted you to know already, that's all."

.

This is becoming quite exciting, she thought as she struggled slowly up the steps next day. The climb had become a real effort now and left her gasping for breath for minutes on end in front of the club entrance.

La Pina's eyes gave nothing away, but the rubbish-dump troops seemed in some disarray. Fräulein Hoffe played at another table, and from time to time Sophie was conscious of her searching gaze. Obviously she hadn't yet made up her mind to join the enemy camp. Sophie decided to make a fight of it, and invited her to dinner. Fräulein Hoffe accepted, hesitantly. Weird old bird, the redhead! Occasionally, when she threw her head back and looked around the room with that peculiar smile on her face, she looked quite beautiful. But possibly not quite all there.

The supper was a success. Lutz and Sophie's "nephew" Karl-Heinz ate with them, and Othello purred blissfully under the table, with four pairs of legs to choose from. Sophie had taken trouble over the food, Lutz got through a bottle of wine and gave imitations of famous musicians, Karl-Heinz served everybody assiduously. They laughed a great deal, and Fräulein Hoffe decided that the redhead wasn't mad, just a bit strange. Was it really true that she and the bridge-club owner . . .

Yes, it was, the ladies assured her the following day, yet they didn't wholly succeed in drawing the newcomer over to their side. Fräulein Hoffe's allegiance hung in the balance for quite a while, she found herself midway across the "bridge," glancing uncertainly from the rubbish-dump brigade to Sophie and back again.

And then, without warning, from one day to the next, she had chosen—and sided with Miss Adultery. And uncompromisingly so. But why? the others wondered helplessly.

From now on Eva Hoffe spent her coffee breaks only with Sophie, brought her sugar, poured her cream, which Sophie now sometimes spilled, wiped up after her, fussed over her, told her she was too thin, helped her into her coat. At first bemused, Sophie gave up looking for explanations, and basked in the pleasure of it. That such a thing could still happen to her—to make a friend! She often felt suddenly drained of all energy, and when she dropped things, simply let them lie there. Eva Hoffe picked them up.

"Thank you, dear," said Sophie. "You are kind."

·

And then, something quite unprecedented happened at the club. What could it mean?

Pina wasn't in her place when Sophie arrived. She was standing in the middle of the clubroom, surrounded by the assembled ladies—and they were all giggling. Fräulein Hoffe wasn't present, she couldn't get away from the office every day.

And where was Umberto? At that moment he came in, carrying a
carton full of brand-new packs of cards, which he distributed among
the tables. He didn't seem to notice the knot of cackling females, but
when he saw Sophie, alone in the doorway, he put down his armload
at once and hurried over to take her coat.

"Ready for you, ladies," he called out, and they made their way to
their respective tables. Pina made a detour in order to pass Sophie's
chair on her way to the cash desk, and said loudly: "Good afternoon,
Frau Reinhold—how are you today?"

Sophie was too amazed to answer, and simply stared at the departing, large and insolently swaying posterior, until her partner's voice
rang out: "Your bid, Frau Reinhold . . ."

.

Today was Wurzerstrasse day. Perhaps Umberto could explain the
giggling and the sudden interest his wife had shown in Sophie's state
of health.

But he shrugged his shoulders. No idea.

"Pina hasn't said anything to you?"

"Nothing, Sophia *adorata*." He, however, had something to say.
Alas and alack! He was going to have to give up Wurzerstrasse. Too
expensive. Such a shame, really.

Sophie turned toward him, her hair tumbling like a red waterfall—
a rather too red waterfall—across her forehead and the surrounding
pillow. She looked at him for a long time without speaking. He felt
quite uncomfortable under her gaze. What was it, didn't his Sophia
adorata love him anymore?

Why, of course, said Sophie. Of course she did.

.

The following evening she went to the English Gardens Park. It
was almost dark. No problem, however, she knew the way.

Then she stopped abruptly. Before her, a vast expanse of grass,
and beyond it the tree, like a huge lilac-colored wig, and underneath,
deep in shadow, the bench, and on the bench two figures, one of
them small and stout and dark-haired, and the other blond. Or was it
her imagination?

She took a roundabout route, crept stealthily toward the bench
and then, taking cover behind a tree, got out her glasses. The bench
was empty.

Chapter 7 Not long afterward two things occurred on one and the same day: first, she saw Eva Hoffe on the other side of Maximilianstrasse and was about to cross the road to say hello, when something unaccountable stopped her. Instead she stood and watched the young woman stroll down the pavement, swinging her handbag. Now she was waiting for the traffic, at an intersection, now the lights changed and she crossed —and turned into Wurzerstrasse.

Sophie looked around. There had to be somewhere to sit down, in this street. A bench—a bench . . .

No bench. Over there, though, on the corner, the Opera Café. Easy now, one step at a time . . . She could see someone coming toward her, just as slowly, in the window of a furniture shop. Who can it be, she thought, and took her glasses from her bag, she looks familiar, a tall scraggy creature with crudely dyed red hair. . . .

Not the Opera Café. A taxi. Home. Lie down.

But as she opened the door of the apartment, the second thing happened: Lutz was standing there. Why? Why wasn't he at the office? For a moment they stared at one another with the same speechless surprise; he obviously hadn't expected her either.

"Sophie—" he whispered. "There's someone in the sitting room—it might be better if you didn't see him."

Too late. A man stood in the doorway to the sitting room, a man Sophie didn't know—or did she knew him after all? Lutz led her toward the doorway and, since the man refused to give ground, virtually pushed her past him into the room, and to the sofa. The man stayed where he was, hesitated, then spoke.

"It's no use, Herr Reinhold, either you tell her now, in my presence, or I go to the police. I'm sorry, but—there *is* a limit." He folded his arms and leaned against the wall.

Lutz sat next to her on the sofa and stroked her hand soothingly, but it didn't help, every heartbeat tolled in her head, for now she knew who the man was: the owner of her little supermarket, where today—and last week—and—

"Sophie, this man says you took a packet of cigarettes this morning. It was just an oversight, wasn't it—you forgot to pay for it, didn't you?"

"She's forgotten dozens of times, Herr Reinhold. Every week for months now, we've had packets unaccounted for, always the same brand. My wife and I simply couldn't believe it, but today I saw it with my own eyes. I let you go, Frau Reinhold, because I wanted to talk to your husband first."

Sophie sat up, holding onto Lutz and shaking her head from side to side, trying to reassemble all the bits adrift inside. "I'll come with you to the police. I'll go to prison."

Lutz tried to force her down onto the sofa again, but she thrust his hands aside.

"Sophie, d'you know what you're saying? D'you know who I am?"

"Don't be so silly, Lutz, of course I know who you are. What's so special about going to prison? Lots of people do, don't they, Herr— Herr—"

The man took a step toward her, rubbing his hands together in embarrassment.

"Of course not, Frau Reinhold, no one wants you to go to prison, I didn't really mean that, it was just in case you tried to deny it. I mean—"

"Deny it?" cried Sophie threateningly, and struggled to get to her feet. "What on earth do you think of me?"

Lutz got up and pulled out his wallet. "Would you tell me how much it comes to, please?"

"Lutz! I forbid you to pay so much as a penny of it. I shall go to prison. I won't let anyone deprive me of my rights." She stood for a moment, then crumpled and fell back onto the sofa. Lutz beckoned to the man, and they left the room to discuss it outside, in whispers.

"No, please, Herr Reinhold, we're not concerned about the money, my wife and I. I say, I'm really sorry about your wife, though. Has she seen a doctor?"

This was the day Lutz brought Dr. Hensch, his own doctor, into the flat; whom Sophie's yells forced to retreat, shrugging his shoulders. "My dear Reinhold," he said, in the hallway, "I'm afraid it'll have to get a lot worse before anything can be done."

.

She had to stay in bed for three weeks, and Lutz looked after her, even supplying her daily cigarettes. But he often had to leave her on

333

her own during the day and in the evenings too, for they needed every penny he could make.

Luckily, Karl-Heinz, the music student, had time to spare. He brought flowers and sat by her bed, discreetly silent. Sophie glanced at him occasionally, and thought: pity. No substance, no vigor. Pale. Reminds me of Turhan.

Tirelessly, he played her records, Mozart, Bach, and they sat and listened. They were the best hours of the day.

Once, as he said goodbye, she kissed him on the cheek.

"Lutz is a lucky man," he said.

"How d'you mean?"

"I wouldn't mind having a wife like you."

She stared at him, then began to laugh and couldn't stop. He blushed a deep red.

"No, no," she said, and stroked his face. "It isn't you I'm laughing at, it's me."

That evening she asked Lutz to tell him not to come to the flat anymore.

"But why? He loves to come, I think he's a bit in love with you."

"That's why. He's so discreet about it I can hardly stand it."

It didn't really work, the business of the "nephews."

.

One morning she woke up and decided that she felt better. In the afternoon she put on her hat and went out. To the club.

Why to the club? she wondered, walking slowly down Theatiner-strasse. What am I after? Umberto? No. Really and truly? Really and truly. Another showdown with the rubbish-dump ladies? God, no! How boring—in fact, how repulsive! She struck herself with her fist, full in the forehead, and a passerby gave her an anxious stare. Drunk? Not a bit of it. Stone-cold sober. Sobered. How could I have lived for these wretched, dreary little feuds for so long! There must have been something more to it, surely, to have kept me trotting down there every day like an old circus horse, full of bounce and energy on the way out, and on the return—but it was never a return, it was more like a retreat, after a costly battle. Thirty marks down the drain, and the sum total of hostile eyes and nasty little remarks which she parried so brilliantly while the game was on, only to feel punctured and out of lifeblood, as she walked home.

So—why on earth am I going there today, with my knees already trembling here on the pavement, and not at all sure I'll make it up the steps?

She stopped so suddenly that two women with shopping bags, behind her, nearly knocked her over. "I'm so sorry—my fault, do forgive me—" All three held onto one another, and the two women were quite friendly about it, laughed, and walked on, deep in their shopping fantasies.

She was still standing on the same spot. Why—go—back—there—again—today? Passersby had to make their way around her, and turned back to look at her. Come along, she thought, you can't stand here like a pillar of salt just because you've finally caught yourself redhanded, and want to get to the crux and "draw the lesson," go and draw it over there, by the display case, people will think you're window-shopping.

Whether or not it was the cool plate-glass window to which she pressed her forehead that cleared her brain and calmed her, she suddenly thought she saw it now, saw if first distantly and a bit dubiously, since it was really quite disgraceful, and yet gradually, inescapably, confirmed: what had in fact drawn her up those three flights of stairs with irresistible force had been the old, old song: addicted again, and this time to cards. She was a card addict. And it wasn't a question of gambling for money, like Papa, she didn't really give a damn about winning the rubber—it was the cards! They had her in their clutches.

She closed her eyes—and there they were. Fluttering in from all sides, thirteen of them, glazed and shiny, smelling of waxy oilcloth, beckoning sanctimoniously but peremptorily, and when had she ever been able to resist anything?

She pulled back her forehead from the glass and saw her face in it, a blurred reflection, calm, almost happy.

.

She was late, because it had taken her a long time to make it up the three flights of stairs, and she had had to sit down on the top step to get her breath back. Then she went in, still so wrapped up in her discovery that before she knew it she'd said "Good afternoon" to a staring Pina. Barely noticing that Umberto rushed up to her and took her coat and plied her with questions, why had she stayed away for so long, had she been ill?

She looked at him absently as he took her hat. Ill? No, not at all,

335

just rather busy. Where am I sitting today? Aha. Good afternoon. Whose deal is it? Here they came now, flying in, the first card, the second, the third—

"One diamond," offered her partner.

"Two hearts," to her right. Sophie next. A pause, while she studied her cards attentively. Normal practice, ten or fifteen seconds might go by before a player committed herself.

Sophie looked up and across the table at her partner, Frau Mahrenholz, who was engrossed in her hand. Handsome woman, Frau Mahrenholz.

"Don't you think they're exactly like doves?"

"I beg your pardon?" said Frau Mahrenholz. Her neighbors gazed at Sophie in silence, one from the right, one from the left.

"*My* cards," said Sophie, "come flying to me, just like doves. Don't yours, Frau Mahrenholz?"

The woman hesitated, frowning.

"You mean—you're not happy about the way the cards were dealt?"

"On the contrary," said Sophie. "I've never seen it done so beautifully."

The three ladies looked at one another. Was the Reinhold woman pulling their leg? Or was she hinting a hand full of spades? The handsome Frau Mahrenholz eyed Sophie uncertainly. (She too had once upon a time sat with Umberto beneath the lilac tree.)

"I don't quite understand—your bid, please, Frau Reinhold. You're holding up the game," she added, though not really rudely, just in the way one spoke to the Reinhold woman. Who looked a bit battered tonight, as a matter of fact.

"Ummm—" went Sophie, examining her cards again with great attention. "What would you like me to say?"

Frau Mahrenholz opened her mouth—and the other two gazed in rapt expectancy—but no vitriolic answer came, for Sophie's smile stopped her in her tracks, a smile she'd never seen from her before, as if she wanted to give her a present.

"Well, what have you got, Frau Reinhold?"

"Oh . . . " said Sophie gaily, "all sorts of things. A club, for instance."

"Good, fine," interrupted Frau Mahrenholz quickly. "That'll do."

"Pass," said the left-hand neighbor.

"Three diamonds," from Frau Mahrenholz.

"Pass." Right-hand neighbor.

With a flourish Sophie spread her cards out on the table, under Frau Mahrenholz's nose. "There now—isn't that beautiful?"

The woman gave her a quick glance, and sighed. There was nothing to be done about the Reinhold woman.

"Don't you think they're just like doves? Have a look at these two, for instance, the ten of spades and the ten of clubs—narrow your eyes a little and you've got ten black doves. Or ten black pigeons—in St. Mark's Square in Venice."

Her smile vanished all of a sudden, and she put both elbows on the table and pressed her fists hard against her chest, just below the neck.

"Frau Reinhold—" said Frau Mahrenholz. "Are you all right? Would you rather go home?" God only knows, she thought, why I'm being so nice to her, she's a shameless old floozie, don't let's forget that. All the same she heard herself say: "Would you like a cup of coffee?"

"No, no," said Sophie. "Thank you so much. You go ahead and play. I like to see them fly, the little doves."

Frau Mahrenholz shrugged and led. Right and left of Sophie, the first cards landed on the table.

"Whee!" said Sophie and laughed. Her partner ignored her and gathered up the first trick.

"Happy landings!" Sophie exclaimed and took a sip from the cup of coffee which had suddenly appeared in front of her.

Her right-hand neighbor could no longer contain herself: "Frau Reinhold—it was Frau Biancamano who brought you the coffee."

"Oh good," said Sophie and took another sip, oblivious of the black looks she was receiving from all sides. The woman didn't even bother to say thank you! The right-hand neighbor slammed a card onto the table to give vent to her fury, the left-hand one rattled hers down beside it. Frau Mahrenholz tentatively added her card, and lost the trick.

"Yes, yes," said Sophie, nodding wisely. "They're cruel, the doves."

She didn't know that Pina was standing behind her chair, nor did she see her walk over to her husband and whisper something in his ear, at which Umberto looked hesitantly across to Sophie, and Pina was obliged to whisper again, louder this time and in Italian.

At Sophie's table the hand came to an end. Frau Mahrenholz had surpassed herself and won almost every trick. But before the cards could be shuffled, Umberto stood up and announced with a broad smile that the coffee break would take place a little earlier than planned, in fact right now. For anyone who felt ready . . .

Chairs being pulled back, with—at Sophie's table—a sigh of relief. All three ladies fled to the buffet counter, and watched from safety as Umberto approached Sophie, who was still sitting at the table, pensively picking out a card here and there, and letting it slip through her fingers.

"Frau Reinhold—" he said, and added softly: "Sophia *adorata*— you don't look at all well. Permit me to take you home."

She looked at him, coolly.

"Pay up first," she said.

"But of course," said Umberto, reaching hastily for her scorecard, and while he pretended to be doing the sums, Sophie reflected what a pity it was that Fräulein Hoffe wasn't there. Miss Adultery No. 2—bon voyage! "Nine marks fifty," announced Umberto—a most unlikely sum, for the rubber had only started.

"I've won," said Sophie, and stood up, satisfied.

·

When Lutz got home that evening he found her in an armchair, fast asleep, her hat still on her head, and Othello in her lap.

"You've been out? Where have you been? For God's sake, Sophie, you haven't been—"

"Yes I have, and I've won. Nine marks fifty."

He stared at her, then went into the kitchen, without a word. She hadn't eaten.

Next day she fell off the chair, with the spoonful of porridge in her hand. The time had come at last.

Chapter 8

That was exactly a week ago.

Kostas was walking down the corridor that evening, to take over for the night. A small plump figure came toward him, Sister Baerbel. He almost didn't recognize her without her nurse's cap. She was going home, lived out, with her parents.

"How was 384 today, Sister?"

"Better. She even managed to eat something, and I stopped the intravenous feeding. She said, 'Thank you very much, sister,' and asked me my name. She also mumbled something about last night and how she was sorry, I think she meant about the clock—"

"She meant about *you*, Sister Baerbel."

"Really?" She blushed, and suddenly looked like a little peasant girl. "Oh, I'm *so* glad. I really am, Doctor. Goodnight."

When he entered the room, Sophie was leaning on her elbow, clutching the bedside table. Her eyes were flickering, her breath coming in gasps again.

"Quick," she whispered. "I need one now, Brother—quickly." She wouldn't even let him glance at the chart on the end of the bed. He could guess what it said: reduce morphine intake. The head physician had established that there was a remission, a temporary improvement, and wanted the dose cut down at once.

He found two vials in the bathroom, and gave her one of them. He'd keep the other in reserve for as long as he could. And perhaps have a word with the head physician in the morning—no, there was no point. It might even be counterproductive. They'd keep a closer watch on her—and on him.

He sat on the edge of the bed and watched her features gradually relax, the closed eyelids stop twitching. The breath came softly now.

"Strange," she whispered. "I seem to be in less pain—is that possible? Or am I imagining it?"

"It's possible."

She opened her eyes. "You're not going to tell me that I—that I'm going to get well again?" He turned his head away. "It's too late for that, isn't it, don't tell me it isn't, I can *feel* it, here—" She took his hand and put it against her left side, below the breast. "There's only a great big hole now, isn't there? Nothing left, it's all eaten away. What are you crying for? Tell me. You can tell me everything, you know that."

Instead of answering he took his glasses off and wiped them.

"Look at me. What do I look like, without your glasses?"

"A bit blurred, but I still recognize you."

"Am I more beautiful—blurred?"

"Of course," he said, and laughed a little.

She took his glasses out of his hand and put them on the bedside table.

"From now on you'll only see me as a blur. Promise me."

He smiled and wiped her hand across his moist eyes. She looked at him with great tenderness and let her hand rest against his cheek.

"I've been trying so hard," she said, "and I just can't find it, perhaps you can help me: I need a closing sentence for my book, it's almost finished now. Did you laugh over Umberto? No?"

"But I cried over Lutz," he said in a low voice.

Her hand fell from his face and rested on the sheet, each finger rose slowly in turn and dropped again.

"You might equally well put it the other way around," she said at last. "Cry over Umberto, and laugh over Lutz. Be careful how you handle the truth, that's what Anita said."

"Perhaps that's your closing sentence."

"No, I'm looking for something that'll explain to me where I went wrong. I had so much to offer, Brother, I had such potential inside me when I started, such ecstasy and appetite and impulse—" She made an attempt to ball her fists, but the fingers only curled feebly. "And I made so little of it, nothing really, nothing at all. You've read the book—do you know why?"

"I can't think without my glasses on."

"Then it's a book without a closing sentence."

"Maybe there's more to come." He immediately wished he hadn't said it.

She studied his face. "You mean, because I'm feeling better? Do people suddenly get better, sometimes, even if they've got—it?" He nodded. "And then—they get by, for a while longer? Weeks? Months?" Whispering: "Years?" He nodded. She turned her head toward the window and said without looking at him, "Will they send me home, as soon as I can eat properly?" And gave him no time to answer. "Who'll give me my injections?"

"Oh," he said as lightly as he could, "we'll find a way. If needs be *I'll* come and do it."

"Where will you get the stuff?"

"From our supplies. Nobody checks them all that carefully."

"Brother!" She gave him a long, hard look. "I was almost ready to believe you," she said slowly. He didn't reply, bowed his head.

She studied him in silence for a long while. He looked up, and they exchanged a long, wordless look of love.

"If Lutz rings up, tell him I'm better. Tell him I'm trying hard."

Then she closed her eyes, and murmured: "Let me have your hand." She embedded her face in his palm and fell asleep, said nothing more during the night, nor in the early morning, when he left the room.

.

Around noon the phone rang at his bedside. Still fuddled with sleep, he picked up the receiver, but couldn't recognize the voice at first.

"*Who* did you say?"

"It's me, Doctor, Sister Baerbel!" Stuttering, gasping with agitation. "Come quickly, quickly! Or shall I call the matron—"

"No! Stay right there. I'm on my way."

He ran down the corridor, buttoning his coat in midstride. Empty corridor. Lunch break. Thank God.

The little nurse was standing by Sophie's bed, with a hand across her mouth like a child who's dropped and broken something. With the other she pointed at the motionless figure on the pillows.

Sophie lay crumpled, with her head thrown back. Her eyes were shut, the mouth open and twisted, a frown on her forehead. No pulse. No heartbeat. Arms and chest already cold.

"When did it happen?" whispered the young doctor.

"I don't know," she whispered back, her hand still across her mouth. "She asked for a cup of coffee—"

"When?"

"Eight o'clock. I was so glad she wanted some coffee! The room had already been done, and she'd been washed; she said she felt better, and she looked better too, Doctor, I don't understand—"

"And then?"

"She took a sip, then wanted to see herself in a mirror. She asked me to bring her handbag—"

"Her handbag?"

"Shouldn't I have given it to her?" Trembling with fright, she pointed to the bedside table. "That's it there, the white one."

The bag was open. He rummaged quickly through it, found a small round cardboard box. Empty.

"Did I do something wrong, Doctor?" He didn't answer, closed the bag and slowly put it down again.

"She didn't want the mirror after all, Doctor," stammered the girl. "She suddenly felt too tired, and sent me away. She said she just wanted to sleep."

He turned toward her, but she saw that his thoughts were on something quite else. He took off his glasses and wiped them on the sleeve of his coat.

"That was all, Sister?"

"Yes, Doctor, absolutely all," she protested, and hoped this would reassure him. "There was nothing else. She only asked me to open the window as wide as possible, she needed fresh air."

He nodded and shut his eyes for a moment. Then he carefully put his glasses on, turned slowly around. No hurry now. There was the window, still wide open, a thin white curtain flapping softly back and forth in front of it.

"Thank you, Sister—go and make out your report." His back was turned to her, and the hoarse, low tone made his words barely intelligible.

"Should I notify the matron?"

She waited, and realized that he hadn't heard her. He was still staring at the window and the swaying curtain.

She took a last look at the motionless figure on the bed. As yet, she'd not had much experience of dead patients, it still took her unawares and gave her the willies, and she couldn't altogether believe it.

"I just don't understand," she whispered again, hoping he would turn around and explain it to her, but he didn't move.

When at last he heard the door open and shut again, he leaned over Sophie. The lips, still soft, were easily closed. But the forehead resisted all attempts to smooth it out, returning obstinately to the same deep crease, as if she were determined to prove that she was trying hard.

He bent down and kissed her gently on the mouth. Eyes closed, he inhaled the faint smell of bitter almonds on her lips. Then he lay his head, just for one brief second, on the pillow next to hers.